Praise for

BETWEEN *the* SAVIOR *and the* SEA

"You could almost forget you are reading a 2000 year old story as you work your way through these pages... The stories come alive with emotion that you might have never imagined being there."

—Russ White, thinkinginchrist.com

"This book is an easy read and a page turner... it turns the Bible into a compelling story without being 'preachy' or feeling like you are being forced to learn."

—Michael Groethem, catholicnerd.com

"I found myself moved quite often. It's faithful and insightful. It gave me much to consider. I really appreciated how Rice showed Peter dealing with his failures... if you like reading about your faith and you like a good story with spiritual insights I think *Between the Savior and the Sea* is for you. I really enjoyed it."

—Matthew Archbold, creativeminority.com

"*Between the Savior and the Sea* accomplishes what every work of Christian fiction should aspire to, namely that as I read it and when I was done I was brought closer to Christ, to His Church, and to His sacraments. At times, I was brought to the point of tears as I contemplated Christ's love and His sacrifices."

—Domenico Bettinelli Jr., bettnet.com

"Besides telling the Jesus story from the perspective of the Apostles, Bob Rice uses the Ignatian spiritual technique of filling out the Gospel scenes with lots of sensory content—the smell of the sea, the sound of a room full of sleeping disciples, etc., etc. Yes, besides being a good psychological writer, Bob Rice is a good descriptive writer... (the book) provides some food for thought, it uplifts the heart and mind, and it can lead us to prayer. And that's a good thing."

—Fr. Gregory P. Houck, O. Carm, carmelitereview.org

BETWEEN
the SAVIOR
and the SEA

by Bob Rice

for my wife

INTO THE DEEP

Luke 5:1-11

You are nothing without me, said the sea.

Simon's hand clenched the side of the boat. Fingernails found familiar grooves under the lip of cedar that curled around its bow. For all his skill, for all his experience, Simon knew he was completely at the mercy of the lake.

He stared into the darkness. There was no moon and clouds hid the stars. A faint light shone from a lamp that hung off the stern of the boat, but it faded quickly into the black.

Simon looked behind him to the other men on the boat. "Anything?" he asked.

James unhooked the lantern and reached his long arm over the water. They saw the net—a large circle held aloft by pieces of cork. It hadn't moved.

Simon looked at the faces of the fishermen on the ship. They were tired. They were frustrated. And there were less of them than usual. His normal crew of eight became six when two of them decided to try their luck to the south. Simon wondered how many would show up tomorrow.

He turned his gaze back toward the water. "Give me your fish," Simon whispered.

The sea answered with silence.

"I'll give you anything."

You have nothing to give, came the response.

Simon drove his knuckles into the side of the boat.

"Simon?" James asked.

He let out a deep breath. "Let's try the north," Simon said. "Maybe we'll have some luck there."

The north proved as fruitless as the other directions they had tried that night. The sky went from black to grey as the sun began its climb over the Gerasene cliffs. Simon looked to the west. The towering hills rolled higher and higher and faded to paler shades of green in the distance. It was as though God dipped His finger at the center of the lake, and the rest of the land rippled upward from that touch.

He looked at the net that lay flat in the lake. Simon had never seen it so empty. He rubbed the water out of his beard, drew his fingers through his tight curly hair, and prayed his brother had better luck than he did. "Let's go home," he said. The boat leaned as fishermen reached out into the water and pulled in the net.

As the others manned the oars, James made his way toward Simon. The vessel creaked and swayed as he sat next to him. James was the only man larger than Simon on the boat.

"Another night and nothing to show for it," he said. "The wife won't be happy."

"My wife is *never* happy," Simon said.

"Well, at least Rachael is a good cook."

Simon didn't respond.

"Look on the bright side," James said. "At least we won't have to pay any taxes to Matthew today."

Simon smiled at that. James went back to the rudder and the boat moved toward Capernaum. The sun broke through the clouds and gave color to the world. The searing heat of summer was gone and the rains began a month or so ago, giving life to everything around. The lake was a bit higher, fed by the rains and the melted snow from the majestic peaks of Mt. Hermon to the north, and poured a strong current out at her southern end into the mighty Jordan River.

Thinking of the Jordan caused Simon to pause. He wondered if the lake was jealous because of his work in the river. But then he thought it better not to think of such things and sat back in the boat to avoid any more conversations with the water. Simon closed his eyes and listened to the birds, and in the distance could hear the beginnings of Capernaum coming to life. There was movement on the dock, stores opened their shops, animals were let out of their homes, and the rooster crowed to bring in the day.

As his ship came into the dock, Simon stood and waved off the merchants before they landed. "No fish today!" he yelled. "NO FISH!"

After some unkind words the people cleared out, revealing a man of short stature that Simon was all too familiar with. He was well fed and his stomach showed it. His bright red robe was lined with golden threads and bright blue tassels hung from the bottom. In his hands were a scroll and a large plume to write with. Simon would have given more thought to slapping the smirk off his face were it not for the Roman guard (more correctly, a hired mercenary from Persia) who stood next to him.

"Shalom Simon," he said as his boat reached the dock, bowing slightly.

"Hello… *Matthew*," Simon said, purposely using his Greek name instead of *Levi,* his Jewish one. The tax collector made as if he were going to step into the boat, but Simon blocked the way. "Like I said, no fish."

"Yes, yes. I heard you yelling it from the lake, but I just had to see it myself," Matthew said with a smile. "I mean, one or two days of no fish is understandable, but this has been happening to you for a few weeks now, hasn't it?" He unbound his scroll and wrote something in it that Simon couldn't see.

"There's no fish, so there's nothing for you here," Simon said. "I'm sure your *master* has another job for you to do somewhere else."

Matthew looked up coldly. "Well, at least I *do* my job, Simon," he said. "You are behind on your quota, and King Herod isn't happy. The other fishermen in the guild seem to bring in fish. Why don't you?"

Simon looked at him in anger but had no reply. Matthew looked around at the others. "I don't know what you are doing out there, but the next time you come to this dock you had better have some fish, *or you are out of the guild.*" He turned around and walked briskly away, followed by the Roman guard.

The fishermen were quiet. Simon felt their stares on him. He put his hand over his eyes to hide the anxiety and replayed the morning's events in his head. *Maybe I should have tried a different place in the lake,* he thought. *Maybe I should have gone out earlier.*

Maybe you should just give up, said the sea.

"BE QUIET!" he yelled, and the fishermen jumped back. Simon swore under his breath. Now his crew thought he was going insane. "Let's finish up and go home," he said.

They hauled the nets onto the dock and began to clean them. Slowly, conversations began and life returned to normal. His brother's boat arrived and moored at the dock. James put his large hand on Simon's shoulder. "He's not going to kick you out of the guild, you know. Not if my father has anything to say about it."

Simon nodded and James went back to tend the boat. Though they didn't like to talk about it, James was related to Matthew. And Papa Zebedee was not someone to mess around with. But Simon wasn't so much concerned about the guild as with his own reputation. What would his father have said? And what will Rachael say when he goes home again with nothing?

"Shalom, Simon." His younger brother's greeting snapped him out of his trance.

"Shalom, Andrew. I hoped you fared better than me."

He shook his head. "Not much," he said, scratching the hairs that were unevenly clumped on his cheek. "I think we are cursed," he whispered.

Andrew was always one to jump at shadows, but this time Simon feared he might be right.

"Let's clean the nets and try again tomorrow." He could tell by the look on Andrew's face that he was hoping for more. "It's all we can do." Andrew nodded and went back to his boat to help with the net.

Simon walked to the end of the dock and looked out at the sea. One of the fishermen from Andrew's boat handed him a small wicker basket barely filled with fish. One slipped out and writhed back and forth against the cracked and weathered wood. Simon watched it die with great sympathy.

He closed his eyes and prayed. *God of my fathers Abraham, Isaac, and Jacob, you know I have been faithful to your covenant. I have kept your commands. Why have you abandoned me? Why have you hidden your face?*

"Sir?"

Simon turned and looked down at a boy no older than ten. One of the fishermen's sons, but he couldn't remember whose.

"Yes?"

The boy pointed to where the dock met the land. "That man wants to speak to you."

Simon looked and saw a man in a light brown robe, facing away from him. Simon handed the basket of fish to the boy and walked toward him.

As he got closer, the man turned and Simon saw his face. Simon was so unprepared to see him that at first he didn't recognize him. The slender build. The long face. The straight hair that fell to his shoulders. He stood taller than most—almost as tall as Simon did. But when Simon caught a glimpse of his piercing green eyes, he knew immediately who it was.

"Jesus!" Simon said.

Jesus smiled. "Shalom, Simon." They embraced. Andrew, James, and his little brother John heard Simon's cry and ran over with joyful shouts.

"Master, it is so good to see you again!" Andrew said.

"How is the fishing going?" Jesus asked.

Andrew rolled his eyes and was about to speak when Simon said, "It's going great."

"Any word on the Baptist?" John asked in his high voice. He was the youngest of the four, having received his bar mitzvah only a year ago. John had the square jaw of his brother but he was shorter and much skinnier.

Jesus put a hand on John's shoulder. "He lives, and is preaching up a storm in Herod's prison."

"Not that it will do any good," Andrew said. "I'm not sure what scares me more, the king or his queen."

"More like his *keeper*," James said as he spit on the ground.

"What of his followers?" Andrew asked. "Have you heard from Philip?"

"Herod hasn't put John in the deepest dungeon, at least not yet. He's allowed Phillip and other followers of his to tend to him."

"What of the ministry at the Jordan?" Simon asked.

Jesus shook his head. "It's over."

Those words broke Simon's heart. The four of them had spent a few months with John the Baptist and remembered the time fondly. That was where they first met Jesus.

"Don't be afraid," Jesus said. "He is on the path God wants him on. That path has led him to Herod. Mine has led me here."

"Why are you here, Master?" James asked.

"To share the good news of the kingdom of God," Jesus said.

"Where? When?" John asked.

Jesus looked around at his surroundings. "I thought maybe…
here. And now."

"Here?" Simon asked. "To whom?"

"To anyone you can get to listen to me."

The fishermen ran through the streets and told everyone to
stop what they were doing because the brother of John the Baptist
had come to proclaim God's word. Capernaum was home to about
fifteen hundred people, and almost all of them came out to hear Jesus
speak. Jesus got into Simon's boat and asked him to pull out a little
from the shore. Then he sat down and taught the crowd from the
boat.

Simon suppressed a smile when he saw people's
disappointment at first seeing Jesus. He remembered feeling the
same when he was introduced to him at the Jordan. To look at him,
Jesus was unimpressive. There was nothing in his appearance that
made him stand out from others, unlike John the Baptist who dressed
in camel skins and had a strong, commanding look.

But when Jesus spoke, no one could move. His preaching
was as gentle as a lamb and as fierce as a lion. He spoke of God in a
way they had never heard—yet it resonated with everything they
ever knew. Capernaum stood still in awe as the carpenter's son from
the little town of Nazareth boldly proclaimed the kingdom of God
from the water's edge.

Hours passed but it seemed like minutes. The only thing that
moved was the sun. Jesus finished his message, led the crowd in a
prayer, and concluded by singing a psalm. Then he sent them on their
way with a promise he would speak again.

Jesus turned from the crowd and sat down in the boat. All
were silent. Simon let out a deep breath—had he been holding it the
entire time Jesus spoke? He looked at his brother, who stared out
onto the lake with his hand on his chest. John wiped away tears from
his eyes. James looked at the floor of the boat, deep in thought.

For a few minutes no one spoke. James broke the silence by
saying, "Thank you, Master." The others echoed the same.

"Thank *you*," Jesus said. "I couldn't have done it without
you."

Simon laughed and saw surprise in Jesus' face. "Forgive me, Master," he said, "but you hardly need our help."

Jesus shrugged and turned his face to admire the beauty of the surroundings. Simon chastised himself for being so rude.

After another moment of silence, Jesus spoke. "Simon?"

"Yes, Master?"

"Put out into deep water, and pay out your nets for a catch."

Simon stammered a bit and sat upright in the boat, not sure how to respond. "I'm sorry Master, what did you say?"

"I said, put out into deep water, and pay out your nets for a catch." It was part invitation, part command.

Simon glanced at the confused looks of the other fishermen. Andrew's face read, *should we tell him?*, as if maybe a carpenter's son wouldn't understand the foolishness of fishing in deep water in the middle of the day.

Then he looked into the sea, and the cry of the gulls sounded like laughter in his ears. *Don't humiliate yourself again,* it said.

Simon agreed. "Master, we have worked hard all night long..."

But Jesus didn't flinch at these words.

"And we have caught nothing..." he confessed.

Jesus looked at Simon more intensely. At first, Simon was afraid Jesus was angry. But as he looked into his face, he saw great compassion and encouragement. Jesus *wanted* him to say yes.

The words spilled out of Simon's mouth. "...but if you say so, I will put out the nets."

They rowed to the deep water and cast out the net in a wide circle. Simon had never been out so far at this time of day. With every moment, the peace he felt since meeting Jesus ebbed away and he questioned his decision.

Time passed, and idle conversation turned to silence. Jesus looked at Simon and smiled. Simon tried to smile back, but it was all effort. Every creak of the boat, every lap of water on the stern seemed to him as a voice that proclaimed his failure as a fisherman, a father, and a son.

Suddenly, Jesus fell on his knees. Simon sat up straight, unsure whether or not he should join him in prayer. Jesus bent over and ran his hand along the floor of the boat. The four leaned over to see what he was doing. Then Jesus looked at them with a joyful expression.

"Amazing craftsmanship. Did you notice the spine of carob wood that runs from aft to stern?"

The fishermen glanced at each other. "I thought it was made out of cedar," James said.

"Mostly, yes," Jesus said. "But there is also a combination of other woods as well. Look here," he said, pointing to another place on the floor of the boat. "Tabor oak strips run parallel to the spine to balance the softness of the cedar. Over here are strips of terebinth and sycamore... I'd say there are about twelve kinds of wood in all."

Simon put his head in his hands. Were they really talking about *wood*?

"Did you ever build boats?" John asked.

Jesus shook his head. "My father and I built many things, but boat building is its own craft." He ran his hand across the side of the vessel. "It amazes me, the complexity that can go into the simplest of things..."

Simon looked to Capernaum in the distance. A group of people watched from the dock. Some hoped to speak to Jesus and awaited his return. Others were the fishermen, unsure if they could go home yet. *They're probably laughing at me,* he thought. *Simon son of Jonah, the fool who fishes in the middle of the day...*

There was a gentle hand on his knee and he turned to see the face of Jesus.

"Don't be afraid."

"What's that?" John asked, and they looked out to the side opposite where the net was. A wave came toward them, unlike anything Simon had seen for it had no crest at the top. It came fast, and got smaller as it approached the boat. By the time it reached them it was a ripple that gently rocked the craft from side to side. They looked into the water all around the boat, but the sun's reflection made it difficult to see beneath.

"Simon!" Andrew cried, pointing to the net. With amazing speed the ropes pulled tight through the cork, the circle closed, the cork pulled together and bobbed for a moment in the water, and then *plop!* The net disappeared beneath.

James and Simon dove into the lake, still wearing their robes. But instead of a diving into a body of water they dove into a sea of fish. Simon felt molested by a thousand scaly hands. He yelled in shock but quickly recovered his senses.

Then John jumped in. He was smart enough to take his robes off and hit the water like a rock, scattering the fish around him.

"Signal the other boat!" Simon yelled. Andrew turned toward the dock and waived madly in the air.

A current of fish slapped against Simon as he and the others finally reached the mesh of rope that bulged with silver fins. Andrew and Jesus rowed the boat closer and reached out as the three of them pushed the net from underneath. The vessel tipped so far over Simon feared it would capsize. Slowly, the fish poured into the boat, leveling it out.

The net seemed ready to tear. The ship was so full of fish it sank deeper into the water. "Where are they?" Simon shouted. His wool tunic added extra weight, and it was an effort to stay afloat and keep the net from falling apart.

Finally, the other boat appeared and men jumped in the water to help. Once Simon's boat was filled to the sinking point, they spilled the net the other way and filled the second boat as well.

They climbed back on their ships and everyone shouted for joy, amazed at what they saw. Two huge piles of fish. Both boats to their sinking points. Simon had dreamed of this moment, to catch more than his father ever did. But once the excitement of getting the fish on the boat passed, so too did the joy of the accomplishment.

Amid the cheers and shouts of his companions, Simon's legs gave out and he fell to his knees, staring at what was before him. All of his hopes and dreams. His salvation from mediocrity. His identity.

A pile of fish.

It was all he ever wanted, and he realized that was all it was.

There, on his knees, surrounded by the things he spent his life to catch, he began to cry. The celebration went silent. Jesus moved toward him, but Simon put up his hand and was too ashamed to even look at his face. "Go away from me Lord," Simon said through his tears, "for I am a sinful man."

No one dared to move. The waves were still. The only sound was that of the fish, twisting around in hope for their life. The sun reflected off their silver scales in a way that made them look dazzling with light.

Jesus went to Simon and put his hand on his shoulder. His touch gave Simon the courage to look up at him.

"There is more to you than this," Jesus said, and his words breathed new life into the fisherman. Simon stared at Jesus' face. It was the same face he knew, same straight black hair, same pronounced nose, same olive skin, but there was also something different. The light reflected off the fish and danced across Jesus' countenance, and something deep within his green eyes seemed to pull Simon away from this world, as if he looked up at the sun from underwater.

How long did that moment last? He felt as if he was both drowning and fully alive. Jesus closed his eyes and put his hands on Simon's head to pray a blessing. Simon closed his eyes as well, and then suddenly became afraid to open them for fear he might awake in his bed and realize this was just a dream.

Can this really be happening to me?

The words of Jesus pierced through his darkness.

"Come after me," Jesus said to him, "and I will make you a fisher of men."

A FISHERMAN OUT OF WATER

A huge crowd awaited their arrival at the dock. They cheered as Simon and Andrew moored the boats, and surged forward with money in hand to buy the fish. Everyone would eat well tonight.

It was a moment Simon always dreamed of, but now he couldn't have cared less. He had found something better.

Leaving the sale of the fish to others, Simon and James pushed through the crowd with Jesus and John behind them. They worked their way through less trafficked streets to get to Simon's home.

They turned a corner and almost ran over a man who carried grain into the city. His name was Amos, a peasant who worked in the fields outside Capernaum. He smelled of filth and stumbled when he walked. Though he didn't want to, Simon thought it best to be courteous and introduce him.

"Master, this is—"

"I know who you are," Jesus said to him. The blood ran from Amos's face. He looked away, mumbled something, and scurried past.

"Well, that's one way to shut him up," James laughed. "I have to remember that next time he wants to go on about the Temple not being the Temple."

The houses in Capernaum were built next to each other and they followed a wall of white, cracked plaster until they came to Simon's dwelling. The synagogue was just down the street and all the doors in this area had "The Lord is God, the Lord alone" written in Hebrew over their doorposts. They touched the *mezuza* and kissed their finger as they entered.

The fragrant smell of fresh bread and olive oil was in the air. They walked into the courtyard. Rachael and their two daughters, Deborah and Hadassah, were lined up to greet them. Rachael looked beautiful. She wore a blue shawl around her head, fastened by a brooch that Simon gave her as part of her dowry. The girls had their heads uncovered. Deborah had her mother's straight hair, while

Hadassah had Simon's curls. Andrew was there as well. He had run ahead of the others to warn Rachael of their imminent arrival.

Rachael bowed, as did the girls. "Shalom, husband."

"As always, you have honored me by having the house so ready," Simon said to her. He leaned forward to kiss her on the cheek. She allowed it.

"It was kind of *Andrew* to let me know about our guest." Then she bowed to Jesus. "Greetings, Master. It is an honor to have you back."

"The honor is mine," Jesus said. Rachael looked at the girls and they headed toward the kitchen. Simon followed and touched Rachael's arm. "Where is your mother?" he asked quietly.

"She wasn't feeling well, so I'm letting her sleep. Food will be ready shortly." And she pushed the curtain back and entered the kitchen.

Simon looked around his small courtyard. A grindstone sat in the middle of it. He still hadn't fixed the thatch roof that gave shelter for their goat. The walls needed to be painted. A stream of mud flowed from the courtyard into the doors that led to their kitchen and bedroom, and he muttered a curse for living on a hill. Simon wished he had more warning that Jesus was coming—he would have prepared the house better.

Where would Jesus sleep? They had only one bedroom, and the rains of winter would make it impossible to sleep outside. The only other room was a small dining area beneath the stairs that led to the roof above their bedroom and kitchen. It would have to do.

The men walked to basins filled with water and washed their hands before sitting down to eat. Rachael and his daughters brought platters of bread, fruit, and milk into the courtyard.

James marveled at all the food. "So much food and only five of us to eat it!" he said. "Could this day be any better?"

They heard a knock at the door and a growing sound of voices from the street. "I think there will be more than five of us before the day is out," Simon said.

Simon's house wasn't large and the courtyard quickly filled with people. Almost every man who arrived brought a gift of food, and a few more women came to help Rachael with the work. The men sat and laughed in the courtyard. The women worked and talked in the kitchen. The children ran around and played in and out of the street. Only the goat was unhappy, and looked weary of giving any more milk.

What surprised Simon most was that a few Gentiles came to visit. Simon knew them because of his work, and showed good hospitality, but never had they entered his house. It made him uncomfortable. They did not bless themselves as they entered. They reached for food off the plate without properly washing their hands. Jesus treated them like any other, but Simon breathed easier after they left.

The door opened again and Simon saw the gaunt face of Jairus, the head of the synagogue, peek in. He nervously looked around before entering the courtyard. Behind him was Judith, his wife, and his twelve-year-old daughter, Sarah. Sarah had the large brown eyes of her mother and the slender frame of her father. She was also best friends with Hadassah.

People immediately began to greet him. Jairus uncomfortably shook their hands and looked around. Simon waved him over to introduce him to Jesus.

"Master, this is Jairus, the head of our synagogue, and also my neighbor," Simon said.

"A great honor, a great honor indeed. For all of Capernaum," Jairus said. "This is my wife, Judith." She bowed to him. "And this is my daughter—where is she?" Simon saw Hadassah and Sarah run out the door. Jairus was clearly agitated.

Judith put a gentle hand on his arm. "I will see to her," she said.

"Yes, yes. You do that."

"Sit with me, Jairus," Jesus said. "I am very impressed by the faith of the people here. I'm sure you have something to do with that."

Jairus blushed. "Oh no, I had nothing to do with that... I mean, I guess I did... Well, if you say so that is."

James started to laugh and slapped his hand against Jairus's back. "I think he means, 'thank you'."

"Yes, yes, that's what I meant. Thank you." Jairus readjusted his robe after the slap from James. "So, you... you're really from Nazareth?"

"Yes. There aren't many of us, but we do exist." Everyone smiled at the comment except for Jairus.

"Well, of course you exist, of course you do. It's just that I've never met, I mean…" He took a deep breath. "Would you like to speak at the synagogue this Sabbath?"

Jesus bowed his head. "It would be an honor," he said. "Thank you for asking."

"No problem, no problem at all. It will be wonderful. Thank you." Jairus smiled and seemed satisfied that his mission was accomplished. He excused himself and quickly left.

"You'll have to excuse Jairus," Simon said. "He's a good man, but a bit nervous."

"I can do that to some people," Jesus said.

"Actually, he's like that all the time!" James said, and they all laughed.

The increasing noise in the street heralded the Zebedees' arrival. Papa Zebedee was a large, barrel-chested man with huge hands and a booming voice. The gentleness and grace of his wife, Salome, provided a sharp contrast to her husband. Their boys marched tall as trees, and spoke at unusually loud volumes.

Everyone stood to welcome them. There were few in Capernaum they weren't related to. The house echoed with loud *shaloms* and the sound of hands slapping on backs.

They greeted Jesus warmly. Salome hugged him like a son and sat next to him.

"How is my sister?" she asked.

"Mother is fine," Jesus replied, "and sends her love."

Simon excused himself and pulled Papa Zebedee aside. "Can I talk to you in private?"

"Why do you want to talk in private?" Zebedee asked, alerting everyone around them of his request.

"Business," Simon replied. That got his attention, and soon the two were walking down the narrow streets of Capernaum together.

They small-talked about the catch he had made earlier that day, but Simon knew it was best to get right to the point. "I'd like to sell you my share of the business."

The request caught Zebedee off guard. "What?"

"I'd like to sell my share of the business," he said again.

Papa Zebedee looked at him sternly. "You mean *your father's* share," he said.

"No," Simon said. "I mean *my* share."

Zebedee laughed. "Why don't we sleep on it and talk in a few days," he said.

Simon was not to be deterred. "Let's do this now. I'm not getting on that boat tomorrow," *or ever again,* Simon thought.

They walked a few more steps in silence. "And what are you going to do?" Zebedee asked.

"Follow Jesus," Simon replied. Just saying it out loud gave him hope and peace.

But Papa Zebedee had the opposite reaction. "Jesus," he snorted. "You're going to be a carpenter now?"

"He's more than a carpenter," Simon said.

"Don't bet on it," he replied. "I know his family. They are not too happy with him right now, you know. They think he's lost his mind."

Simon got defensive. "People said that about the Baptist, too."

"Well, John the Baptist was different," Zebedee said. "He was a prophet through and through. It's all he ever did—it's all he ever was. Jesus probably saw his brother doing it and thought he could do it, too. But let me tell you something. He's no John the Baptist. And he's no Rabbi either. Never went to school for it. Never was someone else's disciple. Just showed up and started preaching. No, that doesn't make you a Rabbi. Is that what you're going to do? Be a Rabbi, too?"

"No, I'm going to be…" and he paused. *A fisher of men* was going to be his response, but as he about to say it he realized it sounded absurd. "I'm going to follow Jesus."

"Follow Jesus, follow Jesus," Zebedee mocked. "Is that all you have to say? This sounds like a great plan. I can't imagine that your father—"

Simon grabbed Zebedee by the arm and spun him around to face him. "Leave my father out of this," he said.

Zebedee didn't blink. "Just because you are doesn't mean I have to." They stared at each other for a moment, and Zebedee stepped closer, right into Simon's face. "I'll buy your share if you can tell me one thing. Are you leaving because you want to follow something, or because you want to run away?"

The question cut Simon like a knife. The wind off the water slapped him in the face. He looked around and realized that their walk had led them down to the lake.

Don't leave me, it pleaded.

He felt uncertain, and a sense of dread came upon his heart. His words failed as he stared out into the sea.

Zebedee grunted with self-satisfaction. "That's what I thought," he said. "Now if you'll excuse me, I have to talk some sense into two of my sons." And he walked up the street back to Simon's house.

Simon stood there a moment, staring at the lake, unsure what to do.

Don't leave me, begged the water.

It sounded just like his father.

Simon turned around and headed home.

James and John fared better with their father than Simon did. They were wise enough to have the conversation in the courtyard near Jesus, where the hospitality of a guest required a more civil tone. It was agreed that they could take some time off, but Zebedee wouldn't agree to anything more permanent. "Wait and see," the father said, and things were settled for the moment.

As the sun began to set, the guests began to leave. Rachael came out with a plate of pomegranates for them to take on their way. It was one of Simon's favorite fruits. He reached for one, but Rachael turned and went back to the kitchen before he could take it. *Did she mean to do that?* Simon wondered. But he was too busy saying farewell to the guests to give it a second thought.

They lit lamps and said the evening prayers. Rachael brought cushions for Jesus to sleep on the floor of the small room they used for meals when the weather was bad. He thanked them and retired for the evening. Rachael gave a courteous bow and went into the kitchen. The girls went to the bedroom.

Simon stood alone in the courtyard. Chickens clucked at his feet, happy to have the place back to themselves. He looked up at the stars and took a deep breath, then headed into the kitchen.

Rachael vigorously scrubbed copper plates. Simon cleared his throat and she stopped, but did not look at him.

"Rachael, you have once again brought honor to our house with your hospitality," Simon said. "Thank you."

"You're welcome, my husband." She did not look up.

"I need to speak to you," he said.

"I'm listening." Her head was still bowed.

"Rachael," he said, and touched her arm. She looked up at him with dead eyes. "I caught two boats full of fish, more than my father ever did." He smiled but she did not respond in kind.

"I heard about it," she said. "I heard about *everything*."

Simon was unsure how to respond. "What's that supposed to mean?"

"The catch. Your *plans*."

Simon took a breath so he didn't yell in response. The walls were too thin and Jesus might hear. "What do you know of my plans?"

"Everyone is talking about it."

"*Everyone?*" Simon asked, "or just your gossiping friends?"

"At least they talk to me," she said. "Why do I have to hear from *them* that you're going to be his disciple? Why do I have to overhear James argue with his father about selling the boats? Are you really leaving everything to follow him?"

Simon slammed his fist on the table and cursed. His head spun and couldn't think clearly. He was just about to break the silence but Rachael beat him to it.

"So it's true?" she asked. There was a hint of shock in her voice.

"He needs me," he said.

Rachael almost laughed. "For what? To lift heavy objects?"

Simon stepped toward her. "You go too far," he said.

"You are the one who wants to go, not me. I'm sorry you aren't the fisherman your father was, and I'm sorry I've borne you no sons—" Her tears choked off her words. Without thinking, Simon raised his hand to strike, and she cowered before him.

He looked at his shaking fist. *What am I doing?* Then he looked at his wife, bent over the counter, crying. He wanted to comfort her. He wanted to kill her. He left the kitchen, and almost ripped off the curtain as he did.

"WHAT DO YOU WANT WITH US?"

Mark 1:21-28

Simon was awake, but wished he wasn't. A sliver of moonlight crept in under the curtain that separated the small bedroom from the courtyard. His wife was next to him, but faced away.

He gave up trying to go back to sleep. Simon rose from the cushions on the uneven floor and reached for his tunic. *How is it that I get up at the same time, every morning, every day?* His father taught him how. He remembered how Jonah shook him awake, often having to slap him to do so.

Instinctively, Simon rubbed his face. His beard felt coarse against his large, calloused hand.

He was ten years old when he first awoke on his own. He remembered the joy of being dressed before his father got up, and the look of pride on his father's face when he came out of the bedroom and found him ready.

Simon moved quietly so as not to disturb his daughters or his mother-in-law, who slept restlessly. As he stepped over his sleeping girls, he lamented that he had no son to wake.

He looked back at Rachael, and felt such a surge of emotion that he had to walk away.

Simon stood in the courtyard and wondered what to do. He should be back in bed. He wasn't a fisherman any more. But the dock felt more comfortable than his bedroom so he headed down to the lake.

The boats were heading out to deep water by the time he reached them. Simon regretted lying in bed for so long.

"Shalom, Simon." He was startled by the voice.

"Shalom, James," Simon said. "What are you doing here?"

James shrugged. "Just making sure everyone got off okay," he said. "You?"

"Me, too." They stood in silence as the fishing boats were enveloped by the night. "James?"

"Hmm?"

"I was lying."

James nodded. "Me, too."

They walked to the end of the dock and sat down, untied their sandals and put their feet in the water like they did when they were kids. Simon and James did not grow up together, but it felt like they did.

"What does Ruth think about all of this?" Simon asked.

James let out a long, slow breath. "Jesus is part of the family," he explained. "There have always been whispers about him. But the Baptist was so charismatic and Jesus was so... hidden. I'm not sure if I can explain it. Anyway, Ruth believes him to be a prophet. If she didn't before, she did when she heard him speak."

"Rachael has never heard him speak."

"Maybe that's what she needs."

Maybe. "He did call me, right? He asked me to be..." Simon couldn't say the words out loud.

"A fisher of men," James said.

Simon nodded. "I don't know what that means."

"Why don't you ask him?"

Simon almost laughed out loud. The solution was so simple he hadn't considered it. He gave it some thought, then shook his head. "I think I'm supposed to know."

The water lapped against the wooden posts of the dock. Simon half expected the sea to speak to him but it stayed silent, and he was torn as to whether that was good or bad.

He recalled the words of Jesus: "There is more to you than this."

But this is all I know!

"You have the greatest prophet in Galilee sleeping under your roof," James said. "Something good will happen."

The days crawled for Simon. He and Rachael did not speak, except in public when they had to. He expected an apology from her, and grew more resentful each day it didn't come.

And then there was Jesus. *What does he need me for, anyway?* There were nicer places in Capernaum to sleep. It was odd he did not stay with his Aunt Salome, though he knew his house would be much quieter than hers.

Guests came and went. There were fewer guests but they stayed longer. John spent so much time around the house it was as if he lived there. And Simon began to miss the sea.

Finally, the Sabbath came. Simon left early with the others to accompany Jesus to the synagogue. Rachael promised to join him after mother woke up. Her fever had gotten worse last night and she wanted her to sleep as much as she could.

Jesus, Simon, Andrew, and John arrived at the synagogue. Stone benches lined the walls and faced each other. But today, woven mats were spread out on the stone floor, ready for a large crowd. In the middle was a small wooden dais, and on it stood a lectern and the seat of Moses, from where Jesus would teach. Jairus paced back and forth in front of it, and showed great relief when Jesus and the fishermen came in. He hastily ran up to greet him.

"Blessed day! Blessed day! Thank you for coming. It is wonderful you are here, truly wonderful."

"I am honored for the invitation," Jesus said.

Jesus and Jairus talked about what Scriptures should be read as people began to gather. It was usually a joyful time of seeing friends, but Simon couldn't help but feel a bit of anxiety. His eyes kept shifting toward the back of the synagogue, hoping to see Rachael arrive with the girls.

She didn't. The space got tighter and tighter. James and Ruth appeared, along with the rest of the Zebedee clan. The men made their way forward and James sat next to Simon. There was no more room inside. People lined up tightly on the benches and on every available space on the floor. The balcony was full. People stood in the doorway and out into the street. *Will she be able to hear the Master from out there?* he wondered. *Doesn't she know how important this is?*

Jairus called the assembly to order. They all stood for the reading of the Torah. Simon continued to look over his shoulder, hoping for a sign of her. His anxiety turned to anger. *She's doing this on purpose,* he thought.

He felt a gentle hand on his shoulder, and he turned and looked into the eyes of Jesus.

"Don't be afraid," he said to him.

"It is my privilege, my privilege indeed, to introduce to you Jesus of Nazareth." Cheers came from the crowd. Jesus walked forward and sat in the chair. The congregation seated themselves on the benches and the floor.

Jesus took a deep breath and proclaimed boldly, *"You will be my people and I will be your God."* He paused, and looked around at the faces in the synagogue. "That is what we heard spoken through the prophet Jeremiah today. God promises us that a new covenant is coming, one that would be written upon our hearts. And what is the result of this covenant? That we would be His people and He would be our God.

"But Jeremiah is not the first to say these words." He gestured to one of the attendants to bring him the Torah scroll. He opened it to the Book of Exodus and read, *"So say to the Israelites, 'I am Jehovah. I shall free you from the forced labor of the Egyptians; I shall rescue you from their slavery and I shall redeem you with outstretched arm and mighty acts of judgment. I shall take you as my people and I shall be your God.'"*

He rolled up the scroll and handed it to the attendant. "God said these words to Moses before the Exodus. Did not the Exodus accomplish God's desire for us to be his people and He to be our God? Was it not fulfilled in His covenant with David that made us a great kingdom?"

Simon could see Jesus was making a good impression on the people. They turned to each other and quietly affirmed what he taught. "If we are truly God's people, and Jehovah is truly our God, then there must be something in God's plan for us that is yet to be fulfilled. Jehovah's work is not finished. Why would Jeremiah prophesy about a new covenant if the covenants we had were enough?"

"I have heard some Rabbis say that the new covenant will merely strengthen the old ones. That doesn't make sense to me. But then again," he said, patting the armrest of the chair, "I'm just the son of a carpenter." And everybody in the crowd laughed.

Simon used the laughter as an excuse to look toward the door. Surely, his wife must have entered the synagogue by now. But what captured his attention was Amos, who sat a few people behind him.

He twitched. More so than usual. And while everyone else smiled at Jesus' preaching, his face was hard and cold.

As the laughter died down, Jesus' tone became more serious. "No, it is not that I don't understand," he said. "It is that the other Rabbis... are wrong."

There were a few gasps at the boldness of this statement. Jairus, who sat in the front, looked around uncomfortably.

Jesus continued. "When God made a covenant with Abraham, was it merely to strengthen the covenant made with Noah? No, it was to do a new thing. It was to make us a people set apart for God's glory. Was the covenant with Moses merely to strengthen the covenant with Abraham? No. It was to give us the gift of the commandments, to give us a law and make us a nation. And when God made his covenant with David, was it merely to strengthen His covenant with Moses? Again, the answer is no. We became a kingdom. Each covenant was built upon the former covenant, but did not repeat it. In fact," he proclaimed, raising the tone of his voice and saying each word with precision, "every covenant God has made with us has been better than the one before."

Simon heard Amos take heavy and deep breaths.

"What's with him?" James whispered.

Simon shrugged and he tried to keep his focus on Jesus. But the hairs on the back of his neck were standing on end. It felt wholly unnatural.

Jesus glanced at Amos, but continued to teach. "In truth I tell you, this new covenant will not just make us a stronger kingdom, but a *new* kingdom. A better kingdom. A kingdom of God." Jesus threw his arms wide and proclaimed, "That kingdom is here! Right now! Repent, and believe the good news!"

At that, Amos stood and howled with a freakish voice. "WHAT DO YOU WANT WITH US, JESUS OF NAZARETH?" he said. "DO YOU *THINK* YOU HAVE COME TO DESTROY US?"

Women screamed. Men crawled over each other to move away from him. Those by the doors of the synagogue ran out of them, yelling for help. Simon and the others jumped to their feet and turned to Amos, but they were immediately frozen with fear. Simon was bigger and stronger than Amos, and a part of him thought that he shouldn't be afraid, that he could take him in a fight. But the fear remained.

Simon looked at James. He was as white as a lamb. John was even paler, if possible. Andrew trembled.

Amos walked toward them. Simon was caught in his midnight black eyes, and he thought he saw different faces floating around in them. Simon opened his mouth to scream but had no breath for noise. It was the most terrifying thing he'd ever seen but he couldn't look away.

Then he felt a hand on his shoulder, and that broke the spell. It was Jesus. He moved him aside and stepped toward Amos. Simon wanted to shout at him, warn him to stay back, but he still had no voice.

Amos froze as Jesus approached. He stared at him for a moment, and then a look of horrified recognition filled his face. "I KNOW WHO YOU ARE! YOU ARE THE HOLY ONE OF G—"

"Be quiet!" Jesus said. Amos was silenced in mid sentence. He moved his lips but no sound came out. He fell to the ground clutching his throat, and when he looked up he was face to face with Jesus.

"Come out of him!" Jesus said firmly. Amos screamed with a terrifying squeal and convulsed on the ground. The sound echoed off the stone walls and a strong wind whipped the inside of the synagogue. The fishermen fell back on the floor. Simon covered his face with his hands.

Then there was the sound of crying. Simon was the first to look up. Everyone was cowered on the ground except for Jesus and Amos. Jesus held him in his arms, and Amos cried like a child. "I'm sorry, I'm sorry, I'm sorry…" Amos said.

Simon could see tears in Jesus' eyes, too. He heard him whisper to Amos, "You are free, you are forgiven, and you are loved."

They stood there, the two of them, weeping in each other's arms. Time stood still in the beauty of that moment. The silence turned to whispers and the whispers turned to murmurs as the people turned to each other to talk about what they had just seen.

Andrew pulled his brother close. "He gives orders even to unclean spirits, and they obey him?" Simon did not know what to say.

Then Jesus began to sing.

"*Hallelujah! Praise God from the heavens, praise Him in the heights. Praise Him, all His angels, praise Him all His host!*"

Those in the synagogue got on their feet, clapped their hands, and shouted for joy. The noise must have echoed into the streets, for people ran into the synagogue almost as quickly as they had run out.

Simon stood in the middle of the celebration, but never felt more alone. Where was Rachael? *How could she have missed this?* If she had seen this, she would know why he needed to follow him.

The noise became deafening. Amos danced and laughed, and people were filled with joy. Men began to dance, and James put a tight arm around Simon's shoulder.

"Hallelujah!" he said.

Just then, Simon saw Deborah make her way to him through the crowd. Her face was swollen with tears.

"What's wrong?" Simon asked. "Where is your mother?"

"Papa, come quickly," Deborah said. "Grandmother is dying!"

Simon's heart almost stopped. Jesus turned and looked at him—he must have heard his daughter's cry. "I'll be right back," Simon said. He pushed through the crowd and into the street.

Simon's house was only two doors down from the synagogue, and he threw open the door and pulled back the curtain to his bedroom. His mother-in-law was on the cushions on the floor, writhing slowly back and forth and muttering incoherently. Rachael was bent over her, sobbing. She wiped her mother's face with a damp cloth.

"She's so hot," Rachael said. "I sent Hadassah to get more water, but it isn't helping."

"Why didn't you call me?" Simon asked, then immediately regretted questioning her at a time like this.

"Why do you care?" Rachael said with glaring eyes. "I know who you love." Her eyes moved over his shoulder. Simon turned and saw Jesus enter the room.

Jesus walked past Simon and knelt by the cushions where his mother lay. Then Jesus looked at Rachael. Simon saw a change come over her. He knew well what it was like to feel pierced by his green eyes. Rachael leaned back and put her hand over her chest, then looked at Simon. Simon began to murmur prayers.

Jesus looked down at Rachael's mother. He gently wiped the hair off her forehead and placed his hands on either side of her face. She grew still, and for a moment Simon feared that she was dead.

But then her eyes opened.

Rachael gave a scream and jumped back, hands over her mouth. Jesus smiled and helped her mother sit upright, though it was more out of courtesy—she seemed stronger than ever.

"What is everybody doing in the bedroom?" she asked. "And what are you boys looking at?" Simon looked over his shoulder and saw Andrew, James, and John in the doorway, mouths open with shock.

Simon and Rachael looked at each other in amazement, and could find no words to speak. Jesus stood and helped their mother to her feet. "We wanted to let you know that we are about to have many guests arriving," he said.

"How many?"

"Probably the whole town."

The mother gasped. "We've got cooking to do!" And she left the room with the energy of a woman half her age, grabbing the arms of James and John and leading them into the courtyard with Andrew right behind. "You boys, come with me! We've got to move things around."

"But… it's the Sabbath!" complained Andrew as he followed her toward the kitchen.

Rachael fell on her knees before Jesus and looked up at him. "Master," she said, "forgive me for not believing in you." Her eyes moved to Simon—she said it to both of them. Simon began to cry. He fell on his knees and embraced his wife.

He held her for a moment. Then he wiped the tears from his face and stood up, hand on Rachael's shoulder. "We will follow you wherever you go," Simon said to him. Rachael looked up to her husband and nodded, and then looked at Jesus and bowed her head.

Jesus smiled, but it was different than before. It was a smile that masked pain. "Yes, you will," he replied. It felt like he was about to say more when Jairus ran into the room.

"Amazing, amazing, absolutely amazing!" he yelled, and then noticed Rachael kneeling on the floor with Simon standing behind her. "I'm sorry, am I interrupting something?"

Rachael got to her feet. "Of course not, Jairus. It is always an honor to have you in our home—"

"Thank you, Rachael. Master Jesus, you must come back, you just must! They are all there waiting for you. This is just amazing. Amazing! Oh, you must come back. Please, Rabbi, please!"

"Yes," Jesus replied. "I'll be right there. I'm more than happy to."

Jairus almost jumped with joy. "Wonderful! Absolutely wonderful!" he said, and ran out of the house and started yelling in the streets, "He's coming back! He's coming back!"

They couldn't help but laugh at his enthusiasm. "Looks like I'll get to finish my preaching after all," Jesus said. Then he walked into the courtyard, leaving them alone.

The husband and wife gazed at each other for a moment, and Rachael slipped her hand into his. The simple touch made him weak in the knees. All was forgiven, all was forgotten. All that mattered was this moment. They began to laugh but didn't know why. Then Simon looked at her and she blushed.

"I still haven't heard him speak," she said.

"Then let's go," Simon said. Together they walked into the courtyard, gathered the rest of their family, and headed to the synagogue with Jesus.

THE PHARISEES ARRIVE

That evening, after sunset, people lined up outside Simon's door. He was amazed at what he saw. All who were sick became healthy again. All possessed by demons were set free.

The next morning, Jesus said, "Let us go to the other neighboring towns and villages, so I can proclaim the message there, too." Rachael gathered some pomegranates for Simon to take on the way.

They left Capernaum with almost four hundred people, and every town and village added more. They came from all over Galilee to see the Rabbi from Nazareth. Even some from as far as Jerusalem had joined the crowd. Jesus went all through Galilee, preaching in the synagogues of every town and driving out demons as he went. By the time they rounded the lake and came near Capernaum again, there were over *two thousand*.

As the numbers grew, Simon felt his importance diminish. Many other men emerged as strong leaders in the group. Matthias and Barsabbas were former disciples of the Baptist. They had great faith and were skilled in proclaiming God's word. David from Tyre was a natural born leader. He came with his twin brother who was not as dynamic as he—most people just called him "the twin". There was also a man named Ioakim from the town of Kelioth in Judea, a brilliant scribe with a talent for gathering money. He and his two apprentices gathered money from the people and distributed it to the poor (they first offered it to Jesus, but he flatly refused to take any of it).

Simon was happy to be a part of the ministry, but felt overshadowed by stronger personalities and the large numbers of people. As they neared his home, Jesus sent Simon, Andrew, James, and John ahead to let them see their families and prepare the town for his arrival. Jesus planned to preach on the mountain the next day and wanted all of Capernaum to know about it.

During a lull in the conversation, it was young John who gave voice to the words they all felt.

"I miss him," he said to the others. "I hope it is not selfish of me to say, but I liked it better when it was just him and us."

James put his hand on his brother's shoulder. "Don't feel bad. I think we all feel that way."

"Let's be thankful for the time we had with him," Simon said. He spoke as much to himself as he did to his friends. "We're fishermen, and he's a great prophet—even greater than John the Baptist. I'm honored he got into our boat that day, and that we got to have such time with him. But things are different now, and I don't see them going back to the way it was."

James and Andrew agreed, but John still had a tough time dealing with it. "I still miss him," he said.

They walked a few paces in silence. Simon drew a heavy breath.

"So do I," he said.

The fishermen were welcomed at Capernaum like heroes returning from war. The townspeople were excited to hear that Jesus would preach the next day and made plans to attend.

As the four turned down familiar streets to come home, Simon could have sworn that someone looked out his door, but it slammed shut as he approached. *Probably one of the children,* he thought. When he tried to open it, the door was locked. He knocked.

"Yes, yes?" said a voice behind the door. "Who's there, who's there?"

Simon was confused. "Jairus, is that you?"

"Simon, Simon, why are you banging my door? You've got the wrong house, the wrong house!"

It was true that the doors looked the same. He stepped back, but still thought it was his. The others seemed equally confused. Then they heard laughter behind the door and it was unlocked and opened.

Philip was on the floor, holding himself in hysterics. He was a scrawny man and looked almost like a boy. Bartholomew stood next to him. He was almost Simon's height, and a large smile emerged from his long graying beard. Soon they were all caught up in gales of laughter as they entered the house and greeted their friends.

Rachael came into the courtyard from the kitchen and met Simon with a kiss. "Welcome home, husband," she said.

"Good to see you Rachael. But I didn't give permission to have dogs in the house while I was gone," he said, pointing to Philip.

"Well, he's *your* friend," she said. "Is the Master coming?"

"Is he? Where is he?" Bartholomew asked.

"He is near, but he probably won't be here until tomorrow night. He'll be preaching on the top of the mountain in the morning."

"Are guests coming?" Rachael's mother yelled from the kitchen.

"Tomorrow!" Rachael called back. "If you'll excuse me, we should probably start baking now. I have a feeling there will be a lot of people. Besides," she said as she headed off to the kitchen, "I think you have some catching up to do."

Simon hugged Bartholomew. Bartholomew was usually a well-fed man, but Simon noticed his tunic hung loosely on him. "It is good to see you," he said. "Are you all right?"

He could see the lines of exhaustion and stress on Bartholomew's face as he smiled. "I have much to tell you, and much to hear," he said.

"By the way, *I'm all right*. Thanks for asking," Philip said. But Simon put an arm around Bartholomew and jokingly ignored him. He, Bartholomew, James, and John walked into the small dining room and reclined against cushions on the floor while Philip and Andrew talked in the courtyard.

"How is the Baptist?" Simon asked.

"Pray for him," Bartholomew said. "And pray for Herod."

"That fox! Why should I pray for him?"

"John thinks he can be converted," he said. "He's in his cell, but Herod talks to him almost every night."

"Convert Herod? It would be easier to convert the devil," James said.

Bartholomew nodded. "But if anyone can do it, it would be John."

"Or Jesus!" John said. "You should hear him preach!"

Bartholomew laughed at his enthusiasm. "Yes, word has even reached the prisons of King Herod about how amazing he is. So John sent Philip and me here to see if we could help."

Andrew popped his head into the room. "Philip and I are going down to the lake to see some people. We'll be right back." Simon nodded.

Bartholomew leaned forward. "So tell me about Jesus. Are the stories true?"

James and John looked at Simon to speak. "Bartholomew, I'm not sure if words can describe what has happened over the past month since Jesus arrived. We were our on our boat, when—" Simon was interrupted by a knock at the door.

James sighed in frustration. "More people," he muttered.

"This happens a lot here lately," John said.

The knocking continued. Simon called to his wife, but she didn't answer. He excused himself from the table to answer the door.

"Is anyone home?" came an older voice from outside the door.

"Yes we are. Who is there?" he asked.

"It's Rabbi Nicodemus with a friend. We are here to see Jesus of Nazareth."

Simon stopped dead in his tracks. Rabbi Nicodemus was one of the most respected Rabbis in Israel, and sympathetic to Jesus' teaching. The others in the dining room heard the voice as well. They anxiously got up from the table and headed for the door. But Simon began to laugh. "How stupid do you think I am, Philip? That doesn't even sound like Nicodemus." He reached to open the door. "You make him sound like a dying old—"

And as Simon opened the door, he saw Rabbi Nicodemus.

"Rabbi!" he exclaimed. The others stood in awe and instinctively brushed off their tunics to make themselves look better.

The old Rabbi smiled. "Not who you were expecting?"

Simon felt his face go red. "My apologies, Rabbi. Please come in."

As he walked in the house, Nicodemus touched the *mezuza* on the doorpost with his finger and kissed it. He was followed by another Rabbi who did the same, but did it more dramatically. "This is my... colleague, Rabbi Dov," he said. Nicodemus was well dressed, but Dov's outfit was even more impressive. He had wide tassels and his tunic was hemmed with gold thread that reflected its color in the late afternoon sun. He stood taller than Nicodemus, almost as tall as James but much leaner.

By now Rachael had made her way into the courtyard, and she quickly called her mother and the girls in for a formal greeting.

Simon introduced himself, his family, and his friends. Rachael offered them food, but Nicodemus politely declined and the women left. Nicodemus looked Simon in the eye and said, "Forgive me, but have we met before?"

"We were all with the Master in Jerusalem last Passover, Rabbi," Simon replied.

"*Master*," Dov murmured. "So, where is he?"

"He is to the south of us, and will be preaching on the mountain in the morning," Simon said.

Nicodemus was pleased, but Dov was not. "It will be good for you to hear him speak, Rabbi Dov," Nicodemus said.

"I don't need to hear a sermon, I just want to ask some questions," he said. Rabbi Dov looked at Simon. "Can you arrange an appointment with him?"

"I can ask him for you Rabbi," Simon said. Dov slightly bowed and left.

Nicodemus's demeanor visibly relaxed at Rabbi Dov's departure. "My apologies for his rudeness," he said. "You have no idea what I went through to get him here. Rabbi Dov is one of the most learned Rabbis in Jerusalem, and his opinion carries much weight among other Pharisees. We arrived two days ago, and have been staying in Jairus's house next door." He looked at Simon and gently touched his arm. "Do what you can to get Jesus to talk to him," he pleaded. "I hope that Jesus can be accepted among the Rabbis. More people need to hear his teaching."

"I'll do what I can," Simon said, feeling awkward about this responsibility. Nicodemus bade them farewell and left. Simon closed the door, and they all took a heavy breath.

"Do you often get the most brilliant Rabbis in Israel knocking on your door?" Bartholomew asked.

Simon shook his head in disbelief. "I guess I should get used to it."

As the sun rose on the next day, the entire town walked up the mount to hear Jesus. Simon led Jairus, Nicodemus, Dov, and seven of Dov's followers up the hill. Those who sat on the ground got up and moved out of reverence for the Rabbis. Simon was in the lead and Jairus walked nervously behind him. Nicodemus and Dov walked side by side, arguing. Nicodemus's cautious optimism was outweighed by Dov's blatant cynicism. Dov moved carefully through the crowd as though he was afraid of catching a disease.

They came upon Ioakim, who was arguing with one of his apprentices. Something about silver. But when Ioakim turned and saw them approach, his entire demeanor changed. "Rabbi Nicodemus! Rabbi Dov! How blessed we are to have such men of great faith and intellect to join us."

He bowed low with an exaggerated flourish of his hand. Then he turned to his apprentice and said, "Judas, tell Rabbi Jesus that these men have arrived." Judas left.

"Do I know you?" Dov asked.

"We have not formally met," Ioakim said, "but I have done much business in Jerusalem with Simeon son of Jethro as well as Abir son of Elezier. And I am related to Saul son of Amichai who works under Caiaphas the high priest."

Rabbi Dov nodded his head with each name. "We are here to talk to Jesus," Rabbi Dov said. He glanced at Simon and then back to Ioakim. "Can *you* take us to him?"

Ioakim did not hesitate to respond. "Of course, honored Rabbis. Please follow me." He ordered people out of the way and led them up the hill, leaving Simon ignored and frozen in his place.

He was speechless. Simon never liked Ioakim, but now he hated him. He turned away in disgust, trying his hardest not to swear out loud. In the distance he saw Matthew, talking to John. The teenager's body language suggested that he only tolerated the conversation. Simon's muscles tensed at the sight of him, and he wondered which one he hated more.

A voice next to him said, "Can it be I've found someone who hates those pigs more than me?"

Simon turned to look at a man a few years younger than he was. The bridge of his nose was slightly crooked, as if he'd been in his share of fights. "Do I know you?"

"Simon, son of Uriel."

"Simon, son of Jonah."

"Yeah, I know. You're like Jesus' bodyguard, right?"

Is that what I am? He looked more closely at the man's face and recognized him. "Were you with that group of Zealots?"

The man looked around. "What would you do if I was?"

"Nothing."

"Are you a friend of the cause?"

"The cause, yes. But not your methods."

The son of Uriel smirked in defiance. "Oh, I forgot that you boys here in Galilee like to cozy up to your Roman owners. But if you came from where I came from, you might have a different view."

The words were meant to arouse anger, but there was something about them that didn't seem sincere. "So where are your friends now?"

He shrugged. "We came here to see if Jesus was the one who would free us from the Romans."

"The Messiah?"

He nodded. "Yeah, well... obviously not. I mean look at him."

Simon crossed his arms. "What's that supposed to mean?"

The Zealot laughed. "Got some fight, I see! I bet you could take down a few guys in a pinch."

"I'm not the fighting type," Simon said.

"Well, neither is he," the Zealot said, nodding to Jesus in the distance. "So my friends took off."

"But you're still here."

"Yeah... I am." A change came over the Zealot as he said those words, like a ray of sunlight that breaks through an otherwise cloudy day. But he quickly regained his earlier bravado. "Let me know if you want to beat up some tax collectors."

Simon nodded, and left to find his family.

Jesus looked with excitement on the gathering crowd. Over three thousand had come to hear him speak, but he didn't see them as a group. He saw three thousand different stories before him, each with their own moments of joy and pain, hope and fear. They were all disfigured by the wounds of their lives, both spiritual and physical. And they were all beautiful. He loved every one.

One of those stories politely called his name, and Jesus turned to look at him. His heart broke to see his face, because he knew how this story would end.

"Shalom, Judas."

Judas stared at him a moment and quickly bowed. "I'm honored you know my name, Master."

"Not just your name but the work you've been doing."

"It's been my pleasure. Master Ioakim wanted me to tell you that Rabbis Dov and Nicodemus have arrived and would like an audience with you."

"All are welcome to come talk to me at any time," Jesus said. "That includes you as well."

Judas nodded. "Thank you Master. I would love to. In fact... can I trouble you with a question?" Jesus nodded and he continued. "I have listened to you preach about the kingdom of God. But you don't mention the kingdom of Israel, as other Rabbis do. Aren't they one in the same? Or do you mean it is something more?"

Jesus smiled and put his hand on Judas's shoulder. "A very insightful question! You remember in Scriptures that it was the Israelites who wanted a king, not God. But he granted it because—"

Then Ioakim appeared with the Rabbis behind him. "Judas, stop bothering the Master!" Ioakim said. Judas quickly bowed his head, muttered an apology, and left.

Jesus looked sternly at Ioakim, but he was oblivious to it.

"Rabbi Jesus," he said with a flourish of his hand, "may I present to you Rabbi Nicodemus and Rabbi Dov."

"Jesus, it is so good to see you again," Nicodemus said. They embraced.

"It is always an honor to see you, Rabbi Nicodemus," Jesus said.

Then Dov politely greeted Jesus. "I have heard much about you," he said, "and I must admit I am impressed by the number of people following you, as well as *some* of your disciples," he said, gesturing toward Ioakim.

Ioakim respectfully bowed. "You are too kind, Rabbi Dov."

Jesus' stomach churned. He saw that the Pharisees had moved many people aside to get to him, and those who had waited for hours were now without a place to sit.

"Please have a seat," he said to the Rabbis.

"Well," Rabbi Dov said, "first I have some questions—"

"Have a seat," Jesus said. His interruption caught Dov off guard and he looked as though he took offense at it. "I will be happy to discuss any questions you have later."

Rabbi Dov nodded, and snapped his fingers. His disciples pulled out a large piece of fabric for them and placed it on the ground so they wouldn't dirty their robes. It took them a few minutes to finally sit down right in front of Jesus. When they were settled, Jesus took twenty steps back and invited those who had been displaced to sit in front of them.

This infuriated Dov and his followers but Jesus paid them no heed. His attention was focused on the rest of the people there and he led them in a psalm of thanksgiving. Then he sat down at the top of the mountain and began to teach.

"Blessed are the poor in spirit," he proclaimed, "for the kingdom of heaven is theirs…"

"WHO BUT GOD CAN FORGIVE SINS?"

Mark 2:1-12

Jesus preached for hours, and Simon hung on every word. What he spoke that day was more masterful than anything he preached before. What amazed him most was how Jesus spoke with such clarity and authority, unlike the scribes who always seemed to be asking questions or making arguments.

"Therefore, anyone who listens to these words of mine is like a man who built his house on rock," Jesus said. "Rains came, floods rose, but the house stood because it had a solid foundation. But anyone who does not listen is like a man who built his house on sand. Rains came, floods rose, and it fell– and what a fall it had!" Then he said a blessing over them and led them in a psalm of thanksgiving.

Simon stood and quickly brought Philip and Bartholomew to Jesus. He warmly greeted them and listened intently as Bartholomew and Philip told him about John the Baptist. When they finished, Jesus exhaled a deep breath. "If anyone can turn Herod, it's John," Jesus said. "He has always had a gift of speaking the truth."

"It runs in the family," Simon said. Jesus graciously nodded.

"Speaking of family," Bartholomew said, "we stopped by Nazareth on the way here."

"And how is my hometown?" Jesus asked.

"Oh, not much has changed," Philip said. "James is bossy, Jedidiah is bitter, and your mother is wonderful."

"They are worried about you," Bartholomew said. He leaned in and said in a softer voice, "To the point where some feel you might have lost your mind."

"By some, I suppose you mean James?" Jesus asked. Bartholomew nodded his head. "I've dealt with James all my life," he said reassuringly. "Don't worry for me. But what about you two? Will you return to John?" Philip and Bartholomew looked at each other, unsure which one should answer.

"He sent us to tell you how he was and do anything you asked of us, Rabbi," Philip said.

"Good, because I can use your help," Jesus said as he looked at long line of people who came forward in need of healing. "I think we are going to have a very busy day."

Jairus struggled to keep up with Dov as he stormed down the streets of Capernaum. The Rabbi's fine garments flapped about as he moved. Nicodemus and Dov's disciples struggled to keep pace as well. Jairus didn't want to leave Jesus' sermon, but it would have been inhospitable to have guests at his house when he wasn't there. Finally, when they got to his house, Dov stopped. His face was red with anger.

"*They* say this but *I* say that," Dov said, mocking Jesus. "Who does this carpenter think he is? Outrageous!"

"Outrageous?" Nicodemus asked, still out of breath. "You want to know what *outrageous* is? You have been nothing but rude and inconsiderate since you arrived here, and now you embarrass Jairus and me by storming out in the middle of Jesus' preaching. You could at least have waited until you heard the whole thing."

Jairus delighted in hearing someone put Dov in his place, but he didn't dare add to it.

"I heard enough," Dov shot back. "And believe me, the other Pharisees will hear about it also."

Nicodemus turned to Jairus and said, "Jairus, I want to apologize for our actions. We have been very rude and not considerate of your town and yourself."

He was shocked at the apology, and realized it was his moment to speak his mind. "Oh, it's no problem. No problem at all." So much for that.

Dov stood still, his face in a sour expression. "Thank you, Jairus. We will not be troubling you much longer." Then he turned to his disciples, "Pack up, we're leaving."

Jairus breathed a sigh of relief, and then worried that he did it too loudly. "It's a shame you didn't get to see Jesus perform a miracle, a real shame." Nicodemus looked at him with surprise and the thought gave him new energy.

"Our host makes an excellent point, Rabbi Dov!" he exclaimed.

I did? Jairus thought.

"The whole area is filled with stories about the miraculous deeds this young man performs. Shouldn't we at least stay to see if there is any truth behind them?"

Dov ran his fingers through his beard and turned to Jairus. "When will his next miracle be?"

Jairus was horrified that something he said might have extended their stay. "Oh, I don't know. They just kind of… happen," he said.

"Do you think one will 'kind of happen' today?" the Rabbi asked.

Jairus looked nervously at Nicodemus and then back at Dov. "Yes?"

"All right then," Dov said. "One more night, and then we leave. Agreed?" he asked Nicodemus.

"Agreed," Nicodemus replied. Dov and his followers went into Jairus's house, leaving Nicodemus and Jairus outside. "Thank you, Jairus. If it wasn't for your quick thinking, we'd be leaving right now."

"Oh please, don't mention it, don't mention it," he said. *Especially to my wife.*

Jesus spent hours healing the sick and laid his hands on every one in need. Simon was amazed at the compassion Jesus showed each person. Beggars lined up to see him and he treated each of them like kings. And it wasn't enough to just heal their wounds or cast out demons. He spoke to them, prayed with them, and whispered things in their ears that often made them break down and cry. The sun slowly fell behind them and cast a deep shadow on the city of Capernaum. There were still more to be cured, but Simon felt it important to stop for the day.

"Master, the sun is going down, and soon it will be difficult to see," he said.

Jesus looked at the sky. "Just a few more," he said. "But tell those who are able to head back to their homes, and I will be available tomorrow."

The fishermen spread the word, and the crowd dispersed.

Another hour passed and Jesus continued to heal. Now it was quite dark. "Is this what Jesus meant by 'a few more'?" Philip asked.

Andrew smiled. "What Jesus means by 'few' is what most people mean by 'many'." In the distance, they saw four lights bouncing up the hill, and when the lights got closer they recognized Matthias and Barsabbas, carrying four lamps.

"Thought you might need these," Matthias said. Then the two of them shouted with joy when they recognized Philip and Bartholomew, who they hadn't seen since the Jordan River.

They were hushed by John, who nodded toward Jesus. He was bent over and having an intense conversation with a family who had brought their son to him.

"Why don't the four of you go down to my house," Simon suggested. "I think we're about done here."

"If we can fit," Barsabbas said.

"What's that supposed to mean?"

"It's packed," he replied. "We had to climb through people just to get these lamps out. Those Pharisees are there, too. Everyone's waiting for Jesus."

Simon breathed heavily and hung his head. "Go ahead of us," he told them. "We'll be there shortly." The four took a lamp and left, leaving the four fishermen behind with Jesus.

The family wept and hugged Jesus, and in the lamplight Simon could see Jesus had tears in his eyes. He blessed them and sent them on their way. There was no one left, and Jesus approached the four.

"Tired, Master?" James asked.

Jesus smiled. His body seemed weary but there was energy in his voice. "How can I be tired? I've waited my whole life for this."

"Well, there are more people waiting to hear you at my house," Simon said.

"Then it's a good thing I have more to say."

They were half way to Capernaum when John muttered a curse and quickly put his hands to his mouth. "Forgive me Master, I just realized I left my prayer shawl at the top of the mount."

His brother handed him a lamp. "Do you want me to go with you?"

"No, I'll do it faster on my own." He didn't mean it as an insult, but the others laughed.

John quickly moved up the hill and searched for his shawl. He had only gotten it a year ago at his bar mitzvah and always feared of losing it. Finally, he found the shawl and began to head down the hill.

John stopped when something made a moaning sound. He froze. *A wild animal?* He wondered if he should extinguish his lamp or if the fire would be good to scare it away. The moan came again.

It sounded like a person.

His curiosity overcame his fear. Holding his lamp high, John headed toward the sound. He came to a large lump of earth and realized that it was a man, lying on his face.

"Hello? Are you all right?"

The body twitched. The hill was steep and John worked hard to keep his footing.

"Can you get up?" John asked.

After a moment of silence, the man responded. "No," he said. "Some men carried me to see Jesus, but left me in the line when it got dark. I slid down here and no one noticed," he said weakly. His breath was labored. "I am accursed by God and deserve to die. Leave me here to be food for the animals."

John's heart broke for the man, not only for his body but for the despondent way he sounded. He was a large man, skinny but tall. *If he's paralyzed then he'll be dead weight,* John thought. *I couldn't carry him, but I bet James and Simon could.* Then he frowned as he surveyed the treacherous landscape. *Might need Andrew as well.*

"I'll be right back," he said. And he ran with great speed toward Simon's house.

Andrew was smart enough to bring a makeshift stretcher, but it still took them over an hour to find the man, lift him off the steep slope, and carry him back to Simon's house. Once word went round that Jesus was preaching again, people lined the streets in hope to hear an echo of his miraculous voice. There wasn't even enough room in the street to make it to the door.

"Well, that settles it," James said, motioning to the others to lower the man to the ground. "We'll just have to wait until later."

Simon scratched his curly hair and began to pace. He was in no mood to wait. The idea of Rabbi Dov and Ioakim sitting in *his* courtyard eating *his* food while he was stuck out at the fringe of the crowd was too much for him.

He took a deep breath to calm his anger and looked toward his home. Over the wall, he saw a head move from side to side, as if a man shifted his position. The movement startled him. How could he see a man's head unless he was sitting on—

"The rooftop!" he exclaimed.

"What?" John asked.

"We can get him to Jesus over the rooftop!"

He looked expectantly at James, who ran his fingers through his long beard. "Not sure," he said.

"Won't we drop him?" Andrew asked.

"Not if we use some ropes," Simon said. "John, go grab some off the boat at the dock." With an excited grin, John dashed off.

James smiled. "It just might work."

"*Might?*" asked the man on the stretcher. It sounded more like an accusation than a question. He said nothing the entire journey, made no sound except for low moans, and the strength of his word startled them. He lifted his head off the ground with considerable effort, but eventually surrendered. The head fell back to the earth, and rolled listlessly to the side. "Leave me to die," he whispered.

The three stood silently and looked with pity at the man. John bounded up the road with ropes in hand, oblivious to the change in mood. "I got the ropes!" he said. He read the looks on the other's faces and fell into an embarrassed silence.

Simon knelt over the man and put a hand on his shoulder. The man did not move. He took his large hand and gently turned the man's head so he could look into his eyes. "Do you want to be healed?" Simon asked.

The man's mouth formed to make a word. He opened and closed his jaw a few times, but no sound came. Tears formed in his eyes. "I don't know if I should," he finally said.

"I do," Simon said. He spoke with such conviction that the man nodded in acceptance. Simon rose and looked at the others. "Let's go."

Jesus had his back against the courtyard wall, unable to move even a step. Philip, Matthias, Bartholomew, and Barsabbas sat in a tight circle by his feet. They tried to use their bodies to give him more room, but it was no use. There were too many people in the courtyard. They hung off the door and sat on the roof. Only a gentle breeze off the lake gave some reprieve from the warmth of bodies and the tightness of space.

The goat bleated unhappily. It too was crammed against the wall and complained that Jesus took her spot. He bent down and gently patted its head. "It seems my lot in life to dwell in the places of animals," he said. "Be at peace." The goat laid down and ceased its complaining moan, but still looked troubled.

He gazed upon the crowd that gathered to hear him speak. The gold and white tunics and turbans of the Pharisees stood in marked contrast to the brown, beige, and blue cloth of the peasants that surrounded them. Skepticism was thick in the air.

Though many of these people had been with Jesus the past few weeks, they had followed the Pharisees their whole lives. As he began to preach, Jesus noticed that much of what he said fell on deaf ears. The crowd became more concerned with the Pharisees' reaction than Jesus' words. In this small, confined space, one could hear every grunt and whisper they made. Occasionally Nicodemus would say, "Well said!" or, "Amen!" But the cold silence of the others made it clear he was in the minority.

Jesus felt as confined by the Pharisees' stubbornness as by the space he was in. Preaching on the mountain that morning felt like flying on eagle's wings—now he felt caged, scrutinized, observed. He raised his eyes to heaven but his view was obstructed by a thatch roof that Simon built to give shelter for the animals. He looked at the smug faces of the Pharisees, and the confused looks on the rest of the crowd. *Father, help me*, Jesus prayed.

The wind blew and a piece of thatch from the roof floated its way down to the ground in front of Jesus. It was followed by another, larger piece. Jesus looked up and saw a large section of the roof lifted back. In its place were the excited faces of Simon, Andrew, James, and John. They awkwardly lowered a man on a stretcher through the hole.

The crowd gasped. Grunts from above gave testimony to the size of the paralyzed man, whose arms and legs hung limply over the crudely made stretcher. In any other situation, this absurd sight would have prompted gales of laughter. But the crowd grew so silent that the only noise to be heard was the sound of the ropes straining to keep the man aloft in front of Jesus' waist.

Jesus bent over to look at him. The crowd disappeared. The Pharisees disappeared. The oppressive closeness, the broken roof, and the fishermen above his head faded into the distance, leaving Jesus feeling intimate and alone with the man.

"What is your name?" Jesus asked.

The man paused. "Josef," he said.

Jesus looked deep into the man's eyes. He saw the pain. He saw the sin. He saw the despair. His soul was in worse shape than his body. He had no faith.

Jesus was troubled. *How can I heal him if there is no faith?* Jesus looked up at the hole in the roof and saw the four fishermen. Their faces were red with the strain of holding the ropes, but they looked down with the expectant belief that their Master would be able to heal.

He smiled. Seeing *their* faith, Jesus looked at Josef and gave him the gift he would never dare ask for. "My child," he said, "your sins are forgiven."

After a moment of stunned silence, tears streamed down Josef's face. He inhaled as if it were his first breath. "Thank you, thank you," he said, and with every breath, "Thank you."

The crowd began to make noise. The Pharisees huddled together and spoke with angry voices. "The blasphemer!" Jesus heard Dov say. "Who but God can forgive sins?"

Looking up from Josef, Jesus addressed the Pharisee. "Why do you have such thoughts in your head? Which is easier to say? *Your sins are forgiven*, or *rise, pick up your stretcher and walk*?"

Rabbi Dov stood and confronted him. "What gives you the right?" he said. "Who gives you the authority—"

"Authority? To prove to you that the Son of Man has the *authority* to forgive sins on earth," he looked down and said to Josef, "Rise, pick up your stretcher and walk."

Everyone stared at Josef, who didn't move. Suddenly, John cried, "I can't hold him!" and a corner of the stretcher dropped, causing Josef to slide off and land on the ground with his feet.

He stood up and looked around in shock. Then he looked down at his feet as he lifted each one and began to shake his arms about.

"I am healed!" Josef screamed, and the crowd erupted in shouts and cheers. Everyone jumped to their feet, clapping and shouting, "Hallelujah!" Josef grabbed his stretcher and waved it high above his head, amazed by the strength in his arms and his legs.

Jesus saw Rabbi Dov and his disciples push their way through the courtyard and out the door, their vacancy immediately filled by people waiting in the street. Nicodemeus was the only Pharisee to stay behind.

Josef embraced Jesus with a strong grip. "Thank you, Master, thank you."

"You *have* been forgiven," Jesus said. "Never doubt that."

"I know," Josef said. "And I never will."

Josef looked up and Jesus followed his gaze. The fishermen looked down through the hole in the roof, arm in arm, faces wet with tears of joy.

"Hallelujah!" Josef cried.

"HALLELUJAH!" the fisherman replied. Jesus caught Simon's eye and nodded his approval. The fisherman smiled.

"Rabbi Nicodemus?"

The old Rabbi opened his eyes and looked around. The celebration had cleared out and he was alone with Jesus, sitting on a bench against the outer wall of the kitchen. "You caught me napping," he said. "The spirit is willing but the flesh is weak."

"Well spoken, Rabbi."

Nicodemus gave a laugh. "It is you who speak well. Your words... I have never heard anything like them. Nor have I seen anything like what I have seen. I am learned in the Law, but I honestly don't know what to make of you."

"And yet here you are," Jesus said.

"Here I am," Nicodemus echoed. He took a deep breath. "Jesus, I must beg you to show some... *restraint*. Especially around people like Rabbi Dov. He is a very influential man."

"I'm not interested in his influence," Jesus replied.

"Well you should be," Nicodemus said. "You have much to learn about the way things work." He shook his head and stood to leave. "I can tell by that look in your eyes you're not listening to a word I'm saying. I probably shouldn't have come."

"I'm glad you did," Jesus said. "And I *am* listening. I just don't agree."

This made the old Rabbi laugh. "If you were one of my students, I'd have you sit at the far end of the circle for such a response."

Jesus smiled. "I'll remember that when I call my own."

The jovial look on Nicodemus's face froze and melted into sobriety. "You have no formal training! It is one thing to have people help you with your ministry… but to formally apprentice students? You go too far. Even your brother never did this."

"I am not my brother."

"Be careful not to end up like him."

Jesus rose from the bench. "We are both where God wants us to be."

"He's in Herod's prison and you are staying in the paltry home of a fisherman!" Jesus glanced toward the kitchen where Simon and Rachael were. Nicodemus lowered his voice. "I did not mean to disrespect the hospitality of this house," he said. "But it is hardly Jerusalem."

"When I get to Jerusalem, you will understand."

"I hope so, because right now nothing makes sense to me." He walked to the door and opened it. "Shalom, *Rabbi*. I hope you know what you are doing."

"Shalom, Nicodemus. I am honored by your counsel and your concern for me. I will pray for you."

Nicodemus softened at those words. "And I for you," the old Rabbi said. And then he left.

Simon and Rachael entered the courtyard. "I hope our conversation didn't disturb you," Jesus said.

Rachael was quick to respond. "Oh, no, didn't hear a word. Too busy cleaning."

Jesus smiled. "Good. It's been a long day, and we have much to do tomorrow. Shalom."

"Shalom," they both answered. Jesus headed into his bedroom. He put his head on the cushion and sleep came at once.

Once Jesus left the courtyard, Rachael felt free to vent her anger. "*Paltry home,*" she said. "What does he expect of us?"

"I think he meant well," Simon said, looking out into the night sky.

"How can you defend that man?" Rachael asked. She looked at her husband and paused. "Simon, what's wrong?"

For a moment Simon didn't speak. "He's calling students, Rachael." He turned his gaze from the stars to her face, and she could see he was about to cry.

"I'm no student." He whispered the words as if he confessed a sin.

Rachael wrapped her arms around him. "I love you," she said. It was the only thing she could think to say.

AN UNEXPECTED DINNER

Mark 2:13-17

Simon could not believe where Jesus was taking him.

A light drizzle fell upon them as they walked to the tax collector's house. Matthew lived on the outskirts of town, on the well-traveled road from Capernaum to Bethsaida. Simon's brother, James, and John were with him, as were Philip and Bartholomew, Matthias and Barsabbas, David and his twin, and Ioakim.

"I find it hard to believe the Master accepted his invitation," David whispered.

"Actually, it was Jesus' idea," Bartholomew said.

"Really?" David asked, looking at Simon.

Simon shrugged.

"He's family," James replied, and for the first time Simon realized it to be true. If Matthew was related to James and John then so was Jesus. This revelation made the trip more palatable, but still difficult.

Just when he thought it couldn't get worse, a large group of well dressed men approached. At the head of them was Rabbi Dov.

"Jesus of Nazareth," he said with a slight bow.

"Rabbi Dov," Jesus replied.

"I would like to introduce you to some friends of mine. This is Rabbi Elezim and Rabbi Zedekiah." They bowed as they were introduced. Each Rabbi had eight to ten disciples, but they were neither introduced nor even acknowledged by the Rabbis.

"I haven't seen you for a few weeks now," Jesus said. "What brings you back to Capernaum?"

"You, of course," Dov said with a tight smile. "We have some concerns that we must address immediately."

"We are on our way to dinner right now," Jesus replied. "Would you like to join us? We could talk there."

Rabbi Zedekiah shook his head. "There are far too many of us to intrude. It would be an imposition."

"I doubt it," Jesus said. "The house we are going to is owned by a very rich man."

Dov looked at the other Rabbis, who smiled. "Lead the way," he said, gesturing with his right hand.

Simon looked at the Rabbi's disciples, wondering if he could ever be like them. They seemed a few years younger than he, and clearly hadn't lived a life of physical labor. As the Rabbis moved, their disciples jostled for position in a single line behind their respective teacher. Simon never thought to follow behind Jesus like that. Most of the time they just walked in a clump.

His distraction only took a few moments, but it cost him a place beside Jesus. Ioakim was next to the Master and David matched him stride for stride. Others scattered around and Simon joined his brother in the rear, right in front of the Rabbis. Jesus led them to the tax collector's house. The Pharisees muttered in admiration when they saw its grandeur.

But they didn't know whose house it was until Matthew opened the door with a warm greeting. Jesus responded in kind, and they embraced. The sight of it repulsed and shocked Simon. As the rest of Jesus' disciples cautiously went in, Dov grabbed Simon's arm and spun him around.

"Outrageous!" he said. "Why does your Master eat with tax collectors and sinners?"

Simon had no answer. He opened his mouth to explain they were related, but wondered if that would be an even bigger disgrace. He was saved by the voice of his brother.

"Simon!" Andrew called from the door. "Come on!"

He bowed to the Rabbis and, without a word, headed into Matthew's house. The outraged Pharisees shouted angrily and spit on the ground as they walked away in disgust.

Simon couldn't help but be impressed with Matthew's house. It was beautiful, but it was also simple. In his mind he imagined Matthew's house would be filled with lavish artwork and statues to Roman gods, but there was nothing of the sort. It felt surprisingly… Jewish.

But the company was not. Many Roman soldiers were there, but few of them were from Rome. The majority were hired mercenaries from Persia, Media, and other places. They had women with them, some with questionable backgrounds. And there were other tax collectors from neighboring villages.

Matthew led Jesus through the crowd and introduced him to various men. But Simon and the rest of them stayed in a tight group by the door. They were trapped in a house filled with people they wanted to avoid. Simon wondered if just being there would make him unclean for the Sabbath celebration.

Matthew's mother, Mary, came out with servant girls holding large platters of food. "Please eat," she said, offering some food to Ioakim.

The corners of his lip curled up in a polite smile and he shook his head. "We're fasting," he said.

The voice of Jesus cut across the courtyard. "There will be no fasting while you are with me." Everyone grew silent and stared at them.

Ioakim was horrified, but quickly composed himself. He grabbed a plum and put it in his mouth. The others ate as well. Conversations in the courtyard returned to normal.

They were called in to dinner. Jesus sat at the head table. Matthew joined him, along with other tax collectors and soldiers of rank. Matthew's family was with him: his younger brother James, who worked with him, and his father Cleopas (also known as Alphaeus). It was obvious that Matthew was Cleopas's son—one was just a younger version of the other. But James and he looked nothing alike. James had a long face with sunken eyes and was very thin. It was hard to tell how tall he was because James usually had his shoulders hunched. His arms hung out from him like branches from a tree.

Simon noted with resentment that Ioakim somehow made it to the head table. So did David and his brother, who seemed connected to his hip. There were two other smaller tables in the room. Lower ranked soldiers and their women sat at one. Simon and the rest of Jesus' followers sat at the other.

The meal started quietly, but soon became loud. The three tables became so caught up in their own conversations they forgot the others were there.

A foreign woman sauntered by the disciples' table and the men averted their eyes. James leaned forward to speak quietly. "Do you know what the difference between a prostitute and a tax collector is?" he asked.

Simon knew the answer and they said the punch line together: "A prostitute earns her money!"

They broke into wild laughter and the rest of the room went quiet. The fishermen stopped. A thick silence hung in the room.

Matthew glared at Simon. Simon stared back. He was not going to be judged by a tax collector, and was ready to say as much until he saw the expression on Jesus' face.

Jesus was furious. His angry stare unraveled Simon and he felt his heart beat twice as fast. The next few seconds passed like an eternity. Simon silently begged God for someone to say anything to change the subject.

His prayer was answered by an unfamiliar voice.

"This is a nice table."

People in the room looked around to identify who spoke. It was David… no, it was David's twin brother, who until this point hadn't said a word. David motioned him to be quiet, and his brother shrugged his shoulders in submission.

"Thank you," Matthew said. "Could you remind me of your name?"

The brother looked to David, seeking permission to talk. David nodded, and he introduced himself. "My name is Judah, but most people call me Thomas," he said, which was Greek for "Twin". "I've built some tables, but none as nice as this one. I really appreciate the strip of cedar that outlines the table. Is it from Lebanon?"

"Are you a carpenter, Thomas?" Jesus asked.

"Yes," he replied. "Though I rarely build furniture. I mostly build boats." This impressed Jesus, and the two of them engaged in a lively conversation about different woods that were used, construction techniques, and other things. Conversations began at the other tables, but Simon stayed silent, still shaken by the Master's angry look.

After the main course was finished, Matthew invited Jesus and Thomas to a private room while the rest of the guests ate dessert. Thomas returned alone. His brother was eager to know everything that Jesus said, but Thomas wasn't much of a storyteller. "He had really beautiful carvings and a lot of religious scrolls," was how Thomas summed up what had happened in the other room. "I think they're talking about how Matthew became a tax collector."

Simon's heart leapt. *That is why we're here,* he thought. He imagined Jesus berating Matthew about being a traitor to his people, and Matthew on his knees in tears. Jesus was gracious to do it in private. He was tempted to take a walk and try to overhear the conversation, but his fear of getting caught kept him in his seat. One rebuke was enough.

Almost an hour passed while the guests quietly ate and continued in their separate conversations. When Matthew and Jesus returned, everyone rose in honor of the master of the house and the guest of honor. There were tears in Matthew's eyes, but not the kind of tears Simon expected. Matthew looked radiant with joy.

"My honored guests," he said, "My apologies for disappearing for so long. I hope my servants treated you well during our absence."

Jesus put a hand on Matthew's shoulder. "Levi, I just wanted to thank you on behalf of my friends for the wonderful hospitality you have shown us tonight. You have truly brought honor to your house."

Levi? Honor? It was not lost on Simon that Jesus used Matthew's Jewish name instead of his Greek one. His throat felt dry and his heart sank into his chest. All he wanted to do was leave.

Jesus could have stayed there all night. Gentiles never came to Nazareth, and when he travelled to Jerusalem he was usually surrounded by family. He warmly said goodbye to each of Matthew's guests, and was grateful for the opportunity to meet them.

Matthew's mother, Mary, came out of the kitchen to talk with Jesus. "How is your mother?" she asked. "We've been praying for both of you since we heard that Joseph died."

"Thank you," Jesus replied. "We both miss him terribly."

"I bet she misses you, too," she said. Jesus nodded, and Mary grabbed his hands to pull him close. "Thank you for coming here tonight," she whispered. "You have no idea what it means for us."

"It was my pleasure," he said to her. "You have raised wonderful boys."

At the compliment, tears rolled down her face. Cleopas came up and put a loving arm around his wife. Jesus blessed them both.

Matthew stood by the door and thanked everyone as they left. Simon again found himself at the end of the group and was one of the last to leave. He couldn't speak or even look at Matthew, and Matthew said nothing to him.

As he walked away from the house, Simon tried to make sense of the evening. Then Jesus called to him. "Simon, come up here and talk to me alone for a minute."

He quickly walked to the front of the group. The others backed away to give them privacy. He feared a rebuke, but there was no malice in Jesus' tone. "I saw you talking to the Pharisees as I entered into the house," he said. "What did they say to you?"

"They asked me why you ate with tax collectors and sinners," Simon answered.

"What did you tell them?"

"Nothing."

Jesus nodded and they walked a few more steps. "And why did I?"

"Master?"

Jesus stopped and looked at him. "Why did I eat with tax collectors and sinners?"

Simon looked down and shuffled his feet. This was the question he struggled with all night. It was about more than family—his kindness to the Gentiles showed him that. And it clearly wasn't to condemn Matthew. He looked up and realized that Jesus was staring at him, waiting for an answer.

"I… I don't know," he confessed.

The muscles around Jesus' eyes tensed as he looked closely at him. "Thank you for your honesty," Jesus said. Then he turned and headed into town. The other followers quickly gathered around Jesus as he walked.

But Simon couldn't move. He couldn't breathe. Everyone passed him except for James.

"What's wrong?" James asked.

The Rabbi just tested me, Simon thought, *and I failed.* "I'm not going to be a disciple," he said.

James stood in silence with his friend and put a comforting hand on his shoulder. The rain began to fall. Simon was glad for it. He was too depressed for tears, so the sky cried for him.

CALLED BY NAME

Mark 3:1-8, 13-19

After a few days of rain, the sun shone to celebrate the Sabbath. But the mood inside the synagogue was dark. Jesus had finished his preaching and the Pharisees began the debate. Simon and the others sat near Jesus, ready to defend him if things got ugly.

Rabbi Zedekiah stood up from amidst the group of Pharisees who had positioned themselves near the middle of the synagogue. "I think everyone here would like to know," he said, "why the Pharisees keep the fast, and why even the disciples of John the Baptist keep the fast, but your disciples do not!" He sat down as the other Pharisees cheered the question.

Jesus replied, "Surely the bridegroom's attendants cannot fast while the bridegroom is still with them? As long as they have the bridegroom with them they cannot fast. But the time will come when the bridegroom is taken from them, and then, on that day, they will fast."

Many in the crowd cheered his answer, but others argued against it. Jesus continued, "Nobody puts new wine into old wineskins; otherwise, the wine will burst the skins and wine is lost and the skins, too. No! New wine into fresh skins!"

Rabbi Elezim stood. "New wine?" he scornfully asked. "Well perhaps the wine of our fathers is not good enough for you. Maybe that is why you dine with tax collectors and sinners!"

Simon winced and looked around nervously. He didn't want anyone to know he ate at Matthew's house.

Jesus put out his hand to calm the crowd. "It is not the healthy who need the doctor, but the sick. I have come not to call the righteous, but sinners."

"How can you call yourself a child of Abraham with such talk?" shouted one of the Pharisees' disciples, and that brought another round of yells and screams.

Bartholomew leaned over and whispered into Simon's ear. "Look at Dov," he said.

Rabbi Dov was the calm amid the storm of Pharisees. He hadn't even raised his voice to challenge Jesus. Next to him sat a man they didn't recognize who looked like a beggar.

"What is he up to?" Simon asked.

"I don't know, but it can't be good."

Phillip, who sat a few people away from Bartholomew, reached over and grabbed his shoulder. "Bartholomew, look!"

Bartholomew looked over his shoulder and swore. Three men in blue and brown tunics had arrived and stood at the back of the synagogue.

"Who are they?" Simon asked.

"Herod's men," he said.

The name sent shivers down Simon's spine.

It was a trap.

Rabbi Dov stood up and addressed the crowd. "Perhaps our great Rabbi can teach us something about the Law," he calmly said, and he signaled the attendant for a scroll of the book of Leviticus. "You will work for six days, but the seventh day will be a day of complete rest, a day for the sacred assembly on which you do *no work at all*!" He thrust the scroll back at the attendant and pointed a finger toward Jesus. "Tell us, learned Rabbi from *Nazareth*, do you agree with this command?"

A confused murmur arose from the crowd, as people wondered why he asked such an obvious question. "I not only follow God's law," Jesus said, "but I have come to fulfill it."

The Pharisees looked like they were going to erupt again when Rabbi Dov silenced them with a sharp motion from his hand. "I have it on good authority that your disciples harvested wheat on the Sabbath, and you did nothing to stop them. Why did they do something on the Sabbath that is forbidden?"

Simon was outraged at the accusation. "That's a lie!" he said. Jesus motioned for him to stay calm.

"They were not *harvesting*, as you claim," Jesus said. "We walked through a field of wheat and they made a path."

"Sounds like they were breaking God's law to me," Dov said, more to the crowd than to Jesus.

"Then you should take the time to study God's law more closely," Jesus shot back. "Have you never read what David did in his time of need when he and his followers were hungry? How he went into the house of God and ate the loaves of the offering which only priests are allowed to eat, and how he gave some to the men with him?"

Rabbi Dov clearly did not appreciate the Scripture lesson. Simon couldn't help but smile.

"So you have no regard for the Sabbath?" Dov said.

"The Sabbath was made for man, not man for the Sabbath; so the Son of Man is master even of the Sabbath."

"How dare you!" one of the Pharisees said. Some of them got up on their feet and Simon and James stood as well, ready for a fight.

"This is the Sabbath!" Jairus cried. "A day of rest to honor the Lord! And this is a place of worship! This is not pleasing to God, not pleasing to God at all!"

The Pharisees looked at Jairus, looked at the fishermen (who stood much taller than they did), and then looked back at Dov who nodded at them. They sat down, and only after they were seated did Simon and James resume their seats on the ground.

"You are right, Jairus," Dov said. "This *is* a place of worship, and this *is* a sacred day. It is precisely because the Sabbath is sacred that I have concerns about this young Rabbi's teaching. But maybe I am wrong. After all, who am I to question someone who does such mighty… *works*."

Rabbi Dov sat down and nudged the poorly dressed man who sat next to him. The beggar seemed reluctant to move, but Dov angrily prodded him again and he stood, hands to his side. His left hand was normal, but his right was a twisted mess of bone and skin.

Simon looked at Jesus and saw his eyes flash with anger. "Is it permitted on the Sabbath day to do good, or to do evil? To save life or to kill?"

Dov and the other Pharisees said nothing, so Jesus addressed the rest of the congregation. "If any one of you here had only one sheep and it fell down a hole on the Sabbath day, would he not get hold of it and lift it out? Now a man is far more important than a sheep, so it follows that it is permitted on the Sabbath day to do good." Then he said to the man, "Stretch out your hand."

It happened so quickly that Simon almost missed it. At one moment the man had his disfigured hand to his side, but by the time he reached it up, it was healed.

The man looked with wonder at his hand. He looked at the front and back of it a few times, then moved his fingers quickly back and forth. The crowd was in awe. The man clapped his hands together and rejoiced at the sound. "Thank you, Master!" he shouted, and kept clapping his hands. People were amazed and shouted for joy. Someone began to sing a psalm of praise, and soon the synagogue was filled with celebration and song.

Everyone got on their feet except for the Pharisees who sat silent with anger. Simon gloated over them, but then noticed that Dov did not seem upset. He saw him look at Herod's men and nod to them.

Andrew put his arm around Simon's shoulder. "Well, that shut those Pharisees up!" Andrew said.

But Simon couldn't share in his brother's enthusiasm. "I have a feeling Rabbi Dov got exactly what he wanted."

Later that afternoon, Dov and Zedekiah walked along the lake away from the town. "Do you really think this is wise, Rabbi Dov?" Zedekiah asked. "I mean, working with Herod—"

"We are *not* working with Herod," Rabbi Dov said. "We have a common enemy, and only Herod has the authority to arrest him. It's the quickest way to solve this problem."

"Herod is dangerous," Zedekiah said.

"And Jesus isn't?" Dov asked. "This is no time for hesitation, Rabbi Zedekiah. We must stop this young Rabbi before it is too late."

They came upon three men, the same men who stood at the back of the synagogue that morning. Rabbi Dov bowed. "Shalom, Hiram," he said.

"Greetings from King Herod," Hiram replied. "These are strange times, that you and I would meet in such a place as this."

"Dangerous times," Dov said. "This young Rabbi is a threat to us all."

"To you, at least," Hiram said. "Has he claimed to be the Messiah?"

"People are starting to talk."

"But has *he* said it?"

"Not yet," Dov said. "But it's only a matter of time. And when he does, there will be many who will believe him."

"He's from *Nazareth*! Who will believe that God would send the Messiah from a dirt farm like that? Even the most common peasant knows the Messiah will come from Bethlehem, not to mention that Elijah must come first."

"The Baptist wasn't from Bethlehem, and people believed that *he* was the one," Dov answered.

Hiram thought about this for a moment and stroked his light brown beard. "What would you have me do?" he asked.

"Isn't it obvious? You must arrest him before he becomes even more popular."

Hiram shook his head. "Has he spoken against the King?"

Dov was incredulous. "Did you not see what he did in there? Did you not hear what he says? If Herod thought the Baptist was worth arresting, how much more so his brother!"

"The Baptist *is* the problem!" Hiram said. "He's a poison to Herod's mind. They talk every night, and the King won't let anyone hear what they talk about. You'd like me to arrest this Jesus and put him in a cell next to his brother? The last thing we need is another prophet getting in Herod's head."

"So we'll do nothing while this carpenter raises an army of dissent? I would think your king would be glad to stop a problem before it starts."

"*My* king?" Hiram snapped. "He is *our* king!"

Dov quickly bowed. "Of course, Master Hiram… *Our* king." He shot a look to Zedekiah who bowed as well.

Hiram took a moment to think about Dov's proposition. "You might be right, Rabbi Dov. I have never seen such things as I did this morning. If he goes against Herod, he will sway many people against him."

"So you'll speak to the king?" Dov asked.

"Not the king," he replied, "but the queen. Her majesty wants the Baptist dead. She always gets her way. Once the Baptist is dealt with, we can put pressure on the King to deal with Jesus."

It wasn't what Dov had hoped for, but at least it was a start. "I'm sure our king will reward you for your foresight."

"I don't need your flattery," he said. "Do what you can to discredit him in front of the people. I'll talk to the Queen. Maybe together we can rid ourselves of this peasant from Nazareth."

When Simon awoke the next morning, he was surprised to find that everyone else was up. He could tell from the warm glow of the curtain door that it was already early morning. He wiped the sleep from his eyes and entered the courtyard. Rachael was feeding the chickens.

"Shalom, husband," she said, giving him a kiss.

"Where is the Master?" Simon asked.

"Not back from his morning prayer," she said. "You're up later than usual."

"I've gotten used to not being a fisherman," he replied. "It will be hard to go back to it."

She put her hand on his shoulder and was about speak when they heard a loud thud on the door. By the sound, they knew immediately who it was. The door opened and Papa Zebedee stormed into the courtyard, with James in tow.

"I need to talk to Jesus," he demanded. "Where is he?"

"Not here," Simon replied. "But he should be shortly."

This answer did not satisfy him. "Then I'm talking to you. In private."

Rachael squeezed her husband's hand and exited toward the kitchen. Simon invited him to the dining room. James tried to follow but his father yelled, "I said, *in private!*" and closed the curtain in his face.

Papa Zebedee paced the room and Simon thought it best to let him have the first word. After a few moments of walking back and forth, he stopped and said, "Has he decided yet?"

"I don't understand."

"The students!" Zebedee said with irritation. "Do you know who he has chosen?"

This must be about selling my boat, Simon thought. "He hasn't said anything—"

"But you know his mind, don't you? He lives here, right?"

"He keeps his own mind."

Zebedee shook his head with a sarcastic grin. "And you'll keep yours, is that it?"

Simon had enough. "I don't know if I'll be his disciple or not, and it's not my place to ask!"

Zebedee looked stunned. "You?" he said in disbelief. "Are you saying that *you* might not be chosen?"

Simon was surprised at his sudden change of tone. "Probably not," he said.

Zebedee sat down in shock and put his head in his hands. "Then there's no hope for John," he said.

"John?" Simon realized that the conversation was never about him at all.

"Sit with me, son," Zebedee said in a quiet voice. Simon obeyed, and saw tears in the old man's eyes. "I just assumed *you* were going to be his disciple. But if you're not going to be, then a young boy like John doesn't stand a chance."

Simon was confused. "Do you *want* him to be a disciple? I thought you said Jesus was—"

"Forget what I said," Zebedee said. "And forget what I want. Much has happened over the past few weeks. I've been in the synagogue, and I've seen the miracles. But the biggest miracle I've seen is in John. He *loves* this man. Will follow him anywhere. Even gets up in the morning to go find him praying somewhere. It's all he talks about. It's all he wants."

Zebedee paused, taking a moment to hold back the tears and regain his composure. "If Jesus doesn't pick him as a disciple, it will kill him. It will *kill* him, Simon." He looked Simon in the eye. "You've got to talk to him. For me. I'll do anything. He's got to pick John."

Simon saw Zebedee in a whole new way. He saw the love he had for his son and it touched him deeply. But it also gave him sadness because he didn't think he could help. "Zebedee, I—"

His words were interrupted by a yell in the courtyard. "The Master summons us! The Master summons us!" It was John, and he burst into the dining room.

"Simon, the Master—Dad!" he exclaimed.

His father toughened up quickly. "Keep your voice down, you'll rouse the whole town."

"Father, Simon, I think he's made his decision! Come on, let's go!" And he was off as quickly as he had come in.

Zebedee and Simon sat quietly in the dining room for a moment. Zebedee drew a large breath. "Well then. What's done is done." They rose to their feet.

"Have hope," Simon said, though the words felt stale in his mouth.

Zebedee nodded. "I will. For John *and* for you." He smiled at Simon and put a heavy hand on his shoulder. "Your father would be proud of you, you know."

The mention of his dad surprised him and he looked away. "I doubt it," he whispered.

"Don't be so sure. For all his faults, he always taught that it was better to be a man who had faith…"

"…than a man who could fish," Simon said. The familiar words cast him back into deep memories. Simon assumed his father would have disapproved of his desire to sell the boat and follow Jesus. But the words of Zebedee rang true in his heart.

He was about to thank him when Zebedee slapped him so hard against his back he almost fell over. "I've got my own sons to tend to," he said. And he left.

Rachael ran in. "Is it true? Has he made his choice?" she asked.

"So it seems," he replied.

She looked up at her husband. "Do you want me to come?"

Simon thought for a minute. If he was to be rejected, he would rather not have his wife see it. "No, but thank you for asking."

She nodded. "I'll make your favorite dinner."

He smiled and kissed her head. "Thank you, Rachael. You are a good wife."

She put her hands on either side of his face. "And you are a good husband. No matter what happens, I love you."

They kissed, and he walked out the door.

Simon's steps were heavy as he walked up the hill. The sky was gray. The wind whipped off the lake and swirled around him like a net that sought to pull him back to the sea. *Surely you have received enough,* the wind whispered to him. *Isn't it selfish to want more?*

His mind thought of all the blessings he received since Jesus came. The miraculous catch of fish. His mother-in-law healed. A deeper relationship with his wife. The miracles he saw. The words he heard. What more could he want? The wind sounded wise in his ears.

Simon turned and looked at the sea. The water was choppy and large waves broke against the shore. *Jesus could take you far away from here,* said the sea. *Isn't it safer to stay?*

For all his troubles with the water, there was comfort there, too. Simon's family lived for generations on this lake. Following Jesus would bring a whole new world of difficulty, even danger. The sea seemed to make sense.

But then the sun broke through the clouds, and Simon felt light upon his face. The sun said no words. It just silenced the other voices. He closed his eyes and listened to the beauty of the world around him.

> *The Lord is my shepherd, I shall not want*
> *In green pastures he gives me repose*
> *Besides restful waters he leads me*
> *He refreshes my soul*

In the distance, Jesus led people in a psalm of praise. He turned, opened his eyes, and began to walk toward Jesus.

> *He guides me in right paths for his name's sake*
> *Though I walk through the valley, dark as death*
> *I shall fear no evil, for you are at my side*
> *Your rod and your staff give me courage*

Simon stepped up his pace. His legs felt lighter now, as did his heart.

> *You prepare a table for me*
> *In the sight of my foes*
> *You anoint my head with oil*
> *My cup overflows*

He broke into a run. The sun shone brightly behind him, and he could feel its rays push him forward.

> *Surely goodness and kindness will follow me,*
> *All the days of my life*
> *I make my home in the house of the Lord*
> *Forever and ever*

Simon made it to the edge of the crowd by the time they sang, "*Amen.*" There were about three or four hundred people gathered, all seated on the ground in front of Jesus. Jesus noticed him and gestured him to come forward. Simon moved through the crowd and sat between his brother and James, who were in front.

"There has been much talk about who my disciples will be," Jesus said. "So let me put your questions to rest. You are *all* my disciples." The people smiled and spontaneously applauded, and for a moment Simon wondered if all his anxiety had been for nothing.

"But I need more than disciples if I am going to continue my mission," Jesus said. "I need some men to be my companions, who can help me proclaim the message and drive out devils."

The crowd began to quietly talk among themselves. "Did he say *drive out devils*?" Andrew whispered.

Before Simon could respond, Jesus spoke again. "So I have chosen twelve of you for this special service. Twelve men, to be my... *apostles.*"

Simon expected Jesus to say "students" not "apostles". He wasn't even sure what an "apostle" was. But he knew he wanted to be one. More than anything in his life. His heart jumped into his throat. Simon became so dizzy with anticipation that he didn't know how he was going to last.

And then Jesus looked at him. The look said it all.

"Simon, son of Jonah."

A wave of relief poured over Simon and he began to cry. Jesus smiled at him. Andrew grabbed his brother's arm. He tried to speak, but the only noise he could make was a low moan.

He felt the large hand of James on his shoulder. "I'm proud of you, Simon," he said. Simon looked in the eyes of his friend and smiled.

Jesus spoke again. "James, son of Zebedee."

James froze in shock. He stared at Jesus. "Me?" he asked. Jesus nodded.

"ME!" he yelled, and his family erupted in cheers. Simon was overjoyed.

"John, son of Zebedee."

"Praise God!" Papa Zebedee said, and he reached forward to embrace his son, who broke down in joyful tears in his father's arms.

"Andrew, son of Jonah."

"Can it be?" Andrew gasped. Simon looked into his brother's face and they quickly fell into each other's arms. Their bodies shook with tears. They were going to follow Jesus *together*. It was like a dream, too good to be true.

Jesus continued calling names. "Philip, son of Efrayim."

Philip began to laugh.

"Nathaniel, son of Tolmai."

Bartholomew put his hand over his heart and bowed in deep reverence before the Master. Simon always thought he was going to be chosen—Bartholomew was well educated and had great experience following John the Baptist.

But the next name caught Simon completely by surprise. "Levi, son of Cleopas."

"Matthew?" Simon asked. He looked back and realized that Matthew was there, sitting with his brothers James and Joses and his parents Cleopas and Mary.

Matthew screamed, "Hallelujah!" His family collapsed around him with joyful sobs and prayerful acclamations. Simon almost felt like asking Jesus if he had made a mistake.

"Judah, son of Samuel."

"Who's that?" James asked. Simon wondered the same thing. He followed Jesus' eyes and it seemed like he looked at David. But it wasn't David. It was David's twin, the one everyone called Thomas. Thomas was pale with shock.

"James, son of Cleopas."

Matthew cried out, "Brother!" and the family of Cleopas began to make even more noise. Simon couldn't believe it. *Two* tax collectors? He knew they were related to Jesus, but this was too much. As he looked back at them, he saw Simon the Zealot stand up in anger and begin to walk away. Simon didn't blame him.

"Judah, son of Jacob."

A man in the middle of the crowd gave a shout of victory. There were confused looks among the fishermen. Nobody knew who he was.

"Simon, son of Uriel."

Son of Uriel? Simon wondered. He immediately realized it was the Zealot. He looked back and saw Simon standing still, almost frozen in mid-step. The Zealot spun around and pointed at his chest as if to say, *do you really mean me?* Then he fell on his knees and nodded yes.

"This is quite a crew," Andrew said to his brother. "How many is that so far?"

Simon had lost count.

"Eleven, I think," James said. "That means there's just one more."

Ioakim was nervous. He fidgeted between Hezekiah and Judas, his two apprentices. He wondered why he wasn't at the top of the list. He was also stunned at who had already been named. *A bunch of fishermen, two tax collectors, and a Zealot? And he chose David's brother, but hadn't yet mentioned David?* He knew there was only one name left and, for the first time, felt a pang of doubt that he might not be picked. *He might pick David, considering how many brothers he's already chosen.*

But to his great relief, Jesus did not look at David but turned toward Ioakim instead. "Thank God," he muttered, putting a hand to his chest. Now he understood—Jesus saved the best for last.

Then Jesus spoke: "Judas, son of Simeon."

It took Ioakim a moment to realize it. Jesus didn't look at him. He looked *next* to him. Ioakim turned toward Judas, who looked back and forth from Jesus to him, clearly without words to say.

Enraged, Ioakim got to his feet. "You picked my *apprentice?*" he said. "Is this a joke to you, assembling this group of *misfits?*" Jesus did not flinch at Ioakim's rebuke.

Ioakim became so enraged that he lost the ability to speak. He growled and stormed away, and Hezekiah followed him. When he broke from the crowd, he turned to glare at his former apprentice. Judas did not look back—he just stared at the ground. *You probably planned this, you thieving backstabber.*

He looked at Jesus and felt like laughing. How could he have ever wanted to follow such a man? Judas over him. Well, he'll find out soon enough. "Watch your money!" Ioakim said, and waved an angry fist in the air. He marched down the mountainside and never looked back.

The shock of Ioakim's outburst subsided and the crowd slowly began to celebrate. But not all were happy. Thomas leaned over and tried to console his brother. "Maybe Jesus mistook you for me," he said.

"*I* mistaken for *you*? That would be a first," he said with a smile, but Thomas could see the pain behind it. David hugged Thomas and whispered in his ear, "I am proud of you, brother. I always knew you'd step out of my shadow someday."

Thomas never loved his brother more than he did in that moment.

Bartholomew was amazed. First, he got to serve John the Baptist. And now he got to be with Jesus. He closed his eyes and thanked God for this tremendous blessing.

"Congratulations, Bartholomew. The Master chose wisely." Bartholomew turned and saw the sullen face of Matthias, with Barsabbas standing behind him. His heart broke for them. They had spent many years serving the Baptist together, and he wondered why he was chosen but not them.

Bartholomew put his hand on his friend's shoulder. "I don't know what to say—"

"There is nothing to say," Matthias said. "We serve as we are asked." Barsabbas slowly nodded his head but said nothing, unable to raise his eyes from the ground.

Bartholomew reached his arms around both of them. "God has a plan," he said. "God always has a plan."

Since Simon, Andrew, James, and John all stood next to each other, the rest of the apostles began to gather where they were. Philip, Bartholomew, and a man Simon didn't know were the first to join them.

"Everybody, this is Judas," Philip said.

"Jude, actually," he said. Jude had light brown hair with a trimmed beard. His tunic suggested that he was not a wealthy man and looked fairly thin. Jude was radiant with joy and eagerly shook hands with each of the fishermen.

"You might not remember this," Jude said to Simon when he shook his hand, "but you carried my mother so that Jesus could heal her when we were in Corazin. I've been following Jesus ever since. It's an honor to meet you."

An honor? Simon felt uncomfortable at the acclamation. "Glad I could help," he said. Simon looked around and saw the Zealot in the distance. He beckoned him to come over.

"This is Simon, son of Uriel," Simon said. The Zealot was not as eager to meet the group as Jude was. He nodded toward them, but didn't shake any hands.

Andrew whispered in his brother's ear. "Wasn't he one of those—"

"Yes," Simon said. "We'll talk about it later."

Thomas approached the group but didn't say much. Matthew and his brother James stood at the edge.

"So," Philip said, "two Simons and two Jameses. How will we keep you apart?"

"Let's call him Little James," said the larger James. He looked at his smaller namesake. "All right with that?"

Little James shrugged. "Fine with me. I'm just glad to be here."

Lucky is more like it, Simon thought.

Philip turned with a large grin to the Zealot. "I guess that would make you little Simon!"

The Zealot crossed his arms in front of his chest. "If *anyone* calls me little," Simon said, "I will kill them."

Philip began to laugh, but stopped suddenly when he realized that Simon wasn't kidding. An uncomfortable silence fell upon the group.

Andrew looked around. "Aren't we missing somebody?"

But no one had a chance to answer. Jesus, who had been speaking to Matthias and Barsabbas, addressed the crowd.

"We can celebrate more tonight," Jesus said. "But for now, I would like to talk to my new apostles." He beckoned toward them and began to walk up the mountain. John jumped immediately behind him.

Simon looked around at the people who had gathered there, the green rolling hills, the town of Capernaum in the distance, and the dark blue lake. He smiled. Simon knew a new part of his life was beginning. He had no idea what would happen next, but there was no fear—no anxiety. Though unsure of the destination, he had complete confidence in the one who would lead him. He felt exhilarated. He felt free.

Heart racing, Simon boldly stepped forward to follow Jesus.

Judas stared at the patch of ground between his feet. The world spun beneath him. He found it hard to breathe. And then he thought he heard a voice call his name. He looked up and one of the fishermen, the one with a patchy beard, was trying to talk to him.

"It's Judas, right?" the man asked.

Words were too hard to speak. Judas nodded.

The man held out his hand. "My name's Andrew. We're going to be apostles together!"

Judas weakly shook his hand. "Good," he said. He meant to say more, but he couldn't think straight.

Clearly this man expected more of a reaction. "Uh, didn't you hear? The Master wants to see us now."

Judas nodded. "Right."

The fisherman considered him for a moment, then headed up the hill.

For the first time since being called, Judas looked around. Ioakim was gone. Hezekiah was gone. The crowd was gone—most were walking down the hill. Jesus and the apostles headed up the mount.

He looked up at the clear blue sky and squinted in the morning light. Birds flew overhead and he heard their song. Judas took a deep breath and exhaled. He still couldn't believe his name had been called. *Why me and not Ioakim?* he wondered.

A horrifying thought took hold of him and his heart beat furiously in his chest. He reached under his tunic and into his coin purse. There he found three silver coins he had stolen from the collection. Judas looked around, worried that someone might see. But no one was there. As he stood, he let the coins roll off his fingers to fall unnoticed in the tall grass.

He breathed again. It was like a great weight had been lifted from his shoulders. *The Lord has given me another chance,* Judas thought. *And I'm not going to mess it up.*

With great hope and confidence he caught up to Jesus and joined the ranks of the twelve.

INTO THE STORM

Mark 3:20-4:41

The courtyard of Simon was filled once again. The twelve sat in a semi-circle around Jesus as he preached. Simon fought hard to keep his eyes open. James was asleep. Most of the others barely hung on.

Nearly a month had passed since the apostles were chosen, but many were still strangers. They had little time to eat or rest. Jesus' fame had spread well throughout the region, and every day hundreds more came to Capernaum to see for themselves what the Nazarene could do.

But Simon noticed a difference in these crowds. The Pharisees had sown so much doubt and suspicion that people were more skeptical of the miracles than surprised by them. Jesus was frequently interrupted by arguments when he preached. And many insulting things were said about the new apostles. "What kind of Rabbi would choose such uneducated students?" they asked.

Simon's stomach felt the dull burn of hunger as Jesus argued with a man about the true meaning of the Torah. Most of Rachael's food was eaten by strangers and nothing was left on the plate by the time it got to them. The combination of sleepless nights, stubborn people, and lack of food had him on the edge of insanity. *How much worse could this get?*

As if to answer that question, Andrew tapped his shoulder and whispered, "Jesus' mother and brothers are here to see him."

Simon quickly rose and awkwardly moved through the full courtyard to get outside.

Once through the door, he encountered four men who were engaged in a fervent conversation. Their robes looked dirty from travel and they all had long, unshaven beards. The men stopped and stared at Simon when he came out of the house. Simon tensed. They looked like they were ready to fight.

But then he saw Mary, Jesus' mother, and felt a wave of peace. She was a short woman with bright green eyes and a beautiful smile. "Shalom, Simon," she said to him. "So good to see you again."

He bowed to her. "I know the Master will rejoice at your visit."

"Some master," one of the men said. Simon stared at him. The smile he had greeted Mary with faded from his face.

Mary blushed at his outburst. "Simon, you remember James —"

"Is it true?" James asked. He stepped closer to Simon and Simon sized him up. He was as tall, but older and not as strong. His long face reminded him of a horse.

"Is what true?" Simon asked.

"Has Jesus formally called students? Does he think himself some sort of... *Rabbi*?"

"He *is* a Rabbi."

James laughed. "He's got you under his spell. You should thank us for taking him out of here."

"What?"

"I've tried to stop them—" Mary said.

"You've had your say, and we've decided," James said. "He is out of his mind and embarrasses our town and family name. It is our obligation to take him home and look after him."

Simon clenched a fist. "It's my house," he said. "I think I have something to say about it."

Mary moved between them. "Peace, all of you." She looked to Simon and touched his hand. "Just tell him that we are here. He'll know what to do," she said.

Simon didn't want to back down from the fight. "For you," he said to Mary. Then he turned and went back into the house.

He pushed his way to the front of the crowd. Simon waited for a pause in Jesus' teaching and came close to his ear. "Master," he whispered, "your mother and *brothers* are outside looking for you."

Jesus paused, looked toward the door, and nodded at him. Simon sat down by his feet between Andrew and John.

Andrew leaned toward him. "That's good, isn't it?"

Simon was too angry to talk about it. He shook his head.

Then he heard whispers in the crowd. Though he had meant to speak softly, people must have heard what he said because soon the whole courtyard buzzed with the news of the family's arrival.

Jesus addressed their concerns. "Who are my mother and brothers?" Jesus asked. And then he pointed to the apostles who sat in a circle around his feet. "These are. Anyone who does the will of God is my mother and brother and sister."

There were gasps in the crowd—did Jesus just disown his own blood? But Simon was struck in his heart with an overwhelming sense of gratitude.

I am his brother. He looked at Andrew, who must have thought the same thing.

"Brothers," Andrew whispered. Simon nodded. He looked around at the other apostles—they were all clearly moved by Jesus' words.

Jesus preached for another hour before dismissing the crowd. The apostles gave him their full attention.

Down by the docks, Rabbi Dov was pleased to see a large group of people turn out for their "announcement". He decided to speak by the water's edge—the same place the carpenter began his blasphemous ministry. With him were Rabbis Elezim and Zedekiah, all of their disciples, and three well dressed scribes. It cost Dov quite a bit of money to get them to make the journey from the Holy City to this miserable village by the lake. But if they could help sway the crowd against the Nazarene, they would be worth every shekel.

"You have been misled!" Dov said to the few hundred people who had gathered there. "We have consulted the Scriptures, and come to the conclusion that this man is *not* a prophet!"

The crowd argued among themselves. Many agreed, but someone asked, "If he is such a sinner, then how can he do such mighty works of God?"

"How indeed?" the Rabbi said. "And it is the answer to this question that gives us the greatest concern." Dov paused and waited for silence so his next statement could have the greatest dramatic effect: "We, the religious leaders and scholars of this area, have determined that Jesus of Nazareth is not a man sent by God, as he claims. Beelzebul is in him! It is by the prince of demons that he drives devils out!"

The name of Beelzebul sent a wave of shock and horror through the crowd. "Could this be?" "God preserve us!" "This can't be true!"

Rabbi Dov reacted in mock sympathy. "I know how hard this is for many of you to hear. He has cured people you know, spoken about God in a way that you think you understand. That is why I invited these scribes from Jerusalem, to make sure what we told you was correct." He made a sweeping gesture toward a group of scholars who arrived in town a few days before.

"It is true," one of them said. "There is an unclean spirit in him."

The crowd panicked. Dov smiled.
Worth every shekel.

Jesus dismissed the people from Simon's courtyard and many of the apostles as well. Only Simon and James remained. As the people left, Jesus' family pushed their way in. Jesus wanted to embrace his mother, but knew he had to deal with his brothers first.

"Who do you think you are?" James said. "Leaving your mother, traveling the countryside, training students? No wonder the Pharisees think you are crazy."

Jesus raised an eyebrow. "So you agree with the Pharisees?"

James scowled. "I'd as much follow a Sadducee than follow their watered-down faith. If your father was alive he'd lock you up and stop this foolishness!"

"That is enough!" Mary said. "I will not have you talk about my husband that way. If Joseph were here, he would be proud of his son. I'm sure I know his mind better than you."

James ignored her. "We're taking you home," he said.

James Zebedee cracked his knuckles and folded his large, muscular arms in front of his chest. "If you wanted to take him, you should have brought more people."

This quieted the Nazarenes. Simon and James Zebedee were large, muscular men, and had an intimidating presence when they wanted to. The Nazarenes were farmers, not fighters. They clearly didn't know what to do next.

The moment was interrupted by a knock on the door. Philip entered the courtyard. "Master, forgive the interruption, but the Pharisees are down by the lake and are saying horrible things."

"I'll be there soon, Philip," Jesus said, and Philip left.

"Maybe, for once, the Pharisees *are* right," James said. "I for one am interested to hear what they have to say about you." He threw the door open and left the house, followed by the other men.

Jesus breathed a sigh of relief at their departure. "We will leave you alone, Master," Simon said. He and James moved into the street and closed the door behind them.

"Come here," his mother said, and she hugged him. Jesus was relieved to be with her and softened at her touch.

"Don't let James get to you," she said.

"I'm used to James," he said. "The problem is these Pharisees. They poison people against the good news."

"You knew this would happen," she gently replied.

"Yes."

She put her hand on his cheek and scrutinized his face. "You look tired."

"I'm fine."

"You need to take better care of yourself."

Jesus laughed. "I'm fine," he said. Mary smiled. But he could see her pain. "Mother?"

She paused, and the silence said it all. "I'm sorry," she said, "The last thing you need is…" She couldn't finish the words. Jesus didn't try to finish them for her. They leaned their heads into each other and embraced a silence that spoke more than anything either of them could say.

The mother broke the silence with song. Her voice was pure and gentle, and though she whispered the words they seemed to fill the whole courtyard. "*The Lord is my strength and my song,*" she sang. She looked up and smiled at her son. "I sing that on the good days."

"And on the bad ones?"

She sang again, this time more somberly. "*My God, my God, why have you forsaken me?*"

Jesus nodded. "Is there anything I can do?" he asked.

"Come home. Maybe we can go to Passover together."

"I will," he said. "You know I can't deny you anything."

She let out a joyful laugh and it lightened his heart to hear it. He bent down and Mary kissed him on the cheek. "I love you, son."

"I love you, too," he said. After a final embrace, Jesus headed toward the door.

"Jesus?" she said.

"Yes, mother?"

"Don't forget to eat. You're all skin and bones." Jesus opened his mouth to reply, but Mary raised a finger to silence him. "And don't give me that *man does not live by bread alone* nonsense. Eat more food."

"Yes, mother."

As Jesus and his apostles came to the docks, Rabbi Dov cried out, "Behold Beelzebul, the prince of devils! Mothers, hide your children! Men of God, be on guard for his tricks! Here is Satan!"

The accusation burned Jesus' heart, but he kept his voice calm. "How can Satan drive out Satan? If a kingdom is divided against itself, it cannot last. And if a household is divided against itself, it cannot last. Now if Satan has rebelled against himself and is divided, then he cannot last either. It would be the end of him."

"The lord of lies!" Dov said. "He will try to convince you that what we say is not true! He is a blasphemer!"

Jesus made his way to the front of the crowd, and stared Dov in the face. "It is you who blaspheme!" Jesus said. "In truth I tell you, all human sins will be forgiven, but anyone who blasphemes against the Holy Spirit will never be forgiven, but is guilty of an eternal sin."

Dov turned to the crowd. "You see!" he said. "He came preaching God's mercy, but when someone challenges him, he talks about unforgivable sins!"

"All sins can be forgiven," Jesus said, also addressing the crowd, "unless you call the one who forgives sins a devil. How can you expect to be saved if you curse the means of your salvation?"

"I will be happy to explain that this Sabbath," Rabbi Dov said, "when *I* preach at the synagogue."

Jesus looked to the back of the crowd and saw Jairus, who went pale and then ran to his house.

The crowd surged forward and Jesus and Dov had to step into the water. Where were Simon and James? They were usually the ones strong enough to hold people back when he spoke. As he looked around for his apostles, he heard a voice from behind him call, "Master!"

Jesus turned and saw Simon, with the other apostles on a boat. He reached out and grabbed Jesus' hand to bring him on board.

"I thought you could use some distance from the crowd," he said.

Jesus smiled. "Well done, Simon. Well done."

He looked at those gathered on the shore. To his right were the scribes and Pharisees, still shouting out various titles of Satan. To his left was his family from Nazareth, arms folded in judgment, waiting for him to say something to prove he was insane. And in the middle was confusion. Even after seeing the miracles and hearing the message, they were many who were unsure about him.

Jesus raised his hand for silence, and everyone but the Pharisees obliged until Rabbi Dov said, "Let him talk, and let his own words condemn him!" Then all was quiet except for the small waves that broke against the shore, and the sound of a strong wind that blew off the lake.

He opened his mouth to speak, but then stopped. *No, I have explained myself enough.* It was time for something new.

"Listen!" Jesus said. "Imagine a sower going out to sow." He looked at the Pharisees. "Now it happened that, as he sowed, some of the seed fell on the edge of the path and the birds came and ate it up." Then Jesus looked at the Nazarenes. "Some seed fell on rocky ground where it found little soil and at once sprang up, because there was no depth of earth. When the sun came up it was scorched and died." Gazing upon the rest of the crowd he said, "Some seed fell into thorns, and the thorns grew and choked it so it produced no crop."

Then Jesus looked down at his apostles who sat by his feet on the boat. "And some fell into rich soil, grew tall and strong, and produced a good crop; the yield was thirty, sixty, and even a hundredfold."

He raised his hands and cried in a loud voice, "Anyone who has ears for listening should listen!"

Then he turned away from them and sat down on the boat.

He heard, or more accurately *didn't hear*, the stunned silence from the crowd. Then a Pharisee cried, "You see! He's trying to confuse you! He's the lord of deception!" And a Nazarene cried,

"He's lost his mind! Lock him up!" More arguments erupted from the crowd, and there were many calls for Jesus to explain himself.

But Jesus wasn't interested in the people on the shore. His focus was on the twelve men in the boat. He looked around at their faces. *Will they understand?* But none of them moved. None of them asked. They kept nervously looking at the reaction of those on the land.

Jesus rubbed his face and felt heavy with exhaustion. The shouts from the water's edge grew louder. "Let's go," he said.

"Where are we going, Master?" Simon asked.

"Away from here," Jesus said. He lifted a tired finger and pointed to the cliffs that framed the eastern side of the lake. "There."

Simon looked at the approaching clouds, and then back at Jesus. "Yes, Master," he said. They picked up the oars and began to row.

Simon stared into the water as they rowed. The sun was already behind the mountain and the sea gave no refection. It looked like a dark abyss. Simon was well aware that this was his first time on a boat since leaving everything to follow Jesus, and the sea was not happy with his decision. Waves rocked them back and forth, and the wood of the boat growled as it adjusted to the weight of the apostles.

As they got out some distance from the shore, John broke the silence. "Master, I don't understand. Why did you speak like that?"

Jesus smiled, as if he was waiting for someone to ask. "Because to you is granted the mysteries of the kingdom of heaven, but to them," and he looked back at the shore, "it is not granted." Staring at the distant crowd, he quoted from the prophet Isaiah:

> *"This people's heart has grown coarse,*
> *their ears dulled, they have shut their eyes tight*
> *to avoid using their eyes to see, their ears to hear,*
> *their hearts to understand,*
> *changing their ways and being healed by me."*

Jesus nodded to Simon, and the fishermen stopped rowing and put their oars in the boat. "Pay attention to the parable of the sower," Jesus told them. "When anyone hears the word of the kingdom without understanding, the Evil One comes and carries off what was sown in his heart: this is the seed sown on the edge of the path. The seed sown on patches of rock is someone who hears the words and welcomes it at once with joy. But such a person has no root deep down and does not last; should some trial come, or some persecution on account of the word, at once he falls away. The seed sown on thorns is someone who hears the word, but the worry of the world and the lure of riches choke the word and so it produces nothing. And the seed sown in rich soil is someone who hears the word and understands it; this is the one who yields a harvest and produces now a hundredfold, now sixty, now thirty."

Andrew leaned into his brother and whispered, "I hope I'm the rich soil."

"Me, too," Simon said.

Simon listened with wonder as Jesus gave them many other parables about the kingdom of God. Twilight faded into black.

Jesus finished and invited them to silently pray for a moment. The moment of quiet became a few moments, and Simon heard a brief snore from one of the apostles.

He opened his eyes and looked at his brother. *Who would dare fall asleep during the Master's teaching?* He worried it was James, but hoped it was Matthew.

It was hard to tell who snored in the darkness. Clouds covered the sky and the moon only gave a faint light. Simon looked to Jesus to see how he might chastise the offender. Jesus didn't respond. He sat peacefully between Judas and John. Simon closed his eyes and tried to return to prayer.

The next snore was louder, and a few of them raised their heads to see who made the sound. "*Sssh,*" Bartholomew said, clearly displeased with the lack of respect.

The timid voice of John spoke. "I think it came from the Master."

Another snore came, and they saw Jesus lean against John, sound asleep. Judas and John helped lower Jesus so he lay in the stern. They would have thought him dead but for the occasional snore he made.

The wind picked up and waves began to rock the boat. There was a flash of lightning in the northeast, and the wind came from that direction as well. The sound of thunder echoed a few moments after it.

Thomas leaned off the edge of the boat and threw up. Philip grabbed him to help with his balance. Thomas shook. "I don't like being on the water," he weakly said.

"I thought you built boats," Philip said.

"On *land*," Thomas said. Then he leaned over the side and threw up again.

Matthew also looked queasy, and the smell of Thomas' vomit didn't help anyone. "Let's go back," he said.

But Simon was tired of running. He stood and faced the approaching darkness of the storm. Waves crested and slammed against the boat.

You are nothing without me, said the sea.

Simon cursed at it. "Grab the oars."

The fishermen obeyed, and John angled the rudder of the ship to turn the boat around and head toward Capernaum.

"No!" Simon said. "We're not going back." He lifted his hand and pointed to the cliff wall barely visible on the other side of the lake. "There."

"*Simon?*" James whispered.

"There?" Matthew asked. "Cross the lake in this weather? Are you out of your mind?"

"It's what the Master told us," Simon said. "Do you want to disobey him?"

"But why would we go where the Gentiles are?" Judas asked. "I hardly think that is what he—"

"What makes you think you know his mind?" Simon said.

"And what makes you think you're in charge?" the Zealot said. He stood to confront him.

James stood as well. "It's Simon's boat," he said.

A strong gust of wind and a large wave almost knocked the three of them over and they sat down, clutching the side of the boat.

"This is suicide!" Matthew said.

"If you want to swim," Simon said, "then be my guest."

Lightning flashed again, and a rolling thunder followed. "We're going to get caught in that storm," Thomas said.

"Then we had better start rowing," Simon said, and the fishermen rearranged themselves to man the oars. There were six oars on the boat, three for each side. Simon and Andrew grabbed the front ones, James and Philip were at the back, and Bartholomew and

Jude got the middle ones because that's where they happened to be sitting. The Zealot and Judas were at the front of the boat, and Matthew, Little James, and Thomas were in the stern where Jesus was sleeping. John was with them, manning the rudder.

"Let's row," Simon said.

Andrew tried to speak to his brother. "Simon—"

"ROW!" Simon heaved the oar into the water, and the others did the same.

John tried to wake Jesus with his foot. "*Master*," he said in a soft voice, "*please wake up*." But Jesus remained asleep.

"Damn fool will get us all killed," Little James said.

Thomas didn't like the sound of that. "People don't really die in these storms, do they?"

Matthew stared coldly at Simon, who rowed with such passion that the others had a hard time keeping his pace. "His father did," he whispered.

The boat was fast, but the storm was faster. Simon cursed the extra weight of the people on the boat. He was used to rowing for seven people, not thirteen.

Bartholomew and Jude had a tough time keeping up with the rowing. The lightning and thunder now arrived at the same time, and the storm was strongly upon them. The rain felt like sharp stones against their faces. Bartholomew got distracted by a blinding flash of light and stopped his row for a second, causing Simon's oar to lock up with his.

"Keep rowing!" Simon said, "or you're going to get us all killed!"

"I'm not the one responsible for this!" Bartholomew said. He turned his shoulder to confront Simon who sat behind him, and as he did a large wave slammed against the side of the boat, causing him to drop his oar.

"The oar!" Andrew cried. James quickly pulled his oar in the boat and reached out his long arms to grab Bartholomew's. He swung the oar back into the boat and accidentally struck Matthew across his side. Matthew fell over the sleeping body of Jesus into John, and he and John crashed into the side of the boat where Thomas was, leaving no one on the rudder. The boat began to spin.

As John tried to untangle himself from Thomas and Matthew, Little James grabbed the rudder but didn't know what to do with it. "Hold it steady!" Simon yelled, but his instructions were lost in another blast of lightning and thunder.

"What?"

Simon stood and moved his hand in a straight line forward and back. "HOLD IT STEADY!" He saw a look of terror on James's face and turned to see what it was.

A wave approached that crested higher than his head. Lightning flashed, and for a brief moment Simon saw himself in its reflection before the water knocked him over, flat on his back, on top of someone. Philip was almost washed off the boat but James and Andrew grabbed his tunic as he slipped over the side.

Simon the Zealot and Judas jumped to the middle of the ship to grab the unused oars. John wrestled himself free and did his best to keep the boat from spinning. There was cursing and swearing and chaos. Waves continued to break into the boat, causing it to flood. Thomas and Little James tried in vain to push the water out with their hands.

Fear gripped Simon's heart. *I'm going to die like my father.* He realized it was his fault these men would die with him. Simon rolled his body over and discovered who he fell on top of. It was Jesus. *Still asleep!* He couldn't believe it. Simon's fear turned to anger, and he grabbed Jesus' tunic and shook him violently.

"Master, do you not care?" he said. Then in the flashes of lightning he saw a darkness move toward him with a white crest on the top. The boat began to pitch to the side and Simon knew they would capsize. "WE ARE LOST!"

Jesus opened his eyes and said, "Quiet! Be calm!"

At first, Simon thought he was being chastised. But he quickly realized—*he spoke to the sea.*

The large wave that was about to capsize the boat fell backwards into the lake. The rain that had pelted them like arrows fell gently on them and then disappeared. The howling of the wind became a whimper and faded into silence. The thunder and lightning ceased. The clouds were pulled back like a sheet, and the first light of morning illuminated a clear sky.

The boat swayed back and forth, back and forth, until it eventually grew still. Everyone on the ship was frozen in his place.

Simon could not believe his eyes. The lake showed no signs of the violent storm they had just been through. It was smooth as glass and silent as the dead. Simon looked in awe and wonder at the calm around him, and then realized he still held on to Jesus' robes. He quickly let go and fell to his knees.

The other apostles did the same. Simon bent low and looked at his hands. They were shaking.

"Why are you so frightened?" Jesus asked.

He couldn't answer. He didn't even have the courage to look up into his Master's face. Simon wasn't sure what scared him more: the manner in which he almost died, or the power by which he was spared. *Did Jesus just speak to the wind and sea, and they obeyed him?* It was too much to take.

Jesus sighed. "Have you still no faith?"

The boat ran aground and it startled Simon. He looked over his shoulder and up at the large Gerasene cliffs. They had made it to the other side.

"We're here," Jesus said. He walked off the ship and into the shallow water of the beach. Simon and his brother looked at each other in amazement.

"Who can this be?" Andrew whispered.

"Come!" Jesus said. Simon and the others stumbled out of the boat and onto the shore.

THERE AND BACK AGAIN

Mark 5:1-43

Jairus didn't sleep well that night. It was partially because of the storms, but mostly he was kept awake with guilt. The Pharisees threatened to boycott his synagogue if he ever let Jesus preach there again. *And Jesus doesn't need a synagogue to preach in,* Jairus rationalized. *He'd rather be outside where he can gather a larger crowd.*

It made sense in his mind, but his heart argued against him. As the storm raged even harder, Jairus fell to his knees. "Oh Lord," Jairus prayed, "if this is your will, please give me a sign." Suddenly, the storm stopped and the first light of morning appeared.

Jairus stepped into his courtyard and gazed at the clear sky above him. *A miracle!* This was the sign he was looking for. The noise of driving rain and thunder had passed, and there was nothing but peace and quiet. Then he heard the sound of heavy coughing.

"Jairus!" his wife said. "Come quickly!"

He ran to the bedroom where his twelve-year-old daughter slept, and found her writhing on the floor, struggling to breathe. The girl saw him and reached out, barely able to say the word, "Daddy!" Jairus felt his heart drop from his chest, and he fell to his knees beside her bed and held her.

"It's okay, it's okay. Daddy's going to make everything all right. I promise, I promise." She coughed so violently that it took all his strength to hold her steady. He looked to his wife who was pale with fear. He kissed his daughter's forehead and ran his fingers through her hair, saying, "Daddy's going to be right back. Everything will be all right, Daddy's going to be right back." Then he ran from the room.

Jairus ran to Simon's door and knocked loudly. After a moment, Rachael opened it.

"Where is Jesus? Where is Jesus?" Jairus asked.

"He's not here," Rachael said.

"Is he praying? Where is he praying? Does Simon know?"

"Simon isn't here either," Rachael said. "They didn't come back last night."

"Didn't come back last night…" Jairus collapsed in tears on the ground.

Rachael knelt beside him and put a hand on his back. "Jairus, what is wrong?"

He looked up with tears streaming out of his eyes. "God is punishing me, punishing me," was all he could say. Then he ran back to his house.

The apostles were in bad shape. Thomas was face down in the sand, thanking God he was off the water. Little James and Bartholomew tended to Matthew, who was in pain from the blow he received from the oar. The Zealot, Jude, and Judas could barely walk because they were disoriented from the journey.

The fishermen were only a little better. Philip shot Simon a harsh look. *I deserve that*, Simon thought. None of them wanted to talk to him. The shock of the miracle had worn off and they realized what happened. They were saved because of Jesus, but should be dead because of him.

The howl of an animal echoed off the rocky cliffs that separated the land from the beach. Everyone was quickly on their feet.

"What was that?" Jude asked.

"There!" John said. A creature leapt from behind the rocks and ran toward them at full speed.

They all jumped back except for Jesus. He stood his ground with firm determination. The creature howled and ran toward them on its hind legs. As it got closer, Jesus reached out his hand and commanded, "Come out, unclean spirit!"

It was as though someone tied a rope around the thing and pulled it back in mid air. It crashed to the ground and writhed in agony.

Jesus walked closer, but the others didn't move. Simon looked at the thing and realized that the creature wasn't a monster.

It was a man.

He was naked and covered in so many scabs and scars that he was hardly recognizable as human. Broken chains dangled around his neck, hands, and legs as if someone tried to chain him but failed.

"WHAT DO YOU WANT WITH ME, SON OF THE MOST HIGH GOD? DO NOT TORTURE ME!" he wailed.

"What is your name?" Jesus said.

The man rolled his eyes in the back of his head and spoke with what sounded like hundreds of voices, each one echoing off the rocky wall. "MY NAME IS LEGION, FOR THERE ARE MANY OF US."

Simon shuddered. He had seen a few people possessed since traveling with Jesus, but none like this.

"Legion, I command you to—"

"HAVE MERCY! HAVE MERCY!" the demons cried. The man was on his knees before Jesus, sobbing hysterically.

Mercy for demons? thought Simon. *Nice try.* But instead of immediately sending the demons back to hell, Jesus hesitated.

"THERE ARE A HERD OF PIGS UP THERE, ON THE MOUNTAINSIDE," they said, pointing to the top of the cliffs. "ARE THEY NOT UNCLEAN ANIMALS? THESE GENTILES WERE GOING TO SACRIFICE THEM TO US ANYWAY. GIVE US LEAVE TO GO INTO THEM. PLEASE, LET US LEAVE THIS MAN AND GO INTO THEM."

Jesus paused. "Go," he said. The man fell unconscious into the sand. Jesus ran toward him and Simon was the first to follow with James right behind him.

It was hard to tell he was naked because he was covered in so many scars. He lay in the sand curled up like a baby.

"James, give me your robe," Simon said.

James took off his outer tunic and they put it over the man and helped him sit upright. It took all of their strength to do it—the man was huge. He began to wake up, as if from a deep sleep.

Jesus knelt next to him. "What is your name?"

The man squinted his eyes to adjust to the daylight. He looked down at his hands and skin as if he wore a new body. "Marcus," he said in voice even deeper than James. "My name is Marcus."

"Marcus," Jesus said, "you are free!"

The man smiled and laughed. Tears of joy ran down his face. The other apostles came closer and breathed a sigh of relief.

"But where did the demons go?" Marcus asked.

Just then, there was a sound of distant pig squeals and shouting men. From atop the cliff, a lone pig jumped off and landed head first onto the beach. Another one followed. Two more after that.

Then Simon witnessed something he would never forget: an enormous herd of pigs charged down the cliff and threw themselves headlong over them. It was like a waterfall of brown and pink, with the sound of squeals replacing the sound of rushing water. Almost a thousand had made the plunge by the time the last one fell. The first few hundred made a pile on the beach, creating a ramp into the water for the rest. Their corpses bobbed back and forth on the sea.

Marcus laughed and raised an angry fist toward them. "Good riddance!" he yelled.

Six men who were in charge of the pigs ran down to the beach. "Who did this?" one of them asked.

Andrew winked at his brother and proudly stepped forward. "Gentlemen, I am proud to introduce to you Rabbi Jesus, from Nazareth. He is a prophet of the Most High God—"

"Get out of here!" the man said.

Andrew was stunned. "What?"

"You heard me. Get out of here! We don't want your kind here!"

"What do you mean by 'our kind'?" Simon asked.

"You know what I mean, *Jew*."

"That is enough!" Marcus said, and he stood to his full height. He was so large and muscular that James's tunic hung above his knees. The men took a step back.

Jesus stepped between them with open hands. "We came in peace, we will leave in peace," he said. "Come, let us go." They walked toward the boat.

Marcus followed. "Please, let me come with you." Simon gave James a worried look. How would he fit in the boat?

Jesus put his hand on Marcus's shoulder and looked him in the eye. "Go home to your people, and tell them all that the Lord in his mercy has done for you." He promised to return someday, prayed a prayer of blessing over him, and sent him on his way.

As they pulled away from the shore, they carefully navigated around a few pig corpses to make their way into deeper water.

"Can you believe that?" Andrew said.

"Last time we try to help a bunch of Gentiles," James said. "You'd think they would at least show some gratitude."

"When people see great power they often react with great fear," Jesus said.

"We shouldn't have gone in the first place," Judas said, malice in his voice.

Simon kept his head down and rowed.

"I wanted to go there," Jesus said. "And I'm glad we did. But now it is time to go home. Let us make haste. We are needed in Capernaum right away."

A woman in a weathered brown robe cautiously approached the synagogue. Her name was Deborah. On hearing about the miraculous power of Jesus, she made a long and dangerous trip to Capernaum. But Jesus was not at the synagogue. She saw a large crowd at the house next door and looked in, hoping to find him.

Deborah stood in the doorway and saw many people, but none of them seemed to be Jesus. A group of Pharisees came in, forcing her to move deeper into the courtyard. She was careful not to touch anyone as she did. Her heart almost stopped as a trickle of blood ran down her foot. Deborah bent over and rubbed the brown robe against her leg, thankful the dark color of her robe would once again hide the stain. Her eyes darted around the courtyard to see if anyone noticed.

But it was hard for anyone in the courtyard to notice anything but the Pharisees. They were there in full regalia, and one Pharisee's trumpeting voice stood in sharp contrast to the hushed and respectful conversations that he interrupted with his arrival.

"We are here to offer our prayers and sympathy to Jairus. Where is he?" asked the Rabbi.

A man came forward and bowed. "Thank you for coming, Rabbi Dov," he said. "My brother is upstairs with his daughter."

"Summon him," Dov said. "We wish to speak to him."

The brother hesitated, then nodded and left. Dov raised his hand to silence the crowd. "Let us pray," he said, "for Jairus and his family at this difficult time. May he be comforted by the words of the psalm: that even *if he walk through the valley dark as death, he should fear no evil for God is at his side.*" And he bowed his head in prayer and led them in a psalm.

He finished and looked around at them. "Yes, God is at our brother's side right now," he said. "But do you notice who isn't here?" He paused and then yelled, "JESUS!"

The crowd began to murmur and argue amongst themselves. Dov raised his voice to be heard over the noise. "Once we revealed who he really was, *he left you!* We have cast that demon from Capernaum, and for that we should give thanks to the One True God of Israel!"

Deborah clutched her chest and felt like she might collapse. *Is it true? Has all my hope been in vain?*

There were shouts of praise and condemnation from the crowd, but they were all silenced when they heard someone say, "How dare you! How dare you!" Deborah stood on her toes to look over the crowd, and she saw a man enter into the courtyard, face red with anger.

"Praise God, Jairus," Rabbi Dov said to him. "Praise God he has set you and your family free from the lies of Jesus."

"YOU ARE THE LIAR!" Jairus rushed headlong at Rabbi Dov and threw him against the wall.

Dov's disciples jumped up to pull Jairus off of him, but Jairus held on to Dov's robes with a grip strong as a vice.

"He's possessed by a demon!" one person yelled. "This is the work of Jesus!"

"The Pharisees are liars!" said another.

It was about to break into a riot when someone came to the door and yelled, "Simon's boat is coming toward the dock!"

The first to move was Jairus, who dropped Dov and burst through the crowd to head toward the lake. The entire courtyard emptied out into the street, and Deborah was caught up with them. Men pushed into her as they left the house, and Deborah began to cry. By touching her sickness, she made them unclean and they didn't even know it. She prayed to God for mercy.

After the courtyard had emptied, Dov's disciples stumbled over each other to prove they had more concern for their master. "I'm fine!" Dov said as he swatted them away.

"Should we go down to the docks?" Rabbi Zedekiah asked.

"I've had enough of these ignorant vermin for one day," he said as he brushed off his robes in disgust. He looked up and realized they were not the only ones in the courtyard. Jairus's wife had tears in her eyes and her brother had his arm around her.

Dov quickly regained his composure and bowed low. "Of course, I was not referring to—"

"Get out," the brother said. He pointed his finger toward the door, hand trembling with rage.

Dov and the others left in haste.

Simon was exhausted and hungry. He, like the other apostles, hadn't eaten since the day before. And none of them had slept except for Jesus, who seemed rested and refreshed as the boat cut across the water toward Capernaum.

The fishermen rowed with tired arms but made good time. Still, it took them hours to make it across the lake. The sun was almost at its highest point in the sky.

"I think I can see a large crowd at the docks," Little James said.

"I hope they brought food," James said.

"Is it the Pharisees again?" Simon the Zealot asked.

Little James squinted his eyes and raised his hand to protect him from the sun's glare off the lake. "I can't see any. But I think I see Jairus, and he seems very agitated."

"Jairus is always agitated," Andrew said, and the others laughed.

But Simon noticed that Jesus didn't. His face had a look of great concern and seemed tense. "Row faster," he said. They quieted down and the fishermen quickened their pace. Knowing the dock was near gave them extra energy to cover the remaining distance with great speed.

As they got within earshot, Simon realized the cause for Jesus' concern. They could hear the voice of Jairus yelling and it broke his heart to hear him wail with such grief. "Jesus, have pity on me! I'm sorry! Don't take my daughter, take me instead!"

"Be at peace, Jairus!" Jesus called to him as the boat approached the dock. He jumped out of the boat and the head of the synagogue fell at his knees.

"My little daughter is desperately sick. Please, please come lay your hands on her that she may live. I know that it is my fault—"

"Jairus, it is *not* your fault," Jesus said.

"Please, forgive me, forgive me…" and he collapsed in tears.

Jesus knelt down next to him and lifted his head. "Let us go to her. Don't be afraid. Have faith."

Jairus looked into his eyes and nodded. They tried to move quickly to the house, but the docks were narrow and the entire town had lined up to see how Jesus would respond to Jairus's plea. Simon and James jumped in front to clear the way, but it was slow going.

The apostles formed a circle around Jesus. There was such a swarm of people that they were pushed to the left and right as they tried to make their way to Jairus's home. As they made it to the narrow streets that lead to the house, the space became tighter and everyone was pushed together.

Deborah felt bodies pressed against her, but once she saw Jesus nothing else mattered. She almost fell a few times, but was determined to keep up with the crowd. *If I can just touch his clothes,* she thought, *I shall be saved.*

Jesus was surrounded by men she assumed must be his disciples. The crowd pushed against them and often caught them off balance. One of them, a small chubby one, fell into a tough looking one.

"Get off me, pig!" the tough one yelled at him.

For a brief moment, she saw Jesus' back. She shot forward like an arrow and reached out to touch him. But then a tall skinny man stepped in her way and she crashed against his shoulder. As they fell forward, she reached out her hand as far as it could go. The tip of her middle finger grazed against the thread of the blue tassel at the bottom of Jesus' robe as she fell face first into the dirt.

And she was healed.

She did not know how she knew it, but she did.

"Are you crazy?" the man yelled at her. A few other bodies fell over them in a pile. Someone roughly lifted her to her feet and pushed her aside. She did not care. Tears streamed down her face. She could go the synagogue again. She could be with her family again. She was saved.

Then suddenly, the crowd stopped. "Who touched me?" someone asked.

It was Jesus. She held her breath. The crowd tried to keep moving forward but he wouldn't budge. He raised his hands and asked again, "Who touched my clothes?"

The crowd grew silent. The only thing Deborah could hear was her heartbeat. A large man with tight curly hair turned to Jesus and said, "Master, all the crowd is pressing against you. How can you ask, 'Who touched me?'" But Jesus ignored him and looked through different faces in the crowd until he came to hers.

She was caught. Deborah came forward, trembling with fear, and threw herself at his feet.

"Forgive me, Master," she said. "Forgive me for defiling you. I had no other hope but you. I have been bleeding for twelve years. I have spent all my family's money on doctors, but was only left worse than when I began…" She choked back tears in order to talk. "I'm sorry I made you unclean, but you were my last chance, my only chance."

She could not control her sobs and bent low to the ground. She could hear the angry whispers of the crowd around her. Then there was silence. She looked up into Jesus' face. She had never seen anything so beautiful.

"I am not unclean," Jesus said. He looked at the crowd. "They are not unclean." And then he bent down and lifted her to her feet.

"*You* are not unclean," he said.

They embraced. She had not felt the touch of another person for over ten years, and she collapsed in Jesus' arms, sobbing with joy.

The only person in the crowd not moved with pity was Jairus. He could see the door of his house from where he stood and anxiously looked back at Jesus. *Why are we wasting our time here?*

As he looked again down the road to his door, his brother Efrayim walked into the street. There were tears in his eyes and a blank expression on his face. As he caught sight of his brother, Jairus shook his head and broke into tears.

"No!" Jairus cried. "No, no, no…" The crowd parted to let Efrayim through. He hugged his brother and they both wept.

"She is gone, Jairus," he said through his tears. "Do not bother the Master any further."

Jairus felt a firm hand on his shoulder. It was Jesus. "Fear is useless," he said to him. "Only have faith." Jesus turned back to the woman and said, "Daughter, your faith has saved you. Go in peace." Then he grabbed Jairus by the arm and pulled him through the crowd toward his house.

Simon passed by his open doorway and saw Rachael and his daughters standing there, crying. "Is it true? Is she dead?" Rachael asked.

"Have faith," Simon said. And he followed Jesus to Jairus's door.

Jesus turned to the apostles. "Simon, James, and John— come in with me. The rest of you, make sure no one enters." Simon looked at Andrew. He could see he wanted to go in as well and looked hurt to not be invited.

The door closed behind them. The courtyard was scattered with family members and mourners who wept and wailed over the girl's death. "Why all this commotion?" Jesus asked. "The child is not dead. She is only asleep." At this, some of them began to laugh.

"Are you mad?" one of them asked.

"The Pharisees are right about you!" another said.

"OUT!" Jesus commanded, and he pointed his hand toward the door.

The mourners left and Jairus led them into the room where his daughter was. He almost collapsed at the sight of her dead body and Simon held him steady so he wouldn't fall. Judith wept by the bed, and when she saw her husband she ran to him and buried herself in his arms.

"She's gone, Jairus, our baby is gone," she cried.

Jairus held her. "Have faith," he said. "Have faith." He stared desperately at Jesus.

Simon looked at the girl's body. She was so much like Hadassah. His heart sank in his chest. She lay motionless and there was no color in her skin.

They were too late.

Jesus walked over to the dead body and stared at it. Then he looked back at the grieving parents. There were tears in his eyes. But they did not notice him. They were too consumed with their own grief.

He knelt down beside the girl and picked up her hand. It hung limply in his and he put his other hand over it. He looked at her for a moment, lovingly. Jairus noticed this and so did his wife. Their tears continued to flow but the wailing ceased. Simon felt something in the air, but he couldn't tell what it was.

The room became completely still. No one dared to move except for Jesus. He bent lower over the girl. Simon could hear the slight creak of leather from his sandal, the swoosh of fabric from this tunic, and even the whisper Jesus spoke into the girl's ear:

"Little girl, I tell you to get up."

He leaned back. Her hand was still limp in his, and her armed swayed like a clothesline in the wind. But then the arm twitched. And the fingers of her hand curled around his. Her chest filled with air and her eyes opened. Her expressionless face transformed into wide eyes and a beautiful smile.

She sat up. Simon and the others jumped back.

Judith screamed. "IT'S A MIRA—" but Jesus raised his hand to silence her. The little girl got up and ran toward her mother, who picked her up and held her tightly.

"Mommy, why are you crying?" the girl asked.

Judith started to laugh through her tears. Jairus fell to his knees. He reached out and kissed Jesus' hand, so overcome with astonishment that he couldn't find the words to say. Judith put their daughter down and she ran to hug her father. "I love you, daddy," she said.

Simon could not believe what he just saw. "A girl raised from the dead!" he said. "Wait until they hear about this!"

"No!" Jesus said, and his stern tone took them all by surprise. "No one must know what happened here."

"But, but Jesus," Jairus said, "people have to know—"

"They will know, Jairus," Jesus said. "But not yet." Jesus looked into the eyes of Simon, James, and John. "Do not even tell the others about this until I tell you to."

John asked the question that Simon was afraid to. "Why?"

James looked condemningly at his brother for questioning the Master. John hung his head and muttered an apology.

Jesus put a hand on his shoulder and John looked up at him. "Because they would not understand," he said.

Am I supposed to understand? Simon wondered. He could not take his eyes off the little girl, laughing and hugging her parents as if nothing happened, as if she wasn't lying dead on the floor a few minutes ago.

"But then what, what should we do?" Jairus asked.

The little girl came up to Jesus and smiled as he ran his hand through her hair. "You should probably give her something to eat."

Jairus's courtyard erupted in celebration when they heard that Jairus's daughter was alive and not dead as they had feared. "What happened in there?" Andrew asked.

"He... he healed her," Simon replied.

"Praise God you got to her before she died!"

"Yes," Simon said. "Praise God." It killed him to not share the miracle with his brother. But the Master had made himself clear.

He looked at Jesus, who laughed and celebrated with the people. Was this the same man he knew a day ago? *He commands the sea. He raises the dead.* He was too tired to think about it.

Simon stumbled out of Jairus's house like a man drunk. He entered his courtyard and Rachael greeted him with a hug. His youngest daughter ran up to him.

"Is it true? Is she all right?" Hadassah asked.

Simon smiled. "She's walking and talking as if nothing happened. Go see her if you'd like." She screamed with joy and ran out of the house.

"You have had quite a day," Rachael said. "You must be hungry."

"Famished," he replied as he sat down on the bench.

"I'll get you some food," she said. She said some other things, too, but Simon couldn't tell what they were. He laid his head against the wall and fell into the welcome darkness of sleep.

HOMECOMING

Mark 6:1-5

"This is a bad idea," James said.

"Do you want to tell him that?" Simon asked. His legs ached as he walked with the apostles along the rocky path that headed east and south of Capernaum.

"I'm sure they'll welcome us with open arms," Philip said. "I mean, other than trying to throw us off a cliff, what is the worst that could happen?"

"That sounds pretty bad to me," Thomas replied, who walked with the Zealot a few steps behind them.

Bartholomew sighed. "It was a *joke*, Thomas." Under his breath, Simon heard him quietly murmur something about how stupid he was.

Not quietly enough. "I'm sorry that I don't know seven languages like you," Thomas said.

"Nine," Bartholomew said.

"That must be convenient when you have to cozy up to your pagan friends," Simon the Zealot said.

"Do you have anything new to say?" Bartholomew said.

The Zealot grabbed Bartholomew's tunic and spun him around. "You're right," he said. "I'm more a man of action than words."

They all stopped. Simon stood behind Bartholomew, ready to help. "Only an ignorant person solves his problems by force," Bartholomew said.

"That's tough talk with your buddies behind you," the Zealot said, keeping his gaze squarely on Bartholomew.

This had gone far enough. "Back down, Simon," Simon said.

"Of course *he* should back down," Judas said. "I mean, you are all friends and family and we just get to tag along, right?"

John ran ahead to get Jesus who was absorbed in a conversation with Cleopas and Mary, the parents of Matthew and Little James. Judas threw his hands in the air. "And there goes the tattletale."

James grabbed Judas by the front of his tunic. "Watch what you say about my brother!" The Zealot sprang to Judas's aid, and Simon and Bartholomew jumped in to break them apart.

"All right, I'm sorry!" Bartholomew said. "Thomas, I shouldn't have called you stupid. Now, can we get back to our traveling?"

"Very heartfelt," Matthew said.

The last voice Simon wanted to hear was Matthew's. "Don't get involved," he said.

"Why not?" Matthew asked. "Am I less of a disciple than you?"

"You're less of a Jew," the Zealot muttered. James couldn't help but laugh, which made Matthew's face grow red with anger.

Little James stepped forward to defend his brother. "So you can insult my brother, but we can't insult yours. Is that how it works?"

"Watch your tone, *Little* James," James said.

"I thought only an ignorant person solves his problems by force," Judas said.

Simon was about to slap the smirk off of Judas's face when the booming voice of the Master froze them all in their tracks.

"What is the meaning of this?" Jesus asked. The apostles quickly went silent and stared at the ground, like children scolded by their father.

Jesus sighed and shook his head. "I hope you will behave more respectably around my family," he said.

They nodded, but shot angry stares toward each other.

"Let us go," Jesus said. "We are almost at Nazareth."

The road to Nazareth was long and unpleasant, for Nazareth was in the middle of nowhere. Most of the followers of Jesus didn't want to come, and Simon didn't blame them. The Essenes had a "we're holier than you are" attitude that none appreciated. And the town was so small that it couldn't provide for the large amount of people who usually accompanied Jesus. Besides, the Passover was only a few days away and they would gather with everyone in Jerusalem soon enough.

The only other people who came with Jesus and the twelve were Matthew's parents (for they had relatives there), and Matthias and Barsabbas—men so devoted to Jesus that Simon wondered why they weren't called to be apostles as well. They were certainly better choices than Judas and Matthew.

Nazareth was a poor village with only about a hundred people and it made Capernaum look like Jerusalem in comparison. Simon counted fifteen poor dwellings that surrounded a small but beautiful synagogue. It was clear that the people of the town cared more about the synagogue than their own homes.

Everyone came out at their arrival. Jesus' brother James stood beside a man that must have been his father. He was a shorter, older version of James. Wrinkles on his face gave him a bitter expression. It looked as though his right arm was missing, but his tunic was large and Simon didn't want to stare.

Jesus bowed to them. "Shalom, Jedidiah," he said to the older man. "Shalom, James."

Jedidiah bowed back. "It is good of you to come home," he said. His words were cold and formal, as if it was the thing he was *supposed* to say.

His son had no such inhibitions. "I must admit that I didn't think I'd see you again," James said. "Nice of you to bring such a small number of your... *followers*."

Jesus avoided his sarcasm. "It is good to be home," he replied.

"I suppose you want to travel with us to the Passover," James said.

Jesus nodded. "It would be an honor."

"And you'd probably like to preach, too."

"If that's all right."

They both looked at Jedidiah. Clearly, he was the elder in the town. Jedidiah looked up at the sky. "Sun's coming down soon," he said. "You can preach in the morning, if you'd like. Not sure who will show up, though."

"Thank you for your hospitality," Jesus replied. They embraced out of formality and Jedidiah walked away with James and the others behind him. Simon took a breath of relief.

They went to Mary's house and the women scrounged up a meager meal, complaining that they didn't have enough warning that such a large group was coming. The other women pushed Mary out of the kitchen so she could spend time with her son. Jesus, Mary, and the other apostles gathered in the dining room that also served as the bedroom. There was lots of singing and laughing, especially as Mary told funny stories of Jesus when he was a boy. There was something about the laughter that united them. Simon looked around the room and realized that there was no crowd of people waiting in the courtyard, no Pharisees calling him a demon in the synagogue, no line of sick people waiting to be cured out the door. It was just… *family*.

Jesus seemed happier than he had been in a long time. He wished Rachael were here to see him this way. The food came in and they were able to eat slowly, like regular people. Simon realized how special this time was and hoped for many more nights like this. They continued their celebration late into the evening as the women gathered the plates together and brought them into the kitchen.

Mary, the wife of Cleopas, helped with the cleanup. When they got to the kitchen, one of the other women said to her, "How wonderful it is that your children are out of that awful tax collecting business!"

"Yes, praise God!" Mary replied. "I can't tell you how happy I was when Jesus called them to be his apostles."

Esther, wife of Jedidiah and mother of James, made a sound of disgust. "*Apostles*. What does that even mean?"

"I think it's great what Jesus is doing," her sister-in-law said. "The only time people hear about Nazareth is as a joke. It's nice to hear that someone from here is doing some good."

Esther turned her large body to confront her. "*Somebody from here* is it? You were the one who said they would never be one of us!"

Mary was confused. "You mean, Jesus wasn't born here?"

"Oh no," came the sister's reply. "Joseph and Mary moved here when Jesus was a child. I think he was born in Egypt."

"No, you've got it wrong," another said. "He was born around Bethlehem, I think."

"Yeah, him and the Messiah," Esther laughed. "No wonder he has so many delusions." She went back to cleaning the kitchen.

Mary gasped in shock, but smiled quickly to cover it. As soon as she was able, she ran to tell the news to her sons.

Matthew and Little James told John the news, but swore him to secrecy. Then John ran and told James and Simon.

"Could Jesus be the Messiah?" he asked.

James's face contorted in doubt. "Look around. How could the Christ come from this place?"

"And where is Elijah?" Simon asked. "The Rabbis always taught the Messiah would only appear after Elijah comes again."

"What if the Rabbis are wrong?" John said. "What if there's nothing he can't do? What if Jesus can restore the kingdom to Isra —"

Simon covered his hand over John's mouth. "*Keep quiet*," he whispered, looking around to make sure no one heard. "The people of this town already think Jesus is crazy, talking about him as Messiah isn't going to help."

"Buh wah ef he es?" John mumbled through Simon's hand.

Simon took his hand away from John's mouth and shook his head. "Your brother is right. God's anointed one wouldn't be born in such poverty, and he wouldn't hang out in Galilee, that's for sure. He's a great prophet but—"

"What if he's something more?" John asked.

"Stop it!" Simon said. He rubbed his beard and took a deep breath. "It's late and we've had a long day. I suggest we go to bed and not talk about this anymore."

That night, they slept beneath the stars. But John had a hard time sleeping. He knew it in his heart: Jesus *was* the Messiah.

Jesus awoke in the comfort of his own bed, an experience he hadn't had in almost a year. For his bar mitzvah, his father bought some wood and together they built his own room as an addition to the house. This room seemed enormous when he was thirteen, but now that he was over thirty it felt a bit tighter.

His prayer that morning was troubled. As much as he loved this room, his house, and the town where he grew up, he knew he would never return here again. When he began his public ministry,

Jesus was aware he started a journey that would slowly strip him of everything he loved until he had nothing left. Now he felt the pain of it.

Jesus prayed about what he would say that morning at the synagogue, and that was also difficult because of the complete lack of faith among the Nazarenes. But the hardest of all was when he prayed for his apostles. As he prayed for each one by name, he clutched his chest and almost fell backward.

One of them was going to betray him, and he knew exactly who it was.

He wept and prayed that it would not be so, but ended with, "Father, not as I would have it, but your will be done instead."

Jesus rose and called his followers together for morning prayer, as was their custom. Then Mary brought out some breakfast to eat before they headed to the synagogue.

When they had finished eating, Jesus told everyone to go ahead to the synagogue before him. Two of the apostles lingered behind: Simon and Judas. It didn't take any prophetic knowledge to know there was tension between the two.

"Judas, would you introduce me this morning?" Jesus asked.

Judas's eyes grew wide and he bowed low. "Thank you, Master! It would be an honor!" As he headed toward the synagogue, he shot a gloating look back to Simon.

Jesus could see the fisherman breathe slowly to contain his anger. "There are many people we do not chose to have in our lives," Jesus said to him. "All we can choose is how to respond to them as God would have us do."

Simon nodded, and Jesus looked toward the synagogue. It was the place where the Rabbis taught him the Torah. It was where he learned to read and write. It was the last place he was with his father before he died.

"Is everything all right?" Simon asked.

Jesus nodded. "Thank you for asking, Simon. It has been difficult for me to return home."

"I'm sure once they hear you preach, they will believe."

"No, they won't."

"Of course they will," Simon said forcefully. "They always do."

Jesus looked at the fisherman. Simon was bold—it was part of his nature. Jesus recognized it to be his greatest strength and his greatest weakness.

"I will preach the word, but they *will not* believe."

Simon had a look of shock. "Then why did we come?"

Jesus turned toward the synagogue and saw Judas had caught up with the others. "Because everyone has the right to hear the good news of the kingdom of God," he answered solemnly. "Even if they reject it."

In the synagogue, John sat next to his brother, James. "He *is*, I tell you."

James shook his head. "He's not. Shut up about it, will you?"

"You never listen—"

James hit his arm. Hard. John tried not to wince in pain.

Judas came in and spoke to the Rabbi in charge of the synagogue. John studied Judas carefully. There was something about him that he didn't like.

Simon and Jesus entered and all eyes were upon them. Simon sat down by John and Jesus stood by Judas.

Judas introduced Jesus and Jesus began to preach. John had never heard him speak with such passion before. His heart leapt to hear his words. How could anyone not be moved by what he said?

But he heard whispers behind him.

"This is the carpenter, isn't it? The son of Mary?"

"Where did the man get all this?"

The comments didn't disturb him as much as the silence that followed. John turned to see what happened. Jedidiah, the old guy with one arm, stood up in the back of the room. His face was bright red with anger. "Who do you think you are?" he asked. The synagogue fell into an uncomfortable silence as he started walking toward Jesus.

"I am the same person you knew growing up—"

"No," Jedidiah said. "I knew a carpenter. I was friends with his father, Joseph. But you, you sound like some sort of... Rabbi."

"He *is* a Rabbi," Judas said. "One of the greatest in all of Galilee." John was happy that Judas spoke up, but he still didn't like him.

"I thought Rabbis had to be trained by somebody," Jedidiah said. He kept his stare focused on Jesus and he lifted his left arm to point an accusing finger at him. "Who trained you?"

"My father," Jesus replied.

"Joseph? He never spoke like this."

John couldn't take this anymore. "If you had seen some of the miracles he's done," he said, "then you would know that he's sent to us from God."

"Miracles?" Jedidiah asked, turning toward the congregation. "Jesus the son of Joseph the carpenter can perform *miracles*?" Then he turned to confront Jesus and continued his slow walk toward him. "You never preformed any miracles here. But maybe we weren't good enough for you. Maybe only strangers and Gentiles deserve it." John wished he had kept his mouth shut.

Jedidiah pulled the robe off his shoulder and revealed a mangled stub where his right arm should have been. "You remember the day, don't you Jesus? You were just a boy at the time but I remember the look of terror on your face as they carried me in from the fields. Could you have healed me then? Or did you enjoy watching me suffer?"

Jesus said nothing.

"I WANT AN ANSWER!" Jedidiah yelled. "Where were your miracles when I became a cripple?" He fell on his knees in mock adoration. "Heal me, Jesus! Heal me and I will believe. We all will."

This is it, John thought. *This is when Jesus shows them who he really is.* John stared at the mangled flesh. He didn't want to miss a moment of watching the muscles weave around the growing bone and see the flesh flow over it.

But nothing happened.

John looked at Jesus. And Jesus spoke two words he never thought he would hear him say:

"I can't."

He can't?

His followers gasped in disbelief. Others in the synagogue started to laugh. The laughter slowly turned into angry shouts, and the apostles were on their feet, expecting a fight.

"Let's take them to the cliff!" one man in the crowd yelled.

Jesus straightened his tunic and walked right past Jedidiah. His apostles and the others followed. John heard the cheers of the men in the synagogue behind them, but no one else followed them out. He tried to keep his eyes on Jesus, but they were blurred with tears. Maybe he wasn't the Messiah after all.

Jesus went to his house and said to them, "Get your things quickly before they make good on their threat."

James and John gathered their things. John found it hard to tie his robes together because of the tears.

"What's wrong?" his brother asked.

"Nothing," John said. He couldn't bring himself to admit that his brother was right.

As they left the house, Jesus saw his mother standing by the door, giving small gifts of food and encouragement to the apostles. As yet she had not looked into his eyes, she busied herself with saying goodbye to the guests. But then they were alone.

She looked at him with bright green eyes and he saw her tears. He felt his heart in his throat and it became hard to breathe. Jesus put his hand on her shoulder, as much to steady himself as to comfort her.

"Will I see you in Jerusalem?" she asked.

His voice felt thick with emotion. "Yes," he said, "in Jerusalem."

She hugged him, and he felt her tight grip on his arms. His head rested for a moment on hers.

"*My God, my God, why have you forsaken me?*" she softly sang. She let go of him, and he wiped a tear away from her eye. She nodded and lifted herself up on her toes to kiss his cheek.

"I love you, mother," Jesus said.

She smiled. "I love you more than you can know."

And there was nothing more to say. Jesus left with a heavy heart. His followers waited outside the town. He said nothing as he passed them and they followed behind.

TWO BY TWO

Mark 6:7-13

For almost an hour there was no noise save that of footsteps on the rocky path. Simon noticed that he and the others, who normally walked closely with their Master, followed a number of paces behind.

When they came to a crossroads, Jesus stopped. He turned and looked at them. "Are you surprised?"

No one dared to answer.

"A prophet is despised only in his own country, among his own relations, and in his own house," Jesus said.

He paused for a moment and looked in the direction of Nazareth. "No one who prefers his family to me is worthy of me," he said. "Anyone who does not take his cross and follow in my footsteps is not worthy of me."

Simon looked at his brother, then at James. He had seen men crucified before—Rome hung them up during all the major religious feasts, a not-so-subtle way of reminding them who was in charge. He shuddered at the image.

"Be prepared," Jesus said. "If they have called the master of the house 'Beelzebul', how much more the members of his household? People will hand you over to Sanhedrins and scourge you in synagogues. You will be brought before governors and kings for my sake, as evidence to them and to the Gentiles."

First crucifixion and now scourging? Simon hoped for some words of comfort or encouragement after what happened in Nazareth. This only made things worse. Andrew looked like he was going to pass out. James clenched his beard. A quick look around the other apostles told him that no one took this well.

"Hand us over?" Andrew asked. "What should we do?"

"Do not worry about how to speak or what to say," Jesus said, "because it is not you who will be speaking. The Spirit of my Father will be speaking in you."

Simon had so many questions he didn't even know where to start. All he could ask was, "How?"

Jesus walked up to him. Simon tensed and regretted asking the question. Jesus put his hands on Simon's head, closed his eyes, and began to pray.

Simon looked nervously around and saw everyone staring at him. He closed his eyes. He heard Jesus whisper something unintelligible. Or maybe it was in a language he didn't understand.

He felt a pressure on his chest, but it wasn't violent. It was warm, inviting. He let it in, and as he did he felt a wave of peace wash over him as if he waded into cool water on a hot summer's day. It enveloped him completely and he relaxed.

Then his heart began to burn. His hands tingled, and he felt like he had the strength to fight a hundred men.

Jesus finished his prayer. Simon opened his eyes and looked at him. Jesus nodded. Then he went over to Andrew and did the same.

While he was praying over Andrew, James mouthed, *what happened?* But Simon couldn't explain. He touched his heart and smiled. James would know soon enough.

Jesus went around to each of the twelve, one by one, laid his hands on their head and prayed over them. When he was done, they stood in silence for a moment. Simon noticed he only prayed over the apostles, and felt bad that Matthias, Barsabbas—and even Cleopas—didn't experience it.

Then Jesus said to them, "I have given you authority over unclean spirits with the power to drive them out and to cure all kinds of disease and illness."

Simon looked at his brother, then looked down at his large hands, then looked back at Jesus.

"Did you say we… we can cast out demons?" Andrew asked.

Jesus nodded. "I am sending you out, two by two," he said. "Do not go into any Gentile or Samaritan territory for now. Go instead to the lost sheep of Israel. And as you go, proclaim that the kingdom of Heaven is close at hand."

He pointed at James. "James, go with Little James. Bartholomew, go with Thomas. Andrew, go with Jude. Simon, go with Matthew."

"Which one?" both Simons asked.

Jesus looked at the Zealot. "Simon, son of Uriel." The Zealot rolled his eyes.

"John, go with Philip. Simon, go with Judas."

Simon almost wished he could go with Matthew instead. "But Master," he said, "who will take care of you? Surely, you shouldn't be left alone."

Jesus gestured to Barsabbas, Matthias, and Matthew's parents. "I'm sure I will be in good hands."

"It will be an honor," said Matthias, bowing low.

"But… the Passover!" John said.

"We will meet you in Jerusalem," Jesus said.

Bartholomew was about to say something, but Jesus held up his hand to stop him. There would be no more questions. "Preach the good news of the kingdom of God," Jesus said. "Whatever town or village you go into, seek out someone worthy and stay with him until you leave. If nobody welcomes you, shake the dust from your feet as you go. I tell you, on the Day of Judgment it will be more bearable for Sodom and Gomorrah than for that town."

Jesus raised his hands. "Look, I am sending you out like sheep among wolves. So be cunning as snakes and innocent as doves. Know that you are in my prayers." And with that, he blessed them and they all went separate ways.

Simon, James, Judas, and Little James headed north. Simon walked with James and Little James walked with Judas. Neither of them talked to his designated partner until they got to the town of Sepphoris. They drew lots to see who would preach there, and the Jameses won. Simon and Judas walked a couple more hours north in almost unbearable silence.

By the time they reached the city of Rumah, it was late afternoon and they had been walking all day. They entered the city and looked around.

"What do we do now?" Judas asked, breaking the long silence between them.

Simon shrugged. "Find someone to stay with, I guess," he said.

It did not take long. A blacksmith named Abraham immediately recognized Simon. "Are you not the fisherman who travels with Jesus of Nazareth?"

Simon was surprised to be recognized. "Yes, I am," he said.

"Praise God!" he exclaimed. "I went to Capernaum to hear him preach. It changed my life! Is he coming here?"

"Sorry," Simon said, "it's just us."

"What he *meant* to say," Judas said, "is that Jesus has sent us to preach the message for him, and has given us the power to cure illnesses and cast out demons."

Abraham's eyes grew wide. "Have you a place to stay? You must stay with me," he said.

"We'd be honored," Judas said with a slight bow.

"I will tell the town you are here," he said. And before the apostles could tell him that they were tired and would rather preach tomorrow, he ran off.

Judas turned to Simon. "*Just us?* We're apostles of the greatest prophet in Galilee. Show some pride."

"Show some intelligence," Simon said. "He's gathering a crowd right now for us to speak to. I haven't even thought about what I will say."

People began to head their way. "Watch and you'll learn something," Judas said. "I'll do all the talking."

As the crowd gathered, Simon hoped desperately that Judas would make a fool of himself. But he didn't. Much to his surprise, Judas was quite good. He gave Jesus' message perfectly—even with the same inflections and mannerisms as the Master.

Simon could tell that people were moved by what he said, and he chastised himself for being so childish as to hope he would fail. *No matter what I think of Judas, these people deserve to hear the message*, he thought. And as he listened to Judas's passionate preaching, his heart softened toward him. *Maybe we're not so different after all.*

"Repent, and believe the good news!" Judas said. "Believe in the message given to us from God through his servant, Jesus of Nazareth!"

"Jesus!" cried out a woman from down the street. "Jesus, heal my daughter!" She broke through the crowd holding a five-year-old girl that was pale and covered in sweat. She looked at Judas and then at Simon. "Which one of you is Jesus?" she asked.

Judas was unnerved by the interruption. "Neither," he answered.

"But I heard that Jesus had arrived."

"We're just… I mean, we *are* his apostles," Judas said. "The Master is in Capernaum."

"She won't make it to Capernaum!" she cried. "Who will save my daughter?"

"They can!" Abraham said. "They told me they have the power to heal!"

She looked with great expectation at Judas, who looked with great anxiety at Simon. "Simon can do it," Judas said, and pointed his finger at him.

The woman ran forward to Simon and put her daughter in his arms. "Please, I beg you, heal my daughter."

He felt the girl's burning flesh against his arms. He wanted to tell her that this was a mistake, but the mother was on her knees sobbing by his feet. Simon looked down at her. *Oh God, I hope this works.*

Cradling the little girl in one arm, he put his hand on her forehead. He could feel the eyes of the entire town upon him. He tried to remember what Jesus did when he healed someone. Usually, Jesus said something out loud. "Oh God," Simon said, "…heal her."

He meant to say something more profound, but that was all that came to mind.

Simon looked down at the girl and saw no change. Her flesh was still hot against his skin. He looked desperately at Judas, and Judas only stared back in shock. The crowd began to get restless, and some commented that Jesus' disciples weren't up to the task.

Judas leaned over and whispered in his ear. "If you don't heal this girl, we're going to be run out of town!"

"If you're so smart, why don't you heal her?" Simon whispered back.

"I preached," Judas said. "You heal!"

The mother overheard this conversation and stood up. She put her hand on Simon's arm and looked into his eyes. "I believe in Jesus of Nazareth," she said. "Please, heal my daughter."

Simon looked into the mother's eyes, and everything else faded into the background. He looked down at this girl who he did not know and felt a love for her as if she was his own. Nothing else mattered now—not Judas, the crowd, fear of failure, or anything. He placed his hand back on her forehead and prayed earnestly for the child.

"Oh God of Abraham," he said, "you hear the cry of your children. Great is your faithful love from age to age. Hear our prayer, and heal this little girl in the name of your servant, Jesus of Nazareth." He closed his eyes and hugged the girl tightly to his chest.

As he held her in his arms, he felt the fever leave. He pulled her away from himself and saw the color return to her skin.

The mother immediately grabbed her and swung her around in her arms. "A miracle! Hallelujah! My daughter is healed!"

Simon and Judas shouted with joy and embraced each other. The whole town cheered and erupted in songs that praised the God of Israel. People brought out their finest food and drink, and they celebrated well into the night.

That evening, Simon and Judas lay on the rooftop of Abraham's small house, gazing at the stars. Abraham was a poor man. He offered to let them sleep in his bedroom, but they decided they'd rather be under the evening sky instead.

"What an amazing day," Judas said.

Simon agreed. "You preached a great message, Judas," he said.

Judas shook his head. "That was nothing compared to what you did."

"I didn't do anything," Simon answered. "In fact, when I stopped trying and let God do the work, that's when it happened."

"Still," Judas said, "it was an act of great faith. I can see why the Master holds you in such high esteem."

That was a generous statement from Judas, and Simon knew it. "Thank you, Judas," Simon said. "I'm sure the Master is proud of you, too."

Judas let out a disbelieving laugh. "Why would you think that?"

"You're an apostle," Simon replied. "Isn't that enough?"

Judas was silent for a moment. "I never thought I'd be called. Not in a thousand years. Funny thing was, I wasn't even trying. And then... *boom.* It was me and not Ioakim."

"*Ioakim*," Simon said. "How did you end up with a guy like that, anyway?"

"Life has not presented me many choices," Judas said. "For all his faults, Ioakim was a great business man. He was amazing with money, and… well, I needed money. So it worked for a while at least. But then he got more interested in power, and realized that no matter how much money he got, he would never get the respect that Rabbis had. He heard about Jesus and off we went. I'm glad Jesus didn't pick him."

"No," Simon said, "he chose you instead."

"I'm not worthy," Judas said.

"And I am?" Simon asked.

Judas hesitated. "You don't know what I've done."

"It doesn't matter," Simon said. "This is a new beginning for all of us."

Judas was silent, deep in thought. "I'm sorry," he said.

"For what?"

"For the times I… I'm not good at taking orders from other people."

"I'm sorry for the times I gave them," Simon said. "You don't need to take any orders from me. The only person we should be following is the Master. You and I are brothers."

"*Brothers*," he whispered. Judas took a heavy breath. Was he crying? "That sounds good to me."

They laid there in silence for a few more moments, looking up at the stars. "An amazing day," Simon said.

"But next time, let's find a bigger house to stay at."

They both laughed, and went to sleep.

Early the next morning, Simon and Judas went to the synagogue and the entire town came see them. Simon noticed that Judas did an even better job preaching than he did the day before. They kept to their winning formula: Judas preached, Simon healed. Simon felt good about this because he didn't like the idea of speaking in front of a large crowd.

Villagers told him about some people too sick to join them, so Simon went off to heal while Judas stayed behind to answer questions and talk more about Jesus.

It felt like a dream. Simon went into house after house, laid his hands on the sick and dying, and restored them to health.

After leaving the home of a former cripple, a man ran up to Simon, saying only, "My son…"

Simon nodded and followed him to his house. He walked in, expecting to see a sick child lying on the floor. But instead he saw a twelve year old boy crouched in the corner, froth coming out of his mouth.

The boy looked at him and gave a deep laugh, far deeper than a boy his age should be able to do. His face looked innocent but his eyes looked ancient. A chill ran down Simon's spine.

"Come out of him," Simon said weakly.

The boy cocked his head to one side. "WHO DO YOU THINK YOU ARE, TELLING ME WHAT TO DO?"

Simon lifted a trembling hand. Isn't that what Jesus did? "Come out of him," he said more strongly.

The boy stood. Simon stepped back. The boy smiled wickedly. "YOU CAN NOT DESTROY ME!" he hissed, and he sprang at him.

Simon threw his arms over his face and screamed, "Stop! In the name of Jesus, STOP!"

The boy did. He collapsed and began to writhe on the floor.

"You're killing him!" a woman cried. Only now did Simon notice her. She was against the wall with her arms around two younger children whose faces were buried in her chest. The mother's eyes were wide with fear.

The father was behind him. "Do something! Please!"

Simon walked over to the boy and looked down at him. The child looked up. His eyes were filled with hate. But Simon also saw something else—a boy who wanted to be free.

He was no longer afraid. "In the name of Jesus of Nazareth," he said, "get out of him!"

The boy shrieked and then went still. The father moved past Simon and fell on his knees by his son. The boy breathed slowly and then opened his eyes, as if woken from a heavy sleep.

The mother ran to her son and bathed him in her tears. Soon the whole family embraced each other and cried with joy. Simon began to tear up as well.

The father looked at him and smiled. "Hallelujah!" he cried.

Simon nodded but couldn't speak. He left the house and leaned against the wall. "I just cast out a demon," he said aloud, though no one was there to hear. He began to laugh—he did not know why. All he knew is he couldn't wait to tell Judas.

Simon found him in the street and excitedly told him what happened.

"That's amazing! But I have even better news," Judas said. "Kaleb, one of the most prominent merchants in town, has asked us to stay at his house. We will sleep well tonight!"

Simon was shocked at Judas's response. He didn't think staying in a nicer house was a bigger deal than casting out a demon. And then he recalled the words Jesus said. "Didn't the Master tell us to stay with the same person until we left?"

"Don't be so literal," Judas said. "Kaleb runs this town. If he believes, everyone else will believe as well!"

"What about Abraham?"

Judas patted Simon on the back. "He'll understand. I bet if he had a chance to stay at Kaleb's place, he would too!"

This didn't sit right with Simon and he was about to say as much when he heard someone in the distance shout something about John the Baptist. They looked at each other and began to head in that direction.

A crowd gathered around a royal messenger in the town square. People cried and wailed. As they approached, one woman turned to Simon in tears. "I can't believe it! How could he do such a thing!" she wailed.

"Do what thing?" Simon asked.

"That cursed fox," she said and spit on the ground. "He murdered John the Baptist!"

Simon's blood ran cold at those words. He pushed through the crowd and grabbed the messenger by the arm. "Tell me what happened!"

"King Herod has executed the one known as John the Baptist," the messenger said. "Please, let me go!"

Simon did and dropped him to the ground. The messenger ran away to carry the message to another village. People in the town cried loudly and beat their chests. Simon fell on his knees and wept.

He's gone, he thought. *I can't believe he's gone.*

Judas put a reassuring hand on Simon's shoulder. "Simon," he said, "I'm so sorry…"

Simon was grateful for his sympathy but this was no time for tears. He wiped his face and straightened up. "We've got to get to Jesus," he said. "If Herod killed the Baptist, then Jesus might be next."

The idea made Judas go pale. "If we hurry, we can make it to Jerusalem by—"

"He won't be in Jerusalem," Simon said. "At least, I hope not. It's too dangerous."

"Where should we go?" Judas asked.

Simon ran his fingers through his beard and then looked to the east, toward the Sea of Galilee.

"Home," he said.

"COME"

Matthew 14:13-33

Simon thanked Abraham for his hospitality and told him they had to leave for Capernaum immediately. Much to his frustration, Abraham and his family said they would come as well. It meant they would have to delay their departure, but how could he say no to the man who had opened his house to him?

Word spread quickly that the apostles were leaving to see Jesus and others decided to join them. Most were already prepared to go to Jerusalem for the Passover, but the Baptist's death discouraged the journey. Rumors flew around about how Herod must be in league with the Romans (for only the Romans had the authority to execute,) and how the Holy City was a trap for all who believed in Jesus. As they began their journey east, Simon and Judas were followed by almost 500 people.

They couldn't make it to Capernaum by nightfall. The slept in Magdala and rose early the next morning. Again, more people joined them.

It was past midday when Simon began to climb the final hill to his hometown. He looked back in amazement. Over a thousand people were right behind.

But he was even more shocked when he made it to the top of the hill and looked down at Capernaum. At first he wondered if it was the right place. People were *everywhere*. They surrounded Capernaum like the white surrounds the yoke of an egg.

Simon gasped. "How many do you think are here?" he asked.

Judas took a moment to survey the crowd. "Ten thousand, at least. And that's only the people *outside* the town."

They took their leave of Abraham and waded through people to get to his house. The journey that would normally take them fifteen minutes took over an hour. He could barely open his door because of the people in the street, and his courtyard was almost as full as it was when he lowered the paralytic through his roof. Simon and Judas moved through people and found Rachael.

"Simon!" she cried. "Oh Simon, isn't it horrible?"

They embraced. She wept, but he was too tired for tears.

"Where is the Master?" Judas asked.

Rachael pointed to the dining room under the stairs.

"Go," Simon said to him. "I will be right there." Judas left.

Simon felt her shake with tears against his chest and he held her tightly. He knew what he was supposed to say at this moment, so he did: "Everything is going to be all right." He was glad Rachael did not look up to see his face—it always betrayed him when he lied.

His words soothed her and he felt her breathing begin to return to normal. She looked up at him and he smiled to give her courage. "Are you all right?"

She nodded. "Don't worry about me," she said. "Worry about the Master. People have flooded the house since we got the news. I don't think he's slept. And we've been out of food since yesterday evening, not that there's been time to eat. And his mood… this news has hit him hard."

"Have any of the others arrived yet?"

"You two are the last ones," she said. She put a hand on his cheek. "He needs you, go to him."

Simon kissed his wife and he went into the room where Jesus was. The apostles lay around the room like soldiers fallen in battle. James was propped up against a wall. Andrew was asleep in the corner, his head on Jude's shoulder. John was the only exception. He sat next to his brother with his leg bouncing up and down like a rabbit.

Only Judas and Jesus were standing. Simon looked in the face of his Master. The lantern that gave light to the room cast deep shadows under his eyes.

Jesus faintly smiled. "Shalom, Simon. It is good to see you."

"Shalom, Master. I am so sorry—"

Jesus held up his hand, as though he could not bear to hear the words. "It is all right," he said. "We have much to talk about, but not here."

"I will clear the courtyard immediately," Simon said. "We will have some privacy."

Jesus shook his head. "There is little chance of privacy in Capernaum."

"Where should we go?" Simon asked.

He expected Jesus to answer immediately and forcefully, tell them that he had a plan and a part for every apostle to play.

But he said nothing.

It troubled Simon to see Jesus this way. Something had to be done.

"The boats, then," Simon said. "The people cannot follow us on the water." He stared at Judas. *Help me out!*

Judas got the message. "A good idea," he said. "Master, you need some rest. We all do."

"I agree," Jude said. His voice awakened Andrew. The other apostles began to stir.

Jesus paused before answering, then nodded. "Yes. We should go to a lonely place and rest for a while."

Simon looked at James, and James got on his feet and nodded back at him. "We'll go in front," Simon said. Then he looked at John. "John, get though the crowd and ready the boat." John jumped up and left.

The apostles moaned as tired bodies began to move, but they were soon on their feet, energized by the new direction and the chance for a quieter place to be. Simon and James lead the way and everyone followed in their wake.

Simon feared it would be hard to move through the crowd, but thankfully people were mostly on the hill, not down by the docks. As they reached the shore, he looked up at the sky and saw storms in the distance. He felt his muscles tense. Simon did not want a repeat of what happened the last time he was on the sea.

He looked at James, who clearly thought the same. "Let's just make sure Jesus stays awake this time," he said to him.

As they got into the boat, people rushed the docks and reached their hands out for Jesus. He blessed them as the apostles pulled the boat away and headed for deeper water. Since the storm was coming from the northeast, Simon headed south. The cries of "Jesus!" faded beneath the noise of wind and sea.

Simon was jubilant to have escaped the crowd and the apostles took a collective sign of relief. For the first time since leaving Rumah, Simon relaxed and even smiled. His brother patted him on the shoulder, thankful that Simon got them out of there.

All were happy on the boat, save the one who mattered the most. While the apostles congratulated each other and celebrated their freedom, Jesus stared at the shore. Simon turned his head and looked in that direction.

Their escape had not gone unnoticed. Thousands and thousands of people ran along the shore waving their hands in the air. Simon could not hear their shouts over the wind, but their actions were desperate and it was clear they wanted him to stay. Simon's elation disappeared and despair felt heavy on his chest. He grabbed his oar tighter.

The other apostles saw the crowd as well.

"Look at all the people!" Thomas said.

"How many are there?" Little James asked.

"I'd say almost four thousand," Judas said.

There seemed much more than that. "Four thousand?" Simon asked.

"I counted families," Judas said. "With the women and children, there's at least fifteen thousand people or so."

The roar of the crowd broke through the driving wind and reached their ears. "Jesus!" "Son of David!" "Have pity on us!"

Simon looked at the storm in the distance. It didn't seem to move, which was good. They might be able to head east without much danger.

"Let's put our backs into it," Simon said to the other men on the oars. "If we push it—"

"No," Jesus said.

Simon was surprised to hear his voice. It was the first word he uttered since leaving the dock. "But Master, I'm sure we could just—"

Jesus looked at him. "No."

It was the voice Simon was used to hearing from his Master. Authority. Conviction. Decision. Simon was glad to hear it again, though he wished it wasn't directed at him.

"Yes, Master," he said, and bowed his head.

"Where is the nearest dock?" Jesus asked.

John pointed to the south. "Tabgha," he said.

"We will moor there," he said.

Simon didn't want to dock the boat. None of them did. But they obeyed.

By the time they arrived at Tabgha, the crowd was almost twice the size that Judas counted earlier.

"It feels like Passover in Jerusalem," Bartholomew said.

Jesus walked to a clearing and the twelve sat in a circle at Jesus' feet. A huge crowd sprawled out behind them and up the hill. It was mid-afternoon by the time the crowd had settled and Jesus began to preach.

He taught at great length. But he did not speak against Herod or his murdering ways. He spoke of mercy. He spoke of love. And then he talked about John the Baptist, and what a wonderful man of God he was. It was moving to hear him speak so personally.

The desire to listen to his Master's words fought against the demands of Simon's flesh. He was hungry. He was exhausted. He looked around at the other apostles and could see they felt the same.

But then he noticed something else. They all sat in different places.

Usually, the fishermen were on one side, the tax collectors in the middle, and the non-Galileans on the other. But now they were all mixed up, most of them seated next to the person they went on their trip with. Even the Zealot sat beside Matthew.

More time passed. Philip leaned over to Simon and Judas. "How much longer will this go on? Someone has got to say something," he whispered.

He looked at Simon, as did Judas and his brother Andrew, who sat on the other side of him. Simon realized that they wanted him to do the talking.

"Do it yourself if it troubles you," Simon said.

Philip seemed surprised at his response, but Simon didn't care. He knew it was his idea to leave Capernaum and it was a disaster. Now they were surrounded by even more people, no roof over their head, no food in sight, and a storm on the way.

Was Jesus mad at him? It was hard to tell. *I was only trying to help*, Simon thought. But he wasn't about to make any more suggestions that might upset the Master.

Jesus spoke for a few more minutes and then seemed to come to the end of a point he was making. Phillip timidly stood up and spoke to Jesus.

"Master, this is a lonely place and it is getting very late. Send the people away so they can go the farms and villages around here to buy themselves something to eat."

Jesus looked up at the sky, as if he only now noticed how late in the day it was. He nodded his head. Jesus looked at the apostles, then back at Philip. "Why don't you give them something to eat yourselves?" he said.

For the first time Simon could remember, Philip was speechless. He looked around at the tens of thousands of people who lined the hillside. "A month's wages wouldn't give each of them a crumb," he said.

"Do you have a month's wages on you?" Jesus asked. Philip looked to Judas who was in charge of the collection and Judas shook his head.

"Then don't start with what you want," Jesus said. "Start with what you have."

Andrew's first instinct was to go to the boat and see if there was anything in it. There wasn't. They had left in such a hurry that nobody packed for the trip. As he came back to the apostles, they all stood in deep conversation about what to do next. Andrew looked at the huge, sprawling crowd that had assembled along the hill that sloped toward the lake. How could they feed all these people? Jesus wanted the impossible.

He felt a tug on his tunic and looked down. It was a little boy with large brown eyes. Andrew looked away from him, hoping the boy would get the hint.

The boy tugged harder. Andrew looked down at him, ready to scold. But his heart softened when the boy lifted up a basket with five barley loaves and two fish that had already been cooked.

"It's for Jesus," the boy said.

Andrew received his gift. "Thank you, child," he said. "I'm sure Jesus will be very happy." The boy smiled wide and ran back to his family.

Andrew sighed. It was a cute effort, but hardly the solution. He walked back to the apostles.

"Anything?" Philip asked.

Andrew shook his head. "Just as I feared."

"Then what do you have there, Andrew?" Jesus asked.

Andrew shrugged, "Oh, just five loaves and two fish that a little boy gave me," he said. "But how will that help with so many?"

Jesus held the basket in two hands and held it up to his face as if it was something sacred. He smiled and looked at Andrew. "It will do," he said. "Good work."

Andrew was pleased at the compliment, but had no idea what he meant by it.

Jesus called the apostles' attention. "Andrew found the food," he said. "Now tell the people to sit in groups of fifty to a hundred."

His brother came up to him. "Where did you find the food?" Simon asked.

Andrew couldn't speak. He felt the blood drain from his face. "But I didn't! I mean, I did I guess... It's hardly anything!" He felt his heart race beneath his tunic.

The other apostles encouraged the people to sit in large groups and Andrew and Simon began to do the same. Andrew felt sick in his stomach. Or was that the hunger? Either way, these people were now expecting food, and they were going to get angry when they didn't get it.

When he returned to Jesus with the others, Jesus had gathered twelve wicker baskets and had broken the loaves and fishes into each one.

"Take these and feed the people," he said to them.

Andrew looked despairingly in his basket, then at his brother. *This is never going to work.*

As Simon feared, his first group nearly wiped the basket clean. He apologetically handed the basket to the second group he encountered. "I'm sorry, but it's all we have." They gave him a confused look, then passed the food around for everyone to eat.

Simon looked down at the basket and it seemed to be about the same amount that he had started with. *They are probably eating small portions*, he thought.

The third group had about a hundred people, and he was convinced that this would be his final stop. "Take only what you need," he said. "I'm sorry there's not enough for everyone."

The head of the family looked in the basket and looked back at Simon. "This will be fine," he said. The basket was passed around and almost everyone in the group took a piece of bread and some fish to eat.

When they handed him the basket, Simon looked down and expected it to be empty. But it looked the same as when he had started. He stared at the basket in amazement and suddenly realized what was happening. Then he ran to the next group, the largest he could find.

"Take as much as you want," Simon said with a grin. They ate their fill.

He looked around. Andrew waived at him, nearly jumping for joy. He saw Matthew trip as he ran from one group to another, and spilt about twenty loaves on the ground as he did.

Word blazed through the crowd that a miracle was taking place. The people dove on the food in celebration and amazement. Cheers started building up in the crowd, and tens of thousands stood and chanted, "Jesus! Jesus! Jesus!"

It took almost an hour for the twelve to make their way through the crowd. By the time they got back, everyone was well fed and joyful. Simon and the other apostles were weary, but happy.

Simon sat down and took a bite out of the bread. It was as fresh as if it had just come out of the fire, and better than anything Rachael had ever made. *Best not to tell her that,* Simon thought.

The crowd's shouting turned to song as Jesus led them in one psalm after another. When he was finished, a line of people gathered to meet him. Simon and the others brought the sickest people forward for Jesus to heal.

A shadow fell on them as the sun made it's way over the hill. Simon felt the wind pick up and he looked toward the sea. Gray clouds faded to black as the distant rain blanketed the eastern cliffs.

"Master, we should be going," Simon said.

Jesus nodded. "Go ahead. I will meet you back in Capernaum."

"But what about you, Master?" John asked.

"There is more I need to do here. Go by yourselves and head back to Capernaum, and be ready for a long journey."

Simon the Zealot stepped forward. "Let me stay with you, Master. There are many people here and you could be in danger."

"I am safe among these people," Jesus replied. "I do not need your protection, just your obedience."

They could tell by Jesus' tone that he would not change his mind, so the twelve got on the boat and started rowing toward Capernaum. Lightning flashed in the distance and Simon knew it wouldn't be long before the storm was upon them.

Thomas looked pale with fear. "Are we heading into a storm... *AGAIN?*"

"It won't be as bad as the last one," Simon said, hoping he told the truth. "But you probably want to brace yourself just the same."

"At least Jesus isn't sleeping this time," James said.

Simon looked at the silhouette of Jesus healing people as they pulled away from the shore. "No," he said. "This time he's not even on the boat."

Jesus healed those who were sick and then went up into the hills to pray. It was his first moment alone since he received the news of John's death, and most of his energy was spent comforting others instead of dealing with it himself.

Nature reflected his mood. Lightning flashed and rain poured down. Jesus cried out in anger at the injustice of the world. He wept with great sadness at the loss of his brother and friend.

That is what happens to prophets, the Spirit whispered. *And it will happen to you as well.*

Jesus knew this. He was never confused about his mission or what it would entail. The rejection of his family and the loss of his friend weighed heavy on his heart. *I have already begun to carry the cross*, he thought. *And still there is such a long way to go.*

He wept aloud. The thunder cried back. He dropped to his knees and let the rain pour over his hair. He became very still—a sharp contrast to the storm that raged around him. He bent down low and put his face to the ground, breathing deep. His robes were soaked and he felt one with the earth.

Jesus closed his eyes and heard everything. He heard the distant thunder. He heard the rain fall on his tunic. He heard his heartbeat and the sound of his breath. And then Jesus heard the voices of the earth.

Save us, they said to him.

Jesus raised his head and heard all creation groan with longing for its redemption. He nodded his head. Then Jesus headed down the mountain.

He walked into the lake and the water rose to his ankles. Then he lifted his foot and put it on top of the water as if he was climbing a step. The lake became firm under his feet, and he began to cross.

The sea did not speak to Simon. *It screamed.* He couldn't make out what it said but he knew it wasn't good.

Waves slammed against the boat as they rowed into the wind. The storm hit with full force in the third watch of the night and they hadn't made much progress since.

Simon, James, Andrew, Philip, Bartholomew and the Zealot were on the oars. John was at the rudder. The others could only helplessly watch and hold on for dear life.

The scream of Little James pierced the noise of the storm. He pointed to the side and Simon saw something walking toward them on the water.

"It's a ghost!" Jude said.

"It's the devil! He's come to get us!" Andrew said.

"WE ARE GOING TO DIE!" Thomas shouted. In his panic, he threw himself toward John hoping he could grab the rudder and turn the boat around. His body slammed to the deck as another wave almost knocked over the ship.

"Have courage!" a voice cried to them. "It's me!" Through the rain, Simon could see a shadowy figure walking toward them.

The fishermen pulled in the oars and they all crouched down on the floor of the boat, afraid the ghost might attack. John began to look over the side, but James pulled him down.

"What are you doing?" James asked.

"I think it's Jesus," John said.

"It's a trick," Philip said. "The devil can mimic other people's voices."

"I *knew* it was the devil!" Andrew said.

"Don't be afraid!" the voice said. It was closer now, about twenty paces from the boat.

"That sounds like Jesus to me," Jude said.

Simon was so scared he could barely breathe. But if it was the devil, he knew what to do.

"In the name of Jesus of Nazareth," he yelled, "be gone from here!" He let out a laugh. *Take that, Satan!*

"I *am* Jesus of Nazareth, Simon." The voice sounded a little perturbed.

"That really sounds like Jesus," Jude said.

All eyes were back on Simon to see what he might do next. "Well, if it is you… tell me to come to you across the water!"

There was not an immediate response. Andrew grabbed his brother by the shoulder. "You did it!" he said. "You showed that ghost!"

Then the voice spoke again. "Come," it said.

The apostles looked at each other in shock. "Did it just say, *come?*" James asked.

Simon lifted his head to see over the side of the boat. Jesus was in plain sight before him. He stood on the water with arms outstretched. The waves that approached him dove under his feet and leapt out of the other side. A calm path of water lay between the boat and the Master.

"Come," Jesus said again.

They all looked at Simon. Simon looked at the water and saw it swirl around the boat. He felt its longing to pull him in. He shook his head. *I can't do this,* Simon thought. *I am not stronger than the sea.*

"Simon," Jesus said. Though the storm was raging, Simon heard his voice as if he whispered into his ear. "Don't be afraid. *Come.*"

He looked at the face of Jesus and everything else faded. Simon rose and began to walk toward Jesus. The look on Jesus' face was so encouraging, so inviting. Simon was lost in the moment.

"I can't believe it," he heard Thomas say. His voice seemed far behind him.

He turned and Simon realized that he was halfway between Jesus and the ship. He looked down at his feet. Simon stood on the sea as if it was dry land.

Suddenly, the wind picked up and the water swelled. The lake roared at him like a lion.

"Simon!" Jesus said.

But it was too late. Simon felt a surge of terror and dropped like a rock into the water.

It took him a moment to realize what happened. It was as though the world had been pulled from him and now he descended into darkness. Simon had no time to catch his breath before he went under. His chest felt tight. He flailed his arms, but his heavy robes made his movement sluggish and pulled him deeper into the black.

You are mine, the sea said to him.

Simon's life flashed before his eyes. He played with his brother in the street. He sat on a ship with his father. He celebrated his wedding day with his wife. He knelt before Jesus on his boat.

Jesus. He could see his face so clearly. The image of Jesus reached out to him and grabbed his tunic. Simon realized that this was not a vision—this *was* his Master. He grabbed Jesus' arms and was pulled out of the sea.

He gasped for air and splashed the water around him. Jesus held him steady. Simon spit out water and collapsed, but the sea did not swallow him again. He put his hand on the water and it was firm to touch, though it was in constant movement. He looked up into the face of his Master.

"You have so little faith," Jesus said to him. "Why did you doubt?"

Simon couldn't believe what was happening. "But the sea —"

"I am stronger than the sea," Jesus said.

He had no answer for this. As they got into the boat, the storm ceased and the wind grew quiet. It was still night, but the clouds disappeared and they were illuminated by the silver light of the full moon.

The apostles were all on their knees. Simon knelt before Jesus next to his brother Andrew.

Andrew grabbed his arm and pulled him close. He said nothing, for he didn't dare break the silence. He looked concerned. Simon nodded to let him know he was all right.

But was he? Simon looked out on the water. *I just walked on you*, he thought.

The sea did not respond. It seemed lifeless to him now, like a whipped dog that was afraid to raise its eyes to its master.

He wanted to rejoice, but his victory of walking on the water was tempered by the fact he nearly drowned in it. He replayed the words Jesus spoke in his head. Was he angry? Disappointed?

Simon raised his eyes to Jesus. He saw him only in silhouette for the moon hung right behind his head. He looked like an angel. Simon was lost in the beauty of the moment and the words fell from his lips: "Truly, you are the son of God!"

The boat slowly turned and the moonlight ran across the side of his face. Jesus looked human again. He also looked tired.

"Let's go back to Capernaum," Jesus said. "We have a long journey ahead of us."

IN FOREIGN LANDS

John 4:1-44

They made it to Capernaum just before the sun rose, and by mid-morning Jesus preached in the synagogue. Rabbi Dov and the Pharisees were there, but even more troubling was the presence of Hiram and other Herodians.

"They've got some nerve showing their face around here, after what they did to the Baptist," James said.

"We must get Jesus to safety," Matthew said. "I worked for Herod and I know what they can do."

"Where can we go?" John asked. "His men are everywhere, he controls all of Galilee."

"Then we must leave Galilee," Matthew replied. "We'll go to the Decapolis, Gaulantis, or even Samaria! These men have tasted blood and they are hungry for more."

"Ridiculous," Simon said. "We couldn't even get as far as Tabgha without tens of thousands following us. This place will be swarming with people once word gets round he's back. Imagine leading that many followers to the Decapolis."

Judas leaned into Simon. "Well, he won't have *any* followers if he keeps preaching like this."

"I am the bread of life!" Jesus said. "I have come from heaven not to do my will, but the will of him who sent me. Whoever sees the Son and believes in him will have eternal life, and I will raise him up on the last day."

Behind him, Simon heard men complain to each other.

"How can he say he has come down from heaven?" someone said. "Didn't he come from Nazareth?"

"Stop that talk!" Jesus said. "No one comes to me unless my Father sends him. Your fathers ate manna in the desert, and they are dead. But this," he said pointing to his chest, "is the bread which comes down from heaven. And the bread I give is my flesh for the life of the world."

The argument among the Jews grew louder, and the apostles grew nervous.

"Do you know what he is talking about?" Thomas asked.

"I'm... sure he will explain it to us later," Simon said.

One Pharisee stood up and addressed the crowd. "This man is insane! How can he give us his flesh to eat?" There was a roar of approval at the question.

Jesus spoke loudly to overcome the noise of the crowd. "If you do not eat my flesh and drink my blood, you shall have no life in you. My flesh is real food. My blood is real drink. Whoever eats my flesh and drinks my blood will live forever!"

Thomas looked at Simon, and Simon had no response. This made no sense. What was Jesus talking about?

Jairus begged the people to calm down and be civil, but it was too late. Jesus left the synagogue and his apostles rushed to keep up with him.

"This is the second time this week we've been run out of a synagogue," Philip said.

The apostles followed Jesus into Simon's house and stood in silence in the courtyard while Jesus paced back and forth.

After a moment, Andrew whispered to his brother, "Do you hear that?"

Simon didn't hear anything. "Hear what?"

"Exactly."

Simon then realized what Andrew meant.

There was no noise. No din of the crowd trying to press around them. No shouts of "Have pity on me, Son of David!" from a sick or dying soul. Usually after preaching in the synagogue, hundreds of people followed to talk or pray with Jesus. But *no one* had followed them, and his courtyard never looked so empty.

Jesus stopped pacing and turned to face his apostles. "This is why I told you that no one could come to me except by the gift of the Father."

The twelve looked at each other, confused by what had just happened and unsure of what to say. "Master," Judas cautiously asked, "what were you talking about in there?"

"Were you not listening?" Jesus asked.

"Yes, of course I was Master. But what did you mean?"

"I meant that if you don't eat my flesh and drink my blood, then you will have no life within you."

"Is that a parable?" Thomas asked.

Jesus' frustration was clear. "How can I speak more clearly? As the living Father sent me and I draw life from the Father, so whoever eats me will also draw life from me."

James and Simon shared a worried look with each other. Jesus saw it and they realized he did. They bent their heads low.

"Then what about you?" Jesus asked. "Do you want to go away too?"

This idea struck the heart of Simon with despair. He looked up and said, "Lord, who else would we go to? You are the only one who has the words of eternal life."

This did not temper his anger. "Did I not choose twelve of you?" Jesus asked. "One of you is a devil!"

Simon had never seen him so upset.

Within the hour, Jesus and the twelve moved with great haste toward Samaria. They didn't use the main road. Jesus instead chose a more direct route that took them over the hills that surrounded the lake. He moved at a brisk pace and the apostles had a difficult time keeping up.

Jesus stopped at the top of the hill. Simon and the others collapsed on the ground to take a breath. He looked around, and could see almost the entire lake with the towns that surrounded it. Below him was Capernaum, and to his left was Bethsaida, the town where he grew up. In the distance he could also see Chorazin, a place they visited on their first trip to the surrounding villages.

His Master's mood hadn't changed. "Alas for you, Chorazin!" he said, pointing in the town's direction. "And alas for you, Bethsaida! For if the miracles done in your town were done in Tyre or Sidon, they would have repented long ago. And alas for you, Capernaum! Did you wish to be raised to heaven? You shall be flung down to hell. For if the miracles done in you had been done in Sodom, it would still be standing today. But it will be more bearable for Sodom on Judgment Day than for you."

Simon's heart shook to hear such a condemnation. Comparing Capernaum to *Sodom*, a town in Genesis known for raping their guests? He didn't dare look at Jesus, nor at anyone else. An uncomfortable silence fell upon the group.

Eventually, Jesus spoke again, this time more gently. "I bless you, Father, Lord of heaven and earth, for hiding these things from the learned and the clever and revealing them to little children."

What children? Simon wondered if he meant them, or if it was supposed to be an insult.

"Let us go," Jesus said. Without a word, they picked up their things and followed him away from the sea of Galilee.

As they travelled, Simon felt his heart race. Everyone he saw along the way was viewed with suspicion. Were they Herod's men? Would they tell him where they were going?

Simon wasn't the only apostle who felt that way. He noticed the Zealot kept his hand on the hilt of his sword and James clenched his walking staff tighter than he usually did. Jesus walked with firm purpose, but the others continued to look nervously around.

As they made some distance from the lake, his fears diminished about who might be following them. But his anxiety increased about the one they were following.

"John's death is really effecting him," Judas quietly said to him. "I think our Master is starting to lose his mind."

"Don't speak such things," Simon said, reluctant to admit the same thought crossed his mind as well.

"What did he mean that one of us is a devil?" Andrew asked. "Is one of us possessed?"

"If we were, he would cast it out," John said. "He can calm a storm with a word!"

"He calmed the storm but he couldn't heal his family," James said. "It just doesn't make sense."

"None of it makes sense," Judas said. "I'm telling you, ever since we went to Nazareth, something has changed."

As the intensity of their conversation increased, so did its volume. "Keep it down," Bartholomew said. And they did. They walked the next few hours in silence until they entered into Samaritan territory.

Simon never thought he would be happy to be in Samaria. He breathed easier knowing that Herod did not control these lands.

But after the initial relief of being safe from Herod's grasp passed, Simon felt unclean. Even the wind felt foreign to his skin.

Knowing they would not be welcomed in any Samaritan village, they camped out that night. It was a dangerous plan. Thieves and wild animals were rampant in the region. They all carried something to defend themselves with. The Zealot had the sharpest sword. James had the largest staff. Only Jesus and Matthew were unarmed.

The moon had only begun to wane and the approaching summer gave the warmth they needed to carry them through the evening. They took turns at watch, but no man or creature stirred against them. In the morning they headed north into Samaria.

The sun rose to its highest point and beat down upon the travelers. Simon missed the wind from the lake that cooled him on days like this. Up a hill in the distance was a town called Sycar, and at the base of the hill sat a well.

Matthew was the first to recognize it. "Is this…?"

Jesus nodded. "It is."

"Is what?" the Zealot asked.

"Jacob's well!" Matthew said. And he ran his stout body toward it.

Simon was not about to pick up his pace in this hot weather. When he and the others arrived, they found Matthew reverently touching the stones that surrounded the well. "This is where our patriarch Jacob met Rachael and fell in love," he said.

"It's disgusting to think of a place like this in the hands of a bunch of half-breeds," Simon the Zealot said.

"Jacob is their father, too," Jesus said.

Little James looked around. "Too bad we don't have a bucket."

"How are we on food?" Simon asked.

"Not well," Jude answered. "Our supplies are low, and there's been nothing to catch or eat since we crossed into Samaria."

Simon sighed and looked toward the village. "Judas, how much money do we have?"

"Buy food from *them*?" Judas asked.

"Do you have a better idea?"

"You will all go together," Jesus said. "I'll stay here."

"Alone?" Simon the Zealot asked.

Jesus nodded. "Now go." They could tell by the tone of his voice that it wasn't up for discussion. None of them wanted to set foot in the Samaritan village, but they were obedient and began the long walk up the hill toward the town.

As they did, they passed a woman carrying two buckets tied to a pole hung over her shoulders. She moved to the side of the path and bowed her head low as they passed. *Why would a woman collect water at this hour?* Simon thought. But he had greater concerns in his mind.

The street grew silent as the apostles entered the village. He saw the Samaritans look down at the blue tassels that hung from their garments, then look up at them in scorn. Simon realized the wisdom of having all of them go together. If it were just a few of them they might not make it back.

They approached the first stand they came to, a wooden cart filled with fresh bread. Next to it was a table of pomegranates.

Judas reached into his tunic and pulled out some coins. The merchant looked disapprovingly at the money.

"That's not enough," the merchant said.

"Not enough?" the Zealot asked. Simon grabbed his arm so he wouldn't reach for his sword.

"A special price for a special people," the merchant said.

Judas moved around the cart and bumped into the table with the pomegranates on it. "Maybe we can—"

"You can back away, Jew," he said. "And be thankful I'm selling anything to you at all."

Simon looked around and noticed other Samaritan men had begun to walk toward them. "Pay the man, Judas, then let's leave."

Judas reached into his purse and handed him the money, took the food, and they quickly left town.

When they got back to Jesus, Simon was surprised to find him with the woman they passed on the way there. Even more shocking was they actually *spoke* to each other. As they drew near, Simon heard Jesus say to her, "I who speak to you am he." Then she jumped for joy and ran past them toward the village.

"At least she left her buckets," Little James said.

They approached Jesus and Judas bowed before him. "Master, we got you some food. You have no idea what we went through to get it!"

Jesus didn't immediately respond. He looked at the Samaritan woman as she ran up the hill. He seemed... peaceful.

"Master?" Judas asked.

Jesus came out of his trance and looked at him. "Thank you, Judas, but I already ate."

"Did somebody bring you food?" Jude asked.

"My food is to do the will of the one who sent me and complete his work."

"Does that mean we aren't gong to eat?" Thomas asked.

Jesus laughed. "No, Thomas, you can all eat."

Simon knew something happened he didn't understand, but he was getting used to that. And he was thrilled to see Jesus so happy. He hadn't seemed this relaxed since their first night in Nazareth.

The apostles sat in a circle and shared bread with each other. Simon sat next to Judas. "I didn't think he was going to sell us his food," Simon said.

"I didn't appreciate the 'higher price for Jews' comment he made," Judas said.

"At least we got some," James said. "I'm glad to never go into that town again."

"Too bad we couldn't afford some of that fruit," Simon said.

Judas reached into his robe and pulled out three pomegranates. "Consider this a gift from our over-priced Samaritan friend."

Simon was thrilled, and didn't think twice about the fact that Judas stole it. They finished the meal and drank fresh water from the well, using the buckets the woman left behind. John looked up and saw a group of people from the town heading toward them. "Isn't that the merchant who sold us our food?" he asked.

Judas panicked. "We've got to get out of here."

The Zealot overheard his statement. "What's going on?"

"Judas stole some food and now the shopkeeper is coming to get us," James said.

The Zealot cursed. "At least we outnumber them," he said, and he drew his sword.

"Put that away!" Jesus said.

"But Master—" Judas said.

"Be calm," Jesus said. "This is who I have been waiting for."

Simon the Zealot put the sword behind him and the merchant arrived with five other larger men. The woman who was at the well was with them. "This is the one," she said, pointing to Jesus.

"My sister tells me that you are…" He looked at his sister and then back at Jesus. "…a *prophet*."

"I am Jesus, from Nazareth."

The man's eyes opened wide. "The Baptist's brother! Now I see why so many Jews would come to Samaria." He folded his arms. "So, you're on the run from Herod?"

"I'm not running from anyone," Jesus said. "I'm here to proclaim the good news."

"And what would that be?"

"That the kingdom of God is here."

The man laughed and shook his head. "By 'here' you mean Jerusalem, right?"

"As I told your sister, the time has come when it doesn't matter *where* you worship, but *who* you worship."

This caught the man's attention. "Which god are you talking about?"

"My Father," Jesus said as he walked closer to the man. "*Our* Father."

Jesus word's amazed the Samaritans but troubled Simon. Did Jesus just suggest that Jerusalem *wasn't* the Holy City?

"Please," begged the woman as she reached out and gently touched her brother's arm.

"Well, I suppose we can talk more about it in the village."

Jesus bowed. "It would be a great honor."

Jesus walked with the men to the village and the twelve followed reluctantly behind.

"I can't believe we are going back there," Judas whispered to Simon. "If the Jews rejected us, how much worse will it be with the Samaritans?"

Simon felt the eyes of the entire town upon him as they reentered the village. He could tell the other apostles were on edge as well.

But not Jesus. His calmness even seemed to unnerve the Samaritans. He walked the streets as though this was a town in Galilee.

Micah, the merchant, began to gather people together in the center of town and a large crowd formed. Jesus stood in the middle and motioned for the apostles to sit in front of him like they usually did.

Simon was reluctant but didn't dare question the Master in front of a group of *Samaritans*. Now his back was to them and that made him very nervous. He tried to focus on Jesus and what he taught, but Simon was distracted by what he heard behind him.

At first there were many murmurs of disapproval from the crowd. They laughed under their breath and spoke the word "Jew" as if they uttered a curse. He clenched his fist and tried to control his anger. *Let Jesus handle this,* Simon thought.

If Jesus heard them he chose to ignore it. He preached boldly about the love of God. Jesus did not waver on saying that salvation came from the Jews, but made it clear that God was doing something new now that His kingdom was at hand.

As he continued to preach, Simon noticed the murmurs were replaced by silence, and silence by talk of a different kind. There was awe in their comments to each other now. He frequently heard the word "prophet" used with reverent acclamation.

Jesus spoke for an hour, maybe two. By the end, the Samaritans were captivated and hung on every word.

He finished and the crowd erupted in cheers and shouts of joy. People rushed forward to meet Jesus and ask for his blessing. Others reached out their arms and embraced the apostles as if they were family. Now Simon felt uncomfortable for a different reason: first he was unwelcome, now he was almost worshipped.

The sick were brought forward to Jesus and he healed them. The miracles added to the joyful hysteria of the crowd. As the sun began to set, everyone went to Micah's house to celebrate.

There was singing and dancing and drinking... *lots* of drinking. The wine flowed too freely for Simon's taste, as did some of the clothes (or lack thereof) that the women wore. He expected Jesus to reprimand the Samaritans, but he didn't. Jesus seemed to be comfortable among them.

Simon was so exhausted that he didn't even remember falling asleep. He awoke on a soft, silk pillow in a room with the other apostles. He sat up and stretched, then saw light under a curtain and quietly got up and opened it. Sunlight flooded the room and he heard Andrew groan and saw Judas cover his eyes. Simon entered the courtyard and closed the curtain behind him.

Micah came up to him with outstretched arms. "Good morning," he said.

"Shalo—, I mean, good morning," Simon said.

Micah smiled. "It is an honor to have such prophets in my house."

Simon nodded, but then considered his words. *Prophets*?

"I'm not a prophet," Simon said.

"No?" Micah asked. "Do you not preach? Do you not heal?"

Simon thought about this a moment. "Well, yes but—"

"Then you are a prophet!" Micah said. He seemed very pleased with himself.

"But not like Jesus," Simon said.

"No! Not like Jesus," Micah said. He drew uncomfortably close to Simon and looked around to make sure no one else heard what he was about to say, not that anyone else was awake. "I know about your Master and what makes him so special," he whispered.

"You do?" Simon whispered back, though not sure why.

Micah nodded and winked as if Simon was supposed to understand. He didn't.

The merchant rolled his eyes. "You don't have to play dumb with me, prophet. I know that Jesus is… *the Messiah*." Then he smiled wide.

"What? Jesus isn't—"

Micah put his finger to his mouth. "Shhh. I understand why you would keep it quiet. These are dangerous times. Your secret is safe with me."

Simon nodded, but only to get out the conversation. This man was insane. Or maybe he was still drunk from the night before. "Where is Jesus?" Simon asked.

"He left early this morning to pray. I will have my wife bring you some food." He bowed and left.

Andrew and James came into the courtyard.

"What was that about?" Andrew asked.

Simon was about to answer, but Micah's wife came in with a plate of bread and fruit. They thanked her and she left.

"They think Jesus is the Messiah," Simon said when she was out of earshot.

"That's because they are uneducated," Judas said, who put a large piece of bread in his mouth.

Andrew scratched his face. "What if he is?" he said.

Judas shook his his head. "He wathant evn bahn en bethatham," he said, wiping the breadcrumbs from his face.

"What?"

"He said that he wasn't even born in Bethlehem," Simon translated. But then he remembered his promise to keep nothing from Judas. "Though he might have been."

Judas swallowed hard. "What?"

"Some in Nazareth mentioned that Jesus wasn't born there."

"Jesus was born in Bethlehem?" Andrew said.

Simon shrugged. "Or near there."

"How long have you kept this from us?" Judas asked.

At that moment, Philip and Thomas came out into the courtyard and squinted in the light of the morning sun.

"Kept what from us?" Philip asked.

"Jesus was born in Bethlehem," Andrew said.

"Isn't he from Nazareth?" Thomas asked.

"Nazareth, Bethlehem—what does it matter?" Simon said to Judas.

"What does it matter?" Philip said. "He could be the Messiah! I spoke to many Samaritans last night who think so."

Judas rolled his eyes. "They also worship on a mountain instead of Jerusalem, so I wouldn't put too much weight on what Samaritans believe. If he's the Messiah, where's Elijah?"

James and John walked into the courtyard and overheard Judas's comments. "Did you say that Jesus was Elijah?" John asked.

"No, but apparently Jesus was born in Bethlehem," Judas said.

"Oh, we knew that already."

Judas turned against Simon. "How many other people did you let into your inner circle? What else are you keeping from us?"

Simon shot James and John a look and froze. He immediately thought of how Jesus raised Jairus's daughter and that they were sworn to secrecy.

Judas must have seen it because his face grew cold. "So that's how it is," he said. Then he turned and walked away.

"Judas…" Simon said, but Judas wouldn't turn back. He left the house and slammed the door behind him.

He wanted to follow him, but what could he say? Simon was a horrible liar and he knew he couldn't say anything about what happened in Jairus's house. His heart broke to see Judas go. He prayed that maybe he just needed a walk to calm down.

He called me brother, thought Judas as he walked down the streets of Sycar. Many Samaritans recognized him as one of Jesus' companions and tried to greet him, but he paid them no attention.

Judas walked himself uphill and out of town. Eventually, he sat and looked at the village below. The town was beginning to wake. Women headed to the well to gather water for the day. Steam bellowed out of the blacksmith's shop and the striking of iron could be heard. Judas heard the bleating of goats and the cackling of chickens as the sun rose high enough to bathe the village in its light.

He closed his eyes and breathed slowly, unable to get the image of Simon and the others out of his mind. *They are probably laughing at me right now,* he thought.

A voice spoke from behind him: "Shalom, Judas."

Judas jumped to his feet and was surprised to see Jesus. He bowed quickly. "Shalom, Master," he said.

"Please, let us sit," Jesus said, gesturing toward the ground.

"Thank you, Master."

They sat down together and Judas felt awkward, like he was caught doing something bad even though he hadn't done anything wrong.

After a moment of uncomfortable silence, Jesus asked, "Judas, are you all right?"

He didn't want to show any sign of weakness. "Yes, Master. I was… just looking for a quiet place to pray."

"Judas, I want you to be honest with me."

"Master, I swear by all the gold in the temple—"

Jesus raised his hand to silence him. "Just let your 'yes' mean 'yes' and your 'no' mean 'no'," he said.

Judas bowed his head. "Yes, Rabbi. I forgot. Please forgive me."

"Always," Jesus replied.

Another pause. If there was something Jesus wanted him to say, Judas couldn't figure out what it was.

"Simon tells me that you are a wonderful preacher," Jesus said.

Hearing the fisherman's name caused Judas to tense. What else had Simon told him? *And why don't I get to have private conversations with Jesus?* he wondered.

He quickly regained control. "Thank you, Master. I just said what you said."

Jesus put a hand on his shoulder. "Make sure you also do what I do."

"Of course," he said. Jesus looked him in the eye, but Judas pulled away. He was always a bit disturbed by Jesus' gaze.

"We should probably go and meet the others," Judas said. "They are waiting for us."

Jesus nodded and they got up and headed back into the village. They didn't speak again, but Judas kept thinking of Jesus' words: *Do as I do.* At first, they were an encouragement to him. But as he mulled them over he grew angry. By the time they reached the house, Judas was convinced that Jesus was disappointed in him.

When Judas saw Simon again, he embraced him and told him everything was fine. But it wasn't. He wondered if it would ever be. Surrounded by the other apostles, Judas never felt more alone.

Every man for himself, he thought. *Just like always.*

"DO YOU STILL NOT UNDERSTAND?"

Mark 8:1-9, 14-21

Jesus and the twelve stayed in the village for a few more days, then spent a month preaching in different towns. They left Samaria and crossed over the river Jordan. Simon dipped his toe into the cold, rushing water. It was refreshing.

They were a day or two's journey north of the Sea of Galilee, and a third day away from Capernaum. The river reminded Simon of home, and he longed to see Rachael again.

Philip jumped into the water—a refreshing antidote to the summer sun. They all relaxed by the bank of the river, enjoying the shade of the trees that were nourished by it. There was much laughter among them, and Bartholomew took the opportunity to take a nap until Philip doused him with water and a chase ensued.

They were now in the area known as Gaulantis, a tetrarchy of King Philip, the brother of Herod. But Philip was *nothing* like his brother, and the two didn't get along. They would be safe here. It was mostly populated by Greeks, but at least there were some Jews and synagogues to worship in.

Simon felt more comfortable among the Greeks. With the Samaritans, there was animosity. With the Greeks, an understanding. Since the Greeks believed in something totally different there was no reason to argue. They did not claim to be children of Abraham, nor did they care about what the Torah meant. And so as they passed through cities with Temples of Athena and Apollo, Simon and the others paid it no heed.

Jesus and the twelve tried to keep a low profile as they traveled through this land. Jesus commanded those he healed to not talk about it, but it seemed that the sterner he told them to be quiet, the louder they would shout his name to others. They relied on the hospitality of the Jews in that region and preached at various synagogues, and all who heard him were amazed.

After heading east, they turned south. Simon knew the Sea of Galilee was to the west of them now, though he couldn't see it. The days grew longer and their travel slowed because they did not want to walk in the heat of the day.

"Why are we going this way?" Bartholomew asked. "At least there were Jews in Gaulantis, but these are all Greeks and Romans."

"Are we safer from Herod?" Thomas asked.

"We've been safe from Herod for the past few months," Bartholomew said, "and we're no safer in the Decapolis than in Gaulantis. Who will open their doors to us here?"

Jesus came to a stop and gathered the apostles together. "Simon and Matthew, go to Afek and let them know I am coming."

Afek was about an hour's walk away. The Zealot and Matthew began to move, but Jesus stopped them. "Simon, son of Jonah," he said.

Simon nodded. He wasn't upset to go with Matthew. Though they hadn't really talked, months together had softened their relationship with each other. Matthew had shown himself to be a man of great faith who rarely complained. This surprised Simon because he always thought Matthew lived a "pampered" life and would not hold up to rough travel.

He thought they made an odd pair to those who would see them. Two Jews walking into a Greek city: one large and muscular, the other short and stout. But Matthew wasn't as stout as he was a few months ago—miles of walking had slimmed his figure.

It was a beautiful morning and Simon knew it would lead to a hot afternoon. He wasn't confident about their mission. "I don't think Gentiles will care that a Jewish prophet is coming to their town," he said.

"The Samaritans came to believe in him," Matthew said. "Perhaps the Greeks will, too."

Simon shook his head and sighed. He looked down at the pale grass. It seemed to long for water as much as Simon longed for home. "I'm tired of being among the lot of them."

"We are not that different," Matthew said.

"But these are not God's chosen people," Simon said. "I think working with them for so long has effected your thinking."

His words stung Matthew and Simon immediately regretted saying them. He opened his mouth to apologize but Matthew was quick to retaliate.

"Did you think it was easy for me? All these months I've heard you and others complain about how *hard* it is to be away from other Jews, how *difficult* it is to dwell among the Gentiles. Well, that was my life! But no matter what you, or your brother, or anyone else says, *I kept the faith*. I was surrounded by them, and *I kept the faith*."

Simon knew he deserved that. If they were supposed to love Samaritans, how much more should they love their fellow Jew? "I'm sorry, Levi," he said. "You are a faithful man, and I have been wrong to judge you."

Matthew stopped dead in his tracks, jaw open in disbelief. "I don't know what to say…" he said.

Simon wasn't expecting Matthew's dramatic response and it made him uncomfortable. He shrugged. "Don't worry ab—"

"I have not been kind to you, either," Matthew said.

They stood for a moment in silence. Simon opened his mouth to speak, but no words came out. He put his hand on Matthew's shoulder and nodded. Matthew smiled. Nothing more needed to be said.

Simon learned two things about Matthew in the hour it took them to reach the city: Matthew talked a lot and he liked to have things organized.

"So what should we say when we get there?" Matthew asked.

Simon shrugged. "The usual," he said.

Matthew shook his head. "Not with Greeks. The 'great prophet of the God of Abraham' or 'brother of John the Baptist' won't work."

"What if we begin by talking about the leper who was healed?" Simon asked.

"Too disgusting. We should start small and build up."

"Casting out demons?"

Matthew shook his head. "For all we know, they might worship demons."

"Well, what about the paralyzed man?"

Matthew thought about this. "That's better, but we need a strong beginning." He snapped his fingers. "Do you remember when Jesus healed the centurion's servant?"

"I wasn't there, but I heard about it."

"*That's* a great beginning because he healed a Gentile! So, after I tell them about Jesus, the great holy man from Galilee—"

"Not Jesus of Nazareth?"

Matthew rolled his eyes. "They probably haven't even heard of Nazareth, and if they did they wouldn't be impressed. As I was saying, I'll announce Jesus of Galilee, then tell them about the centurion's servant being healed. You tell them about healing the paralyzed man—"

"Me?" Simon said.

"Of course," Matthew said.

Simon shook his head. "I don't talk."

Matthew looked at him with surprise. "What did you do when Jesus sent us out before?"

"I healed. Judas preached."

"Hmm," Matthew said. He stroked his beard. "Well, I think we should both do the preaching and the healing. That's what Simon and I did and it worked well."

Simon ran his fingers through his curly hair. "What will I say?"

"After I talk about the servant, you can talk about the paralytic, and then I'll close with the leper."

Simon nodded. He could do this. All he had to do was say what he saw, and Matthew would do the rest.

They came upon the city gates of Afek and passed Roman soldiers as they entered. It was a larger city than Capernaum. Many of the houses had detailed woodwork and large walls. The streets were paved with cobblestone. Simon saw many kinds of faces: Greek, Roman, Persian, even Egyptian. There was not a Jew in sight.

Simon and Matthew followed narrow streets until it opened into the center of the city. It was filled with people who haggled with merchants in numerous languages. There were many statues. Whether they were of gods or just people Simon couldn't tell.

He felt sweat run down his back. He wasn't sure if it was from nervousness or the heat of the day. Some shops began to close and people moved through the town square to escape the bright summer sun. It was now or never.

He expected Matthew to look flush with heat but instead he was pale with fright. Simon put a comforting hand on his shoulder. "You can do it," he said to him. "If anyone starts fighting, I'll protect you."

Matthew looked at him in horror. "Do you really think they'll start fighting?" he asked.

"No, no," Simon said. "I'm just saying… if they did, that's all."

Matthew closed his eyes and took a deep breath. Then he raised his voice. "Good people, gather around! I have come from far away to tell good news!"

A crowd assembled. First ten, then twenty, then fifty, then about a hundred. Simon did not expect that many people to gather so fast. They looked curious, but also impatient. Matthew waited for them to be silent before he spoke.

"People of Afek," Matthew said, his voice nervously cracking. "I have come with a message of good news! Good news indeed!"

"You've already said that," someone yelled from the back of the crowd. "What is the news?"

Matthew was unnerved by the interruption, but he bravely carried on. "I wish to tell you about Jesus, the great holy man from Galilee. I myself witnessed a Roman centurion—"

"Are you talking about Jesus of Nazareth?" a woman said.

Someone knows him? Simon wondered. He could see Matthew was also surprised.

Matthew straightened his tunic. "Yes, well—"

"The brother of John the Baptist?" another asked.

Matthew's jaw dropped open. "How do you—"

"The one who casts out demons?"

"Stop!" Matthew said, and the crowd grew quiet. He cleared his throat. "As I was saying, I myself witnessed—"

"Do you know him?"

"Are you his disciples?"

"Is he coming *here*?"

Matthew looked at Simon with a plea for help.

"Uh... yes," Simon said. "He'll be here in a few hours." At this, the crowd erupted in shouts and cheers and the people ran down the streets, shouting the news of Jesus' imminent arrival. Simon and Matthew couldn't believe it.

A Greek woman came up to Simon. "I am so excited to meet him. Everyone's been talking about him since that man came to town."

"What man?" Simon asked.

"I wasn't here. My sister told me about it. I've got to tell her!" And off she ran.

In the excitement of Jesus coming to town, the apostles were almost completely ignored. They quietly left the way they came.

Simon and Matthew went back to the others, who were sitting in the shade.

"Did they kick you out that quickly?" Bartholomew asked.

"No, they started screaming and shouting with joy," Simon said.

Philip laughed, thinking that Simon was telling a joke.

"How can this be?" Little James asked.

"Master," Matthew asked, "have you sent someone to this town before?"

"Not that I know of," Jesus said.

"Then someone is preaching in your name."

"Should we find him and stop him?" Simon asked.

"No," Jesus said. "Do not stop him. Whoever is not against us is for us."

"But we don't know who he is or what he's said about you!" Matthew said.

"Then let's find out," Jesus said.

Simon could barely keep up with the others. His legs felt like anchors. Of course, the other apostles had rested in the shade while Matthew and he walked to Afek and back. He couldn't help but wonder: *Who would dare preach in the name Jesus without his permission?*

As they neared the city, Simon saw a man approach surrounded by children. As they got closer he realized they weren't children, but small adults. Then he realized that they were regular sized adults and the man was a giant.

Now he knew.

Tears of joy ran down the giant's face and he called out, "Master!"

"Marcus! It is good to see you again!" Jesus said. Marcus was so large that as he hugged Jesus, Jesus almost disappeared into his robes.

Marcus looked very different since they last saw him on the shore of the Gerasenes. His open wounds had healed. There were no shackles on his hands or wrists. His body looked as fierce as ever, but it was clearly inhabited by a gentler spirit. Joy radiated from his face, revealing a smile of broken teeth.

"What a joy that you and I should be at the same city! I have been to all ten cities, and they all know of the marvelous works you have done. Give me a week, and I will run to every town and tell them you are here. They must hear what you have to say!"

Jesus gave Marcus his blessing, and off he ran.

A week later, they gathered in a remote place, about half a day's walk from Afek. Simon couldn't believe how many people had come to hear Jesus preach.

"What do you think?" Simon asked Judas.

Judas surveyed the crowd. "There are some wealthy people here," he said. "We should collect quite a bit of money."

Simon was surprised by his answer. "No, I meant how many *people* do you think there are?"

"Oh, right," Judas said. "I would say four thousand families, maybe twenty or thirty thousand people."

Amazing, Simon thought. There were almost as many Gentiles gathered to hear Jesus as the Jews who gathered on the other side of the lake almost five months ago.

Marcus sat in the circle around Jesus' feet with the twelve and Simon sat next to him. He marveled at the scarred giant and felt small—not just physically, but spiritually. Marcus's encounter with Jesus was brief yet it was enough to change his entire life. Simon thought of the woman at the well who had a similar experience.

He thought of his own journey. Simon had been following Jesus for over a year now… *but they seem to have greater faith.* Through the long hours of preaching that followed, Marcus couldn't help but stare at Jesus, and Simon couldn't help but look at Marcus. Tears flowed from the giant's face and he absorbed every word.

Simon looked around at the other apostles and was horrified at what he saw. They all looked tired, even disinterested, as if it were another day at work. *May I never treat Jesus so casually*, he prayed. James was almost asleep next to him. A sharp elbow brought him back to life, and he did his best to focus on the Master.

Jesus had a lot to say. Because he spoke to Gentiles, he spent most of the first day talking about the existence of the One True God and told the history of how God had saved his people. The second day he talked of how the kingdom was open to everyone, Jew and Gentile alike. And on the third day he talked about the importance of the Ten Commandments as well as other moral teachings.

When he finished, the crowd was in awe. They had never heard anything like it. Some cheered, some wept. There were those who didn't agree, but they seemed to be the minority.

It was late in the day when Jesus finished. He gathered the twelve close. "I feel sorry for these people," he said to them. "They have been with me for three days now and have nothing to eat. If I send them off home hungry they will collapse on the way."

"Where could anyone get these people enough bread to eat in this deserted place?" Matthew asked.

"Jude, how much bread do we have?" Jesus asked.

"Seven loaves," Jude answered.

Jesus smiled. "It will be enough. You all know what to do."

Simon grabbed a basket and headed toward the crowd, excited to participate in another miracle. "Take as much as you want," he told the people.

There were seven basketfuls of scraps left over when they were done.

One of the people from a costal town let Simon borrow a boat to go back to Capernaum. It was big enough to bring Marcus with them, but to Simon's surprise he didn't want to go.

"There are more places I can tell about Jesus," Marcus said to him. "I hope you know how blessed you are, Simon. Take care of him."

Simon was amazed at his faith. "I will," he said.

They embraced, and Simon felt like a little boy being hugged by his father. Then Marcus and Jesus stepped away as Simon and the others prepared the boat. When Jesus came back, there were tears in his eyes.

The sun was setting as they left and they could see the lights of Capernaum by the time it disappeared. The weather, for once, was perfect. There had been some light rain during their time in the Decapolis, but now the moon was half full and the sky was clear.

Simon rowed in the back of the boat and felt Jude move behind him. "What are you doing?" Simon asked.

"*Shhh,*" Jude said. "I think I forgot the bread scraps and only have one loaf. Are they over by you?"

"We'll be in Capernaum in a couple hours," Simon said. "I think we can manage without bread until then."

Simon looked at the water. The lake was black beneath the boat, and the reflection from the night sky made him feel like they floated in stars. Everything was beautiful, and the sea did not speak a word.

"Master?" his brother said.

"Yes, Andrew?"

"Will we be safe in Capernaum?"

Jesus paused. "Why would we be in danger?"

The answer seemed obvious. Simon wasn't sure if he was feigning ignorance to teach them a lesson or if he really had no fear of Herod and his men.

"Then why did we leave Capernaum?" Andrew asked.

It was hard to see Jesus' reaction in the moonlight. But he shifted his weight a bit and paused long enough to make them all feel uncomfortable. "Why do *you* think we left Capernaum?"

"To flee from Herod?"

"I thought I made it clear in Samaria that I was not running from Herod," came the reply.

"You meant that?" Judas said. "I thought you were—"

"Thought I was what?" Jesus said.

"Nothing, Master," he quickly replied.

"So why *did* we leave Capernaum?" Thomas asked.

"Because *the stone which the builders rejected has become the cornerstone,*" he said.

Simon didn't understand what he meant by that. Apparently, Thomas didn't either.

"So we *meant* to go to Samaria?" Thomas asked.

"Of course I *meant* to go to Samaria," Jesus said. "Just as I *meant* to go to Gaulantis and I *meant* to go to the Decapolis. Did you not see how quickly they embraced the message, or were you too busy looking over your shoulders, worrying that Herod might arrest us?"

The twelve said nothing, and Simon was thankful that Thomas spoke no further. They stopped rowing and the boat gently swayed back and forth on the lake, wood creaking as it did.

Jesus gave a discouraged sigh. "If you thought the kingdom of God was just for you and not for others, then you have been listening too much to the false teachers of the Law. Keep your eyes open. Look out for the yeast of the Pharisees and the yeast of Herod."

Jude cursed. "I knew I should have brought more bread," he whispered to Simon.

Jesus must have heard it because he stood up on the boat and harshly rebuked them. "Why are you talking about bread? Do you still not understand? Have you eyes but can't see, ears but can't hear? Or do you not remember? When I broke the five loaves for the five thousand, how many baskets of scrap did you collect?"

The disciples were hesitant to answer.

"HOW MANY?" Jesus asked. His words echoed across the lake.

"*Twelve*," came the muted reply.

"And when I broke the seven loaves for the four thousand families, how many scraps did you collect?"

"*Seven*."

"Do you still not realize?"

All were quiet. Jesus collapsed into his seat and put his head in his hands.

Simon did not know what to make of it. He hated to disappoint the Master, but he was also frustrated that he didn't understand. He looked around at the others. Judas had his arms crossed and looked angry. Thomas shook his head. He could see by John's trembling shoulders that he silently wept.

For the first time, Simon questioned his decision to follow Jesus. Jesus seemed so much different now from when he first called him on the lake. It had been a long journey in foreign lands, and all Simon wanted to do was to go home and see his wife and children.

He picked up the oar and put it in the water. The others did the same. They silently rowed through the stars toward home.

Nobody spoke. Jesus did not look at them and his lips moved like he was praying. Or maybe he was angry and talking to himself.

Who is this man, anyway?

As they rowed, a warm wind blew. It felt to Simon as if it were a breath on his neck, and it whispered to him a solitary word:

Messiah.

PETER

Matthew 16:13-23

Simon shared the word with no one, and over the next few months questioned if he even heard it. He tried to forget about it, but the memory persisted.

Messiah.

He wasn't about to ask Jesus if he was the Christ. Such a statement would border on blasphemy and probably get a strong rebuke. He feared that Jesus might even kick him out for believing such a foolish thing.

Since the voice was clearly wrong, Simon started to focus not on what was said but what said it. Was the sea trying to trick him? It didn't sound like the sea. It had spoken to him in a voice he had never heard before yet felt intimately familiar with.

As weeks went by, the word echoed in his head even louder than when he had heard it on the lake.

One day, while doing ministry by the shore, Simon found a rare moment alone with Jesus. "Master, has creation ever… spoken to you?" Simon asked.

"Of course, Simon," Jesus said, and Simon felt great relief. "*The heavens tell of the glory of God, and the sky shows forth the works of his hands,*" he said. "*The meadows are covered with flocks and the valleys are mantled with grain– they shout for joy, yes they sing.*"

Simon's heart fell. This wasn't what he meant. "What about the sea?"

Jesus nodded as if he had asked an insightful question. "The sea is speaking now. Can you hear it?"

Simon immediately tensed. What did it say to Jesus? "I don't hear anything," he said.

Jesus stood with eyes closed and hands outstretched before him. "Close your eyes and listen."

Simon did so reluctantly. Thankfully, the sea wasn't speaking to him now. "All I hear is the water breaking against the shore."

"Yes!" Jesus said. "That sound: *shhhhh*. It is like a mother hushing her young child to sleep. It says, '*Be still and know that he is God.*'"

"That's what the water says?" he asked, convinced now more than ever he was losing his mind.

"Yes. The water is very quiet."

Not to me, Simon thought.

As if he read his mind, Jesus said, "The sea is more about action than words. It speaks little, but reflects much."

At first, the townspeople of Capernaum were happy to see them again. But as months passed there grew a greater tension than before and, though Judas was loathe to admit it, the Gentiles had been more open to Jesus' message than the Jews were. The most devoted people were the poor, a fact that bothered him to no end.

"These people are intolerable," Judas said to James and John. "The Gentiles were more generous."

"The Gentiles had more money," James said. "These people give what they have."

"We used to attract a better class of people," Judas said. "Poor Jews, rich Gentiles, Samaritans… does this bother anybody? Why are we still in Capernaum and not in Jerusalem?"

"We've been to Jerusalem," James said.

"Sure, to celebrate religious feasts like everybody else. I mean we should *stay* there, and not hang out among…" he waved his hand across the Galilean landscape, "…this."

"We go where he goes. Isn't that enough for you?" John said. "Besides, many of these people believe—"

"Oh, they believe all right. They have nothing else to believe in. Some even believe he is the Messiah, of all the foolish things."

"It's not so foolish," he said. "He cures the sick, casts out demons, raises the dead—"

"Wait," Judas said, "Did you say *raises the dead*?"

John froze and gave a telling look to his brother who looked at him sternly. "I meant that… well, people talk about it and…"

"No, I understand," Judas said with a sympathetic smile. "The people believe all sorts of crazy things. That was actually my point."

John agreed, too quickly, and excused himself to leave with his brother. Judas could hear James chastise John as they left. "You're lucky he didn't notice," James said to him.

But Judas did. He vividly remembered when Jesus took Simon, James, and John into Jairus's house to heal his daughter. And he knew the three fishermen kept secrets from the rest of them. It all added up.

She had died, Judas realized, *and Jesus raised her from the dead!* The only other person in Scripture who was known to raise someone from the dead was... *Elijah.*

That was it! Jesus was really Elijah, the one who was to come before the Messiah appeared. His heart leapt in his chest. *I am a disciple of Elijah!*

Judas could hardly contain his excitement.

Should he tell the others? No, they weren't to be trusted. Besides, there must be a reason why Jesus kept it quiet. Did the fishermen know? They were too stupid to figure it out.

Unless Jesus told them, he considered. But they didn't act like they were in the presence of Elijah. And they seemed too simple to cover up something that big.

Perhaps Jesus was waiting to see who would figure it out first, and even name that person as his chief disciple. The thought of this thrilled Judas, and he fantasized about taking his rightful place as the head of the apostles.

But the timing had to be perfect. Jesus mentioned they would soon head to Bethsaida and continue north to Mt. Hermon. That was it. It would be a long journey that would provide plenty of opportunity to show the Master who his smartest disciple was.

They were almost six months away from the Passover feast and Jesus was concerned. He knew exactly what would await him there, but that's not what he was worried about.

The apostles weren't ready.

They had shown little progress over the past twelve months. He had prayed that one of them, any of them, would understand who he was. But so far, his prayers to his Father had gone unanswered.

He led them north and they came upon the city of Caesarea Philippi. It took them about a week to get there, and they were tired from the rugged terrain.

The sun was still high in the sky, so Jesus knew they could make it to another town by nightfall. He told them to sit down and eat. Though happy for a chance to rest, Jesus could see the apostles were not comfortable to linger here. Caesarea was to the Gentiles what Jerusalem was to the Jews. It was their holy site, and people traveled thousands of miles to offer sacrifice to their gods.

Jesus looked up at the huge rock wall that the city was built against. In one part of the cliff, a large cave opened up into a bottomless pit. The Gentiles thought it was a gateway to hell. King Herod's father built a large and beautiful temple dedicated to the god Pan and set it against this opening, so that sacrifices from the temple could easily be thrown into it. Jesus heard the cries of goats and lambs echo off the rock as they descended into "hell", followed by the cheers of Gentiles who felt their god was appeased.

Statues of Greek gods were everywhere, especially that of Pan. He had cloven hoofs and played the pipe, dancing with a look of mischief on his face.

"Who is Pan the god of?" Simon asked.

"Shepherds and sheep," Bartholomew said.

Almost as if on cue, a shepherd passed by followed by thirty or forty sheep, heading into town toward the temple.

"I have a feeling many of those sheep won't make it back alive," Philip said. The others laughed.

Jesus watched the flock closely as it passed. "I tell you the truth, anyone who does not enter the sheepfold by the gate, but climbs in some other way, is a thief and a bandit. But the one who enters through the gate is the shepherd of the flock. The sheep hear his voice, and one by one he calls them and leads them out. They will never follow a stranger, because they don't recognize the voice of strangers."

He turned to look at his apostles. Blank, confused expressions were on their faces. *Will they ever understand?*

"I am the gate," he said. "All who have come before me are thieves and bandits, and they have come only to steal, kill, and destroy. But I have come that they may have life and have it to the full. Anyone who enters in through me will be safe and find good pasture."

He looked at the statue of Pan that hovered over them in a portico against the wall. "*I* am the good shepherd," Jesus said, "and the good shepherd lays down his life for his sheep. I know my own, and my own know me."

The apostles nodded as if they understood, but Jesus wasn't convinced. *Do you really know me?* he wondered.

It was time to find out.

"Who do people say that I am?" Jesus asked.

Judas immediately spoke up. "Some say that you are Elijah…" It seemed as though Judas wanted to say more, or maybe wanted Jesus to react to the statement. When he didn't, Judas looked around at the others and awkwardly sat down.

"I have heard people say you are John the Baptist back from the dead," Philip said.

"One person thought you were Jeremiah, if you can believe that," Little James said. Some of them laughed.

"What about you?" Jesus asked. "Who do *you* say that I am?"

An uneasy silence fell over the apostles.

Bartholomew stood and bowed to him. "You are a great prophet," he said. "If I may say, one of the greatest in all of Israel. And we are honored to serve you." The others nodded in agreement.

It was a bold proclamation and Jesus took it graciously. He looked around to see if anyone had something else to say. Everyone was still except for Judas and Simon. Judas looked anxiously around. Simon looked flushed and sweated profusely.

Jesus sighed. *The greatest in all of Israel*, he thought. *At least they are getting closer.* "Let us go," he said. Jesus stood and turned to gather his things, and the others began to as well.

From the moment Jesus asked the question, Simon's heart began to race. But he didn't dare speak. His face grew red and he felt sweat roll down his back. When the others began to gather their things, Simon's heart screamed to him: *SAY IT!*

He could bear the voice no longer. Simon stood up and burst out, "You are the Christ, the Son of the living God!"

Everyone froze, including Jesus who was turned away from him at that moment. Simon gasped for air, only then realizing that he had been holding his breath since Jesus asked the question.

Jesus turned and Simon did not know what to expect. He looked as surprised as the others. Then Jesus bowed his head and put his hands together over his mouth as if in prayer. He opened his arms wide and looked radiantly into the sun as if to say: *thank you.* Then he turned his gaze upon Simon.

"Blessed are you!" he cried out. "Simon, son of Jonah, you are a blessed man!" And he walked up to him and gripped his shoulders. Simon stood as one dead, unsure of what was going on. "My Father spoke to you, didn't he? You didn't get this from any man, but my Father in heaven."

The Father? Was that the voice he heard on the boat?

Jesus hugged him and Simon found the strength to return the embrace. Jesus looked around at the others and then toward the large rock face that dominated Caesarea's landscape. "You are no longer to be called Simon," he said to him. "I say this to you, you are Peter, *the rock*, and upon this rock I will build my church."

As if to compete with the sacred moment, the wail of an animal was heard, followed by the cheers of those who had thrown it into the pit. Jesus looked toward the temple of Pan and proclaimed, "And the gates of hell will not prevail against this church!"

He then turned his attention solely toward Simon, who fell on his knees before Jesus just as he did when he first called him on the boat. But this time, no words could come to his mouth.

You are *the Messiah,* Simon said to himself, reviling in the wonder of it all.

Jesus put his hands on Simon and blessed him. "Peter, I will give you the keys to the kingdom of heaven. Whatever you bind on earth will be bound there, and whatever you loose on earth will be loosed in heaven."

Simon looked up at him in amazement. He wasn't completely sure what was happening, but knew in his heart that his life would never be the same. Jesus looked at him with such joy and love that Simon wished he could gaze upon that face forever. His mind had thousands of questions, but his heart had never felt such peace.

Jesus raised him up and they embraced again. Simon turned and looked at the others. They seemed frozen in shock.

"You are the Messiah…" John said.

Jesus smiled and nodded.

John jumped up and down. "You are the MESSIAH!"

Jesus held out his hands to silence him. "Be quiet and tell no one about this. There is more for you to know. But here," he said as he glanced around at the surrounding statues, "is not the place. Let us go."

They traveled east and walked along the southern border of Mt. Hermon. The sun was behind them and they hurried to find a hospitable town before it set. Simon walked as if he was in a daze. He looked to his left and saw the beautiful snow capped peaks of the mountain. A layer of white clouds surrounded the peak, as if a shearer had clothed it with wool. Then he looked to the humble carpenter in front of him who led the way. He was not sure which sight inspired more awe.

He had walked for almost an hour before he noticed James's stare.

"What?" he asked.

"Nothing… *Peter*."

"I'm still Simon."

"You *were* Simon. Now you're Peter."

Simon wanted to argue, but to do so would contradict the Master's statement. And he couldn't help but feel a great sense of pride about it. "I guess so."

He looked around, and for the first time realized that everyone followed behind him. Normally, unless they plowed through large crowds of people, he and the other fishermen hung in the back, with people like Judas in the front. Now it was just the opposite.

Simon saw his brother's joyful face, and behind him John and Matthew were excitedly talking. Philip, Jude, and Bartholomew conversed with each other in quieter tones. The Zealot walked alone, as he usually did, but had a look of pride on his face. Thomas, Little James, and Judas were at the back of the line, and Simon thought they walked a little farther back than usual.

Jesus led them through two towns but neither had what he desired: a synagogue. Finally they made it to Kela, a small village by Lake Phialah which sat at the foot of the mountain. As they approached, Jesus was happy to find the head of the synagogue, a short and skinny man named Saul, leaving for the night.

"Yes, I have heard stories about you!" Saul said. "It is such an honor to have you and your disciples here. You must stay at my house while in our town."

Jesus bowed graciously. "Thank you Saul. We would be delighted. But I have another favor to ask of you."

"Anything for the great prophet of Galilee."

"I'd like to use your synagogue."

"Of course. Tomorrow morning, I will tell the whole town and we will delight to hear your preach."

"No, I mean tonight."

Saul scratched his long beard. "Most people are going to sleep now. It would be hard to gather—"

"I'm not looking for a crowd. I'm looking for a place to teach my disciples. In private."

Saul agreed, but only on the condition that he would preach to everyone the next day. He went home to prepare their lodgings, and they went into the synagogue and closed the door behind them.

It was a small synagogue, but well kept. The ornate tabernacle that held the sacred writings stood in contrast to the simple surroundings. There was one torch lit, and with it they lit another. Flames danced shadows across the room and Jesus sat down to teach. His apostles formed a circle around his feet.

Jesus asked Matthew to fetch a scroll of the prophet Isaiah, and Matthew did so with great reverence.

Unrolling the scroll, Jesus proclaimed:

"Look, my servant will prosper, will grow great, will rise to great heights.

As many people were shocked when they saw him, he was so inhumanly disfigured that he no longer looked like a man.

He had no charm to attract us, no beauty to win our hearts

He was despised, the lowest of men, a man of sorrows, familiar with suffering,

One from whom we averted our gaze.

Yet ours were the sufferings he was bearing, ours the sorrows he was carrying.

We thought of him as someone being punished and struck with affliction by God,

But he was being wounded for our transgressions and crushed because of our guilt.

The punishment meant for us fell on him, and we have been healed by his bruises."

Jesus' voice filled the room and there was no other sound to be heard. He paused and took a deep breath, then continued.

"Ill treated and afflicted, he never opened his mouth.

Like a lamb led to the slaughter house,

Like a sheep dumb before the shearers.

Forcibly, after sentence, he was taken,

Which of his people was concerned that he had been cut off from the land of the living?

Or having been struck dead for his people's rebellion?

He was given a grave with the wicked, and his tomb with the rich,

Although he had done no violence, though he had spoken no deceit."

Jesus felt overwhelmed and could speak no more. He handed the scroll back to Matthew as if it had grown heavy with weight, and Matthew reverently put it back in the tabernacle and returned to his position by his feet.

In the dancing light he looked slowly at each of his companions. The silence was unbearable but no one dared to speak.

"What I have to tell you now will be troubling to you. I need you to listen, not with your human ears, but with your faith. We have been together for some time now, and you have seen many things you never dreamed of. Now I tell you that you will see greater things, but the path to glory is heavy with suffering."

There was no way to gently tell them what they were about to face. "The passage I read was about me. I am the suffering servant of God."

His followers were shocked and murmured about this. Jesus did not relent. "We will go to Jerusalem, where I will suffer grievously at the hands of the elders, the chief priests, and the scribes. They will put me to death, but I will rise on the third day."

The twelve looked at each other in horror. Audible gasps and unintentional curses flowed from their mouth. Matthew put his hands to his head and rolled backward, almost passing out. John had to put his hands in front of him to steady himself. James's jaw hung loosely from his face as his body slumped to the ground. Simon looked stunned.

Jesus' heart broke for them. "It is enough for tonight," he said. "We will talk more about it in the morning."

For Simon, his hope became a horror. He was too shocked to think. He stumbled to his feet and began to follow Jesus out of the synagogue. Maybe he would wake up tomorrow and realize it was all a dream.

A sharp pinch on his arm reminded him that he was awake. He turned and saw his brother's anxious face.

"You've got to say something!" Andrew whispered.

Philip, Bartholomew, and Simon joined the conversation.

"This is madness," Bartholomew said.

"May my family be cursed for a thousand generations if I stand idly by and let him be killed," the Zealot said.

Andrew repeated his plea. "Talk to him, Simon."

"Why me?"

"Because you're *in charge!*"

James, John, and Matthew came and stood next to him as well. It seemed the consensus was that something must be done.

"All right," he said.

Jesus had already walked out of the synagogue and Simon ran to catch up to him. "Master, may I speak to you?"

"Of course, Peter," Jesus said. Simon looked around. The other apostles kept a distance behind.

Simon looked into his Master's face and he began to feel the significance of his words. *Suffer at the hands of priests? Handed over to death?* "Heaven preserve you, Lord," he said. "This must not happen!"

Jesus stepped backward as if he had just been struck across the face. Simon immediately wished he could return the words to his mouth.

"Get behind me, Satan!" His words echoed down the quiet village streets. "You are an obstacle in my path because you are thinking not as God thinks, but as human beings do!"

Jesus looked at the apostles, none of whom dared to return his gaze. He looked back at Simon and then turned and headed toward Saul's house without another word.

Simon's knees felt weak and he feared he might pass out. It was all he could do to not unravel on the spot.

No one spoke during the short walk to the house. Inside, food was served and some engaged in casual conversation. But Simon remained silent in spite of his brother's attempts to get him to speak.

His mind replayed the day's events over and over, and left him with more questions than answers. Was he a rock or the devil? Was Jesus the Messiah or the suffering servant?

Was this a dream or a nightmare?

Exhausted though he was, sleep did not come easy to him that night.

ON THE MOUNTAIN

Luke 9:28-36

The commotion in Saul's house provided easy cover for Judas to step outside and take a walk. Clouds covered the stars and the moon looked pale in the distance. The lights in many courtyards grew dim. One man looked suspiciously out his door but then closed it quickly when Judas returned the stare. Kela was home to about three hundred people, and it wasn't long before he walked every street in town.

He knew that Jesus was not the Messiah. It confused him as to why he would say he was, but since he seemed honest in every other matter, the only logical reason was that he truly was insane. Or maybe he was possessed, as the Pharisees claimed. Either way, Judas was in a mess.

Should I leave? Those who believed in Jesus would see him as a traitor. Those who didn't believe would laugh at him as a fool. He had given over a year of his life to this man and hadn't even a drachma to show for it. Never had he seen so much money and received so little. The Greeks were especially generous, but Jesus wouldn't keep any of it. Had Jesus given any thought to his disciple's future? At least Ioakim had paid him well.

The thought of his old master caused him to laugh. *How lucky you were to not have been picked,* he thought. *God blessed you after all.*

His heart burned when he thought of Simon. *An uneducated fisherman as the head of the apostles?* Bartholomew would have been a more tolerable choice, but choosing Simon was insulting. *Simon probably knew it from the start*, Judas thought. He would *never* call him Peter.

There was no reason to follow Jesus anymore. He could leave, change his name, and start a new life somewhere else. But the idea sickened him. He had already started a new life when he apprenticed under Ioakim, and then again when he became a disciple of Jesus. How many new lives must he live to get away from his old one? Poverty seemed a curse he was destined to.

"Give me a sign!" he cried aloud to no one in particular, but certainly not to God. A door opened and a man looked out. It was the same man who looked at him before. Judas realized that he had walked in a full circle.

He wasn't in the mood for games. "What do you want?" he said.

The older man came out of his house with a bowed head. "Excuse me, but are you the prophet from Galilee?"

This is the last thing I need right now, Judas thought. "No, I'm just a disciple of his," he said.

"But he is here?"

Judas nodded because speech was too much effort.

"My wife has been suffering from horrible back pain. Could he heal her?"

"I'm sure he will in the morning," Judas said, using a tone to inform the man he had better things to do. "And he'll even do it for *free*." The last word made him sick to his stomach.

"Oh, no, I can pay," he said. The man reached under his robes and lifted three silver coins. "See? They are all I have left, but I would gladly give them to have my wife be healthy again."

The coins shined in the moonlight and were beautiful to Judas. This was the sign he was looking for. He grabbed them and quickly put them in his purse under his tunic.

Judas put his arm around the man as if he was his best friend. "I will personally see to it that your wife will be as good as when she was young."

"Do you swear?" the man asked.

Judas flashed a reassuring smile. "I swear by all the gold in the temple."

Early the next morning, Andrew found his brother sitting by a small brook that flowed from the lake. Simon threw in one pebble after another, deep in thought.

"Simon, I've been looking everywhere for you." he said. His brother did not respond. Frustrated at his silence, Andrew decided to have the conversation by himself. "*Good to see you, Andrew.* Yes, it's good to see you too, Simon. *What have you been up to this morning?*

Oh not much, just frantically running around this little village because I've been worried sick about my brother. How about you? *Just throwing pebbles into this brook here*—"

"Did you hear what he called me?"

Andrew decided to feign ignorance. "What, you mean the rock?"

Simon looked coldly at his brother. "No. The *other* name."

Andrew tried his best to shrug it off. "Oh. *That*. Well, I might have. But I doubt the others even—"

"Hello, Andrew!" Philip called from the distance. "I see you found your brother." He waved to Simon. "Hello, Satan!"

Simon threw a pebble at him. It missed far to the left.

"Good thing you fish better than you throw. The Master is waiting."

Simon turned away from him and shrugged.

"He specifically said he wouldn't start without Peter."

"We'll be right there, just give us a minute," Andrew said. Philip headed back to the house.

Simon threw another pebble in the brook. "Do you remember what the Master said in Capernaum? That one of us was a devil? From the moment he said it, I was afraid it was me. Turns out I was right."

Normally, mentioning the devil was enough to set Andrew in a panic. But his concern for his brother superseded his fear. "Don't be stupid," he said. "The Master said you were the rock upon which the gates of hell would not prevail. One comment said in anger doesn't take that all away. He doesn't think that about you. And neither do I."

Andrew sat next to his brother. Now it was his turn to throw a pebble into the water. "This probably wouldn't have happened if I hadn't asked you to talk to the Master in the first place."

Simon shook his head. "I'm sure I would have said it eventually. I have the tendency to speak before I think."

"Really? I hadn't noticed."

After a pause, they both broke into laughter.

Simon leaned back and sighed, staring at the pale blue sky above them. "Why me, Andrew?"

Andrew shrugged. "Why any of us?" He exhaled a deep breath, and emotion welled up within him. "Brother, I must confess something to you," Andrew said.

Simon looked at him. "What is it?"

"I've been jealous of you," Andrew said.

"What?"

"From the moment Jesus invited you, James, and John into Jairus's house and left me outside. I wondered what I did wrong."

"Andrew, I—"

"No, it's all right," he said. "But now you're *Peter*. And Jesus is the Messiah. And we're going to Jerusalem where he'll be killed? What will happen to us?"

Simon put his hand on Andrew's shoulder and looked at him. "I don't know what being 'Peter' means. I don't know what is going to happen to us. But know this: I will *always* be your brother."

Andrew found comfort in his brother's eyes. Simon gently slapped him on the face the same way their father did when they were boys. Andrew felt peace. Simon had a way of making everyone around him feel secure. He might not know that about himself, but the other fishermen did. And then Andrew realized: *This is why he is the rock.*

"Let's go, *Peter*," Andrew said. They stood up and headed back to the house.

The town turned out in large numbers to hear Jesus preach and many were healed. Word went around the region that he was there, and people started to make their way toward Kela to see him. There were many people, but not so many that Jesus felt overwhelmed by the numbers. He was pleased to find his message was welcomed with joy and the ministry was fruitful.

The evenings, on the other hand, were difficult to bear. Every night, Jesus took his apostles in the synagogue and gave them hard teachings, bracing them for what was to come.

"If anyone wants to be a follower of mine, let him renounce himself and take up his cross and follow me," he taught. Jesus had said those words before, but now they took on a deeper and more troubling significance.

"What does it gain for someone to gain the world but lose their soul?" Jesus asked. "And indeed, what can anyone offer in exchange for his life? For if anyone in this sinful and adulterous generation is ashamed of me and my words, I will be ashamed of him when I come in the glory of my Father and his angels."

Jesus kept a steady eye on each of the apostles, and prayed for them vigorously. He made sure to have quiet moments with each one as the week progressed. He knew they struggled. Some doubted that he could be the Messiah. Those who did believe had a hard time accepting the type of Messiah he claimed to be.

His main focus was on Peter. The mantle of leadership was heavy on his shoulders. Jesus knew his rebuke had stung him deeply and that self-doubt ate at him. When Simon walked on the water, the wind and waves distracted him and he almost drowned. Even now Jesus could tell the fisherman was starting to turn his head.

Something needed to be done to keep Peter's eyes fixed on him. *My Father's voice helped him once,* Jesus thought. *Maybe it can do so again.*

In the middle of the night, Simon awoke with a violent shake. "*Peter, I command you to get up!*" said a frustrated whisper.

"How dare—" he began to say, but his voice was muted by a hand quickly placed over his mouth. As his eyes adjusted to the darkness, he realized it was Jesus. James and John stood behind him.

"Grab a heavy tunic and follow quietly," Jesus told him. "We have a long journey ahead. Do not wake the others."

As Simon reached for his tunic, he saw Jesus lean over Andrew who slept next to him.

"Are you awake?" Jesus asked him.

Andrew muttered something.

"Your brother, James, John, and I are going on a trip. We will be back late in the evening, maybe tomorrow. You're in charge."

Andrew muttered something else, then rolled over.

The moon was full and the four of them quietly walked through the courtyard, careful not to rouse the animals that slept. They gently closed the door behind them and made their way north through the town.

"Master, where are we going?" Simon asked.

Jesus smiled and pointed to the top of the mountain. "Up," he said.

Simon, James, and John looked at each other in shock.

"How far up?" James asked.

"Follow me," was the only answer they got.

The journey was slow. *This is why I spent my life on the water,* Simon thought. They zigzagged their way up the slope of one of the lower peaks, walking up steep trails. At times the slope became so severe they had to climb and pull each other up.

They often ran out of breath and stopped numerous times. Jesus and John fared the best. Simon did all right. James had the toughest time.

Everyone was covered with sweat. The sun rose and arched over their head as the morning turned into the afternoon. Dark storm clouds threatened, but only a light rain appeared. The water slowly drenched their clothes, right down to their inner tunic, and made them heavier with weight.

The clouds hung low, and eventually they hiked into them. The path became treacherously narrow and they could only see the person in front of them.

"Don't be afraid," Jesus called out. "We are almost there."

Simon heard the sound of rocks falling. He looked behind him and saw James lose his balance. He grabbed James's shoulder and threw him against the rocky ledge. Small stones and dirt were loosened upon the impact and showered the fishermen's heads. The sack he carried fell off his shoulder and disappeared into grey blackness.

They leaned against the wall for a moment, stunned at what would have been a deadly fall. Simon kept his friend's shoulder in an iron grip, until James gently nodded his thanks. Simon turned back to the path and could see no one in front of him.

"Master? John?" he called. There was no response but a roll of thunder and an increase of wind.

They continued their climb. Within a few moments, the wind died down and the fog disappeared. They found themselves on a plateau *above* the clouds. Jesus and John were there, admiring the view.

The sun quickly dropped out of sight to the west, and darkness settled in. James plopped down on the ground and wrung out his robe. "I feel like a prune," he said, observing his waterlogged hands. The ground was muddy underneath him.

"Speaking of prunes," Jesus said, "what have we got to eat?"

"Dropped my sack on the way up here," James said. "It had most of the food."

"I have some bread," Simon said. But when he pulled it out, it was soggy and fell apart in his hands.

John had some fruit that survived the journey, and they ate. As the sun dropped from the sky so did the temperature. They were cold, wet, hungry, and exhausted. "How high are we?" Simon asked.

"High enough," Jesus said. "Let's get some rest."

It was the best news he heard all day. The dark blue sky faded into black and the stars shone brightly above their heads. They lay on their backs and looked up to the heavens.

"Look up into the sky and count the stars if you can," Jesus said. *"So too will your descendants be."* Simon knew the quote from his childhood. It was what God said to Abraham when he made His covenant with him.

"That's a lot of stars," John said.

The four of them moved close to stay warm and slowly fell into sleep.

Simon felt something move beside him and thought it was Rachael. But the cold mountain air quickly reminded him that he was nowhere near his home or wife. Looking up to the sky, he noted that the stars and moon had moved but the sun had not yet risen.

He lifted his head and saw Jesus standing a short distance away, arms lifted in prayer. Simon's muscles ached and his entire body fought the idea of being awake. Every movement brought a blast of cold air into his tunic, which was still wet. *I'll just wait until the sun rises*, he thought. His mind went back to Rachael and Capernaum, imaging the softness of his pillow and the smell of bread.

Simon's eyes were half open, gazing upon the night sky. The stars seemed brighter somehow. A cloud hovered overhead, brilliant white. Rain fell from the cloud in slow motion, reflecting sunlight as it fell.

But there was no sunlight. And it was not rain. Slowly, like a feather, pieces of light fell from the cloud and landed upon Simon. Whatever it touched became immediately dry and warm, until

Simon's robes felt like he just pulled them off a rope on a bright summer's day. The mud beneath him turned into dirt.

He sat up and rubbed his eyes, not believing what he saw. Jesus stood before him, bathed in the light that fell from the cloud. Simon looked to the others to see if he was dreaming. John was awake and tried to rouse his brother.

"What?" James asked. He sat up and immediately fell on his face in amazement.

Jesus stood transfigured before them, clothed in a white brighter than any wool Simon had ever seen. It looked like Jesus, but at the same time it didn't. It looked *better* than him.

And he was not alone.

There were two people, also clothed in white, standing beside him. *Are they angels?* Simon wondered. The three of them talked while flakes of light gently fell to the ground around them like pedals off a flower. The mountain peaks and the starry night gave a majestic background to the picture. It was, quite simply, the most beautiful thing he had ever seen.

Simon thought he heard music, or at least the echoes of music, as he strained to listen to their conversation. Jesus turned to the man on his right and mentioned his name.

Moses.

Simon's heart almost stopped. The man was old, with a long beard and rays of light that shone from his head. His prominent nose stood out above a square jaw, and his beard accentuated the sharp angles of his face. He was tall, taller than Jesus and the other man. In his hands he held a large staff. *The staff that parted the Red Sea?*

Moses talked with Jesus about his upcoming exodus. Then the man to the left of Jesus spoke up. This man was shorter, but stronger—a hairy man with a belt of leather around his waist. Whereas Moses looked sharp and regal, this man looked like a wild animal. There was something reckless and dangerous about him that inspired fear and awe at the same time.

Jesus spoke his name: *Elijah.*

John fainted. James buried his head in the ground and outstretched his hands, tears streaming from his face. Simon stared in amazement. Never had he imagined such glory or beauty. He wanted to stay in that moment forever.

It was impossible for him to tell how long they talked, but eventually their conversation came to an end. John had come to and was on his knees, clutching his chest. James never moved.

Don't go, Simon thought. He hadn't dared to speak, but as they said goodbye to each other he couldn't help it.

"It is so good for us to be here!" he said. They all turned and looked at him, as if noticing him for the first time. He felt undone by their gaze. *What am I saying?* "Master, if you want me to, I could build three shelters. One for you, one for Moses, and one for Elijah."

Moses looked at Simon and then at Jesus. Jesus nodded.

Then the cloud above them burst forth a light so blinding it pushed them to the ground. And from the cloud they heard a voice.

"THIS IS MY BELOVED SON, WITH WHOM I AM WELL PLEASED. LISTEN TO HIM."

Simon immediately recognized the voice. It was the same voice he heard whisper on the water. It was the voice of the Father.

He knew that no one could see the glory of God and live. But he was so ravished by the beauty he saw that he would have chosen that death over any pleasure he could experience in this life. Simon opened his eyes and looked at his hands that were beside his face on the dirt. He was still alive.

He looked up. The sun shone brightly and it was a clear day. Jesus stood alone, no longer dressed in glory but in his plain beige and brown robes. His eyes were closed and his face had the look of ecstasy. He opened his eyes, looked at Simon, and smiled.

Simon stood. On hearing his movement, James and John looked up and realized they were alone. Simon walked forward with trembling legs and fell on his knees before Jesus. James and John lay a few paces back, prostrate on the ground.

For a long time, no one said a word.

When they did speak, they could only use clips of words and phrases. It was a while before they could put full sentences together. At times they laughed like drunkards and then fell into a solemn silence. Tears came and went—they had no idea why. They had nothing in their life to compare the experience to. They were totally and utterly amazed.

Eventually, Simon found his voice again. "Why do the scribes say that Elijah must come first?"

Jesus smiled. "He already came."

John gasped with sudden realization. "John the Baptist?"
Jesus nodded.

James, who had just found the strength to stand, had to sit down again.

Simon breathed heavily. He had been a disciple of Elijah, and now was the head disciple of the Messiah! It was greater than anything he could have even fantasized about.

But the man he saw next to Jesus didn't look like the Baptist. "John was Elijah?" he asked.

"He played the part," Jesus said. "Elijah is indeed coming and will come again, but I tell you that in the Baptist he has come already. They did not recognize him and treated him as they pleased." His face grew sullen. "I will suffer a similar fate."

Jesus looked intently at Simon, and Simon could still see the transfigured glory in his eyes. "I *will* be delivered into the power of men, and they will put me to death. But on the third day, I will rise again."

He didn't want to hear it. But the words of the Father, "LISTEN TO HIM," spoke to his heart as loudly as "*Messiah*". He nodded. Simon wasn't sure what would happen or what "rising again" even meant, but believed in faith that what Jesus said was true. He would not oppose or rebel—he would follow.

Jesus swore them to secrecy about what had just happened. He got no argument. Who would believe them anyway? They turned to go back the way they came and were struck at the beautiful landscape that lay before them. The clouds were gone and they could see as far as the sea of Galilee and beyond.

"It that Jerusalem?" John asked, pointing out into the distance.

Jesus laughed at his enthusiasm. "No, you can't see it from here. But it is that way," he said, and aimed John's finger toward the right direction.

"Where are we going now, Master?"

Jesus paused before giving his reply. "Down," he said.

"To Jerusalem?" Simon asked.

"Not just yet," Jesus replied. "Let's go home for a few months first. We'll go to Jerusalem for the Passover with everyone else."

They hadn't eaten, but weren't hungry. The trip down would be much quicker than the way up, especially with such beautiful weather. Jesus and John led the way. James motioned for Simon to go before him, but Simon said, "Oh no, I'm not going to have you fall on me." James laughed and slapped him hard on the back, then started down the mountain.

Simon was the last to leave the plateau. He looked back to where Moses and Elijah had stood.

"Sim—I mean, Peter! Let's go!" James said.

The path sloped down before him. Simon breathed in the peace of the mountaintop, knowing that there was doubt, confusion, and despair down below. He was reluctant to leave.

The voice of the Master called to him: "Peter?"

And he began the journey down.

SUNDAY

Luke 19:28-38

From his view atop the southeast tower of Antonian Fortress, the young Roman soldier was awe-struck by the majesty of the Jewish Temple. Its enormous white marble walls were trimmed with ornate wreaths of gold. Before coming to Jerusalem, someone mentioned that the Jewish Temple stood taller than anything even in Rome. "I'll have to see it to believe it," said the doubting soldier.

Now he did.

Its huge marble face reminded him of a tomb. Their temple stood in the center of a large courtyard, which had walls that broke the space into smaller courts.

His admiration for the Jewish Temple only fueled his hatred for the Jewish people. They did not deserve such beauty. They bickered among each other, had bizarre eating and cleaning rituals, and mutilated their young boys in a manner that made him thank the gods he was Roman.

After being in Jerusalem for three months he decided it was as bad, if not worse, than they said it was. The Roman fortifications at Jerusalem were comprised of two kinds of soldiers: the young who weren't related to someone who could get them a better assignment, and the old who were sent there as punishment. He was one of the young ones and hoped (like most) to be gone in a few years.

The soldier saw something in the distance that troubled him. He bounded down stone steps to report to the centurion, Longinus. Longinus was the only man who seemed to *enjoy* being in Jerusalem. He sat at a wooden table with a few other senior soldiers. There was wine, and it was late in the afternoon. The soldier didn't want to interrupt their revelry, but after a few moments decided it had to be done.

"Sir, a report from the tower!" He stood at attention and struck his chest with his right fist.

The centurion turned toward the guard with a serious expression and looked at him with his one good eye. "Riot in the Temple?"

"No, sir. A large group of people heading toward the city from the northeast."

"You're supposed to be watching the Temple," the centurion said.

The young guard's heart beat heavy in his chest. "Yes, sir."

"The Temple is to the south of us, isn't it?"

"Yes, sir."

"So why are you looking to the north?"

The warm sweat he had gathered by running down the tower stairs had now turned into a cold chill. He stared at the centurion but tried not to. Longinus was a frightening man to look at. Scars arched across his large shaved head, and his right eye was a murky white puddle.

"I... I... I..."

The centurion suddenly stood and the wooden chair flew backward as he did. "Are you making fun of my eye?" he said.

"No sir! No sir! I would never do that! Sir!"

At this, the other soldiers howled and fell off their chairs. Even Longinus began to laugh. The guard realized that the joke was on him, but was still too petrified to react.

Longinus grabbed a wineskin and took a long swig. He wiped his mouth and said, "All right, soldier, spit it out."

"A large group of people coming from the northeast, sir."

One of the soldiers who had been sitting at the table turned his ugly face toward the young man. His name was Quintus, captain of the Roman soldiers and second-in-command. "Have you been informed of the upcoming Jewish feast, soldier?"

"Yes, sir."

"You're going to see a lot of Jews heading for the city these next few days."

"I understand, sir."

"So why are you reporting this to us as if it is something important?"

The soldier felt as if his knees were about to buckle. There was a part of him that thought, *just say you are sorry and leave.* But then he felt like he would be derelict in his duty.

"They seem to be marching, sir. In large numbers."

This got the centurion's attention. "How many hundreds?"

"More like thousands. They come from a village outside the city."

"Bethany," Quintus said. "Do think it's the Zealots?"

Longinus had too much to drink and steadied himself on the table. "The Zealots are cowards," he said. "They hide in shadows and strike when nobody's looking. They wouldn't march on us in the afternoon and there aren't enough Jews who like them enough to make that big of a crowd. Take some soldiers and check it out."

Quintus gave a slight bow and put his fist to his chest. Longinus dismissed him with a wave of his hand but did not return the salute. The young soldier began to head back up the stairs to his post but Quintus grabbed him by the shoulder. "You're with me," he said.

Six other soldiers mounted horses. There were two gates to the fortress: the western gate that headed into the city, and the eastern gate that faced out. They spurned their horses to a gallop as they exited the city and in a short time came upon the crowd.

The young soldier halted his horse and listened to their chants. "What are they yelling? *Ho-sawn-yah?*"

"It's an acclimation for a king," Quintus said.

The soldier reacted in alarm. "Is this one going to try to overthrow Herod?"

Quintus laughed and pointed to the skinny man on a donkey in the middle of the crowd. "If he is, then someone had better get him a real horse."

"Hosanna! Hosanna to the son of David!" the people cried. They waved palm branches in the air and laid their cloaks down in front of the ass that carried Jesus. Peter and James were, as usual, in front trying to clear a path for the Master. The other apostles surrounded him on the side and back.

"Blessed is he who comes in the name of the Lord!" a man shouted. James pushed him to the side.

"Hard to 'come in the name of the Lord' with all these people in the way," James said over the din of the crowd. The few hundred people who began with them in Bethany had grown into a few thousand.

"At least they're not trying to kill us," Peter said.

"Well, not *yet*." James pointed to a group of Pharisees and Sadducees who stood by the Golden Gate. Peter could tell by their body language that it wasn't going to be a warm welcome.

There was lots of pushing and shoving. Matthew fell into Simon the Zealot, who caught him. His face was red with embarrassment. "Thank you, friend," he said.

"Are you buddies with pigs now?" said a voice from behind Simon. He was about to strike the man who said it, but then he recognized him.

"Reuben!" he said, and they embraced. But their joyful greeting was interrupted by a sea of people that pushed against them. "This is a bad time, Reuben," Simon said, "Can I find you later?"

"I'll find you," Reuben said. Then Reuben pressed his lips close to Simon's ear. "*Barabbas* sends his regards," he whispered. Then he disappeared into the crowd.

Hearing Barabbas's name sent chills down Simon's spine and brought back a flood of memories of a life he once lived. Of all the Zealots, Barabbas was the most dedicated, the most respected (at least among the other Zealots), and the most violent. A few years ago, he would have been thrilled to be recognized by him. But not now.

He looked at Matthew, worried that he might have heard. Matthew was busy trying to move people out of the way. *Why should I feel guilty?* Simon thought. *I haven't done anything.*

But the guilt remained. He felt like his old life had just reached out and wanted to pull him back in.

Judas couldn't help but stare at the well dressed Pharisees and temple priests who came to witness the spectacle. Their fine garments made him realize how pedestrian he looked, and felt even more shame that his "Messiah" rode on a donkey with his usual off white and brown tunic. He thought he could hear them laughing, though they were a distance away and the crowd chanted so loudly he could hardly think straight.

The crowd surged, and a woman fell into him. "Idiot! Watch where you are going!" he shouted. Little James looked at him disapprovingly, and Judas reminded himself he needed to be careful not to betray his true feelings. He looked again at the richly dressed Pharisees and saw their disciples standing behind them, arms crossed in judgment. *What I wouldn't give to be there instead of here,* he thought.

At the back of the circle were Philip, Thomas, and John. Peter and James were so impenetrable at the front that many tried to reach Jesus from behind. In the chaos, the apostles found themselves bumping into each other more than once.

"All right, listen!" Philip said to the other two. "Thomas, stay on my right and John, stay on my left. Let's keep moving!" An old woman grabbed Philip by the tunic and nearly choked him until he was able to wrestle it free.

He rubbed his neck and looked to his left, where he saw Thomas coming up behind John. Anger built up in him. "Can't you follow a simple instruction? You are to be on my RIGHT! Over HERE!"

"I thought *I* was supposed to be on your right," Thomas said. Philip looked to his right and, sure enough, Thomas was there. Philip did a double take. He looked back to his left, and he saw Thomas standing there also. It was hard to breathe with all the people surrounding them. *Am I hallucinating?*

"Thomas!" cried the one.

"Brother!" cried the other. And the twins embraced and laughed.

Philip's relief of not losing his mind was quickly disrupted by another wave of people that threatened to knock them over. "It's great to see you, David," he said, "but can it wait?"

"Need help?" David asked.

"Yes!" both Philip and Thomas said. David smiled and worked with the others to form a protective circle around Jesus.

"You see how they respond to him," Rabbi Dov said. "He grows more popular with every trip to Jerusalem."

Annas stayed quiet, but ran his fingers through his long, silver beard. He observed the scene with alarm before him, but did not want to give the appearance of being *too* concerned. "He comes, he goes, just like every other peasant who doesn't have the sense to live in the Holy City."

"I have never seen a peasant enter the city like this," Dov said. "With every trip to Jerusalem, he becomes more popular."

"With the visitors, yes, but not the inhabitants."

"You *do* realize that there are more people who live outside of Jerusalem than there are who live in it," Dov said.

Yes, but who cares? Annas thought. "I haven't been high priest for years now," he said, throwing up his hands in mock surrender. "You should talk to my son-in-law, Caiaphas."

"No!" Rabbi Dov said. "You are the man! When you were high priest, you fought strongly against heretics and Zealots alike, made peace with the Romans, and courageously upheld the Law. You have Caiaphas's respect, and ours as well. If you acted, there would be none to stop you." The other Pharisees around him echoed similar sentiments.

It was exactly what Annas wanted to hear. He knew of his power and influence—he just wanted to make sure that others knew it, too. It was difficult when he surrendered the office of high priest. He hoped to play the puppet master with his daughter's groom, but Caiaphas proved too strong willed for it. But this crisis of the carpenter provided an opportunity to regain some of the power he once had.

He bowed humbly. "I'll see what I can do," he said.

Finally, they made it to the Golden Gate, the largest and most beautiful entrance into the city. Peter stared at the large pillars of bronze that shone like gold and the enormous, ornate doors that were so large that they needed twenty men to open them.

They slowed the pace. There were almost three thousand people with them now, and the crowd was forced to narrow as they came through.

The gate was tall and formed a huge arch at the top. Peter thought of a psalm:

O gates, lift high your heads
Grow higher, ancient doors
Let him enter, the king of glory!

As a child, he imaged the Messiah would be so large that even these gates would have to expand to let him in. But as his eyes went at the top of the arch and then behind him at the carpenter on a donkey, he had to laugh.

Who would have thought?

They passed through the gates and into the outer wall, which was more like a building than a wall. It was comprised of many rooms, most of them used by soldiers. The shouts of *hosanna* nearly deafened him in that enclosed space. His eyes adjusted to shadows and torchlight as they pushed through.

When they came to the other side, his ears rang from the noise and he squinted to adjust to daylight again. The crowd spilled into the courtyard with chants and cheers. It was an incredible experience. But the numbers that seemed so vast coming through the Golden Gate suddenly felt small. The courtyard of the Temple could easily hold tens of thousands of people.

The Temple stood tall before them. It glowed with the light of the setting sun behind it. A purple sky contrasted brilliantly with its white marble face. Smoke from the evening sacrifice ascended from the inner court and floated slowly upwards. People arched their necks to see the full view.

With the exception of the few thousand who came with Jesus, the Temple was fairly empty with most people having gone home to eat. The soldiers followed the crowd on horseback, eyes moving back and forth. Peter felt uncomfortable beneath their stares. In his hometown, the soldiers were hardly ever seen. Here, they were everywhere.

Jesus allowed the cheering to continue as the rest of the crowd came through the gate. He blessed them and encouraged everyone to have a good meal and prepare well for the upcoming Passover feast. Then he got back on the donkey and left the city in the same way he came. Peter and James made their way to the front of the crowd again, but it was much easier going than it was coming.

The fishermen sat against the wall outside Simon the leper's house in Bethany. As Peter looked to the southwest, he saw the walls of Jerusalem with the Temple behind them. He was lost in its beauty when James nudged him.

"I think he means you," James said.

Peter turned and saw a young boy hold a plate of pomegranates.

"Are you Simon? I was told to give this to you. It's from your wife."

Peter smiled. In the months since he was named head of the apostles, he no longer felt like Simon the fisherman. He was Peter, the rock. The only one who still called him Simon was Rachael.

He reached for the plate and nodded his head. "Thank her for me," he said. The boy bowed and left.

Peter took a bite out of the fruit and thought about Rachael. Though absent more these past two years than in their entire married life, he was more deeply in love with her than ever before. He knew his travels were hard on Rachael, but she never complained. She made it easier for him to follow Jesus—and for that he was truly grateful.

Philip cleared his throat and Peter realized all eyes were upon him. He bit off most of the pomegranate and threw the remaining piece at Philip. Unlike the stone he threw by the river, this one hit him square in the head. Everyone laughed.

Matthew came out. "Has anyone seen Simon?"

"The leper?" John asked.

"We really should call him the *former* leper," James said. Jesus had healed him on one of his earlier trips to Jerusalem.

"No, the *apostle*," Matthew said.

"He's probably around here somewhere," Peter said. "Good luck trying to find him." Bethany was overrun with people from Capernaum and other cities and towns. Every able Jew and their family had made the annual pilgrimage to Jerusalem for the Passover feast. Every house and courtyard was full, and people lined the streets to sleep.

"Well, let me know if you see him," he said.

"Good luck," Peter said. Matthew went back into the house.

Bartholomew stretched. "What a day," he said. "I've never seen people so excited before."

"I was afraid that they might turn on us," John said. "You know, like Jesus said they would."

John was too young to realize it was inappropriate to break a jovial mood with such words. For a moment no one said anything.

"It was a good day," Peter said. "And it's worth being thankful for. All we can do is take one day at a time."

They agreed and the subject was quickly changed. But John had given voice to the fear Peter had in his heart and he wasn't able to sleep that night without thinking about it.

MONDAY

Mark 11:12-19, John 12:1-8

In the morning, they headed into Jerusalem. Jesus walked among the apostles to avoid attention from the crowds. There was no triumphal procession into the city this day. He was a pilgrim like the rest.

The morning meal they had was sparse and Jesus felt hungry. In the distance, he saw a fig tree in leaf. It was an unusual sight because it was not the season for figs. His mouth watered at the thought of eating the fruit.

"Let's go this way," he said.

They headed north and arrived at the tree. Its gray bark looked soft in the morning sun and its branches cast a large shadow on Jerusalem's wall. The tree was full and beautiful, and stood at twice the height of James. Sheep grazed around the grass where it stood.

Jesus grabbed one branch with excitement, then another. He continued this all the way around the tree and grew more discontent with each branch. There were no figs to be found, just leaves.

"May you never bear fruit again," Jesus said.

He led them toward the Sheep Gate, a wide entrance that shepherds used to bring lambs into Jerusalem for sacrifice. The Pool of Siloam was on their right (used to wash the lambs) and Antonian Fortress was on their left. Thousands of lambs were everywhere, ready for the slaughter. They passed through the gate and beheld the Temple. It faced east and the rising sun shone so bright against it that it reflected a blinding white light. The twelve gasped in amazement and began to talk about how beautiful it was.

Unlike his followers, Jesus' attention wasn't focused on the Temple but on the large group of people who were assembled in front of it. In the distance he could see animals and wooden carts, and he could hear the sound of men shouting.

The closer they got to the Temple, the denser the crowd became. The stench that struck his nostrils was only slightly less offensive than the noise that hit his ears. The courtyard was filled with sounds, not of psalms, but of people haggling over prices. Cages of turtledoves hung from carts. Bulls and heifers groaned against a wooden gate that gave them no room to move. Sheep roamed everywhere, and their droppings followed with them.

Large tables were lined with money boxes and those working behind them were elaborately dressed. Though the bleating, chirping, and groaning of animals made quite a noise, it was nothing in comparison to the shouts that came from the people at these tables. Those selling the animals accepted nothing but the Jewish currency that only the moneychangers could offer, and these men had no sympathy for the poor pilgrim who couldn't afford the high exchange rate.

Jesus felt a burning in his chest and began to breathe heavily. He had seen this many times before with every Passover feast, and each time he restrained his anger. But no more. This was not some side street or marketplace. This was his Father's house.

He decided to speak to them in a language they would understand.

Walking into the Temple courts was something Peter could never tire of. It was lined with enormous candelabras made of pure gold and almost ten times the height of man. Banners hung from pillars of bronze that lined the outer court and glowed with the light of the morning sun that began to ascend over the eastern wall.

There were many animals in pens, in cages, tied to tables, or just roaming around. Men and women haggled loudly with merchants, but Peter was used to that. The court was full of people and Peter knew it would only get busier as Passover approached.

Wide, circular stairs led the way into the inner court, and behind its large doors stood the Holy of Holies, the place where God dwelt. Peter couldn't wait to bring the Passover lamb into the inner court and get a closer look at it. It was the tallest, most dramatic part of the Temple. Within it hung a large tapestry that separated the people from the presence of God. This was where Abraham sacrificed Isaac. This was where the Ark of the Covenant once dwelt. This was where they became God's chosen people.

Everything was so large and majestic that Peter felt out of scale, like he was a tenth of his usual size. He had to arch his neck back to take in the whole view.

A man bumped into him. "Watch where you're going!" he snapped.

"Sorry," Peter said. He looked at James and shrugged. Then he looked at Jesus…

…but Jesus was gone.

"James, where is the Master?"

James turned and surveyed the crowd. The other apostles grew anxious at Jesus' disappearance.

"I thought he was right behind me!" Andrew said.

"Has someone taken him?" John said.

"Let's spread out," the Zealot suggested.

"There he is!" James said.

Peter looked toward the entrance of the courtyard and saw Jesus move through people to get to them. He took a breath of relief.

"Master, please don't leave us again. You had us worried," Peter said. Then he noticed a piece of leather hanging from Jesus' hand. It kind of looked like a whip. "What is that?" he asked.

"A whip," Jesus said. "Stay here and do not interfere." Then he passed the apostles and disappeared into the crowd, heading toward the animals and moneychangers.

"Did he say, *a whip*?" Philip asked.

The crack of leather that pierced the air answered his question.

The next few minutes were utter chaos. People screamed in anger and in fear. Bulls and heifers broke from their pens and stampeded through the crowd. Turtledoves swirled around in the air before disappearing in the bright blue sky. Sheep bleated loudly and ran about in confusion, causing many people to trip over them as they tried to escape.

Hundreds of people ran toward the doors of the outer court and pushed against Peter and the others as they left. Little James and Thomas fell on the floor and a number of men and women went with them. A large ram began to bolt and chase its owner with its huge horns. He screamed and hid behind the pillars to escape its wrath.

More cracks of the whip. Peter saw some men try to stop Jesus, but he swung the whip around his head and they dove for cover. Jesus went to the moneychangers' tables and lifted them off the ground. The men fell backward on the steps. Their tables spun in the air and splintered on the floor. The *clink-click* of a thousand coins echoed in the courtyard as people dove to collect the money.

Peter felt like he was frozen in place, unable to comprehend what he witnessed. The outer court of the Temple looked like a battlefield of broken cages, overturned tables, frightened animals, and shocked people. In the middle stood Jesus, who looked around to see if anyone would oppose him. None did.

Jesus pointed his whip at the moneychangers. "Get all of this out of here and stop using my Father's house as a marketplace!"

It grew very quiet. One of moneychangers crawled on the ground, so obsessed with collecting coins that he didn't pay attention to the Master's words. He followed a trail of money to the foot of Jesus. Then he looked up in horror and melted backward under Jesus' angry gaze.

Jesus threw the whip on the floor and walked away in disgust. He walked past the apostles and headed out of the court.

For a moment, no one moved. Then Peter ran to catch up to Jesus, and the other apostles did the same.

The stunned silence turned into angry shouts. Men ran toward Jesus waving their fists and demanding money.

"You destroyed my cart!"

"All my animals have escaped!"

"Just who do you think you are?"

Peter jumped in front of Jesus and the apostles formed a circle around their Master to keep him from being attacked. They tried to move him away from the angry crowd but a man with a round face and square beard blocked the way. He was so fat that Peter had a tough time moving him aside.

"How dare you insult the Temple of God!" he said.

"Tear it down," Jesus said, "and in three days I can rebuild it."

This set off an explosion of arguments. Insulting the temple was akin to insulting God himself. Peter was finally able to push by the fat man and lead Jesus toward the Temple gate.

The inner chamber of the high priest's palace had no windows. Oil lamps hung symmetrically from the ceiling, throwing light on tapestries and sacred relics that had been handed down over hundreds of years. There were plates from Solomon's original temple, brought back after the Babylonian exile. A sword hung on the wall that was used by King David. Against another wall were jars holding sacred texts that survived the Greek persecution.

The high priest stood by the large wooden table that sat in the middle of the room, face red with anger. Caiaphas was known for his calm disposition, so his advisors uneasily shifted as they waited for him to respond. Only Annas had a slight smile on his face. This was the reaction he was hoping for.

"Who does he think he is?" Caiaphas said, straining to keep his question under the level of a scream.

"The larger question is, what should we do about him?" Annas said.

Caiaphas looked coldly at his father-in-law. "Well father, *if you were high priest*, what would you do?" he asked.

Annas feigned a smile. "I would get rid of him."

"He will be hard to imprison with the people hanging on his every word."

"I'm not talking about imprisonment," he said grimly.

Caiaphas looked at him, dumbfounded at his implication. "The Romans would kill us."

"Herod could do it. He's done it before."

Caiaphas laughed. "Yes, and when he killed the Baptist, Pontius Pilate had a fit and threatened Herod that the next time he does something like that it could be *his* head on the platter. Or hadn't you heard?"

Annas hadn't, and it stung him that Caiaphas knew more about such things than he. "Then we'll let the Romans do it," he said quickly.

"I don't think the Romans are eager to do our dirty work," he replied.

Annas pointed to the direction of the Temple's courtyard. "You saw what he did! He becomes more aggressive with every trip to Jerusalem. They say the last time he was here he raised that man Lazarus from the dead!"

"You don't believe that nonsense, do you?"

"It doesn't matter what I believe. It matters what *they* believe."

Caiaphas thought about this. "I won't make this decision on my own. We need to bring in more people to discuss the matter."

Annas rolled his eyes. The former high priest had hoped Jesus' outburst in the courtyard would spurn Caiaphas on to immediate action. He sighed in realization that he would do nothing without the approval of others.

A messenger walked in the door and Caiaphas looked at him with an annoyed expression. "This is a private meeting," he said.

The man bowed. "It is important."

Caiaphas eyed him warily. "It's Malachi, isn't it?"

"Malchus, sir."

"What is your message?"

"Barabbas is in Jerusalem," Malchus said.

All grew silent at the news. Annas almost had to lean against the table to steady himself. "It will be a bloodbath..." he muttered.

"How do you know this?" the high priest asked. "Tell me everything."

"Last night, I observed Jesus and his disciples in Bethany, as ordered, when I recognized Reuben, son of Isaac, a known accomplice of Barabbas. He contacted one of Jesus' disciples, a Zealot named Simon, and they both headed toward Jerusalem. Seeing no activity with Jesus I decided to follow him. They met with Barabbas and others of his men in the eastern quarter of the city."

"Jesus is in league with Barabbas!" Annas said.

"Don't interrupt!" Caiaphas said. He beckoned the servant to continue.

"I don't think he is," he said, answering Annas's concern. "The disciple moved quietly away from Bethany, as if he didn't want to be discovered by the others. I couldn't hear what they were saying, but their conversation was intense. Then some of his men came upon my position, so I hid and only recently had an opportunity to escape undetected."

"You did well," Caiaphas said. "Go now and get some rest." The servant was clearly honored by the high priest's praise. He bowed and left.

Annas raised an eyebrow toward his son-in-law. "Having Jesus watched?"

"I'm not as foolish as you think I am," he said. "But now we have a bigger problem. If Barabbas tries to pull something, Rome will harshly retaliate."

"Do you think he's working with Jesus?"

"I'm not as worried about Jesus right now."

"You should be."

Caiaphas slammed his fist upon the table. "He's an uneducated peasant from Nazareth, isn't he? Do we not have the greatest scholars in the world in Jerusalem? Debate him. Humiliate him. Show the people the farce he is."

"And if that doesn't work?"

"We'll arrest him."

"And then?"

"We'll decide tomorrow, when we meet about it. Thank you, father. It was good that you brought this to my attention."

"But—"

"*Thank you,*" Caiaphas said. "As you can see, I have more pressing matters to attend to."

Annas bowed and left. He was desperate to know what would be done with Barabbas, but knew he had outstayed his welcome.

It was a cool, clear night, and the mood was festive. Cheers greeted Jesus and the apostles as they entered into the courtyard of Simon the leper's house. Peter was grateful to be away from the Temple after the day they had there.

The women were lined up and greeted them as they entered. There was Mary, the wife of Cleopas. There was Martha, the sister of Simon, and her sister Mary. It was hard not to admire Martha's beauty, and it only made her sister's defects that much more apparent. There was another Mary too, a woman from Magdala. She was thin with a long face and dark eyes. Peter didn't feel comfortable around her. Jesus had cast out not one but *seven* demons from her, and Peter could never forget the demonic howls that came from her mouth as Jesus prayed over her.

But finally, Peter came to the woman he cared most about.

"Rachael," he said. They embraced. It was good to be in her arms.

"How was your day?" Rachael asked. "I heard there was some kind of trouble in the Temple."

"Nothing we couldn't handle," he said.

Then she gave him that look. The *I-know-you're-lying-but-we'll-talk-about-it-later* look. She kissed his cheek and went into the kitchen with the other women.

Peter wished he was a better liar. He did not want Rachael to worry. But what should he have said? "*I spent the day in absolute terror that we would be arrested at any moment*," wasn't a good way to start the evening.

And besides, he didn't want to talk about it. The courtyard was set for a large feast. Food was spread out on many tables. Musicians joyfully played the lyre and flute in the corner. People buzzed with excitement at the chance to meet Jesus. There was no reason to dwell on the tension of the day. They were safe here.

Peter sat down on a bench and sighed as he ran warm water over his feet. His brother sat next to him and did the same. Peter noticed that Andrew's hands shook a bit as he wiped his feet clean. "Andrew, are you all right?"

"I'm fine," he said.

Peter noticed he didn't look him in the eye. He put his hand on his shoulder and felt it tense. "It's going to be all right, Andrew," he said. "Nothing is going to happen to the Master. Not while we're here."

And now Andrew did look at him. Peter had such strong memories of him as a boy it was hard to see him as a man. But the lines of worry on his face reminded him he wasn't a child anymore.

"But his warnings," Andrew said. "He will be arrested and killed? Why would he say such things?"

"So we would be on our guard," Peter said. "So we could prevent it from happening. And we will, Andrew. By my life, we will."

Andrew nodded. Peter's conviction seemed to bring him some peace.

"Come on, let's eat."

They got up and sat at a table that was quickly populated by the other fishermen. The music continued to play and they began to laugh together, especially when Philip mimicked the looks on the moneychanger's faces after Jesus flipped their tables over.

Peter looked at Jesus. He had never seen him so angry as when he was in the Temple, but now he seemed totally at peace. Jesus was a mystery to him. Sometimes it felt like the more time he spent with him, the less he knew.

A man came next to him. "May I eat here, or is it only for fishermen?"

Peter smiled. "We would be honored if you ate with us, Lazarus."

"Thank you," Lazarus said, and sat down. He looked very similar to Jesus in height and frame. Even his beard looked the same. The only major difference were his large ears that stuck out the side of his head.

"To be honest," Lazarus said in a low tone, "I'm just glad to sit with people who won't keep asking me about what it was like to be raised from the dead."

There goes my next question, Peter thought.

It had only been a few months since Jesus called Lazarus out of the tomb after being dead for four days. He was glad the others now knew Jesus had that power. But even after witnessing it, there were still some who remained unconvinced.

Peter scanned the courtyard to look for the other apostles. James, John, Andrew, Philip, and Bartholomew all sat near him. Simon and Jude stood in a corner, talking in private. Judas spoke to a well-dressed man from Arimathaea, a more recent follower. He could see Little James with their younger brother Joses and the back of Matthew's head.

He thought about Joses for a moment. He had the lean figure of James but the face of Matthew. Matthew had shared with Peter how Joses didn't share in his family's belief that Jesus was the Messiah, and how much that pained his heart. Was he jealous to be the only brother in his family to not be called as one of the twelve?

Twelve. Peter looked around the courtyard and counted the apostles. Someone was missing.

"Where's Thomas?" he asked.

"With his brother and the rest of his family. He'll be back in the morning," Philip said. Then the man who Peter thought was Matthew turned around, and he realized it wasn't Matthew at all, but his father Cleopas.

Before he could wonder where he was, Matthew appeared in the courtyard, clearly agitated. His eyes darted around until they rested on Peter and he moved with great haste toward him.

Peter stood as he approached. "What's wrong?"

"I just spoke with a friend at the temple," he whispered. "They're gathering the guards. And they know where we are, Peter. Apparently, they have been having us watched."

Peter swore and clenched his fist tightly. The others couldn't hear their conversation, but they could see by his body language that something was wrong. Conversations slowly began to stop as Peter walked to where Jesus was sitting and whispered in his ear.

Jesus saw the seriousness with which Peter approached and prayed for him. He knew these next few days would be the most trying of his life.

Peter knelt beside him. "Master, we should leave this place. You are in danger," he whispered.

Jesus shook his head. "It is not my time yet, Peter."

"But they might be coming for us *tonight*," Peter said.

"Let them come!" Simon the leper said in a loud voice. All in the courtyard were silent now and focused on them. "We will not let you go without a fight. They will have to kill us first."

"Agreed!" Lazarus said. Men began to stand and echoed similar sentiments.

Jesus put his hands out to silence them. "Thank you my friends, but it is not necessary. Nothing will happen this evening."

"I meant what I said, Lord," Simon said. "I would die before letting you be taken by them."

That is what I'm afraid of, Jesus thought. He looked in Simon's eyes and knew he meant every word of it. He loved Simon and his family, and it grieved him to think that harm might come to them. "It will not come to that, my friend. This is the last night we will be staying with you."

Simon looked hurt by the statement. "Where will you go? Where will you celebrate Passover?"

"Someplace safe."

"You will be safe if you stay here!"

"But *you* will not be."

Simon grew angry. "I was a leper and had nothing until you touched me. My brother was dead! Lying in a tomb until you called his name! And my sisters—"

"Yes," Jesus said. "Think of your sisters. Think of Martha and Mary. Think of their children."

"You might be killed!"

Jesus put a steady hand on Simon's shoulder and looked him in the eye. "There is nothing that can stop that now," he said.

He heard a gasp and the clang of a copper plate that fell to the ground. He turned his head and saw her. She looked at him with a stunned expression. Tears welled up in dark eyes. Her nose bent at an odd angle and her round face ended in a flat chin. Her black hair, long and straight, hung flatly off her head. She was a woman the world would never call attractive, but she was one of the most beautiful women Jesus had ever known.

"Mary," he said. But she turned and ran back to the kitchen.

"Forgive my sister," Simon said. "She—"

Jesus held up his hand to stop him. He opened his mouth to speak but did not know what to say.

His throat felt thick with emotion. Jesus had hoped to have one more night of celebration, one more night where he didn't have to worry about what was going to happen. But now he knew that moment was gone. The flute and the lyre would no longer play. There were none in the mood for singing.

The silence of the courtyard was broken by the sound of women crying in the kitchen. Out of the kitchen came Simon's sister Mary holding an alabaster jar. Her head was bent low. Her shoulders shook with every sob.

People respectfully moved out of her way. When she came to Jesus, she knelt and opened the jar. A strong smell of perfume filled the courtyard. It was intoxicating. She poured a little of it on his feet, then paused. Then she poured the entire contents on him and smashed the jar on the ground.

People in the courtyard gasped at her action.

"The fool woman just spent a year's wages!" he heard Judas say. He didn't speak loudly, but there was such silence in the courtyard that even a whisper seemed like a scream.

Eyes turned toward Judas and he quickly justified himself. "I'm just saying that we could have sold it to feed the poor."

"Leave her alone," Jesus said to him. "You have the poor with you always, you will not always have me." Judas briefly met his gaze and hung his head.

Jesus might have said more, but he felt something brush against his feet. He looked down and realized what Mary was doing. She bathed his feet in her tears and dried them with her hair.

Such love.

He did not try to stop her. He could see that people wanted to protest her actions. It was embarrassing. It was humiliating. That her love caused such a scandal only made it that much more sweet.

Jesus sat still and kept his gaze lovingly upon her. When she finished, she looked up at him. Her face was swollen from crying. Her eyes were red with tears. Mary's hair was a mess of water, dirt, and oil. She wiped her runny nose and tried to push her hair back, but made it only worse.

He looked into her puffy eyes. She tried to smile but the tears came again.

Jesus embraced her and did not let go until he felt her sobs subside. As she grew quiet, he whispered, "Don't be afraid."

She pulled back and nodded. Jesus kissed her on the cheek. Mary bowed, picked up the pieces of the jar, and went into the kitchen.

Sounds of revelry and song were heard outside in the street but in the courtyard no one moved. The aroma of costly perfume lingered heavy in the air. Women (other than Mary) returned to the courtyard with food, eyes red from tears. With food came conversation and Jesus motioned to the musicians to play again. They did, though more somberly than before. No one made any further comment on what occurred. There was nothing more to say.

When Rachael came by with food, Peter followed her into the kitchen and reached for her hand. She turned to him and collapsed in his arms, tears flowing freely.

"Simon, I am so scared. What is going to happen?" she said.

Peter was silent. He hadn't told her of the prophecies, not wanting to burden her before it was necessary. "Don't be afraid," he whispered to her. It was the only thing he could think of saying.

She looked up at him, eyes filled with tears. "But now you are leaving? Where will you go?"

"I go where he goes," Peter said. She opened her mouth to protest but he put a gentle finger on her lips. She closed her eyes and the tears rolled out. She again leaned into her husband.

"I am honored to be your wife," she said quietly.

"And I your husband," he said.

Now *he* felt the tears coming. He looked around to distract his sorrow and noticed the other women watching him. Embarrassed with such public affection, he began to push away from Rachael.

She pulled him back. "Not yet," she said.

He felt her shake under his large arms. He rested his head on hers. No longer caring about what others thought, he allowed himself to cry and bathed her head with his tears.

That night, Peter asked the two best fighters in the group, James and Simon the Zealot, to sleep with him in the courtyard near the door. Peter and Simon had swords. James had a large staff. Jesus said nothing would happen, but he didn't want to take any chances. They barred the door with a beam of wood for extra protection.

At the temple, Malchus gathered twenty guards. There was tension in the air. Caiaphas appeared and they bowed reverently before him. He slightly returned the bow, and turned to Malchus. "Is everything ready?"

Malchus stood at full attention. This was his best chance to impress the high priest. "Yes, sir," he said.

"And they know what to do? We can't have any mistakes."

"They understand."

He turned his gaze upon the temple guards. "Take him alive. No matter what happens. I don't care about his followers." They nodded their understanding and Caiaphas left.

The moon was almost full, and its silver light reflected brightly off the guard's spears and golden tunics. They walked over sleeping bodies in the streets of Jerusalem, and their boots echoed down the cobblestone paths of the city. Eventually the cobblestone made way for dirt, and the shadows from houses gave them more cover from the moonlight.

Their plan was simple: catch them by surprise, overwhelm them with greater numbers, and take the leader alive. After some walking, Malchus pointed to a door and they gathered around it.

"Open it," Malchus whispered. One of the guards tried, but the door was immovable.

"They must have a piece of wood blocking it on the inside," the guard explained.

"Break it down," Malchus commanded. The guards drew their swords.

Peter heard a voice on the other side of the door. Someone was trying to open it. Then something pounded on it. The men jumped to their feet as the door shook. Simon and Peter drew their swords. James held his staff at the ready.

"Who is there?" Peter said in a harsh whisper, trying his best not to awaken anyone.

"Open the door!" came a voice, heavy with breath.

"Reuben?" Simon asked. He reached to remove the wooden bar, but James put his hand on his shoulder.

"Is this a good idea?" James asked.

Simon shrugged him off. "He is a friend," he said. As soon as the beam was removed, the door burst open and Simon fell backward. Reuben held his sword over his head and swung down for a fatal blow. Simon raised his sword in the nick of time and sparks flew from the steel. James hit Reuben in the stomach with his staff and he fell to the ground. Then he kicked the sword from his hand and lifted him by his robe like a mother dog would carry her pup. Peter looked outside to see if there was anyone with him. The street was empty.

"Traitor!" Reuben said. "Betrayer!"

Even in the pale moonlight, Peter could see Simon's skin turn white. Simon stood with his sword pointed at Reuben's chest, but his eyes darted back and forth from Peter to James.

Peter recalled the words of Jesus that someone would betray him. He stared at Simon. "You?" he said.

Simon nervously shook his head, but he had the look of a man who had been caught.

Reuben twisted his body and James let him go. He fell to the ground but quickly got on his feet. Peter noticed that one side of his face was stained with blood, as was his tunic. He lifted his left arm and the robe fell to his elbow, showing a gash that still bled. "A gift from your friends at the Temple."

"What are you talking about?" Simon asked.

"I barely escaped with my life. How dare you betray Barabbas!"

"Barabbas?" Peter said. "Are you in league with that scum?"

Reuben laughed, and then coughed as he did so. "Didn't Simon tell you? We were all going to overthrow the Romans together. Weren't we, Simon?"

"It's a lie!" Simon said. "I agreed to nothing."

"You met with *Barabbas*?" James asked. He turned slightly toward Simon, and it was enough for Reuben to make his move. He elbowed James in the chest, then grabbed his staff. Reuben swung it at Simon's head but Peter raised his sword to block the staff in mid-air. Doubled over in pain, James reached up and grabbed Reuben by the collar and pulled him down hard.

Reuben fell flat on his back and his head slammed against the ground. Simon jumped on his chest and aimed his sword at his neck, ready to drive it through his throat.

"No!" Peter cried, stopping Simon from following through. Simon dropped his sword and his hand shook. He staggered backwards and fell on the ground.

Reuben tried to get up, but James's foot pushed him back in place. Reuben coughed up some blood. "You told them where we were," he muttered. "Now they'll kill him."

"I said nothing," Simon said.

"Are they coming after us?" Peter asked.

Reuben eyed him with contempt. "Do you think I care about you or your Rabbi from Nazareth?"

Peter nodded to James and he picked him up off the ground. Reuben cursed loudly as James threw him into the street. By now the most of the house was awake, as were the neighbors. Realizing he attracted too much attention, Reuben staggered away and ran into the darkness.

Simon the leper came into the courtyard. "What is going on?" he asked.

"Nothing," Peter said. "A friend of Simon's got a bit drunk, that's all. There's no problem here." He saw Rachael's concerned face appear by the stairway where the women were sleeping. She shot him a glance that said, *are you all right?* Peter nodded, and she with the others headed back to bed.

Peter and James sat on the ground. They breathed slowly as their heartbeats returned to normal. James moved and bent sharply in pain from where he was hit. Peter touched his shoulder, but James signaled he was all right.

Simon looked as one dead and stared blankly toward the door. Peter moved toward him and he cowered.

"I didn't betray anyone," he said. "Neither Jesus or Barabbas."

"But you met with him," James said.

Simon nodded. "Reuben and I… we go way back. He took me to Barabbas. He wanted to know if Jesus was the Messiah. I told him I didn't know."

"It was good that you lied to him," Peter said.

"I didn't lie to him! The truth is, *I don't know*." The fire began to return to Simon's voice. "You might have received some prophetic knowledge about it, but not me. Doesn't this whole thing strike you as bizarre? Why are we knocking down tables in the temple when we should be knocking together Roman heads?"

"So you side with Barabbas?" James said.

"No!" He realized his voice had gotten loud and went back to a whisper. "I told him that Jesus wasn't the man they were hoping for," he said quietly, "and that I wasn't either."

Peter stared at him and tried to determine the truth of what he said. "All the same," Peter said, "it would be best if you handed over your sword."

Simon's face grew red with anger and he stood and held his weapon. James and Peter stood as well, unsure of what he would do. With a quick move, Simon thrust his sword between Peter and James and drove it into the door, where it embedded itself into the wood. Then he spat on the ground and walked away.

TUESDAY

Mark 12:1-34, Matthew 24:1-3

The rooster's crow only vaguely echoed in Peter's head. It was when someone tried to open the door that he jumped to his feet, alert and ready to fight.

"Peter, it's me!" Jesus said.

Peter looked down and realized he was holding a sword. He quickly put it behind him. "Forgive me, Master... I was having a, uh, bad dream."

Jesus looked at him just like Rachael did when she knew he was lying.

"Did something happen last night?" he asked.

Peter paused. Was he the only one in the house who slept through the commotion last night? *Probably*, he thought. *After all, he slept through a storm.*

"As you said, no one came for you," he said.

James yawned and sat up. He stretched his arms and rubbed his face. "Shalom, Master," he said.

"Shalom, James. I hope you both got some rest last night. We need to pack up and be on our way."

Peter heard footsteps and turned to see the Zealot approach. He did not look Peter, or James, in the eye.

"Master, may I speak to you in private?" he said.

"I was just going to take a walk," Jesus said. "Why don't you join me?"

Simon nodded, and Peter stepped aside to let them open the door. As they left, the Zealot gave Peter a cruel stare and Peter closed the door behind them.

"Should we have told him?" James asked.

"It's between them," Peter said.

James looked around. "Where's his sword?"

Peter picked his robe off the ground and drew the Zealot's sword out of it. "Here. But there's no way he's getting this back. I don't trust him."

James nodded.

Rachael came out and hugged her husband. He calmed her fears, and she went into the kitchen to work. Other disciples staggered into the courtyard, allowing the crisp air to awaken them as they rubbed their eyes against the rising sun. The smell of bread was in the air and the town slowly came to life.

An hour or so passed before Jesus returned with Simon. Peter kept his distance.

It was difficult to say goodbye to Simon the leper and his family. Harder still was Peter's goodbye to Rachael. After a long embrace, he kissed her head and they said a prayer.

"Promise me you'll come back," she said.

"Rachael, I—"

"*Promise me*," she pleaded. "I can't help but feel something horrible is about to happen."

He nodded. "I promise." They kissed, then parted ways.

Jesus and the twelve left Bethany and headed into Jerusalem, and for a moment Peter thought they were going in a different way than they had before. As they got to the gate, something seemed new and yet familiar at the same time. He looked around and saw nothing unusual except a blackened stump with withered branches.

"Look, Rabbi," Peter said, "the fig tree that you cursed has withered away!"

The apostles quickly gathered around what was left of the tree in amazement. Yesterday it stood tall. Today it was lower than their waists.

Jesus shook his head and laughed. "You've seen me raise the dead, and you're impressed that I killed a tree? Have faith in God. In truth I tell you, if anyone says to the mountain, 'Be pulled up and thrown into the sea,' with no doubt in his heart, but believes that it will happen, then it will."

He reached out and grabbed a branch. It snapped off easily at his touch. "I tell you, everything you ask and pray for, believe that you have it already, and it will be yours." Jesus stared at the branch as he rolled it between his fingers.

He seemed lost in thought. Then he said, "And when you stand in prayer, forgive whatever you have against anybody, so that your Father in heaven will forgive your failings, too. But if you don't forgive others, your Father will not forgive your failings either." He threw the branch on the ground. "Now let us go."

Peter did not need a look from Jesus to know that his words were directed toward him. Simon must have known it too. They both lingered behind as Jesus went into the city.

He unfastened Simon's sword from under his tunic and handed it back to him. "Here," he said.

Simon took the weapon and looked at it thoughtfully. "Did you tell Jesus what happened?"

Peter shook his head. "I thought that should be between you and him."

Simon nodded. "I wasn't sure what you had said to him. Jesus didn't react when I told him the story, but he can be tough to read sometimes."

"Tell me about it," Peter said. "If the Master has no quarrel with you, I don't either."

Simon tied the sword under his tunic. "You're a good man, Peter. I'm glad Jesus put you in charge."

His words had a great impact on Peter and almost brought him to tears. But after a stressful night and an emotional goodbye to his wife, he knew that he was more susceptible to emotion than usual.

"It's an honor to be with you, as well," he replied. They clasped hands, and then walked together into Jerusalem.

Jerusalem buzzed with news about the capture of Barabbas. It was the first time that Peter could remember someone being talked about *more* than Jesus. People were relieved and even euphoric at his capture. Whatever he planned to do against the Romans would have had severe consequences for the Jewish people. Many were bitter that *he* always escaped but innocent Jews died in retaliation for the Zealot's actions. Jerusalem breathed a collective sigh of relief to know that he was not going to cause trouble any more.

As they headed toward the temple, a huge throng of people approached, crying "Murderer!" and "Crucify him!" In the center of the crowd, Roman guards beat back people that stood in their way as they pulled a man bound in chains.

"Is that him?" Peter asked Simon. Simon nodded. Peter arched his neck over the crowd to get a look at him.

He was surprised at what he saw. He expected Barabbas to be a giant, fierce creature but instead he looked... normal. His face was shaven, which was unusual for a Zealot, but then he remembered stories of how Barabbas often disguised himself as a Roman to prepare for his attacks. He had no memorable features except for a scar on his left cheek and strong chin that was bloodied either from his capture or harsh treatment from the soldiers. Though he occasionally flinched when something was thrown at him, he walked regally, like a man willing to die for what he believed in.

"Crucify him!" Little James shouted, swept up in the emotion of the crowd. He had his fist in the air when he turned to look at Jesus and froze. Slowly, he lowered his arm. Jesus' expression was one of sadness tinged with horror. Unsure why he felt that way, the apostles were less sure how to act. Amid the shouting, cheering, and cursing, the thirteen stood silently as Barabbas passed them by on the way to be condemned by Pontius Pilate, the Roman governor of Jerusalem.

On the other side of the crowd, Caiaphas spoke with Malchus. "How is he?" he asked, a look of concern on his face.

"He'll live, but he might lose his arm. I don't think we'll be so lucky with Aaron."

Caiaphas hung his head. The capture of Barabbas had been bloody, but at least it was successful. "Have you slept?"

Malchus shook his head.

"Get some rest. Give the guards my thanks. They preformed exceptionally last night and they will be well rewarded, as will you."

The servant gave a weary smile and bowed. As he walked away, Annas came up to Caiaphas, clapping his hands.

"Well done, Caiaphas. I didn't know you had it in you. But why not just tell the Romans and let them do the fighting?"

"We don't need others to clean up our own garbage."

"And now they owe you a favor."

Caiaphas smiled. "The thought had crossed my mind."

As the crowd passed by, they saw Jesus and his disciples head toward the temple. "You might need that favor sooner rather than later," he said.

Caiaphas's face soured. "We'll see how he fares today. Then we'll decide tonight."

Peter felt a thrill of excitement as they entered the courtyard of the Temple. All eyes turned their way. Tension was palpable in the air. Jesus found a place in a portico along the eastern wall and the twelve sat around his feet.

Normally, arguments were spread throughout the Temple. The Herodians would argue with the Sadducees about the Davidic dynasty. The Sadducees would argue with Pharisees about the resurrection of the dead. The Pharisees would argue with the priests and scribes about the role of Jerusalem and the establishment of synagogues. It was the highlight of the year. Let the Romans have their gladiators and the Greeks have their Olympics. Religious debate was the lifeblood of the Jewish faith.

But on this day it was different. Today they all came together against a carpenter's son from Nazareth. A crowd quickly gathered and Jesus wasted no time.

"A man planted a vineyard, which he leased to tenants and went abroad," he said. "When the time came, he sent a servant to collect from the tenants his share of the produce. They viciously beat the servant and sent him away. So he sent another, and they had him killed. Then others followed. Some were killed, some were beaten. But he still had someone left: his beloved son."

Peter looked around at the crowd. There were many quite eager to hear what Jesus had to say. They sat on the ground behind the apostles, dressed in common robes and tunics. But there were others who only wanted blood. They stood in the back with fine garments and arms folded in judgment, ready to tear him to pieces.

Jesus continued his parable. "The master thought, 'They will respect my son'. But the tenants said to each other, 'This is the heir! If we kill him, the inheritance will be ours!' So they seized him and killed him and threw him out of the vineyard."

The crowd murmured at the upsetting nature of the story. Those standing shot curious glances to each other, wondering what Jesus meant. Jesus looked down at those seated and addressed them softly, like a father telling a story to his child. "Now, what will the owner of the vineyard do? I'll tell you what he'll do." Then he looked up with fire in his eyes and addressed those who stood behind them. "He will make an end of them," he said sharply. "And he will give the vineyard to others."

The apostles needed no explanation to understand this parable, nor did anyone else in the Temple. An explosion of outrage erupted among the scholars.

"What is he doing?" Jude asked, stunned by Jesus' aggressive tone.

"Drawing first blood," Peter said.

"What gives you the right?" yelled one of the scribes. He screamed the question a few times until the other voices died down so he could address the young Rabbi. "You knock over tables in the Temple, you speak with insolence to your elders. Tell us with what authority do you do such things!" The scholars cheered and the eyes of the crowd went back to Jesus.

Jesus lifted up a finger and pointed it at them. "And I will ask you a question, just one. Tell me what you have decided about my brother, John. What was the origin of the baptism he did: heavenly or human? Answer me that."

The question surprised them, and a group of temple scribes quickly gathered to come up with an answer. Bartholomew laughed.

"Brilliant," he said.

"What do you mean?" Peter asked.

"If they say it was from heaven, he'll ask why they didn't believe in him. If they say it wasn't the crowd will turn on them. Everyone respected the Baptist."

The man who posed the question shook his head and turned back to Jesus. He cleared his throat and tried to stand as tall and as proud as he could. "We need more inquiry to ascertain the validity of his endeavors," he said.

Jesus tilted his head to one side. "I'm sorry, I don't understand."

The man didn't move, except for his eyes that darted uncomfortably around him, hoping to find a way to escape the question. "We don't know," he finally admitted.

"Ah," Jesus said, nodding his head. "You don't know."

"But you still haven't answered *my* question!" said the man, pointing an accusing finger toward him.

Jesus raised his hands in surrender. "Of course, of course," he said. "I tell you what. Once you figure out where John got his authority from, then I'll tell you from where I get mine."

The crowd erupted in cheers at his answer and the scribes' faces grew red with anger. Many of them left. People in the crowd laughed, repeating the answer to each other and mimicking their angry response.

One of the Herodians stepped forward and applauded his answer. "Well said, Rabbi. It is clear that you are an honest man and unafraid of anyone, because human rank means nothing to you and you teach the way of God in all honesty." Jesus looked at him sternly, but the man continued his pretense. "Since you are so devoted to God and have no concern with someone whether they be a scholar, a priest, a king, or even an *emperor...*" He let the last word hang so to gain the full attention of everyone. "Tell us, is it permissible to pay taxes to Caesar or not? Should we pay?"

The crowd briefly conversed among themselves before looking at Jesus. This was a hard fought argument among Jews. Jesus put out his open hand. "Have you a denarii? Let me see it."

Surprised by the command, the man reached into his purse, pulled out a coin, and handed it forward through the crowd to Jesus. When it reached him, Jesus flipped it around in his hand and looked as though he had never seen one before. "Whose face is on this coin? Whose inscription?"

The Herodian shrugged, unsure whether not to answer such an obvious question. "Caesar's," he said.

Positioning the coin on his thumb, Jesus flipped it back to the man who caught the coin with both hands. "Then give to Caesar what is Caesar's and give to God what is God's."

The man's face was motionless as the crowd cheered the answer. He angrily put his coin back into his tunic and stormed out, followed by some of his companions. The Pharisees and the Sadducees looked at each other, wondering which one was going to go next.

A Sadducee raised his hand to speak. "Master, Moses told us that if a man dies without a child, his brother must marry the widow. Now, we had a case where a man had seven brothers. He died childless and the woman married the next. Then his brother died without a child and so she married his younger brother. This happened through all *seven brothers*, until eventually she herself died."

The crowd broke into small conversations about the tale. *Was it real? What are the chances of that happening?* Jesus kept a patient expression on his face while the Sadducee enjoyed the crowd's reaction to the story. "Thank you for your story," he said, "but is there a question you'd like to ask?"

The Sadducee smiled. "Of course, Rabbi. My question is simple. At the resurrection of the dead, whose wife will she be?" The Sadducees cheered and shook his shoulders at such a clever question, but he kept his eyes fixed on the young Rabbi before him. A look of smug arrogance radiated from his face. The crowd turned to each other, and then to Jesus, with growing excitement.

The Pharisees squirmed and shot condescending looks at the Sadducees. For the first time today, Rabbi Dov hoped Jesus had a good answer. He knew the Sadducees disregarded the resurrection as superstitious nonsense. The question was meant not only to rattle Jesus but them as well.

"If Jesus doesn't have a good answer, we need to respond!" Rabbi Zedekiah said.

"And what should we say?" asked another.

"This isn't about us, it's about *him*," Rabbi Dov said. "Say nothing." Others in the crowd voiced their agreement and they turned their attention back to Jesus.

Dov noticed that Jesus sought no council and didn't even seem to struggle with his response. He waited for the crowd's noise to die down before he spoke. When he did, it was clear and deliberate.

"You are wrong, because you neither understand the Scriptures nor the power of God." The crowd held their breath and the Sadducees were stunned at such a rebuke. Jesus went on. "And as for the resurrection of the dead, have you never read what God himself spoke to you? 'I am the God of Abraham, the God of Isaac, and the God of Jacob.' He is God, not of the dead, but of the living. You are very much mistaken."

The people seated on the floor cheered louder than ever. *Amazing,* Dov thought, but he quickly chastised himself for thinking anything good about that carpenter. The Sadducees yelled back in anger, but couldn't be heard above the crowd. They left, shaking their fists as they did. Of his detractors, the Pharisees were the only ones left. They pulled close to each other to decide their question.

"We should challenge him on the Sabbath," one suggested.

"We've done that before," Rabbi Dov said. "It didn't work in Capernaum and it probably won't work here."

"Let's call him a devil!" Rabbi Zedekiah said.

"With this crowd?" Rabbi Dov said. "They're falling in love with every word he speaks." He rubbed his face with his hands. "He's just a *carpenter.* There must be some aspect of the law where we can trip him up!"

"Master, what is the greatest commandment of the law?" someone asked.

Rabbi Dov spun around. The words, "Who asked that?" were formed on his lips but his eyes told him the answer. It was another *Pharisee,* a young Rabbi named Jeremiah.

Dov was furious. This was not an approved question. Violent thoughts ran through his head of what he would do to Jeremiah when this was over. He cleared his throat but Rabbi Jeremiah paid him no heed and kept his focus on Jesus.

Then Dov looked at Jesus and saw something on his face that he hadn't seen all morning: *Surprise.*

The crowd grew still as Jesus considered the man before him. He ran his fingers through his beard and looked deeply at him, though it was hard to tell from his expression what he was thinking.

"Love the Lord your God with all your heart, with all your soul, and with all your mind," Jesus replied. "This is the greatest and first commandment. The second resembles it: You must love your neighbor as yourself. On these two commandments hang the whole Law, and the Prophets, too."

Rabbi Jeremiah pondered Jesus' answer. "That is well spoken," he replied, speaking to himself as much as he was to Jesus. "To live out these commandments are more important than any burnt offering or sacrifice."

Jesus' eyes grew wide and he pointed a finger toward the man. The Pharisee took a step back in expectation of a rebuke. But one did not come. "You... are not far from the kingdom of God," Jesus said. And he bowed to the Pharisee.

The crowd applauded with delight. The Rabbi humbly returned the bow and looked at Dov. Dov thought his head might burst and ground his teeth. The young Rabbi quickly left.

A hand was on his shoulder. "We should go," Rabbi Zedekiah said.

"No!" Dov said. "We can defeat this Nazarene."

But the other Pharisees were already starting to leave. None of them looked him in the eye.

"Cowards!" Dov said.

Zedekiah moved close to him. "Stay calm, Rabbi Dov. At least we weren't embarrassed like the rest of them."

The Rabbi patted him on the shoulder and left. Jesus began to teach the crowd and there was no one left to challenge him. "A carpenter from Nazareth," whispered Dov. He spit on the ground and walked away.

From a balcony accessible only to priests and temple servants, Caiaphas and Annas sat in silence.

"I have never..." Caiaphas began, and then he stopped. Jesus was now teaching unopposed by anyone and it was clear the crowd delighted in every word he said.

He looked at his father-in-law and, maybe for the first time in his life, found him speechless. Malchus came in and greeted them both.

"I thought I told you to get some sleep," Caiaphas said.

"Forgive me, sir. But I got word that Jesus is not planning to return to Bethany tonight."

Annas stood in concern. "Where is he going?"

"No one knows, or at least they're not telling."

Caiaphas ran his fingers through his beard. There was no way they could arrest Jesus during the day because of the crowd, but there would be no way they could find him at night if he fled to the surrounding hills of Jerusalem for shelter. "Have them followed. I want to know where they are at all times."

"I will see to it personally," Malchus said. He bowed and left.

Caiaphas stood and addressed his father. "We will meet tonight in my palace. See to it that Rabbi Dov and any others you think necessary are there."

Annas nodded. "Do you realize the danger now?" he asked.

Caiaphas put up his hand. "I have much to think about," he said. Annas gave a slight bow and left. Caiaphas sat back down and watched Jesus as he taught the crowd.

"I have never…" he said again, and then fell back into silence.

Malchus fought off sleep over the next few hours as Jesus continued to preach. He wanted desperately to sleep, but he didn't want to miss an opportunity to please the high priest. A few days ago, Caiaphas didn't even know his name. Now Malchus was his most trusted servant.

But he was bored out of his mind. He would have fallen asleep if it wasn't for the occasional prodding of Jerrod, a relative of his and fellow temple guard. Jerrod was a large man with an ape-like face. Not smart, but good in a fight.

As Malchus leaned his head against the wall and closed his eyes, Jerrod gave him an elbow in the ribs to wake him. "I think he's finishing up," Jerrod said. Jesus sang a psalm with the crowd and blessed them. After that, many stood and surrounded him, making it tough to see where he was.

Malchus feared losing Jesus in the large crowd, and the fear brought him back to his senses. "Can you see him?" he asked.

Jerrod stood on his toes to see over the crowd. "He's wearing a brown tunic and he just flipped it over his head. There's a bunch of men from the house he was staying at with him. Look, they're heading out of the southern side."

"Let's go," he said. They followed them out of the Temple and on to the streets.

Jesus and his disciples moved slowly so at first it was easy to follow them. But suddenly, as if planned, they moved with determined speed and split down different narrow streets.

Malchus and Jerrod looked at each other, neither sure which group had Jesus. "Follow them, I'll follow the others," Malchus said, and he pushed his way through the busy Jerusalem streets to catch up.

He turned a corner and feared he lost them until he caught sight of the Zealot. He would know that face anywhere. Quickly looking at his companions (there were about seven of them,) he recognized Jesus with the hood of his brown tunic pulled over his head. He breathed a quick prayer of thanksgiving and kept up the pursuit, occasionally stepping behind a cart or into a doorway to avoid detection.

Jesus and his followers made a sharp turn off the busy streets and Malchus followed, but as he rounded the corner he found them waiting for him. The Zealot stood in front.

"Looking for someone?" he asked.

"I command you by the order of the high priest to tell me where you are going."

"Just walking around with my friends here, that's all."

Malchus looked at his companions, and then at Jesus. Jesus stepped forward and pulled the hood off his head, revealing two large ears. It was only then that Malchus realized he hadn't followed Jesus, but that man named Lazarus that everyone had been talking about. Enraged, he waved an angry fist toward them.

"Keep interrupting in Temple affairs and you'll be dead," Malchus warned.

"Already was," Lazarus said, a huge smile on his face.

Furious, Malchus turned and walked away.

As Jesus sat upon the Mount of Olives waiting for the twelve to arrive, he took off his sandal and pushed his toe against some fertile soil. Pulling it away, he saw it teemed with life: an uncovered earthworm twisted to find its way back into the dirt, some ants ran frantically back and forth, and a beetle jumped and flew by his head to find a quieter place. He raised his eyes from the dirt to the city of Jerusalem that stood before him in all its glory. It, too, teemed with life. The Passover feast was two days away and the population of Jerusalem would grow to over a million people—ten times it's normal size.

The people looked like ants from his vista on the hill. Before him was the Temple and at this height he could see into its walls. Its gilded spires pierced the peach-colored sky. Beside it, the Antonian tower buzzed with soldiers, lighting lamps for the evening.

The city of Jerusalem was built on two hills with a long wall that surrounded them. The eastern hill was Mount Moriah, the place where Abraham offered his son Isaac and where the Temple was built. The western hill was Mount Zion, and this is where much of the population of the city lived. A small valley ran between the hills, and there that is where the poor dwelt, packed in small houses no bigger than a room. But the wealthy lived near the top of Mount Zion, where the palaces were larger and the view more spectacular. The tiled roofs of the wealthy and the thatched roofs of the poor created a rich tapestry that blanketed the city. The walls looked impregnable, and the orange rock on which the city sat seemed like bronze.

Jesus pondered a saying of the Rabbis: *He who has not seen Jerusalem has never seen a beautiful city.* Even in the time of David and Solomon, Jerusalem never looked so radiant.

He heard movement among the trees. *"Master?"* a voice said.

"Over here," Jesus replied. Peter stepped out from behind one of the trees with a look of relief.

"When you said to meet you at the top of the Mount of Olives, you probably should have been more specific."

Jesus smiled. "Won't happen again," he said.

"I'll collect the others," Peter said. As he walked away, Jesus' smile faded. *I should tell them now,* he thought. *They need to know.*

He didn't want to. He knew what he had to say would shake them to the core and even break their spirit. With everything else going on, why tell them now?

It's because of everything else, he reasoned. The apostles gathered with laughter and joy. They exchanged stories of how they had eluded the temple guards.

Spirits were high. Jude pulled out some bread and a wineskin was passed around. They sat in the grass and ate their meager dinner, impressed by the magnificent view before them.

Judas stood next to him and marveled at the sight. "Master, look at the size of those stones!" he exclaimed. "Look at how large the buildings are! Isn't it incredible?"

Jesus sighed. *It was time.* "You see those great buildings?" he said, waving his hand across Jerusalem's landscape. "Not a single stone will be left on top of another. Not one. Everything will be pulled down."

The noise of the forest suddenly became deafening as the apostles fell into complete and total silence. "How... When?" Peter asked.

"When you see Jerusalem surrounded by armies, then you must realize that it will soon be laid desolate. Then those in Judea must escape to the mountains, those inside the city must leave it, and those in country districts must not take refuge in it. For this is the time of retribution when all that Scripture says must be fulfilled." He shook his head with great sorrow. "Alas for those with child, or with a baby at their breast when those days come."

Thomas gasped. Philip clutched his chest. Jesus continued. "Great misery will descend on the land and retribution on this people. They will fall by the edge of the sword and be led captive to every Gentile country, and Jerusalem will be trampled down by the Gentiles until their time is complete."

"Even the temple?" Matthew asked.

Jesus nodded.

"But then you'll build it again? In three days, right?" John asked. Jesus shook his head. John put his head in his hands and wept as quietly as he could. Others had tears in their eyes as well.

"The Temple will not be rebuilt?" Peter asked.

"I will rebuild it," Jesus said, "with you."

The apostles looked at each other, wondering what he meant. "I will build a temple of living stones," Jesus said to them, "and you are to be its foundation."

Judas looked at the sturdy walls and magnificent buildings of Jerusalem. Then he looked at the carpenter, skinny and meek, and the pathetic group of men who followed him. His mind was made up. *Jesus is insane.*

Jesus continued to speak at some length about "the appalling abomination" and "when the Son of man comes in glory", but Judas paid no attention to it. It had become a liability to follow Jesus. The money he had taken from the collections was useless because he had no opportunity to spend it and no place to properly save it. And now Jesus ranted like a mad man. *He will be laughed out of Jerusalem if he talks like this in public,* he thought, *and his followers will be exiled with him.* His mind raced to find some way out of being an apostle.

But where could he go? He couldn't work for the Temple after what Jesus did to it. The Sadducees were so enraged that they would never take a former disciple of Jesus. The Herodians? Even he wouldn't stoop so low.

No, his best bet was the Pharisees. There were some who supported this young Rabbi and might like to have one of Jesus' disciples by his side. At least Jesus hadn't humiliated them like he did the others.

Given his limited options, it was his best bet. Judas decided to leave the ranks of the twelve as soon as he possibly could.

The soundproof walls of the high priest's chamber were tested to their limit. Around the large table, men were on their feet and angrily shouted at each other. Annas noted with great dismay that the group was out of control and Caiaphas remained seated, neither saying a word nor doing anything to stop the chaos.

The Sadducees were in favor of killing him, and so were some Pharisees—especially Rabbi Dov. The Temple's treasurer had his new assistant rattle off the numbers of how much money they had lost because merchants were afraid to sell animals with Jesus and his followers around. The scribes and priests agreed that Jesus must go. But Hiram made it clear that Herod would have no part of it. The king was still upset that he killed John the Baptist and was afraid that Jesus was his reincarnation. Since no one had the authority to kill without Rome's immediate retribution coming down upon them, it would have to be Rome that did the deed.

This heated up the debate. They all hated Rome and a few of them hated Rome more than they hated Jesus. To hand Barabbas to the Romans was an obvious move—he deserved every lash and nail he would receive. But some thought it was too cruel for Jesus, and those who were uncertain about Jesus' fate spoke out strongly against handing him over to the Romans.

The Pharisees were the most sharply divided. There were even some who approved of Jesus after they saw him dismantle the Herodians and the Sadducees in public. And so the argument went round and round, each time at a louder volume. Some thought he should die by any means. Some agreed with death, but not through the Romans. Others thought he should receive a lesser punishment through the Sanhedrin.

Finally, Caiaphas stood. The room grew quiet, waiting for him to speak. "It is one thing to kill a criminal, but it is quite another to put a righteous man to death. I listened to him speak today, and I was moved. Never had I heard someone so eloquent about the Law and the prophets."

Annas feared all was lost. Rabbi Dov almost exploded, but Caiaphas calmly raised his hand to keep him silent. "However, I also agree that he threatens to rip apart the fabric that holds us all together, and he has no problem humiliating us in public and raising doubts in the people's mind of whether we are fit to lead them. The people *need* us and our leadership, or else the Romans would overtake us completely. Are we perfect? No. But God has put us in this place, and no carpenter from Nazareth will take it away from us."

Some objections began to rise, but a cool stare from Caiaphas held their tongues. He looked solemnly at those around the table. "It is better for one man to die for the people. We will give him to Rome."

"But how?" one of them asked. "The people will revolt."

Annas snorted with disgust. "The people will do what we tell them to. Besides, we'll have Jesus arrested at night. We've been having him watched and know where he is. We'll send Temple guards to get him right away."

Caiaphas tensed and looked angrily at his father-in-law. "We *don't* know where Jesus is," he said. This was new information for Annas and he realized that Caiaphas was furious for forcing him to reveal it in front of everybody. "He went into hiding and eluded our guards this afternoon."

"Then we'll arrest him at the temple!" one of the Sadducees said. At this, almost everyone in the room raised their voice to support or argue against the idea. Some thought it was the perfect way to show that they weren't afraid of someone from Nazareth. Others feared violence on the Temple floor.

Caiaphas pounded on the table to regain order. "We will *not* arrest him in the Temple. Not while I am high priest." He said it with such conviction that there was no room for any argument. But still the problem remained.

"Then how will we find him?" Annas asked.

Caiaphas paused. "He's sure to preach in the Temple tomorrow, we'll follow him then."

"If it didn't work today, what makes you think it will work tomorrow?" Rabbi Dov asked. "We're almost at Passover and then he will be gone. If he leaves Jerusalem without punishment he will be a hero for these peasants, and we will be the laughing stock."

Everyone agreed with this statement. Caiaphas lowered his head and put both hands on the table. "I'm open for suggestions," he said.

The table grew quiet. Annas desperately wished that he had an idea, that he would be the one to solve the problem. But he was as silent as the rest of them.

The Temple treasurer spoke up. "May my assistant speak?"

His assistant? It was unusual for someone of such a low stature to volunteer something at this kind of meeting. Caiaphas motioned for him to come forward.

"I think I know a way to find him," the assistant said, "but it will cost money. Maybe even one hundred silver pieces."

Caiaphas considered this. A hefty sum, but worth it. "That won't be a problem. And you are?"

"My apologies," the man said as he bowed with a flourish of his hand. "My name is Ioakim."

WEDNESDAY

John 8:2-11, Matthew 23:13-32

They were up late talking about the end of the world, and such thoughts made Peter feel smaller than a star on a cloudless evening. A pall was cast over all the apostles that night. They did not choose to go to sleep—sleep pulled them into darkness.

They made camp close to the valley. When Peter woke, he was surrounded by mist and couldn't see more than a body away from him. His first thought was for the Master, who slept between James and John. James he could see... but not Jesus. Drowsy, he crawled toward James to look for him and his knee landed firmly on James's outstretched hand.

James immediately awoke and swung a fist at Peter, but he was quick to dodge it. Only then did James realize he struck at his friend and muttered an apology.

"Where's Jesus?" Peter asked.

"Praying," said the soft voice of John through the mist.

Peter moved close and saw him, first his silhouette and then his young boyish face. "You saw him go?"

"No, but look," he said, pointing to the place where Jesus had laid. His outer tunic, which also served as a blanket, was folded tightly into a perfect square. The three of them, now awake, looked at his folded robes with great admiration.

"I wonder how he does that," John said.

For Peter, the sight gave some relief. It was a sign that he wasn't taken, but had left of his own free will. But what if Jesus came to some trouble while in prayer? He thought to go look for him, but it seemed foolish to do so with the mist, the trees, the twilight of morning, and the unfamiliar terrain.

The sun rose. Slowly, the haze began to clear and the rest of the apostles awoke, though none were concerned with Jesus' absence more than Peter. James noticed his friend's agitation.

"Relax. He'll be here," he said.

Peter did not respond. As the head of the apostles, it was his job to keep the Master safe. He was convinced that all of Jesus' talk about being arrested was to encourage them to greater vigilance. *After all, why talk about something if there was nothing we could do about it?*

When Jesus finally appeared, he did not experience relief but anger. "Where have you been?" Peter asked. "Master, I insist that you no longer leave without telling one of us where you are. It is far too dangerous."

Jesus looked at him calmly and paused before responding. He pointed into the distance, the direction from which he came. "There is a large rock surrounded by olive trees just down the mount over there," he said. "When I pray there again, I'll take you with me."

"Well… good," Peter replied, a little surprised that Jesus didn't offer more resistance to his demand. The quick victory left him without anything else to say.

"Let's eat," Jesus said. He patted him on the shoulder as he walked by to join the rest of the twelve. After a simple breakfast and morning prayer, they headed back to the Temple where a large crowd had gathered to hear Jesus teach.

"Hold her tighter!" Rabbi Zedekiah said as he pulled the woman through the street. His young disciple was far too gentle and she continued to wrest her arm away from his grip. "Idiot! Keep your eyes on her!"

The young disciple averted his gaze. "She is all but naked!" he said. The women was clothed only with a sheet that kept falling off as they pulled her along.

"So are animals," Zedekiah said. With a yank he pulled her forward and dragged her knees along the cobblestone street.

A crowd gathered behind them. Shouts of "Adulterer!" and "Whore!" echoed off the narrow streets until they made their way into the Temple courts. Zedekiah looked around and saw where the people had gathered. That was where Jesus would be.

He tried to drag her there but the stubborn girl dug her heels into the ground. She screamed something, it didn't matter. He kicked her legs out from under her and she fell backward.

Zedekiah let her go and spit on her. She tried her best to cover herself with the sheet. *As if she had any dignity*, Zedekiah thought.

He looked with distain at his sweaty hands. There were more than enough men to carry her now. Zedekiah motioned them to grab her and they were more than happy to oblige.

Zedekiah led them toward the Nazarene. This was *his* triumphal procession. All eyes were upon him as he crossed the courtyard. He past the crowd of Pharisees and caught the approving look of Rabbi Dov.

The Rabbi walked right up to Jesus. Even the carpenter went speechless when he saw him approach. The crowd before him parted like the Red Sea. With a flick of his wrist, the men threw the woman at his feet. People shouted in anger but Zedekiah held out his hand for silence.

"*Rabbi*," Zedekiah said, "this woman has been caught in the very *act* of committing adultery. Now in the law, Moses ordered us to stone women of this kind. What do you have to say?"

Zedekiah looked up and saw the Roman guards in Antonian tower pointing and starting to move. He looked into the courtyard and saw Jewish men running toward them, eager to watch. Fingers scraped the floor for anything that could be thrown with deadly force. A pile of stones, set aside for the continuing construction of the Temple, was quickly depleted as men grabbed them and passed them to others.

The crowd became a mob, and he loved it.

Zedekiah couldn't hide his smile, delighted at the trap he had sprung. He knew Jesus had only two options: obey the Law and face Rome's swift and deadly retribution; or seem weak by telling them not to kill her, and lose the high opinion of the crowds. He would be killed by Rome or discredited by the Pharisees. Either way, Jesus was finished. And he, not Dov, would get all the credit.

Jesus stood motionless and stared intensely at Rabbi Zedekiah. Then he did a completely unexpected thing:

He bent down on the ground and wrote in the dirt with his finger.

The sudden movement startled the Rabbi and he looked back in confusion at Rabbi Dov, who stood in the back with other Pharisees. Dov wasn't any help—he was as surprised as he was.

Zedekiah turned back to Jesus who continued to scribble in the dirt. The woman was in front of him and obscured his view as to what he wrote. Zedekiah didn't know what to make of it, and felt all eyes upon him.

He's stalling. "What have you to say, Rabbi? I demand your answer!"

Jesus calmly looked at him, then stood. "Let the one of you who is without sin be the first to throw the stone." And he gestured toward the woman huddled on the ground before him with an open hand as if offering an invitation to do so. Then he bent down and continued his writing.

For a moment no one breathed. All eyes turned back to Zedekiah, who now began to sweat. His mouth hung open, unable to utter a word.

Zedekiah was a Pharisee, a teacher of the Law. He was confident he had no sin in him. Someone handed him a rock and he looked down at it. Then he looked up to the tower where Roman guards pointed and gestured toward the Temple. Soldiers ran into the courtyard with their swords unsheathed, ready to cut through anyone who got in their way.

If I throw this stone, the Roman's will kill me. But if I don't, I'm publicly admitting that I am a sinner! Now *he* was caught in a trap. As the Romans drew nearer, his fear overcame his pride. Zedekiah threw the stone on the floor and walked away. The rest followed him out.

The woman was huddled in a ball, her sheet barely covering her nakedness. All she could think was, *I will be killed and go to hell.* She knew the punishment for her crime and knew what she had done was a serious sin against the Lord. She could hear nothing above her sobs. She tensed and waited for the first stone to strike, praying that it might knock her unconscious so that she wouldn't feel the pain of the rest.

She felt something on her shoulder and flinched, thinking it was the beginning of the end. But it was not a rock, it was a hand. *His* hand. She looked up and saw Jesus. Then she turned around to see what the mob was going to do.

The portico was empty. She could not believe her eyes. Stones marked the places where people should be. They had all left.

In one of the most public places in Jerusalem, she was alone with Jesus.

She released a deep breath and put her hands on the floor to steady herself, inadvertently letting the sheet slip off her. She felt the warmth of cloth and looked to see Jesus cover her with his outer tunic. The sweaty, dirty, and torn sheet that covered her body fell to the ground as she was wrapped in the man's garment.

Jesus took her by the hand and gently lifted her to her feet. "Woman, where are they? Has no one condemned you?" he asked.

She looked around again. "No one, sir," she replied.

Jesus came closer and she was captured by his penetrating gaze. She had slept with many men, but never felt the kind of intimacy she had in this moment. It both excited and frightened her, and she didn't know what to do. His lips formed to make words, and her heart froze—what would a righteous man like this say to a woman like her?

"Neither do I," Jesus said. Her fears melted away. "Neither do I condemn you," he said again. She felt like she was going to faint. Tears streamed down her face.

Jesus raised his finger and wiped a tear off her cheek, and then cupped his hands around her chin so that her head rested in them. "Go now," he said to her, "and *sin no more*." This was said in a different tone than before. It was a command, but not one she felt belittled by. In fact, she felt encouraged—no, *empowered* by it—as if he filled her with a power to walk away from the sinful life she led.

She backed away, bowing and giving thanks, still in shock over what had just occurred. In her years of prostitution, she had let men touch every part of her body, but this was the first time that a man touched her heart. There was a warmth inside her that she never felt before, like the beginning of a new life. Tears of sadness turned into tears of joy as she thanked Jesus again and ran home.

Peter and the other apostles waited outside the portico. When he saw the woman leave, he came back in. He saw Jesus, radiant with joy and tears in his eyes. But then a dark look covered his face and his muscles tensed. Peter was afraid. The last time he saw Jesus with such a look he was fashioning a whip.

"Master? Are you all right?" he asked.

"Please invite Rabbi Zedekiah and his friends back here," Jesus said. "I have something to teach them."

Peter backed away and dutifully obeyed.

When Jesus gave the look for the apostles to leave the portico, Judas was the first on his feet and into the courtyard. Israel's greatest Rabbis uncomfortably milled about, and it seemed a perfect opportunity to find a new master.

He picked one who had all the important qualities: near Jerusalem, had money, had ambition. Judas approached him and bowed low. "Rabbi Elias, may I speak with you?"

Rabbi Elias was a large man with meaty hands and a bulging stomach that even his long robes couldn't fully cover. "Does Jesus wish to speak to me?" he said loudly, gaining the attention of all who were near.

Judas grimaced. He did not want the extra attention. "It's a private matter, honored Rabbi," he said quietly. Elias nodded and they began to walk around the walls of the Temple together.

"Now then, what does your Master want?" he asked.

"It's not about my Master, it's about me. I know it is forward of me to ask, but I was wondering if you were taking on any disciples. If so, I would be honored to be one."

Rabbi Elias stopped dead in his tracks. "You wish to leave Rabbi Jesus?"

Judas nodded.

"For me?"

Again Judas nodded.

"You wish to leave Jesus... *for me*." A smile ran across his fat face. "What is your name?"

"Judas, sir."

"Well Judas, your idea has merit. I think I might be able to find room for you among my disciples. You know you'd have to move to Jerusalem."

Judas's heart leapt at the idea, but acted like it would be a sacrifice. "If that's what I must do to learn from you, then I will do it, Rabbi."

"Good, good," said the Rabbi. He patted Judas on the back. "Yes, I think we can make it work. But not before the Passover, I'm far too busy. Talk to me after that."

Judas smiled and tried to contain his excitement. "Thank you Maste– I mean, *Rabbi*." He did it on purpose, and Rabbi Elias smiled.

"Talk to me after the Passover," he said again. And then he went back into the Temple courtyard.

Judas wanted to run through the streets of Jerusalem, shouting for joy. All his hard work and patience had finally paid off. *My time with Jesus wasn't a waste after all*. Soon, Judas would be the disciple of a prominent Rabbi, live in Jerusalem, and could finally spend some of his money.

"Greetings Judas!" came a familiar voice. He spun and saw Ioakim, dressed in fine garments. Judas was completely caught off guard and unnerved by Ioakim's presence. To add to his confusion, Ioakim actually *bowed* before him—something he had never done before.

"What are you doing here?" Judas asked.

"I'm a treasurer of the Temple," he said. "You know Judas, I was pretty upset when last I saw you, but it was the greatest thing that ever happened to me in my life."

"It was?"

"Yes, of course! I wasn't sure if I should focus on religion or money, but now I work with religious money! And *lots* of it." He laughed. "Of course, I've been stuck in Jerusalem the last year, while you got to travel the country. How has that been?"

"Wonderful," he said, trying his best not to show how jealous he was of Ioakim's situation. *If I had stayed with Ioakim, I might be here with him*, he thought. "Where's Hezekiah?" he asked.

Ioakim hesitated. "Oh, well, it didn't work out with Hezekiah. After you left, I realized that you were the one who really did all the work, so I had to let him go."

He had been far too complimentary and now the spell was broken. "What do you want, *Ioakim*?" He enjoyed calling him by his first name without having to say "Master" before it.

Ioakim's face fell as if he dropped a mask. The familiar coldness returned to his eyes. "I'm giving you an opportunity to serve the people of God—"

Judas laughed. "I'm not so stupid, Ioakim. You wouldn't do anything if it didn't benefit yourself. Goodbye." Judas walked away and entered the Temple courtyard where Jesus had already begun to teach.

Ioakim chased after him. "Listen to me, Judas, and listen well. That so-called Rabbi of yours won't live through the end of the week. I'm a man of some influence in the Temple and can offer you a handsome sum if you help us. One hun—"

"You think I don't have a way out?" Judas shook his head in disgust. "You always thought little of me, Ioakim. But let me tell you something. I don't need you. I don't need your help. And I don't even need your money."

The blood drained from Ioakim's face and Judas enjoyed the sight of it. "Shalom," he said triumphantly. Judas turned his back toward Ioakim and walked away. He wanted to replay the moment in his mind, but was distracted by the sound of angry shouts that came from the portico where Jesus taught.

As he rounded the corner, he was filled with dread.

"Alas for you, scribes and Pharisees!" Jesus said. "You are like a whitewashed tomb that looks handsome on the outside, but inside is full of dead bones and filth!"

"You are a child of the devil!" one of the Pharisees yelled.

"And you are the children of those who murdered the prophets!" Jesus said. He beat his chest and opened his arms wide, as if inviting them to kill him on the spot. "Very well then, finish the work your fathers began!"

More shouts followed, with curses and cries of blasphemy by the Pharisees. They left in disgust and took much of the crowd with them. Judas watched in horror as Rabbi Elias passed him by. The angry stare the Rabbi gave him made it clear to Judas that he would *never* be his disciple. Some people moved forward to argue with Jesus, others left, but Judas couldn't move. The din of the crowd faded in his ears, and all he could hear was his breath and the furious beat of his heart.

No Rabbi would take him in now. *Jesus did this on purpose, to ruin me.*

Judas spun around and caught a glimpse of Ioakim walking out of the Temple gate. He ran to catch him and grabbed his shoulder.

Ioakim was surprised by the move and pulled away from him. "What do you want?" he said.

"How much?" Judas asked, panting for breath. "How much if I hand him over to you?"

Ioakim smiled. "How about… thirty pieces of silver?"

PASSOVER

John 13:1-14:11, 16:16-22

Peter awoke to the song of birds and a brilliant blue sky. He could not help but feel excited. It was the fourteenth day of Nisan, the first month in the Jewish calendar, and that evening they would celebrate Passover in the Holy City with the Messiah. His heart raced in his chest when he thought about it.

He sat up and breathed in the cool air of morning. Jesus and John were already awake, dressed in white. Thomas and Matthew were putting their white tunics on and others began to stir. He counted heads. All were there except for Judas who spent the night in Jerusalem with some of his family.

Soon they all were awake and gathered together for prayer. Jesus led them in a psalm:

My God, my God, why have you forsaken me?
The words of my groaning do nothing to save me.
My God, I call by day but you do not answer,
At night but find no relief.
Yet you, the Holy One, who make your home in the praises of
Israel,
In you our ancestors put their trust,
They trusted and you set them free…

Peter sang along but paid little attention to the familiar words. He thought it odd that Jesus would sing a psalm of lament on a day set aside for praise, but the psalm spoke of freedom and that was what the Passover was all about.

He looked up and saw Jerusalem through the trees. The Temple cast a shadow over the Western part of the city. The walls of Jerusalem were surrounded by the white tents of pilgrims—it looked like a city built on clouds. Could such beauty truly be destroyed? His excitement turned into fear when he recalled Jesus' words.

Peter looked at the Master and the Master looked at him. Peter suddenly realized that he had stopped singing. He quickly bowed his head and finished the psalm with the others:

And to those who are dead, their descendants will serve him,
Will proclaim his name to generations still to come,
And these will tell of his saving justice to a people yet unborn:

He has fulfilled it. Amen.

Jesus prayed a blessing over them, and they began to eat some of the food left over from the night before.

When everyone was finished, Jesus said to Peter, "I would like you and John to go into Jerusalem and make preparations for the Passover."

Peter nodded. Since he was in charge of the others, he expected this honor. John, however, could barely contain his excitement. Peter laughed to see the joy on his face.

"Need any help?" James asked.

Peter was about to accept but Jesus shook his head. "Thank you James, but just Peter and John are needed."

Then Peter asked a question that had been on all the apostles' minds. "Master, where will we eat the Passover meal?"

"When you go into the city, you will find a man carrying a water jar. Follow him. He will lead you to a house, and when you get there tell the owner, 'The Master says this: Where is the room for me to eat the Passover with my disciples?' He will show you a large upper room furnished with couches. Make the preparations there."

Peter hesitated. "A man with a water jar?"

"Yes," Jesus said. Peter could tell by his tone that there would be no further discussion about it.

Judas made his way up the Mount of Olives to where Jesus and the apostles were when he caught sight of Peter and John on their way down.

"Morning, Judas! How was your family?" Peter said.

"What? Oh, excellent, brother," he replied. He had almost forgotten the lie he told so he could meet with the high priest. "And where are the two of you off to?"

"We're going to make preparations for the Passover!" John said.

Judas froze. Since he was in charge of buying things, he assumed that he would be sent for the job. Maybe Jesus knew what he did last night and that's why he sent Peter and John instead of him. "I'll come with you," he quickly suggested.

"No need," Peter said. "The two of us can manage."

"I insist," Judas replied. He realized he spoke with too much desperation. Peter looked at him quizzically.

"The Master said it was just supposed to be me and Peter," John said.

"He *was* quite specific," Peter said apologetically.

"We must always listen to the Master," Judas said, trying to look as relaxed as possible. "I was just trying to help. I'll see you this evening."

Peter navigated through the chaos of Jerusalem. He hated crowds. Tens of thousands of people lined crowed streets and brought their sacrifices to the Temple. More than once he was afraid he lost John. Everyone was dressed in white, making it that much harder to find him in a crowd. Thankfully, John was one of the few men who didn't have a beard.

One of the shepherds they met by the Sheep Gate gave them his best lamb, and it truly was a beautiful creature. Then Peter and John waited in a long line that went all the way around the Temple. Hours later, they were brought in with about thirty other men into the Temple's inner walls where the altar of sacrifice lay.

The men lined up in two rows and came before the altar. John held the lamb steady while Peter quickly twisted its neck causing its instant death. They handed it to the priest who carried it to the altar and stabbed its side, causing a jet of blood to flow out of it. Much of the blood was captured into silver and gold cups that were poured upon the altar with trumpet blasts and the shouts of "Hallelujah!" The rest of it spilled on the ground. As they walked through the Temple, John was careful to avoid the shallow pools of blood, but Peter paid them no heed. The blood drenched his sandals and feet. They handed the lamb over to be burnt and its roasted flesh was returned to Peter and John for the Passover meal.

On leaving the temple, they were passed by a man carrying a water jar. They followed him to a house and asked to see the owner. Peter felt uncomfortable with Jesus' command, but the owner's face immediately brightened and he led them to a large upper room with a long table and cushions around it. A line of columns divided the room and the ceiling arched between each one. Peter and John smiled at the man and clasped his hands. As he left to prepare the meal, they marveled at the room.

"I can't believe it," Peter said. "It's just as the Master said it would be."

John laughed. "It's *always* as the Master says it will be."

Peter began to laugh with John, but they both grew quiet. Jesus also said that Jerusalem would be destroyed and the Temple leveled to the ground. That one of them would betray him. That he would be handed over to death.

Peter quietly prayed that Jesus wasn't *always* right.

As the sun began to set, the other apostles joined them in the upper room and marveled at the beauty of it.

"Where is the Master?" Peter asked.

"Talking to the master of the house," Philip said. "From his tone I'm guessing it might be one of his long conversations."

Peter nodded. He quickly counted heads and all twelve were there. But there was something missing. The room grew quiet and Peter realized that for the first time in weeks they were together *without* Jesus.

Simon noticed it, too. "All right, men, where do we stand?"

"On what?" John asked.

"*On what?*" Simon repeated. "On this Messiah stuff."

Matthew immediately tensed. "Watch your tone, Simon—"

"No, let him talk," Little James said. Matthew looked at his brother as if he was betrayed. "I think it's about time we discussed it among ourselves."

"It's the Passover," Philip said. "We should be celebrating."

"The timing could be better," Bartholomew said, stroking his long beard. "But with Jesus around us all the time we don't have much opportunity to openly discuss the matter."

"Is it so terrible that Jesus is around us all the time? We should be honored," Jude said.

"I didn't mean *that*. I was just acknowledging that Simon has a point."

"So where do we stand?" Simon asked again.

"What, are we taking a vote?" Andrew asked. "If the Master hears us talk like this—"

"Talk like what?" Simon asked. "There's nothing wrong about my question."

"But you waited for Jesus to leave the room before you asked it."

"Do you question my integrity?"

"That's enough," Peter said. He thought for a moment and said, "There's nothing wrong with the question. Those who wish to answer it may."

There was silence. Matthew was the first to speak up. "I believe he *is* the Messiah," he said, almost with an air of defiance.

"Me, too," John said.

"And I," James said.

Andrew nodded.

Silence again.

"I think he is," Jude said.

"I'm sure he is," Judas said.

More silence.

Bartholomew exhaled a loud breath and began to pace about the room. Little James covered his face in his hands. Matthew put a gentle hand on his shoulder. "Brother?"

Little James was on the verge of tears. "I don't know, all right? It's not a yes. It's not a no. I just... I wish I had your faith." Matthew embraced him.

Philip went to talk with Bartholomew in a corner of the room. Andrew looked at the Zealot. "What about you?"

Simon cracked his knuckles. "I've waited so long for the Messiah to come and kill these pagan dogs that desecrate our Temple and insult our fathers," he said. "But is this the man to do it?" He opened his mouth to speak again, but nothing came out. Frustrated, he turned and kicked the table with an angry grunt.

Philip and Bartholomew were in a heated conversation in the corner. What they said was mostly inaudible but had something to do with the Baptist. Thomas had his arms crossed and looked down at the floor. When he looked up, he realized that all eyes were upon him. He looked at Peter.

"Do I have to answer?" he asked.

"No."

"Then I won't." And he looked back down at the floor.

Philip and Bartholomew returned to the others. "Okay," Philip said. "This is where we're at—"

"And where is that?" asked the voice of Jesus.

The apostles froze. No one heard him come up the stairs. How much had he heard? Philip opened his arms wide. "We're... here! In this beautiful room!" His smile was frozen on his face.

"Since we're all here," Jesus said, "let us begin our meal."

The long and narrow rectangular table sat low to the ground and was made with the finest Lebanon cedar. Peter sat to the right of Jesus. James was going to sit on the left but John quickly squeezed in between them. James didn't mind. The others gathered in their usual order.

Peter thought it was strange to be sitting in such a wide rectangle instead of a circle. Judas usually sat at the far end of the circle, now he was directly across from him. Servants entered, and the food was laid out on beautiful dishes before them: the roasted lamb, the unleavened bread, the bitter herbs.

Jesus held up a cup of wine and said, "Blessed are you, God of Israel, who has created the fruit of the vine! Blessed are you, God of the Universe, who has chosen us from among all people, exalted us above all languages, and sanctified us with your commandments! Blessed are you who led your people out of slavery from Egypt! You have preserved our lives and brought us safely to this season."

They all responded, "Amen," and drank their cups of wine. A servant brought in a basin of water. As he left, Jesus asked him for his towel. The servant was confused but obeyed. When they were alone in the room, Jesus stood up, removed his outer garment, and put the towel around his waist.

This was *not* part of the Passover meal. Andrew leaned into his brother. "What is he doing?"

Peter had no answer. Jesus moved behind John.

"Master?" John asked.

"John, please turn around," Jesus said.

John gave a helpless look at those around the table and then turned his body to face Jesus. Jesus reached for his sandal and John instinctively pulled it away. Jesus looked into his eyes and John slowly moved his foot back toward him. Jesus untied his sandals and washed his feet in the basin, then dried them with the towel around his waist. John's mouth hung open and he couldn't speak, couldn't even turn back to the table. Jesus moved behind James and did the same.

Peter did not know what to make of it. He watched the different reactions on the apostle's faces as Jesus made his way around the table. James looked humiliated, Jude was in shock, Thomas looked anxious and Philip nervously laughed. Judas's response, to him, seemed the most sensible. He untied his sandals and had his feet ready so when Jesus got there it took him less time. *Maybe I should do that,* Peter thought. *Just get it over with as fast as I can.*

Something inside him rebelled at that idea and his heart burned with anger. By the time Jesus made it to him, he had made up his mind.

"Peter?" Jesus asked.

Without turning, Peter said, "Lord, Are you going to wash my feet, too?"

"I know you don't know what I'm doing right now, but later you will understand."

Peter pounded a fist upon the table and the plates vibrated on the cedar. "You will *never* wash my feet!"

Jesus paused. "Peter, if I don't wash your feet, then you can have no part with me."

Peter turned to look his Master in the eye. He was serious. Fear struck Peter's heart. He looked around at the others, but they were of no help. Many had tears streaming down their faces—some had their heads in their hands. They were stunned, angry, humiliated, and confused.

He looked back at Jesus. The idea of being cut off from him was too much to bear. "Then not just my feet, but my hands and head as well!"

Jesus began to untie his sandals. "A person who has had a bath does not need washing," he said as he lifted Peter's feet into the basin. Peter looked at them and was embarrassed. Not only were they caked in mud, but also in blood from his time at the Temple that afternoon. As Jesus poured water over his feet, the blood made the water pink and even tinted the white towel he cleaned them with.

"Now you are clean," Jesus said as he straightened up. "Though not all of you are."

What did he mean by that? Is there someone here who is unclean?

Jesus returned to the table and they grew still. "Do you know what I have done?" Jesus asked. "You call me Master and Lord, and rightly so. If I, your Lord and Master, have washed your feet, you must wash each other's feet. I have given you an example so that you may do to others what I have done to you. Blessed are you if you behave accordingly."

Jesus was quiet for a moment and the apostles dared not break the silence. "Scripture says: *He who shares my table takes advantage of me.* I tell you this now so that when it does happen, you may believe that I am He." He paused, then looked around the table. "One of you is going to betray me."

Judas's heart stopped. The apostles erupted in angry shouts and denied it vehemently, but to Judas it was all silence. He could not help but stare at Jesus, who whispered something to John. *How does he know about me?* Judas wondered.

Or does he? Jesus had not named his betrayer. Maybe someone from the Temple told him an apostle was betraying him, but he didn't know which one. It was not like Jesus to play games—when he knew the truth he said it. He still might have a chance to get out of this alive.

Judas stood and joined in the shouts of his peers. "Outrageous! How could you suggest such a thing?" But his hands trembled and he found it hard to control his voice. A cold sweat ran down his back.

"I will not allow it!" Peter said. He looked around at the reddened faces of the apostles, all of whom protested in similar ways. Could one of them really betray Jesus? But now he knew that Little James and Thomas didn't believe, and the Zealot had different ideas of his own. "Who is the betrayer?" he asked Jesus. "I will kill him with my own hands!"

But Jesus did not respond to him or anyone else. He sat calmly, as if oblivious to the noise around him. Jesus reached for the bitter herbs and dipped them in a cup of salt water before he ate them. Then he beckoned Peter to sit and Peter did.

Jesus handed him the herbs. Peter ate them and was overwhelmed with the strong taste. He passed them to Andrew who sat next to him.

The ritual calmed the apostles. One by one they sat and a heavy silence fell over them. When the bowl had passed all around them, Jesus took it from John and placed it back on the table.

Then Jesus looked at John. Silence hung in the air as if something was expected of him. Then Peter realized that John was the youngest person in the room.

John realized it, too. "Oh! Uh… Why is this night different from all other nights?" he asked, clearly remembering the words as he said them. "For on all other nights, we eat leavened bread, but on this night, why do we eat only unleavened bread? On all other nights, we eat many kinds of herbs, but on this night, why do we eat only bitter herbs? On all other nights, we eat meat roasted, stewed, or boiled, but on this night, why only roasted meat? On all other nights we dip the herbs only once, but on this night, why do we do it twice?" Then John took a breath of relief. James put a hand on his shoulder.

"Good job," James said.

"I haven't said that since I was ten," John said.

Philip smiled. "So that would make that, what? Last year?"

The table erupted in laugher and even John joined in. Peter laughed, too. The tension was so unbearable that he needed to.

Jesus smiled and waited for them to grow silent again. "My father was a Syrian, ready to perish," he said. And beginning with Terah, the father of Abraham, he told the story of their faith.

Peter had heard it told a hundred times, but never like this. Jesus spoke with such passion and unusual detail that Peter felt like he was right there. He saw the look on Isaac's face as Abraham lifted the knife to sacrifice him. He felt the warmth of the burning bush that blazed but did not consume. He heard the screaming of Egyptian mothers while the Jews huddled safe inside their houses.

"And tonight we remember what God has done for us," Jesus concluded. "Blessed be the name of the Lord."

They all said, "Amen". It was only when Peter heard the watchman's call outside the window he realized over an hour had passed. *Could that be possible?* He looked outside the window and marveled that the stars had moved. It seemed only a moment ago when... when what? He remembered feeling angry, but now he felt in awe of what the Lord had done for his people. One thing was sure —he hoped this night would never end.

It was the longest night of Judas's life.

He winced as Jesus painstakingly detailed each and every single patriarch in Scripture. *And the way he added all those fictional details...* the man was truly insane. The end of this meal could not come soon enough.

The servants returned with roasted lamb, unleavened bread, and more bitter herbs. The glasses were filled with wine. Jesus raised his goblet and said, "Therefore, we are bound to thank, praise, laud, glorify, extol, honor, bless, exalt, and reverence Him, because He has brought us forth from slavery into freedom, sorrow into joy, from darkness into a great light." And then with much excitement he said, "Let us sing before him: Hallelujah!"

All the apostles yelled back, "Hallelujah!" Then they began to sing:

Praise, servants of the Lord, praise the name of the Lord!
Blessed be the name of the Lord, now and forever!
From the rising to the setting sun, praised be the name of the
Lord!

They clapped and sang and beat their hands on the table to the rhythm of the song. Judas sang along and began to relax as he studied the others. They were so taken by the celebration that they seemed to forget all about the betrayal.

At the end of the psalms they drank their second cup of wine. Jesus took one of the two loaves of bread and gave thanks. He broke it and handed half to Peter on his right and half to John on his left. Both sides went around the table until it came to Judas—but somehow they miscalculated and there was nothing left for him to have.

Thomas, who sat beside him, began to rip his piece in half but Jesus stopped him.

"Here," Jesus said. He tore a piece of his bread, dipped it in the bitter herbs, and handed it across the table to Judas.

For the first time that evening, Judas looked into Jesus' eyes. And with horror Judas realized…

…*he knows.*

"What you are going to do, do quickly," Jesus said.

Judas ate the bread. An explosion of bitterness filled his mouth but he did not flinch. He was frozen in Jesus' stare. It was Jesus who first looked away, and Judas almost fell backward like he had been cut from a line. He straightened his robes and headed toward the stairs.

Each step was an agony. He imagined Jesus whispering to the others that he was the betrayer. Any moment he would feel the strong hand of James on his shoulder or the sharp sword of Simon at his back. When he got to the top of the stairs, he looked back to see why they hadn't reached him yet.

What he saw astonished him. The apostles were busy passing the lamb around and having conversations as if nothing important was happening. Jesus carried on with the rest of them. No one thought it strange that he left the table or even seemed to care that he was gone.

Good riddance, Judas thought. He pulled his tunic around him and headed down the stairs into the darkness outside.

Jesus breathed easier when he heard the door slam at the bottom of the stairs. It was hard to be so near to Judas all evening, not because he was angry but because he loved him so much. He knew what Judas had done, he knew what he was going to do, and he knew there was nothing he could do about it.

The roasted lamb was delicious and perfectly prepared. He savored the last piece of meat in his mouth and thanked the Father for a final comfort. From now on, he would be stripped away until there was nothing left. Only one more thing remained to do.

The servants came in to clear off the table and filled the glasses again with wine for the "blessing cup" which followed the main meal. Jesus motioned to one of the servants to leave a loaf of bread on the table. The servant looked confused but did as he asked. They left the room and Jesus was alone with his eleven apostles.

He reached forward and picked up the loaf. It was flat and round like a dish, the center of it a darker shade of brown than its edges. Jesus lifted it up. He held it there for a moment and time stood still. Then Jesus slowly, carefully, ripped the loaf in half. He stared at the two pieces in his hands for a moment. Then he looked up to his apostles.

"Take this, all of you, and eat it," he said, raising the bread again but this time holding it flat in his open palms. "This… is my body." He gave the bread to Peter and Peter hesitated—according to tradition, they shouldn't eat anything after the lamb was consumed. Jesus nodded and Peter bit into the bread.

Everyone stared at Peter as he chewed. He was surprised to find that it tasted like… bread. Peter knew this must have something to do with what Jesus talked about in Capernaum, but he couldn't make the connection. He passed the bread to Andrew and it went around the table.

Then Jesus took the wine, the blessing cup. "Drink this, all of you, for this is my blood, the blood of the new covenant. It will be poured out for many for the forgiveness of sins. From now on, I shall never drink wine again with you until we drink the new wine in my Father's kingdom." He drank from the cup and handed it Peter who did the same. It went round the table and John emptied what was left.

Jesus took the cup from John and placed it on the table. "Whenever you do this, remember me," he said.

Remember you? Peter thought. *Why is he talking like that?*

"I give you a new commandment," Jesus said to them. "Love one another. You *must* love one another just as I have loved you."

Peter noticed Jesus used a Greek word for love: *agape*. It was the highest form of love, greater than *eros*, the love between husband and wife, or *phileo,* the love between brothers.

Jesus' voice became thick with emotion. "Little children, I shall be with you only a little while longer. Where I am going, you cannot come."

This was too much. Peter knew something important was happening, but he was frustrated that he couldn't understand. "Lord, where are you going?" Peter asked.

Jesus looked at him solemnly. "You cannot follow me now, but later you will."

"Not even me?" He had grown accustomed to going places with Jesus that other apostles did not.

"You will all fall away from me tonight, for the scripture says: *I will strike the shepherd and the sheep will scatter.*"

The apostles reacted first with shock and then with anger. Simon stood and pounded his fist on the table. Matthew went white at the thought.

"I will never leave you!" James said.

"Nor I," Jude said.

Peter could not contain his anger. "How can you say such a thing? I have given my life for you!"

"Simon," Jesus said, "Satan has gotten his wish to sift you all like wheat. But I have prayed for you that your faith may not fail. And once you have recovered, you in your turn must strengthen your brothers."

Peter was stunned. *Why did he call me Simon?* "Even if *they* fall away from you, I will not. I will never disown you."

Jesus hesitated and looked into Peter's eyes. "In truth I tell you," Jesus said, "before the cock crows you will have disowned me, not just once, but three times."

Peter felt as though he had been stabbed in the chest and the sword pierced him straight through. He looked around at the others but only found harsh stares in return. He didn't care. Nobody loved Jesus more than he did, he was sure of it. He would rather die than disown him.

The apostles began to argue with Jesus but he silenced them. "Do not let your hearts be troubled," he said. "You trust in God, trust also in me. There is a place for you in my Father's house. After I have gone and prepared it, I will come back for all of you. You know the place where I am going."

"No, Lord, we don't!" Thomas said. "We have *no idea* where you are going. So how can we know the way?"

Jesus pointed to himself. "*I* am the way. I am truth and life. No one can come to the Father except through me. If you know me, you know my Father, too. From this moment you know him and have seen him."

Philip was clearly torn. "Lord, show us the Father, and then we will be satisfied."

Jesus looked him in the eye. "Have I been with you all this time, and you still do not know *me*?"

Philip leaned back in his cushions with shock, absorbing what the Master said.

"What I say to all of you is not of my own accord—it is the Father, living in me. You must believe me when I say that I am in the Father and the Father is in me. Or at least believe in me because of what you have seen."

"But you are leaving us," John whispered.

He put a hand on John's shoulder. "I shall not leave you orphans," Jesus replied. "I will ask the Father, and he will send you the Spirit of truth. In a short time you will no longer see me, but then a short time later you will see me again."

He is in the Father and the Father is in him? We won't see him soon but later we will? Peter felt like the room was spinning. It was all he could do to not throw the table over and scream with all his might.

Jesus closed his eyes and breathed deeply. He opened his mouth and said, "Be at peace."

And suddenly, Peter was.

The tension left from his shoulders. His breath became steady. Peter looked around at the others and he could see they experienced something similar.

"This peace I give you is my own," Jesus said, "so do not let your hearts be troubled or afraid. You will weep and wail while the world rejoices. You will be sorrowful, but your sorrow will turn to joy."

Jesus stood and the others rose as well. "I have other things to tell you, but you cannot bear them now. When the Spirit comes, he will lead you to the truth. But now we must go."

"Why?" Peter asked.

Jesus looked at him. "Because the prince of this world is on his way."

IN THE GARDEN

Matthew 26:36-46, Luke 22:39-51, John 18:10-11

They moved silently through the streets, now empty while everyone celebrated the Passover meal. They exited the city through one of the Southern gates and headed into the Kidron Valley. There was a heavy mist about and they descended into darkness. The apostles grabbed hold of each other so that no one would be lost. Jesus led the way.

After a while, the steep slope bent upward and they began to climb the mount. The mist above them whitened, illuminated by the full moon. They saw the ground again, and each other. Jesus navigated them to their camp and they collapsed with exhaustion and grief.

Peter did a quick head count. Everyone was there, except for Judas. *But Judas has always been good with his bearings,* Peter thought. *I'm sure he'll find his way through the mist.*

Many of the apostles were already sleeping. He was ready to join them, hoping a good night's rest would make everything clearer in the morning. Jesus faced away from him, looking up at the moon. "Good night, Master," he said to him.

Jesus turned, and the look on his face was one Peter had never seen before. Jesus' hands trembled. Tears streamed down his face. His olive skin seemed pasty white in the moonlight. He looked sorrowful to the point of death.

"Master?" he asked, reaching toward him.

Jesus grabbed his arm as if he were about to collapse. Peter had never seen him look so weak, so frail. It scared him.

"Come and pray with me," he asked.

"I'll get the others," Peter said.

Jesus grabbed his tunic tightly and stopped him. "Just James and John," he said. His chest heaved up and down with each uneven breath. Peter nodded that he understood.

The four of them walked through the mist until they came upon a large rock surrounded by olive trees. Peter noticed that this was the place that Jesus had told the others to find him when he prayed.

"Stay here and pray not to be put to the test," Jesus said. They sat down and leaned against a tree while Jesus went to the rock.

"I've never seen him like this," John whispered.

"I've never seen *anyone* like this," James said.

Jesus' mouth moved as if he was talking, but Peter couldn't hear what he said. His breathing seemed laborious. He looked up at the sky and then buried his head in the rock. Jesus seemed desperate, and at times he writhed around like an animal caught in a trap. It was a disturbing sight.

"Do you think they'll take him tonight?" John asked.

"In this mist?" Peter said. "No. Nothing will happen tonight. Not while we are here, at least." He reached beneath his tunic and rested his hand upon the hilt of his sword.

They were silent for a moment. Jesus lifted his hands up to heaven and seemed to shout at the sky, but the words were only desperate whispers. Then he was down again, arms outstretched upon the rock.

John couldn't bear the silence any longer. "Do you think he was right? About all of us running away?"

Peter felt his heart began to race again.

"No," James said. It was clear he didn't want to talk about it.

John looked at Peter for a response. "But Jesus is always right, isn't he?"

Peter had no intention of answering him.

"Peter?"

"*Not tonight,*" he said softly, fist clenched around the hilt of his sword.

"What?"

"I said—NOT TONIGHT!" He pulled out his sword and drove it into the ground.

His yell echoed through the clearing. Even Peter was shocked by the noise. He held his breath and looked toward Jesus, terrified that he interrupted his prayer.

Jesus didn't seem to notice. He breathed again. Peter left his sword embedded in the grass.

Peter steadied his breath and tried to calm his anger. *I will not betray him*, he thought. *Why would Jesus say such a thing?* The thought of denying Jesus twisted his stomach. *It must be some sort of test*, he thought. He was determined not to fail, even if it meant giving his life.

The mist came in thick and Jesus seemed veiled in a white light. He was surrounded by the knotted, twisted trunks of olive trees. They looked like deformed hands breaking through the earth, desperately reaching to be healed.

He looked at James and John. They seemed as scared of him as they were of the Master. "I'm fine," he said to them. "We should pray."

They nodded and bowed their heads. Peter closed his eyes but found it hard to concentrate. His heart still thumped in his ears. He breathed slowly, in and out. He began to calm down.

Peter tried to quiet himself and listen as Jesus had taught him to. What he heard caused him to jump.

Save us, the world cried.

Its voice was deep and ancient, yet it whimpered like a child. He looked at James and John to see if they heard it as well, but they were motionless. In fact, he wondered if they were asleep.

He stared at Jesus, who lifted himself off the rock. He was soaking wet, and he could see the sweat fall off of him as if they were drops of blood. Jesus nodded as if he agreed with something.

Peter leaned back against the tree. Had he heard anything at all? It must have been his imagination.

His eyelids felt heavy with exhaustion. With every blink his eyes closed longer. Looking at Jesus on the rock in the distance, he closed his eyes. When he opened them again, Jesus stood right in front of him.

"Simon, are you asleep?"

Peter quickly sat up and rubbed his face. "No," he said. He felt drool on the side of his lip.

"Could you not stay awake with me for one hour?" Jesus asked.

James and John now sat up as well, both mumbling apologies. "Stay awake, and pray not to be put to the test," Jesus told them. "The spirit is willing, but human nature is weak." Then he went back to the rock.

"Yes, Master," Peter said. He opened his eyes wide, determined not to fall asleep again. He sat up straight and focused on Jesus. It was not long before he awoke to Jesus' face again.

"What are you doing?" Jesus asked.

"Sorry, Master…" But he could hardly sit upright. James was out cold. John's eyes were open, but he stared up at the sky.

"Try to stay awake," Jesus said. Peter nodded, but he couldn't even remember Jesus making it back to the rock.

Jesus knelt on the stone and looked at the sky. Every ounce of his humanity wanted to give up and run away. He did not want to die. The thought of it made his chest feel empty and his muscles go weak. Jesus was afraid.

No, *terrified*. He came to experience the fullness of humanity. He knew what it was to be loved. The joy of a beautiful day. The satisfaction of hard work. The difficulty of learning new things. He knew what it was like to have friends, and also to have enemies. He knew what it was to lose someone who was close. How it felt to be misunderstood. Even betrayed by someone he loved.

And now he knew fear. Terrible, relentless, oppressive fear. He worried about his apostles, and especially Peter. But Judas troubled him the most. Was there anything more he could have done?

No, he consoled himself. *Judas was an* apostle. *He was as close to me as any of the others. I could not have loved him more or given more of myself to him.* And he grieved deeply.

He heard something move among the trees. It would be any minute now.

"Father," he begged, "for you everything is possible. Take this cup away from me."

But there was nothing but silence.

Jesus repeated his request.

Nothing.

He collapsed upon the rock again. "Not as I would have it," he said aloud, "but your will be done."

Jesus shook and found it hard to breathe. "Help me," he said.

An angel appeared to comfort him. It was filled with light yet radiated none of it. Jesus continued his prayer with great anguish and the angel's presence gave him strength. Eventually, his hands stopped shaking. He breathed deeply and slowly.

He looked up—the angel was gone. Jesus slowly lifted himself back to a kneeling position on the rock. His arms hung limply by his side, hands open in surrender.

"Your will be done," he said.

Peter had the sensation of falling, and jerked awake. He saw Jesus rise from the rock and head toward them. The others were asleep. He hit James, and James woke John.

"I'm sorry, Master," Peter said, stumbling to his feet. "We will keep praying."

"There is no need," Jesus said. "It is all over. The time has come."

The question, *what do you mean?*, was forming on his lips when Peter heard someone approach. Fear woke him like a bucket of cold water splashed on his face.

The dense mist made it impossible to see beyond a tree or two. He saw James grab his staff. Peter reached into his tunic for his sword, but realized it was stuck behind him in the ground. A solitary figure approached and became clear in the moonlight.

It was Judas.

Peter relaxed and released a deep breath while James let out a laugh. "Judas, you scared us half to death!" Peter said. "Are the others with you?"

Judas approached but never looked at them. His eyes darted from tree to tree. "Simon, James, John! How good it is to see you!" he said, with a volume that struck Peter as louder than necessary.

"Master!" Judas said. He approached Jesus with arms outstretched. Judas put his hands on Jesus' shoulder and kissed him on the cheek.

Jesus never moved, never offered a kiss in return. "Is that how you betray me, Judas?" he asked. "With a kiss?"

Just then, lanterns appeared around them and three armed figures came through the mist. It was not hard to tell by their helmets that they were Temple guards. James brandished his staff.

Even though he was unarmed, Peter thought they could probably take care of them. But then three more came. And three more. And ten more. He stopped counting at thirty. Then one of them stepped forward.

"Guards!" he yelled. And they all drew their swords at the same time. It was an ominous sight and filled the fishermen with fear. James and John turned and ran into the darkness.

Peter turned and began to run as well, but only took a few steps when he came upon his sword still planted firmly in the ground. He looked and saw that Jesus was not moving and guards were almost upon him.

This is it, Peter realized. *This is the test!*

"NO!" Peter pulled the sword out of the ground and rushed headlong to the guards. He raised it over his head and brought it crashing down on one of them, but the guard moved to the side at the last minute and Peter severed his ear clear off his head. The man screamed and put his hand to the wound. Blood gushed out between his fingers.

Peter's muscles tensed and he raised his sword again as the guards rushed at him. He knew he would not survive. *But I can take one or two of them out to give the Master some time to escape,* he thought.

"Put the sword away!" Jesus said. His words froze everyone except for the injured man who writhed on the ground like a fish out of water. Peter looked at him with shock. Why hadn't he run?

Jesus bent over and put his hand on the wounded man's head. Slowly, he grew still. When Jesus pulled back, the ear was healed.

While Peter stared at Jesus, one of the larger guards took the opportunity to grab him by the neck and knock the sword out of his hands.

"Am I a bandit that you have to come after me with swords and clubs?" Jesus asked. He looked at the man whose ear he just healed. "If I am the one you want, let the others go."

The man stood, his hand still rubbing the side of his face. He gave a look to the guard who held Peter. The guard let go and Peter staggered back, clutching his neck. Peter and Jesus looked at each other. Without knowing what else to do, he ran away and was quickly enveloped by the fog.

Judas moved behind the guards, hoping not to be confronted by Jesus or the others. As the guards tied Jesus' hands behind his back and pushed him forward, he looked for Malchus. Malchus was on his knees, running his fingers along the ground.

"Malchus?" Judas said. Malchus didn't respond, so Judas said his name again. This time Malchus stood up, and showed Judas what he had in his hand.

It was a severed ear.

"Do I have two ears on my head?" he asked with a dazed expression. "And if so, then where did this come from?"

Judas didn't have time for this. "Where is my money?" he asked.

Malchus didn't pay any attention to the question. "I was healed... Jesus touched me and I was healed. It's a miracle—"

"Yes, yes, I've seen them happen all the time," Judas snapped. "Now where is my money?"

Malchus looked at Judas and stared at him coldly. He untied a purse from his leather belt and threw it hard against Judas's chest, almost knocking him over by the blow. "The high priest thanks you for your service," he said. Then he turned to catch up with the rest of the guards and disappeared into the mist.

Judas didn't care what Malchus thought of him. Or the apostles. Or Jesus. His fingers twitched so anxiously over the purse he could barely get it open. A hysterical laughter built in his chest. He looked into the purse, but couldn't see the beautiful shine of silver because a branch from an olive tree cast a shadow upon it.

He moved to a clearing and tripped over a large flat rock. Coins scattered everywhere and clinked upon the stone. Judas screamed and dove forward, scooping the coins from the ground and pulling them close to his chest.

27... 28... 29... 30. All there. He breathed a sigh of relief, but it was cut short by the sound of laughter. He covered the money with both arms, like a mother protecting her infant. Judas looked around and saw shadows among the trees.

He stood to get a better look. "Who's there?" he asked. A piece of wood cracked behind him, then branches swayed to his left. Judas turned in circles. Dizzy, he was no longer sure which way he faced when a hideous face appeared out of the mist. Judas yelped and fell backward. Some coins bounced from the purse as he hit the ground, but he caught them with his hands.

He looked down at the money. A cloud moved across the moon, and the silver turned to black. When the moon appeared again, they reflected the color of blood.

Judas screamed in terror. And the devil laughed.

IN THE COURTYARD

Luke 22:54-62, John 18:12-27

Peter had not run far before his wits returned to him. He circled back to where the other apostles had slept and found it deserted. The mess they left behind was a clear sign that they had departed in haste. He ran down into the valley toward Jerusalem.

A snapping branch ahead of him let him know he was not alone. He stopped for a moment. *If it was a group of guards they could not be so quiet*, he thought. "Who's there?" he whispered.

There was no response at first. Then a voice eventually spoke. "Peter?"

"Yes, it's me."

John walked out of the mist and faded into view. "Peter, what should we do? I can't find James or any of the others. And I almost walked into the guards when I looked for them."

"Which way were they heading?"

"Toward Mount Zion. But I think the others must have—"

"If they're heading there then they must be going to the high priest's palace," Peter said. "Doesn't one of your family work as a servant there?"

"Abijah still works in the kitchen, I think."

"And you know him?"

"I doubt he'd remember me, but he'll know my father."

Peter grabbed him by the arm. "Let's go."

"But what about the others?" John asked.

"They'll fend for themselves."

"Won't they recognize us?"

"You're just a boy," Peter said. "They won't mess with you."

"But what about you?" he asked.

"It doesn't matter about me," he said. "We've got to help the Master."

The guards had a head start but they moved slower than Peter and John. They caught up to them by the time they reached the high priest's palace. The main doors were closed when they arrived, so John knocked on the servant's entrance and Abijah let him in. "You can stay by me and I can keep you out of trouble," he said to John, "but I'm not sticking my neck out for your friend."

"I can take care of myself," Peter said. He threw the top of his tunic over his curly hair and entered the courtyard. It was cold and dawn would come soon. *This is about the time I used to get up and go fishing*, he thought.

About twenty elders, scribes, Sadducees and Pharisees gathered around an ornate wooden chair that had been put in the middle. Peter noticed that Rabbi Dov and Rabbi Zedekiah were there. He pulled the tunic over his face and walked to an opposite corner of the courtyard where some people warmed themselves by a charcoal fire.

A servant girl came by with some fruit and unleavened bread that were left over from the night's feast. Peter took some food and thanked her for it, but caught a look in her eye that made him think he was recognized. He turned away and put his hands over the fire to warm them. *You're probably just imagining it,* he said to himself. But when he looked back, he found her still staring at him.

"Didn't I see you with Jesus in the Temple?"

Peter's heart beat quickly. "I don't know what you're talking about," he said.

"But I'm sure that I—"

"Go away," he said.

She closed her mouth and left. Peter looked around the courtyard and realized he was trapped. The main doors were shut. The kitchen was on the other side. The only other exits led deeper into the high priest's house. *This might be a huge mistake.*

Jesus was led into the courtyard. He was still dressed in his seamless white tunic and didn't look like he had been beaten or badly treated. The high priest's father-in-law, Annas, entered the room. A man stood at attention. Peter recognized him as the one who's ear he cut off.

"Thank you Malachi, that will be all," he said.

"Will Master Caiaphas be joining us?" the servant asked.

The former high priest seemed insulted by the question. "Caiaphas didn't want to give the appearance of working on a holy day, so for now *I* am in charge. Understood?"

The man quickly bowed. "Of course. Forgive me."

Annas sat in the wooden chair. "I would like to thank our distinguished leaders who have joined us at this late hour," he said. "This is an informal gathering. The full Sanhedrin will meet in the morning… but we have some questions for you, young Rabbi." He leaned forward and looked at him intently. "Do you realize what kind of trouble you are in?"

He spoke in a condescending manner, like a storekeeper might lecture a child he caught stealing fruit from his cart. Jesus did not respond, did not even look up at him. His eyes were focused on the ground.

Annas sat back in his chair and rolled his long fingers on the wooden armrest. Then he smiled wickedly. "Maybe my question was too broad for you to comprehend. So let me ask simpler questions that someone from Nazareth might understand." The crowd laughed at this. "Have you ever been a disciple of a Rabbi, and if so, what is his name?"

Jesus did not respond.

"I'll take that as a no," Annas said, and the crowd laughed again. "What about your disciples?"

Peter tried to steady his breath. *They don't know who you are,* he said to himself.

Annas continued the questioning. "If you have never been a disciple, what gives you the right to form your own school of disciples?"

No answer.

At the word, "disciples", one of the men standing next to Peter asked. "Aren't you one of his disciples?"

Peter acted insulted at the question. "Me? I don't even know that man," he said firmly. The man shrugged, and focused his attention back to the interrogation.

Sweat ran from Peter's forehead into his beard. He stared at Jesus for fear that looking in any other direction might get him caught.

"And what of these teachings you give? Do you tell people to not keep to the fasts and break the law? To not listen to their leaders?" Again, there was no answer and Annas spoke more forcefully. "What, have you nothing to say? Or do you save all your words for uneducated and easily manipulated peasants?"

Then Jesus looked up, and the look took Annas by surprise. "I have spoken openly for all the world to hear," he said, "both in synagogues and in the Temple. If you want to know what I taught, ask someone who listened to me."

At this, the guard who stood next to Jesus slapped him across the face. Peter winced. The courtyard grew silent, and heads angled themselves in the crowd to get a better view of Jesus' response.

The slap split Jesus' lip, and he spit out a bit of blood. Peter cursed, wishing he had his sword on him. He would kill that guard right then and there.

But Jesus showed no anger. He looked at the man who struck him. "What did I say that was offensive?"

The guard looked around, but had no answer.

"If there was nothing I said that was wrong," Jesus continued, "then why did you strike me?"

"You are a child of the devil!" Rabbi Dov said. "You turn the people against us and against the God of Israel. You are a traitor, an insurrectionist, and a blasphemer!"

At this the crowd exploded with noise. Men raised their fists in the air. Peter had a hard time seeing what was going on.

There was a tap on his shoulder. He turned and was face to face with the slave girl. Behind her stood a large guard with an ape-like face. "This is the one I was talking about," she said.

The ape-faced man pointed a finger at Peter. "Yeah, that's him. I just saw you in the garden."

Peter began to swear loudly. His curses were lost in the general din of the crowd. He swore at the slave girl and told her to mind her place—what kind of way is this to treat a guest of the high priest? He cursed at the guard that he would dare to think that he would be associated with such a blasphemous traitor as the Rabbi from Nazareth. He swore by all the gold in the Temple that they were mistaken.

Annas raised his hands to quiet the crowd, but Peter didn't see him and continued his tirade, until only his voice could be heard: "I DO NOT KNOW THE MAN!"

Then Peter saw Jesus turn and look at him. He felt his heart stop in his chest. Everything around him froze as he stared into the face of his friend. Jesus' eyes were wide, as if he wanted to tell him something but couldn't. Peter opened his mouth to speak—what could he say? He didn't mean that, he was just pretending. Surely Jesus couldn't believe—

Then a cock crowed.

Jesus turned and faced Annas, who berated him with more questions. Peter's heartbeat came back, but this time with a furious pace. He looked around at the faces in the crowd. Every one was an enemy about to strike. The courtyard began to spin.

He heard a knock at the door and saw a servant open it to allow a man into the courtyard. Peter ran to the door and slid into the street before it was closed again.

The entrance was sealed with a large thud. He walked a few steps away, but had to reach out his hand and balance himself against the wall.

I denied him.

A few more steps and his legs felt like jelly. He could barely stand.

I denied him.

His vision became blurry and he wiped his eyes, but the blurriness returned. He was crying uncontrollably.

I denied him.

Over his tears, Peter heard cheers and laughter in the courtyard, and a man yell, "Prophesy to us! Who hit you!"

They are beating him, he thought. *I should go back.*

But then he heard the squeak of the door opening and his heart leapt with fear, thinking that someone was coming after him. He ran down the street and fled.

ON TRIAL

Luke 22:66-23:12, John 18:28-40

A frantic knocking at the door awoke James the Nazarene from his sleep. Their journey to Jerusalem had been long and the Passover "celebration" was anything but.

That evening, his father Jedidiah had joyfully recounted the wonderful works of God... but all eyes were upon the mother of Jesus. Mary held a tremendous sadness within her that ruined the whole evening. What was worse was that she never cried. *That would have been better*, James thought, *if she collapsed in tears like the other women do.* Then she could have been excused from the meal and nobody would have to think about it. But there she sat, almost regal in her suffering. The bitter herbs seemed pleasant compared to the sorrow he experienced looking into her eyes.

Someone called his name. He got out from the warm blanket that covered him and felt the cold chill of the morning. The other men in the room stirred uncomfortably as he pulled back the thick fabric that was a door for the room and let in wisps of morning light. He saw Salome. Her face was red with tears. John, her youngest son, stood next to her and looked as white as wool.

"Where is my sister?" she said.

James pointed to the room where the women were and she ran into it. He heard muffled cries of, "They've taken him!" and the sound of women shrieking in grief. Everyone was awake now, but few dared to move.

"What happened?" James asked. It was the first words he spoke that morning, and his voice was still rough with sleep.

"We were betrayed," John said in a stunned whisper. "Judas led them to us, and Jesus is being put on trial as we speak."

At this time in the morning? James thought, looking at the sky. But it suddenly made sense to him. They could not have done anything last night because it was the Passover. And when the sun went down tonight, it would be the Sabbath. All that they wanted to do to him had to happen during the day.

"What are they planning to do to him?" James asked.

John looked as if he was about to burst into tears. "One of the servants said they were planning on handing him over to the Romans."

Crucifixion. It was the only reason to hand him over. A cold chill ran across James's skin, and he felt sympathy for the teenager before him who was desperately trying to be strong.

James had an idea this would come. Jesus had become delusional and blasphemous and deserved what was going to happen. But he was surprised at the emotion he felt hearing the news. Memories of their childhood came flooding back to him.

He deserves it, his mind said. But his heart spoke something different. He thought of the little brother he sat next to while their fathers taught them the Law, and imagined unclean Gentiles nailing him to a cross. No one deserves to die like that. No one.

Mary and Salome came out of the room. The other women stood by the door but did not follow. Salome shot James a hateful look but Mary calmly approached.

She bowed before him and gently said, "With your permission, I would like to see my son now." He could not see if she was crying, for she did not look up from the ground.

A lump formed in James's throat. "God be with you," he said. She bowed again, and the three left.

"God be with all of us," he whispered to himself. He woke the rest of the house to lead them in prayer for his brother.

Caiaphas marveled at himself in the mirror. His turban and tunic had streaks of royal violet, his outer garment was made of crimson cloth sewn with golden thread. He wore golden shoulder pieces with two pieces of onyx on which were engraved the name of each of the twelve tribes of Israel. He combed his beard and placed on his head a golden diadem that had the words "Glory to God" inscribed upon it. Now he looked perfect.

His outfit had been a part of the Temple ceremonies for centuries, and was made up of items from even before the exile. Rome also knew its value—which is why they "kept it safe" and only allowed him to wear it on high holy feasts. This thought burned

Caiaphas's heart with rage. He should not need permission from Romans to wear what was rightfully his.

"Master Caiaphas," Malchus said.

Caiaphas turned and Malchus looked with awe at the high priest. Satisfied with this reaction, Caiaphas asked, "Are they ready?"

"They are all here, Master."

"Then let's not keep them waiting... Malchus, are you all right?" He seemed pale.

"I'm fine, Master," he answered.

Caiaphas knew it was a lie but had bigger things to worry about. He entered his courtyard and the Sanhedrin stood and applauded him. All seventy-two men were there, composed mostly of Sadducees and some Pharisees. He was impressed they were gathered at such an early hour. It was a bit cramped to have them meet at his palace but gathering at the Chamber of Hewn Stone in the Temple's outer wall was too public for what they needed to do.

After allowing a few moments of applause and adoration, he quieted them and sat in his chair. "Bring in the Rabbi from Nazareth," Caiaphas said. Jesus was led in.

There were gasps in the crowd when they saw him. His white tunic looked as if it had been dragged across the floor. His lips were cracked and wet with bleeding, and there was dried up blood around his nose. His right eye was red and almost completely swollen shut. His hair was a mass of sweat, blood, and dirt.

Caiaphas shot an angry stare at his father-in-law and motioned him over. "He was in your charge. What happened to him?" he asked.

Annas shrugged. "Perhaps he resisted when they came to get him."

The high priest shook his head in disgust and he addressed the Sanhedrin. "I call this trial to order," Caiaphas said. "What case have you against this man?"

With that question, the courtyard erupted in shouts.

"Silence!" Caiaphas ordered, and slowly the crowd obeyed. "This is a court of law, and we will have order. I need two witnesses to give testimony against this man. Come forward and make your claim."

Men came forward, one by one.

"He's possessed by a devil!"

"No, he casts them out!"

"He works on the Sabbath!"

"He teaches against the Law!"

The accusations grew more outrageous with every man, and witnesses began to contradict each other. Annas whispered in his ear. "Surely, you have heard enough."

"Enough?" Caiaphas said. "This is an insult to the Law. Mark my words, I will not convict without a serious claim."

Annas's jaw hung open for a moment. Then with grim determination he walked over to a group of Pharisees and began an active conversation while witness after witness came forward about how Jesus was the devil, broke the law, cursed children, or supported Rome.

The high priest couldn't keep his eyes off the Rabbi from Nazareth. He noticed that Jesus barely moved and kept his eyes toward the ground. There was no fight in him. Where was the man who preached so fearlessly in the Temple?

He felt a great surge of pity for the man. He looked so meek. Was it right to hand him over to the cruelty of Rome? It was hard to believe that a man so eloquent and knowledgeable about the Law could ever blaspheme. It was clear to him by now that most claims brought against him were exaggerations or outright lies.

Then the Pharisees brought two men forward. One had a round face and a square beard. "I heard this man say that he could tear down the Temple and rebuild it in three days. I swear by my life."

The man next to him agreed. "I heard him say it also. I swear by my life."

The courtyard grew quiet. It was the first time two witnesses agreed on anything. Caiaphas leaned forward in his chair and addressed Jesus. "Have you no answer to that? What is this evidence these men have brought against you?"

Jesus gave no response.

Insulting the Temple was serious, worthy of flogging or imprisonment, but not death. He looked at Annas with an expression that said, *Is this all you have?* Annas wrung his hands but had no response. Normally, he would have enjoyed seeing his father-in-law in such straits, but this moment was too important.

Caiaphas stood and walked toward Jesus. "No answer? Then let me dare to ask the question everyone else seems afraid to: Are you the Christ, the Son of the Blessed One?"

The courtyard became deathly still as they awaited Jesus' response. The question hung in the air for what seemed like an eternity.

Caiaphas regretted asking it, and his mind raced to think what he could do if Jesus didn't respond, or if he responded "no". Rome would demand some kind of evidence to execute him, and the witnesses they had were weak. The governor owed him a favor for handing over Barabbas, but it was doubtful he would kill a man because he was asked to. And if they couldn't convict him, then the Sanhedrin would lose faith in him…

Then Jesus spoke. "I am," he replied.

The crowd gasped. Caiaphas staggered back. "What?"

Jesus continued. "And you will see the Son of Man seated at the right hand of power and coming with the clouds of heaven."

Caiaphas looked with horror at the devil before him. "Blasphemy," he muttered, and then shouted, "BLASPHEMY!"

He reached below his rich outer garment and ripped the tunic he wore underneath. "What need have we of witnesses?" he cried. "You have heard for yourselves! What is your verdict?"

"Death!" echoed the people. They struck him and spit at him and almost ripped him apart. Caiaphas motioned to the temple guards to remove him. If Jesus got killed in his house he would most likely be blamed.

They burst through the main doors and into the street where a large group of people had gathered. Guards pushed Jesus through the crowd. Caiaphas proudly led the way. Never was he more convinced that a man deserved to die.

By the time John, his mother, and Mary made it to the high priest's palace it was empty except for a few servants who cleaned up the mess. Abijah was still there and told them what happened.

"Where did they take him?" John asked.

"To see the Roman governor," he said.

They stepped outside the palace. It was built on the side of a hill that sloped down and rose on the other side where the Temple was situated. John saw a mob of people head toward Antonian Fortress.

"If we hurry, we can catch them," he said.

"We aren't as fast as you!" his mother snapped. "Give us a moment, won't you?" She sat down, weary from traveling and grief.

John looked longingly in the distance as the crowd moved closer to the Roman fortress. Mary put a gentle hand on his arm.

"It's all right," Mary said. "We'll see him."

John didn't want to look at her for fear he would cry. All he wanted to do was to run away as fast as he could and scream until his voice became hoarse. Mary's gentle touch felt heavy upon him. John did not want to witness her grief because he barely felt he could carry his own.

His mind flooded with excuses for him to leave. *I should try to find the others*, he thought. He looked at Mary to tell her this, but his open mouth was struck silent as he looked upon her face.

In that moment he realized: Jesus had his mother's eyes.

John had never looked at Mary this closely before, but the resemblance was clear and gave him a renewed strength. He recalled the fondness with which the Master talked about his mother and decided he would do anything to help her.

"I'm ready when you are," he said. After a few moments, they headed down the hill.

Longinus was warned of the approaching mob and he had a large group of soldiers ready when they arrived. He held up a hand and expected immediate silence. When it did not come, he ordered the soldiers to draw their swords. The sounds of metal against their scabbards achieved the desired effect.

One of the Jews, dressed in so many jewels that he had to be the high priest, stepped forward. "We wish to speak to Governor Pilate on a matter of great urgency."

"About what?" the centurion asked.

"Our highest court has convicted this man to death for blasphemy and treason."

Longinus sighed. "Show me the prisoner."

The Temple guards pushed Jesus forward and he stumbled toward the centurion. "What's his name?" Longinus asked.

"Jesus, from Nazareth," Caiaphas said.

"Kill him!" someone shouted from the crowd. Longinus strained his head to see who said it, but no one else dared to speak.

He waved them forward. "Come on," he said, and began to walk into the fortress. The priest cleared his throat. The centurion turned and realized he wasn't following.

"We can't enter a Gentile house, or we would be unclean for the Sabbath. Please tell the governor we wish to speak to him here."

Longinus wasn't sure whether to swear or laugh. He decided to do neither. He shook his head and spoke to a soldier next to him. "Tell the governor the high priest would like to speak with him *outside*."

Pilate rubbed the stubble on his face and considered not shaving. Maybe he should grow a beard. *Some hair on my chin might make up for the hair I'm losing on my head,* he thought. The governor didn't mind his receding hairline—it made him look older. And he always felt his baby face kept him from higher positions of command.

He had to bend down to see himself in the mirror. The previous governor must have been a midget. But he refused to change the mirror, the gaudy décor, or anything about the fortress. That would give the impression he might be *staying*. He planned his tenure in Jerusalem to be a short one, and now that he was executing Barabbas, the terror of Judea, he hoped his departure would be sooner rather than later.

There was a knock on the door, and Governor Pilate called the soldier in. "A large group of Jews, led by the high priest, desire to speak to you."

Ah, Caiaphas. He normally wouldn't have entertained such a request before breakfast, but he did owe him a favor for capturing Barabbas. Or did he? They were probably saving their own skin. For every Roman Barabbas killed, they killed a hundred Jews. Pilate wondered why they hadn't turned him over sooner.

They probably want to have some part in the execution. He would let them, of course. Good relations with the locals would only make his career look better.

But what he saw as he walked outside gave him pause. He didn't like the size of the crowd that had gathered outside his door. Archers lined the top of the fortress, bows at the ready. He looked at

Caiaphas and almost laughed aloud. The high priest wore the regal vestments usually kept at the fortress, but the tunic underneath them was torn, giving him a disheveled look.

"Caiaphas, I hope you are having a good Passover," he said.

"The Passover was last night, your excellence. Today begins the feast of Unleavened Bread."

Whatever. "How can I help you?"

Caiaphas pointed at the prisoner. "This man, Jesus of Nazareth, has been found guilty of blasphemy and according to our law must be put to death."

Pilate looked at Jesus with a frown. "Your laws are not always our laws, high priest."

"But he claimed to be our Messiah, our king. The one who is to liberate us from any... *oppressors.*" Pilate raised his eyebrows at the statement. "Surely such a man must be seen as not only a danger to us, but also to you."

Pilate rubbed his hand against his chin and scratched the stubble. He took a few moments to look at Jesus and consider what he should do.

He turned to Longinus. "Bring him inside," he said. Then he looked back at the high priest. "Unless you object to him being *unclean.*"

The high priest said something in response, but Pilate was already walking back through the door.

Inside the fortress, a servant handed him a pomegranate. Pilate eagerly bit into it. Jesus entered, flanked by Roman guards. The angry screams of the crowd became muffled as the door closed behind them.

"So, you are the king of the Jews?" he asked.

Jesus stared at the pomegranate for a moment, then looked at Pilate. "Are you asking for yourself, or because others have told you?" he asked.

Pilate laughed. "Am I a Jew? It's your people who turned you over to me."

"Mine is not a kingdom of this world," Jesus said. "If my kingdom were of this world, my people would have fought for me."

The governor shook his head and took another bite. He wiped the juice off his mouth. "I can see why they don't like you. Nobody likes a self-proclaimed king. Especially Caesar."

"I never said I was a king," Jesus said.

"Not a king? Then what kingdom are you talking about?"

"The kingdom of God."

Interesting. "Are you willing to die for this 'kingdom of God'?"

Jesus nodded. "I was born for this. I came into the world for this."

"To die?"

"To bear witness to the truth. And all who are on the side of truth listen to my voice."

"Truth?" Pilate laughed. "What is that?"

The prisoner didn't seem to get the joke and said nothing. Pilate was amazed at his calm demeanor.

The governor took a moment and considered the man before him. He looked like a beggar but spoke like a prince. Pilate had interrogated many men who faced execution. Some were defiant in anger, others writhed on the ground begging mercy. But this man did neither. He had never seen a man look so... gentle.

Pilate folded his arms and shook his head. This Jew was a problem. Pilate had been around enough guilty men to know that he was innocent. He would *not* kill an innocent man, and resented Caiaphas for putting him in this position.

He did not believe in God or "truth", but was a firm believer in the law. It was the law that made Rome so superior to the civilizations that preceded it. Killing people over religious differences is what the barbarians did. It was the very reason Rome took that power away from them.

Pilate began to pace, trying to think of a way out of this situation. He couldn't just release him—that might spark violence and damage his career. If there was only a way to make them not want him dead. He abruptly stopped pacing when the idea came to him.

"Centurion!" he said. Longinus snapped to attention. "Take the prisoner out front and place my chair on the steps of the fortress."

Longinus gave a slight bow but did not salute. The governor endured the affront the same way he always did, by saying nothing.

"I have good news for you," Pilate said to Jesus. "You won't be dying today."

The prisoner closed his eyes for a moment and Pilate stared at him, expecting *some* reaction of joy. But when his eyes opened, his demeanor hadn't changed.

The soldiers turned the man around and led him out. "You're welcome," Pilate said under his breath.

The din of the crowd turned into a roar when Jesus was led out of the fortress. His right eye was so swollen he could barely see out of it. Sweat from his brow got into his other eye, and he could not wipe it away because of his bound hands. Jesus shook his head to clear the sweat away. He saw men shake their fists at him in violent motion. But Jesus paid them little notice. He looked for people who stood still. Those would be his followers.

Simon the Zealot was in the front to the right. Jude stood in the back to the left. Thomas was somewhere in the middle. None of the Galileans were there. Jesus thought of Peter and said a prayer for him.

He continued to look through the crowd. In the back, separate from the mob, were three women. No—it was two women and a young man between them. The man must be John. The woman, face to the ground on her knees, must be Salome. And the woman who stood still…

…was his mother.

Jesus felt both joy and dread. He didn't want her to see this anymore than he wanted to go through with it. *But she has her own cup to drink*, he thought. *Father, your will be done.*

Mary lifted a hand toward him. He nodded to her, and the hand came down. His heart felt as if it was going to break.

He saw John put his arm around her shoulder. For the first time that morning, Jesus faintly smiled. The scabs on his lip pulled as he did so, but he didn't care. *Well done, John,* Jesus thought. *Well done.*

Pilate came out of the fortress and quieted the crowd. He sat down on the large stone chair that the soldiers had put out for him. "This morning," he said in a loud and clear voice, "your elders brought to me this man, Jesus of Nazareth, for his false claim of being King of the Jews."

At this, the crowd began to roar again. Pilate allowed it for a few seconds, but then beckoned for silence once more. "After interrogating the prisoner… I find no guilt in the man."

The crowd protested in outrage and Caiaphas, who stood at the front of the crowd, looked like his head was going to explode. In contrast, Pilate calmly motioned to a servant for something to drink and a servant brought him a cup of water.

Pilate sipped from it while the crowd whipped themselves into a frenzy. People who heard the noise ran out of the Temple to see what the commotion was about. There were almost a thousand people now.

The additional numbers tried to push the crowd forward but the Roman soldiers, who formed a line between Pilate and the mob, lifted their swords. This gave everyone pause, and the roar of anger diminished into a dull hum.

Pleased with their response to Roman force, Pilate spoke to them again. "I understand that this man is troublesome to you. So I have a proposal for you all to consider. It is customary for your Passover feast that I release a prisoner for you. So who shall I release? Jesus, the king of the Jews…"

At this many people started to yell, "Crucify him! Kill Jesus!"

"…or Barabbas?"

The crowd grew deathly still. Pilate focused all his energy in not allowing his face to break out in a smile. The priests and Pharisees in the front had their jaws open in shock.

From the back, a faint voice yelled, "Release Jesus!"

"No!" Caiaphas roared, and he turned to face the crowd. "Give us Barabbas! We want Barabbas!"

The other priests and elders quickly did the same, until the entire crowd was chanting, "BARABBAS! BARABBAS! BARABBAS!" Caiaphas waved his arms to the rhythm of the chant, and the crowd followed along.

Pilate felt the blood drain from his face. *Release Barabbas? Are they fools?* It never occurred to him they would ask such a thing. He considered asking the question again, but he knew he had lost.

Caiaphas turned and gave the governor a smug look. For a moment, Pilate imagined ordering the guards to forcefully retrieve the priestly garments off of Caiaphas' back.

But he quickly regained his composure. Two can play at this game. *If I can't kill my terrorist, you can't kill your king.* Pilate stood and, without a word, turned his back to the crowd and walked toward the entrance of the fortress.

One of the guards at the door asked, "Sir, what should we do with—"

"Have him scourged," Pilate said, and then disappeared in the building. The crowd cheered with victory as the soldiers took Jesus and led him inside. The other soldiers also retreated and the large wooden doors of Antonian fortress slowly shut with a loud thud.

AT THE PILLAR

John 19:1-16

Jesus sharply inhaled as the felt the cold, rough marble pressed against his bare chest. His tunic was pulled down to his waist, and a soldier stretched Jesus' arms around one of the large pillars inside the Roman fortress. They tied the leather straps on his wrists to a round metal hook that hung well above his head on the other side of the column.

He was bound so tightly to the pillar he could lift his feet off the floor and not slide down. He could only breathe in shallow breaths. The pain subsided in his wrists as his hands became numb.

From behind him, Jesus heard men laughing. A soldier walked to the side of Jesus so he could look at him. He was a large, bald man with a scar over the right side of his face.

"It's an honor to meet you, *your majesty*," he said. There was laughter and the man looked around as if to thank them for their applause. "My name is Longinus. Forgive me if I miss your back and hit you in the face. You see, I can't see out of this eye," he said, and he pointed to a milky cloud in his right eye. "The other one isn't so good neither."

Longinus backed away. Jesus couldn't see what was going on behind him. Though his face was to one side, he had instinctively turned his head to the left so his swollen eye wouldn't be pressed against the stone. Jesus heard Longinus swing the whip around, heard its whistle in the air, and even felt it breeze across his bare back.

"Are you ready?" Longinus asked.

Father, help me… Jesus was determined not to cry out or show fear.

"Here we go!" the soldier said.

The whip cracked and Jesus tensed, clinging even tighter to the pillar if that were possible. But there was no blow. He had just cracked it in the air.

The soldiers erupted in howls of laughter. Jesus relaxed for a moment.

And then the first hit came.

It hit with a sharp thud and knocked the wind out of his lungs. He tried to arch backward in pain, but they tied him too tightly around the pillar to move. Jesus gasped but did not scream.

Then another blow, this time from the other side. It came too quickly to be from Longinus—there was another man helping him. Then Longinus struck from the left. The whip hissed and thudded against his back. Jesus winced when it made impact.

Spirit, give me strength.

The blows continued from side to side. One of them smashed against his face.

"Nice shot," one of the guards said.

"He can't say I didn't warn 'em!" Longinus said with a laugh. Others laughed as well.

"I think he's ready to go at any moment," the other soldier said.

Jesus wasn't sure what he meant by that. And then he did.

The centurion struck him with the whip, but it didn't fall away like the other blows did. A sharp piece of bone tied to the end of the whip got caught in his skin. He heard the murmuring approval of the watching soldiers. Then the whip was yanked away and it peeled a strip of flesh from his back.

Jesus opened his mouth and gasped as if he was going to scream. He felt the cold morning air against the wound and the blood run down his back. He took a few quick breaths and swallowed hard. One of the soldiers came up to him and looked at his face.

"He singing yet, Quintus?" Longinus asked.

"Almost," he said.

"What blow was that?" the centurion asked.

"Twelve, I think."

Twelve. Jesus thought of his apostles, and he decided to pray for each one by name. As the whip cracked for the thirteenth time, Jesus closed his eyes and clung tightly to the rock, whispering the word, "Peter…"

"Get up you drunk!" A wrinkly old woman with a weathered shawl around her head faded into view. "Can't you stay sober, even on Passover? God will judge you!"

Peter stared at her with blurry eyes and took in his surroundings. He was outside the city, leaning against one of the many poor houses that surrounded it. He looked behind him and recognized the southern wall of Jerusalem. Peter staggered as he got to his feet.

"God will judge you!" she said again, and then went back into her house.

What time is it? How long have I slept? The last thing he remembered was the look on Jesus' face and running through the streets with his eyes full of tears.

He thought of what the old woman said. *God will judge me*, he thought. The reality of his denial came back to him, and he would have cried if he had any tears left to shed. His chest felt hollow and he felt sick.

Even if everyone else denies you, I will not! Had he said that the night before? It seemed like a week ago. What happened? They celebrated the Passover. They went to the garden. Jesus kept waking them up. And then...

Judas.

He greeted Jesus with a kiss. And Jesus said something about betrayal. Did Judas hand them over?

Peter rubbed his temples with his hands. It was inconceivable. Judas was one of the best preachers among the twelve of them. He collected money and was generous to the poor. He was... a traitor?

He shook his head as if he argued with someone. It made no sense. Judas must have been forced to do it. They must have captured him and threatened to... what? Kill him? Was he so cowardly that he gave the Master's life to save his own?

If that was the case, he should have died for him, Peter thought.

But you *didn't,* said the sea.

He spun around. There was no water to be seen for miles, but he was sure he heard its voice. "I tried to," he said, "in the garden. I was ready to die—"

You were scared by a slave girl.

His heart recalled the fear he felt in the courtyard and he couldn't deny it. He stammered to find words but none came to his mouth.

You are no rock.

Simon agreed.

He hung his head and continued his walk, letting gravity pull him down into the Kidron valley. As he got to the bottom, he saw someone move among the trees.

Simon froze, wondering if his eyes deceived him. He saw a shoulder behind one of the trunks, and then it turned away.

His first instinct was to run. But what if it was one of the other apostles? "Who's there?" he asked.

The man did not respond, but Simon saw a shoulder appear and disappear again behind the tree.

Though Simon was gripped with fear, something pulled him forward, step by step, toward the man. He heard the wind blow through branches and the creaking sound of pulled leather. The man must be tall because his shoulder was as high as Simon's head.

"James?" he asked.

When Simon came round the tree, the man spun toward him and Simon looked into the pale and horrified face of Judas.

Simon screamed and fell backward. Judas turned away. Then he turned back. Simon saw a leather belt around his neck tied to a strained branch that kept Judas's feet of the ground. The wind turned him back and forth, back and forth.

"Judas…" Simon whispered, and he stared at the face of his former friend.

Judas's eyes were wide with terror, and his mouth was open as if frozen in mid-scream.

"Come join me," Judas said. His mouth did not move.

"What?" Simon asked, both shocked and intrigued by the request.

"Come join me," Judas said again, this time with a darker voice. Simon considered the belt that hung Judas from the tree, and realized he had one of his own. He wondered if his belt could hold his weight and his fingers reached to take it off…

"NO!" Simon screamed. The dead body didn't flinch. Then the wind turned Judas's back to him.

Simon ran as fast as he could up the hill. Branches slapped across his face and body. His heart pounded in his chest and he breathed heavily as he made his way up the mount.

He stopped to catch his breath in a clearing where there was a large rock. It was a familiar place, but he had never come at it from this direction before.

This is where they took him.

He saw the blood on the ground where he had cut off the servant's ear. He could imagine Jesus praying on the stone, and he looked over to the trees that the three of them slept against.

Stay awake, Jesus told them, *and pray not to be put to the test.*

Simon crawled on the rock and assumed the same posture that Jesus had the night before. "I'm awake now, Master," he said. "I'm awake...."

But it was too little, too late. Simon collapsed. He knew he had to go back to Jerusalem, had to see what they would do to him. But he hadn't the strength to move. Simon lifted his head to heaven and prayed the words that Jesus taught him to pray.

"Our Father, who reigns in heaven, holy is your name. Your kingdom come, your will be done..."

A group of priests, Sadducees, and Pharisees huddled by the large granite steps that led into the fortress. People stood on their toes and arched their heads to get a better view. The crowd grew by the minute.

Caiaphas felt intoxicated. Never had he dreamed to rally a crowd this close to the Roman fortress. He raised his hands for silence. "Children of Abraham! We have found Jesus of Nazareth guilty of blasphemy. We have brought him to Pilate for punishment, but he does not want to put him to death, and by doing so spits in the face of Moses, David, and all that we believe in!"

The crowd roared in anger.

"How much longer shall we be subject to an authority that would protect the lives of men like Jesus and Barabbas, who are enemies to us and all that we believe in?"

Another wave of angry yells rippled through the mob. For many who had joined the crowd late, this was the first time they heard that Barabbas was set free, and they were enraged.

"They are scourging him now, as if that would satisfy our Law. But does it? DOES IT?"

"No!" the crowd yelled.

"What must they do?"

"Crucify him!" they shouted.

"WHAT MUST THEY DO?"

"CRUCIFY HIM!"

As far as Longinus could make out, the blur of white flesh that hung against the pillar had become a blur of red. They lost count of how many times he had been struck, but still this man hadn't made a sound. Longinus was impressed that Jesus hadn't screamed by the twentieth lash, but by the thirtieth lash his admiration turned to anger.

He had done everything he knew to make him sing: he quickened the pace of his lashes, changed sides, and used all his might to embed the bony claws more deeply into Jesus' back before dragging them across his body.

By now it was getting hard to find a place where the sharp edges would bite. He walked closer to the prisoner to get a better look. Jesus' back was so bloodied that his flesh hung from it and revealed bone. He looked like a dead animal that had been picked apart by crows.

Longinus was determined not to finish until he was satisfied. He let the whip fly again. The prisoner absorbed the blow as if he was a corpse.

"Longinus," Quintus said quietly.

"Come on, Jew! Scream!" He stood directly behind Jesus and the whip cracked again. The blow to his spine caused Jesus' legs to convulse.

Quintus walked over to Longinus and grabbed his arm. "I'm not taking the blame if he dies."

Longinus shook him off. "I know what I'm doing!" He figured he could survive at least one more hit.

He aimed for the head. With deadly accuracy the whip caught Jesus above the ear, and the pieces of bone got caught in his hair. With a roar, Longinus spun his body and the whip pulled free. He felt the end of his lash—there were chunks of hair and scalp on them.

Longinus ran a few steps forward to listen, hoping for a moan or a quiet plea for mercy. He only heard a series of quick, shallow breaths. In disgust, he threw the whip against the floor and drew his sword. He went to the other side of the pillar and cut the leather bonds free.

Jesus had no strength to stand. He fell backward and landed in a pool of his own blood. Jesus arched his back to keep it from making contact with the cobblestone floor.

The centurion's boot crashed down on his chest and knocked the air out of him. Jesus gasped for breath. The centurion slowly turned his foot, and Jesus' back twisted against the ground. Jesus looked at him but found it hard to focus. All he could see through the blur of sweat and blood was the crooked teeth of Longinus's twisted smile.

"We're not done with you yet, *your highness*." He lifted his foot and spit in his face. There was a circle of men tightly around him now, all of them laughing and spitting. They lifted him up and pulled his tunic, which had been pulled down to his waist, back over him.

Jesus shook with pain as the fabric rubbed against his back, but at least the tunic kept the dangling strips of his flesh in place. The blood sealed the tunic to his skin like a bandage. A little strength returned to his legs.

The circle of soldiers opened and one of them brought in a purple robe. The soldier bowed before him and put it over his shoulders, clasping the brooch in front of his neck. The others tried their best to play along, but many couldn't keep a straight face.

Longinus held up with a branch of thorns. "What is a king without a crown?" He said. He circled the branch around Jesus' head.

"Hmm…" he said looking at him. "It doesn't seem to fit." Then, taking a stick, he slowly pressed the thorns into his flesh.

Jesus' legs buckled, but two soldiers held him up. The centurion continued his slow push of the thorns into Jesus' head. As he did, Jesus felt blood run down his face and drip out of his beard.

After circling Jesus and making sure that all the thorns had dug firmly into his scalp, he put the stick in Jesus' hand and bowed. "Hail to the king of the Jews!"

"The king of the Jews!" the soldiers cried in response.

"Let's put him in a royal procession!" someone said. There was immediate approval at the idea. The two soldiers holding Jesus began to walk Jesus around in a large circle, and they all chanted, "Hail to the Jewish king!" Some of them fell over because they were laughing so hard. Jesus tried his best to keep pace with the guards, but they moved too fast and often dragged his feet along the ground.

"What is the meaning of this?" boomed a voice. It was the governor's.

The soldiers immediately stood at attention. Pilate looked at Jesus and his upper lip curled in disgust. He spoke to the soldiers holding him. "Can he stand on his own?"

They let go of Jesus, and steadied him before releasing. "Walk forward," the governor commanded.

With great agony, Jesus took two steps forward and stopped.

Pilate folded his arms. "Who is responsible for this?"

Longinus stepped forward. "I am, sir."

The governor smiled. "Excellent job, as always."

"Thank you, sir."

"I will go out and introduce him. Then open the door wide and lead the prisoner out." He looked again at Jesus. "Keep the crown and robe. They're a nice touch."

"Yes, sir."

Pilate walked away.

A soldier turned to Longinus. "He didn't say anything about the scepter."

Longinus went up to Jesus and grabbed the long stick from his hand. "All hail to the king," he said, and beat the stick against Jesus' head.

Others did the same.

Fifteen Roman guards came out of the fortress and formed a perimeter at the bottom of the steps. At the sight of them, the crowd's volume increased. Pilate came out and motioned for silence. The crowd obeyed.

Pilate looked at the size of the crowd and tried to hide his amazement. It had grown three or four times larger. He felt beads of sweat on his forehead. "Behold the man!" he yelled, and pointed toward the door with a dramatic gesture. The large wooden door opened wide and Jesus stumbled out, stopping at the front of the step.

The people gasped. Many wondered if they looked at a thing or a man. Pilate held his breath and continued to survey the crowd. He had hoped to elicit pity from the crowd toward the young Rabbi so he could have him released. To scourge *and* crucify someone was a torture reserved for only the hardest criminal. Even Barabbas wouldn't have gone through that.

The governor cared little about Jesus—he was just another Jew. But he believed him to be innocent and hated Caiaphas. It was the latter reason that drove him more.

A slow murmur began to rise from the crowd that caused Pilate's heart to sink into his chest. They chanted with greater and greater volume: "Crucify him! Crucify him! CRUCIFY HIM!"

"Why? What harm has he done?"

"CRUCIFY HIM! CRUCIFY HIM! CRUCIFY HIM!"

"Swords!" Pilate commanded, and the soldiers drew their blades. But it only threw the crowd into a greater frenzy.

"Archers!" Twelve more soldiers appeared atop the wall over the door, bows taught and ready to fire. But still the crowd chanted ever more loudly.

Pilate saw the soldiers looking side to side at each other. He also noticed that they stood with weight on their back foot, more ready to retreat than to fight.

He quickly did the math. Rome's hold on Jerusalem was more psychological than physical. He didn't have enough guards to quell an all out assault, especially not at a time of the year where the population was ten times larger than usual. He glanced behind him and saw the large fortress door was open wide. He cursed himself for his theatrics.

Pilate imagined the angry mob rolling over the line of soldiers and flooding into the fortress. They would whip him worse than this Rabbi, and *he'd* be hanging on a cross by the end of the day.

His mind still revolted against his emotion. *How can you be afraid of the Jews?* The Jews were a doormat, a disease passed from one empire to the next, important only because the Arabian dessert to the east and the Mediterranean Sea to the west made them a necessary land bridge for Rome to extend her power from north to south. They had been called many things, but never a *threat*.

The governor glared at the young Rabbi. This was *his* fault. There is no way people would feel such hatred for a simple teacher from Nazareth.

"Where have you come from?" he asked the prisoner. "Why do they hate you so much? What have you done?"

No answer. The crowd's chants grew louder and Pilate's anxiety grew higher, as did the pitch of his voice.

"Don't you know I have the power to release you or to crucify you?"

Jesus coughed. Or was it a laugh? He looked at the governor —green eyes pierced through his crimson stained face. "You would have no power over me if it wasn't given to you from above. That is why the man who handed me over to you has the greater guilt." Then he looked away.

Pilate turned and looked at the front of the mob. Caiaphas was there along with chief members of the Sadducees and Pharisees. He could see in their eyes that they longed for blood. So he made a decision:

Better him than me.

He called for a servant who brought out a large bowl of water. Pilate pushed his hands in the water and it splashed off the sides, then he rubbed his hands in the air.

"I wash my hands of this man's blood!" he yelled, and he flicked his hands so the water droplets flew forward. "It is on you!"

"Let his blood be on us and on our children!" Caiaphas answered, and many others said the same.

Pilate turned toward Jesus and the soldiers who stood behind him. "Crucify him with the others," he said, and then briskly walked into the fortress. Behind him he heard the mob cheer in celebration, and their noise even echoed in the courtyard after the large wooden door was shut.

As she saw her son led back into the fortress, Mary began to cry. She felt John and Salome's arms around her. Behind the sound of their groans and tears was the jubilant sound of celebration.

She took in deep breaths to control herself. This was no place to fall apart. There was too much more to come. Mary gently pushed them away and nodded, wiping her tears with her blue shawl that covered her head.

"Let us go," she said. They held hands so as not to be swept away by the crowd and made their way toward where they knew Jesus would be next: the *via Delarosa*, or "the road of the cross".

THE CROSS

Luke 23:26-43

Longinus was furious. Never had he faced such humiliation. "Are we Rome or are we not? To think you turned tail to a bunch of Jews," he said.

"It's easier to be brave when you're nearly blind," murmured one of the soldiers.

Longinus heard the whisper and lifted the man up by his breastplate. "My hearing works fine." Only a string of desperate apologies caused him to release his grip and the soldier crashed into the ground.

"Where are the other prisoners?" Longinus said.

The soldiers brought forward two men whose hands were tied behind their backs. One was taller than the other. They were bruised but not bloodied.

A soldier came up to Longinus and handed him three wooden tablets. Longinus handed them over to Quintus.

"Thief and murderer," Quintus read aloud. He looked up at the two prisoners. "Which one of you is the thief and murderer?"

The men looked at each other and then looked back at the captain.

"Come on now, don't make this hard on yourself," Quintus told them.

The soldier that brought out the tablets whispered in Quintus's ear, and he looked at the next tablet. "Oh, I see we've got *two* thieves and murderers here. You friends?"

The smaller of the two men began to say, "No! I do not—"

"Shut up," Quintus said. He handed the tablets to the soldier who nailed them on two staffs.

The centurion surveyed the two men. The smaller one whimpered and the other was tense with hate. He smiled. It was more satisfying when they had a little fight left.

"You first," he said to the tall one.

From behind, a soldier shoved him forward so forcefully he almost lost his balance. Then they pushed him down and his bare knees thudded against the hard stone floor.

Three large beams of wood leaned against the wall with a pile of rope beside them. After they cut his hands free, two soldiers lifted a beam, put it against the prisoner's back, and then tied rope around his elbows to make sure it would stay in place. They lifted the man to his feet by grabbing the wooden beam and pushed him forward.

By now, the other soldier had fixed the tablet to the staff and stood in front, lifting the staff high so the words, "Thief and murderer" could be read in the three languages it was written in: Greek, Hebrew, and Latin.

Next came the other. But when they pushed him forward he fell down on the ground and made no motion to get up. Longinus rolled his eye. He was going to be one of *those*. He motioned two soldiers to lift him up. The man was crying, begging, and pleading not to be put to death. He would not open his eyes.

"Look at me," Longinus said.

The man shook his head, eyes still closed.

"Look at me!"

He wouldn't.

Longinus released a heavy breath, and then pulled out his blade and placed the side of it against the man's cheek. "Open your eyes or I'll cut your eyelids off," he said.

The man opened his eyes.

"That's better," he said.

Longinus put a hand on the man's shoulder as if he was a friend. "I'm sorry for your troubles, I really am. But I've got a job to do, understand? You go along, and I'll make it as easy for you as I can. But you give me trouble, and you might end up looking like him."

He pointed to Jesus, and the man looked at him with horror. Then he slowly nodded. The tears were gone now, replaced by a kind of numb expression that had lost all hope in life.

"Good boy," Longinus said. The soldiers moved the prisoner into position. They pushed him to his knees, though not as harshly as they did with the taller man, and tied the rope to his elbows. Another soldier with the placard stood before him, ready to lead him to his crucifixion.

Longinus felt some pity for the man. True, he found a kind word to a scared man could make his job much easier—it's a lot of work to drag a man kicking and screaming to Calvary. But he did feel a connection with those he tortured and executed. He held their life in his hands and it made him feel like a god. It was the closest thing to a religious experience he had ever felt.

But he did not feel that way with Jesus, the only remaining prisoner before him. Jesus didn't scream, didn't curse, didn't whimper. And right now, he didn't even look back at him. Longinus never met anyone like this.

"Now let's see what Pilate charged you with," Quintus said. He read the tablet and began to laugh. "I don't believe it! The King of the Jews!"

Soldiers began to howl in hysterics. Even Longinus began to laugh.

"All right, your majesty, you know the drill," Quintus said. He handed the tablet off to one of the soldiers. They pushed Jesus to his knees. He jolted with pain as the wood pressed against his skin and the rope tightly pulled against his arms. One of the soldiers helped him to his feet.

The other Romans picked up their shields and drew their swords. There were four in the front, two between each prisoner, and four at the end. Longinus and Quintus placed themselves at the rear.

Longinus wanted to drive nails into flesh as soon as possible. "Let's go!" he commanded.

The fortress door opened as wide as it needed to, letting the soldiers march down the steps, with the tablets of the prisoner's crimes held high before each one of them. The noise was deafening, but no one got in their way.

Caiaphas stood at the front of the crowd, jubilant with victory. But when he saw the tablet that preceded Jesus he became enraged. After they passed by, the high priest grabbed a soldier and demanded to see the governor.

"About what?" the soldier asked.

"The judgment! It should read, 'He *claimed to be* King of the Jews.' This is an insult!"

The soldier shrugged. "I'll tell him," he said, and he went into see Pilate.

As Caiaphas waited for a response, the crowd left to see the crucifixion. The high priest wanted to go as well, but felt this injustice must be dealt with immediately. Pilate took a long time to respond. By the time the Roman soldier appeared to hand him a note, only Malchus remained to attend him.

Caiaphas grabbed the parchment from the messenger's hand, furious that the governor wouldn't speak to him in person. The note read: "What I have written, I have written. Return your priestly vestments to this soldier. Now."

He crumpled up the paper and threw it on the fortress's steps with an angry growl. Malchus helped him removed his breastplate and turban and handed them to the messenger while Caiaphas cursed under his breath.

The streets narrowed as they moved through the city. Shouts of anger echoed off tightly packed houses and it was almost impossible to think straight. Longinus wished he had brought his whip to get the line to move faster.

They had expected a large amount of people to turn out for the execution today because they were supposed to be killing Barabbas. But the vehemence they showed for this prisoner was greater than Longinus had ever seen. He couldn't understand how a religious teacher could be hated more than a murderer. Shouts of "blasphemer!" and "devil!" rang in their ears.

In many ways, Jesus looked like the devil—more a monster than a man. The prisoner walked with his shoulders hunched over so the weight of the crossbeam wouldn't pull him to the ground. His face and body were red with blood. The crimson crown of thorns looked like horns that protruded from his skin.

Only occasionally did they hear someone say, "Son of David!" and at one point Longinus thought he heard someone yell, "Son of God!" Raised fists came down on that voice before it could utter another word.

"Son of God," Longinus laughed.

Quintus heard it, too. "Like Hercules," he said.

"I think Hercules was a bit stronger," the centurion said, and he kicked Jesus in the back to keep him moving forward.

He kicked him too hard. Jesus went face first into the cobblestone road with the weight of the cross beam behind him and went unconscious.

Quintus and another solder picked him up. Jesus hung limply from the wood, still breathing but doing little more.

"He's not going to make it," Quintus said.

Longinus cursed. It was his job to keep him alive until they crucified him. He pushed his way into the crowd. The Jews screamed and swore as he knocked them over, but didn't dare stop him. When he came back he had a bucket of water.

"Time to wake up!" he said. He threw the water on Jesus, and by doing so drenched Quintus and the other soldier who held him. They swore as the water hit and Longinus laughed. Jesus coughed and opened his eyes.

The crowd grew quiet. The water had washed the red away, and for a brief moment Jesus looked like a man. But then the crimson began to flow from his thorned head and he became the monster. The crowd screamed with new vigor for his death.

Longinus looked around and tried to get his bearings. They weren't yet outside the city, and it was clear Jesus wasn't going to make it on his own. It was beneath the dignity of a Roman soldier to carry a cross, so he went into the crowd and grabbed a tall, strong looking Jew.

"I didn't do anything!" the man yelled.

"Don't care," Longinus said, throwing the man on the ground in front of Jesus. "Help your king."

The man looked at Jesus with disgust. "He's not my king! I don't even know this man!"

Longinus drew his sword.

"But his blood will make me unclean for the feast!"

"His blood or yours," the centurion said. "Your decision."

John and the women waited by the city gate. This was the closest gate to what the Romans called Calvary but the Jews called Golgotha—the place of the skull. John remembered having nightmares about it as a child. Golgotha was a hill outside Jerusalem that had three oddly shaped indentations that looked like the holes in a skull for the eyes and the nose. Five tall wooden posts were permanently fixed into the hill. No one was there when they arrived except for a small amount of traffic that came in and out of the city.

Salome was frantic. She paced back and forth and wrung her hands. They had been joined by the two other "Marys". Mary, the wife of Cleopas, tried to control her sobs. Mary Madgelene looked like one struck dead. Her flesh was pale and she seemed as if she might collapse any minute.

John could hardly think straight. *Why would God allow this to happen?* He felt like his heart was being torn in his chest.

Then he felt a hand upon his shoulder. Warmth seemed to radiate from it and it gave him peace. He looked and saw Jesus' mother standing next to him. He was again reminded how much she looked like her son.

"Have faith," she said.

Mary bore a great sorrow, but she was not crushed by it. John marveled at her words. *He* should be comforting *her* at this moment, not the other way around.

He inhaled and his chest shook with tears. "But why—"

She closed her eyes and held up her hand as if she could not bear the question. He put a hand on her shoulder, furious at himself for asking such a foolish thing. His brother always chastised him for saying things out loud that should be kept silent. "I'm sorry," he said.

Mary looked up at him with tear-filled eyes. "God's will be done," she said.

John looked down the road. The wait was agonizing. He wanted to be back on a boat in the Sea of Galilee. He wanted to be sleeping next to his Master by a campfire in Samaria. He wanted to be celebrating the Passover meal in the upper room with the apostles. He wanted to be anywhere but here.

Slowly, people began to gather. They could hear the echo of yells in the distance. The growing crowd tried to dislodge them from their place by the gate, but they didn't move. If they could stay next to the gate, they could be close to Jesus as he passed by. They might even be able to touch him.

More waiting. Finally, they caught sight of a wooden placard that said in three languages, "Murderer and Thief", carried by a Roman guard. A tall man wearily walked up the hill toward the gate, surrounded by a few soldiers. Whenever one of the Romans prodded him forward his eyes flashed with hate and he swung the crossbeam tied to his shoulders as if he would hit them. But he didn't dare. And he hadn't strength to keep the rage alive for more than a moment.

But then he saw, as he approached the gate, the place of the skull. He screamed and locked his knees, determined not to go another step.

The soldiers were ready for it. They positioned themselves behind him, grabbed the ends of the crossbeam, and relentlessly pushed it forward as the man tried to dig his heels in vain. He thrashed back and forth and a torrent of profanity spewed out of his mouth. But it did no good. They were almost carrying him now, leading him though the gate, leading him to his death.

Behind him came a soldier carrying a placard that said the same thing. This man was smaller, and moved timidly like a whipped dog. He saw the same sight and he collapsed. The soldiers grabbed him and dragged him forward while he whimpered. As he passed by the women, he looked at them with a desperate stare. *Help me*, he seemed to say. John knew he would never forget the look on that man's face as they carried him out of the city.

There was a pause. Shouts were heard, but no one moved. It seemed like an eternity, and in that moment John had a thought of hope that he didn't dare say out loud. *Maybe he got away. Maybe he worked a miracle!* This hope cut his heart more violently than any weapon could.

And then, despair. A soldier appeared with a placard that read, "King of the Jews". Mary of Magdala clutched her hands to her heart. The wife of Cleopas fell to her knees wailing. Salome raised her hands and began to shout, "NO! NO! GOD HAVE MERCY, NO!"

Mary clung to John, her face now drenched with tears. The guards came closer and blocked their view. Through the crowd they saw the crossbeam, which seemed at a sharp angle, and it looked like two figures were slowly moving forward. The soldiers tried to push them aside, but they didn't budge. Not thinking them a threat, they let them stay where they were as they passed through the gate.

Jesus came into full view: hideous, disfigured, limping, and covered with blood. A man helped him carry the cross. All the women screamed except for Mary, who sobbed but would not hide her face. They came to a stop before them. Jesus weakly raised his head and spoke to the women.

"Do not weep for me, daughters of Jerusalem. Weep for yourselves..." and then he caught his mother's eye, "and for your children." Mary nodded. John held her tight.

"Keep moving!" Longinus yelled.

He saw Jesus lift up one of his legs and step forward. It slipped beneath him, but the Jew helping him grabbed him before he fell. Then Jesus lifted the other leg and put his foot on the ground. It held, and he took another step forward.

He was almost walking now, and his head was up—looking directly at the place he was to be crucified. Longinus could hardly believe it. Jesus could still not bear the full weight of the crossbeam, but there was an immediate difference in his strength. Unlike everyone else he had ever crucified, Jesus *gained strength* as he kept his eyes focused on the hill.

Incredible.

Jesus was through the gate now and they headed up to Calvary. The other soldiers waited for them to arrive. At Longinus's command, the ropes that tied the prisoner's arms were cut. The wood fell to the ground and so did the prisoners, exhausted at the weight they carried.

"Rome thanks you for your service," Longinus said to the Jew who had helped the prisoner carry the cross. He was covered in blood. "Sorry to make you *unclean*."

The man missed the sarcasm. "I'm not," he said, a stunned expression on his face. He stared at his bloody hands. "He told me I'm not."

This was the last thing Longinus needed. He nodded to a soldier who grabbed the Jew and pushed him down the hill where a bunch of women were wailing. A large crowd was gathering to see the crucifixion. It was cold out and clouds were gathering. Best to do this quickly.

He signaled to his men. Soldiers grabbed the first prisoner and ripped his tunic off him, leaving him naked. They threw him down on the crossbeam and put their knees on his arms while one of the soldiers drove a huge stake through his right wrist. He screamed. Longinus breathed in the sound.

As they positioned the next nail, other soldiers came for the second man. Again, the clothes were ripped off. He fell to his knees and begged for mercy, but no one would respond, or even look at him except for Jesus. They pushed him backward and kneeled on his arms. The hammer sounded against the nail and the nail cracked against the bone. His back arched and he wrenched his other hand free from the soldier.

"Hold him!" Longinus said. The soldier dropped his foot into the man's chest and the breath left his body. In that moment of shock they grabbed his arm again, and now two men knelt to put it in place.

The first man was lifted up onto the vertical wooden beam that stood permanently in the ground. There was a large notch on it that matched a corresponding notch on the crossbeam. A man on a ladder was ready to tie them together as they fell into place. Then they came for Jesus.

One of them pulled at his tunic but it didn't tear. "Wait a moment," Quintus said. "Look at this! It's seamless."

"Let's not rip it," another said. "We'll cast lots to see who gets to keep it."

They agreed. Quintus was about to pull the tunic over Jesus' head when Longinus stepped forward and stopped him. Quintus backed away and Longinus grabbed the bottom of the tunic, looking Jesus in the face.

"One more chance to sing," he said. And then with a fierce yank he pulled the tunic over Jesus' head.

The garment was sealed to Jesus' back like a bandage, and scabs had already started to form. Pulling the tunic ripped his wounds open again. His whole body shook and he collapsed naked to the ground. The soldiers that surrounded him laughed—except for Longinus. He stared at the prisoner's face to see if he would finally cry out in surrender. Jesus opened his mouth wide, as if a scream was about to burst from his chest... but no sound.

Who is this man?
"Nail him down," he commanded.

As the nail broke through his wrist, a burst of pain went up Jesus' arm and into his neck. His jaw locked, and he couldn't turn his head to see the other nail go in. On feeling the pain in his other arm he lurched forward, all muscles tense.

Suddenly, he was being dragged. He looked at his hand. There was a rope tied to the beam. He assumed there was one on the other side, too. Then his body was lifted up. His feet scraped on the ground until they dangled in the air. Two soldiers grabbed them and pressed them on to the wood of the center beam. He heard the sound of nails and he winced. But no—they were just fastening the beam on to the post.

Then another nail rang, and this one was driven through his ankles. He bent forward in so much pain that he thought the nails in his hands would rip out.

Jesus' body sagged and his legs lost all strength. It was hard to breathe, and the only way to catch a breath was to push himself up by the nails on his feet. As he did, he felt the rough wood scrape against his open back. He gasped and collapsed again.

His head dropped and his eyes surveyed his naked body. He was covered in blood. Many of the lashes he received at the Roman fortress had curled around his waist and made open holes in his chest. His right eye was so swollen it was useless, and blood had caked around his left one, making it difficult to see.

Jesus found it hard to breathe so he again lifted up and drew in a sharp breath, trying his best to stay in that position for as long as he could. But it was only a moment before he slid down again. Splinters of wood held stubbornly to pieces of his flesh. Darkness began to surround his vision, but he would not give up. Not until he had given all.

He heard the soldiers laugh at the three of them, directing many of their comments toward their circumcisions. A large group of people had gathered at the base of the hill and cheered to see the soldiers finish their work.

Jesus raised his head to look at the heavens. "Father," he said, "forgive them. They know not what they do."

Once the soldiers were satisfied that everything was in place, they allowed a few people at a time to ascend the hill and gaze upon the dying men. The first in line was Rabbi Dov, with a group of other Pharisees and their disciples.

Dov beamed with victory. Looking at the others he said, "Is this our Messiah? Is this the king of the Jews?" They all laughed. "He saved others, but he could not save himself."

Then he turned to Jesus. "Well, Jesus, I'll give you one last chance to prove yourself. Let the Christ, the king of Israel, come down from the cross now for us to see and believe."

Jesus looked at him but said nothing. It was getting hard to breathe again.

Rabbi Dov leaned forward as if to hear a response. "Nothing? No great teaching, Rabbi? We are all ready to learn, O great teacher from Nazareth!" They laughed at him. "You came to save your people right? Then save us! Show your miraculous power! Come down off that cross and we will follow!"

The thought crossed Jesus' mind that he *could* come down off the cross, *could* command a legion of angels to set him free, *could* show Dov, the Pharisees, and all the crowd who he really was.

But the thought passed quickly. He already overcame that temptation and it held little power over his heart. He pushed himself up on the nails to catch a breath and then slid down the wooden post again. Flesh from his back hung like ribbons and he shook in pain.

The Pharisees' laughter turned to anger as they accused him of blasphemy. The Romans stepped up and forced them to move along.

The line continued, all were focused on Jesus. Pharisees, Sadducees, scribes, and Herodians all came to pay "homage" to the king of the Jews. Jesus lost his focus in a blur of insults and curses. It was getting harder to push himself up to catch a breath. *Was it even mid-day yet?* He prayed for strength as face after face came forward to spit, curse, and insult him.

A woman came forward and began to scream. "You killed him! You killed my husband! I hope God lets you burn for a thousand years!"

How did I kill your husband? Jesus lifted his head and realized that for the first time that day someone wasn't yelling at *him*. She screamed at the man to his left, the shorter one who had whimpered his way to the cross. The words that came out of her mouth were unbecoming of a woman. Her eyes were wide with hate. Her family had to hold her back from tearing the man apart. Jesus turned his head and looked at the man.

The man was crying.

"I'm sorry, I'm sorry, it was an accident, I didn't mean to, I'm sorry—" he said.

This apology only angered the woman even more. "I will not forgive you! I will never forgive you! You will burn in hell forever!"

Her fingers reached out and looked as though she would claw the flesh off the man's body. The soldiers stepped forward, but her family had already restrained her. A younger man who might have been her son had to carry her away.

But as they began down the hill she broke free and ran toward the man with a violent shriek. A soldier stepped in her way and pushed his shield against her, knocking her to the ground. Her family responded with anger—some went to pick up the mother, others clenched fists and charged the soldiers.

Swords were drawn and orders were shouted. Most of the family was pushed back while other soldiers drew a tight circle around the prisoners. The family brushed themselves off and with spits and curses moved down the hill. The centurion halted the next group of people in line until he got things under control.

The taller man on Jesus' right cursed the Romans as well. "You dogs! Beating up a grieving widow! Who do you think you are?" One of the soldiers took the blunt end of a spear and drove it into his stomach, silencing him.

The hill grew quiet as the soldiers regained order. The only sound to be heard was that of the smaller man's wails. He cried so hard his entire body shook, and his cross vibrated back and forth beneath him.

Jesus prayed for him and for the family of the man he had killed. The look of rage on the mother's face was a painful sight to see. *He killed them both that day*, Jesus thought. He said a prayer of thanksgiving that his mother didn't react the same.

Mother. Where was his mother? He looked around and saw her standing at a distance from the base of the hill. He prayed earnestly for her, offering up his pain for her strength.

At what should have been the brightest time of the day, the sky grew dark and a cold wind blew. *It is getting closer*, Jesus thought.

But not yet, the wind told him.

The line had resumed. No one else addressed the men to either side, all the focus returned to Jesus. Eventually, Caiaphas, Annas, and the other chief priests with their servants came before him. Caiaphas was dressed only in a torn tunic. His hair was frazzled and he hadn't put on any other garments. He looked insane, yet his speech was calm and collected.

He pointed off into the distance where the top of the Temple could be seen. "So! You would destroy the Temple and rebuild it in three days?" And then he addressed the other priests and all those who had gathered to watch the crucifixion. "Let this be a lesson to anyone who dares put themselves before God and his dwelling place!"

The crowd cheered and he carried on like this for a good portion of time, more for the crowd than for Jesus. Eventually he and the other priests walked away, spitting on the ground as they did.

As they dispersed, Jesus saw the high priest's servant stare at him, hand unconsciously cupped around his left ear. Then he realized that the rest of the group had left and moved quickly to catch up with them.

The man to the right of Jesus began to laugh, though it sounded like more of a cackle. "You really thought you could destroy the temple? You really think that you are the Son of God?" He spit out blood on to the ground. "I don't know what is worse. Being put up here by Roman dogs or being forced to die next to an insane blasphemer."

"HAVE YOU NO FEAR OF GOD?"

The man on the cross was stunned by the rebuke and looked around to see who said it. The soldiers did the same.

"HAVE YOU NO FEAR OF GOD?" came the voice again. It was the other thief on the cross, to the left of Jesus. They looked at him in disbelief, shocked he had the strength (or the will) to make such a noise.

He leaned forward and his arms trembled. "This man is innocent! Innocent! He got the same sentence as we did. But we deserve it... I deserve it..." He could hang forward no longer and slumped back against the cross where he took some heavy breaths.

"Jesus," he said with a dry voice. "Remember me when you come into your kingdom."

Jesus strained to answer. He pushed himself up to catch a breath to speak, and shook as he did so. "I promise you, today you will be with me in paradise."

Jesus tried to pull himself up for another breath, but his left arm wouldn't seem to cooperate. He twisted on the cross like a snake grabbed by its head, and finally managed to grab a breath.

He knew that soon he would breathe his last.

"WHY HAVE YOU FORSAKEN ME?"

John 19:25-29, Matthew 27:45-56

Simon shivered in the cold wind and tightened the tunic over his face. In the distance he could see the shadow of the cross, but he dared go no further for fear of being recognized. He sat outside the wall of Jerusalem and imagined what was happening on that cursed hill. Part of him wanted to go closer. Another part wanted to run far away. So he did neither and stayed where he was.

The wall behind him was rough and the rocks beneath him were uncomfortable to sit on. Simon had no desire for comfort right now, and even less desire for company. When a drunk man sat next to him it took all his strength not to tell him what he could do with himself. *Drunk at this time of day,* he thought. What kind of man would do that?

But he quickly realized that he was in no place to judge. After all, maybe this was a punishment from God. The man reeked of sweat and wine, and looked like some people had roughed him up recently. *Maybe he will go away when he realizes I have no money to give.*

He looked back to Golgotha. He could see a long line of people at the foot of the hill. *I bet Rabbi Dov is there.* His heart burned with hate. Then he saw Jesus' body shake and writhe up and down on the wood. His anger was replaced with horror and shame.

I should be up there, Simon thought. *I should be on the cross, not him.*

"I should be on that cross, not him," the drunk said.

Simon was shocked. "What did you say?"

"I should be on that cross, not him," he said again.

Could this man read his mind? Was this an angel sent from God to condemn him? He looked closely at the man's face and saw a long scar across his cheek. Simon realized it was no angel.

"Barabbas," Simon said. He stood and violently grabbed him by his tunic, lifted him off the ground, and raised his fist to strike.

Barabbas did not try to defend himself from the impending blow. He gave Simon a confused look. "Did I do something to you?" he asked.

Simon let go. His hands shook. It was a totally irrational act, and he rubbed the temples of his forehead as he muttered an apology. Barabbas staggered to his feet and looked at Simon's face intently.

"I know who you are."

Simon's blood ran a few degrees colder.

"You're one of his," and he pointed to the hill in the distance. "Peter, right?"

Simon couldn't look him in the eye. "Simon," he replied.

Barabbas rubbed the stubble on his face. "Yeah, I knew Simon, too. The back-stabber." His laugh carried the sharp stench of alcohol. "But I guess that's what all you disciples do well, huh? At least *my* followers fought for me."

Simon grabbed him by the throat and pinned him against the wall, digging his fingers into the nape of Barabbas's neck. Simon was bigger than he was and crushing his windpipe was not going to be a problem. Barabbas shook but did not fight, and Simon was just about to kill him when he caught a look on Barabbas's face.

It said, *do it.*

Simon let go. Barabbas collapsed to the ground, hands cradling his neck. "Are you a man or a coward?" he coughed.

But Simon wouldn't take the bait. "If you want to die, do it yourself."

Barabbas looked at him and smiled. He tried to respond, but it took him a moment or two get his throat properly working again. "Not my style," he rasped. "That's not how Barabbas is going to go."

They stared at each other for a moment, but there was nothing more to say.

Without a word or a nod, Barabbas walked away, steadying himself against the wall as he did. Simon watched him as he left. After a few paces, Barabbas turned around.

"Want to know something?"

Simon didn't, but was determined to not say another word.

"When I heard them shout my name, I thought it was 'cause they wanted *me*. Funny, isn't it?" His eyes moved from Simon to Jesus in the distance. "But they just hated me less than him." He shook his head in disbelief and walked away, leaving Simon alone with his thoughts again.

Simon looked to the hill in the distance and saw shadows of people pass in front of the cross. *What were they saying to him?* he wondered.

What did he say to them?

Were any of the other apostles there?

His curiosity almost led him forward, but his fear held him back as he wondered:

What if they recognize me?

What if I'm arrested?

And the worst thought of all:

What if he sees me and turns away?

No closer to a decision than before, Simon fell against the wall and sat on the ground, pulling his tunic tight around his face to keep out the cold.

Jesus had no idea what time it was. If the sun moved in the sky, it was impossible to tell through the thick layer of dark gray clouds that stretched from horizon to horizon. It seemed as though a storm was upon them, but he felt no rain.

He felt the wind, though—a sharp cold wind that numbed his flesh. It was a small comfort but one Jesus was grateful for.

The soldiers built a fire and huddled around it. Steam wisped out of their mouth as they complained about the weather and wondered how much longer they would have to stay.

The line of people who wanted to accuse Jesus had finally disappeared. Jesus fought to stay conscious to hear every insult, just as he did with every physical blow. The weather drove only the most zealously angry to remain, but even they left after having their say.

The only people left now were the faithful at the bottom of the hill. They had been joined by more women from Bethany. He couldn't make out their faces, but he could hear their cries. Rachael was among them. Martha was there as well, but he didn't hear her sister Mary and assumed she hadn't come. *This would be too much for her,* Jesus thought. *She already said her goodbye.*

The storm clouds swirled around the cross and the wind whipped around the hill. The soldiers whispered about the gods being angry.

Jesus hung awkwardly off the cross. His legs were mostly numb, but would occasionally awake with sharp bursts of pain. Jesus leaned to his left. His legs were so weak that to breathe he had to not only push, but *pull* himself up on the nails in his hands, and could only pull himself up a little to get a shallow breath. His left arm had all but failed him now and involuntarily twitched against the wood. Darkness encroached on what little vision he had.

Is it time yet? he prayed.

Not yet, the wind responded. *You have to give it all.*

Give it all? What had he left? He had no money or home to speak of. His followers abandoned him. He looked down at his mangled naked body—they had even taken the clothes off his back. What could he possibly have left to give…

And then he saw her. She leaned against John amid the wailing women at the bottom of the hill.

"Mother," he said. But he couldn't say it loudly, and he stuttered with pain.

He lifted up to try to draw a deeper breath. "Mother," he said again. It was louder this time but still barely more than a whisper. He tried one more time.

"*Mom!*"

Longinus heard it. Jesus looked at him, then looked at his mother. Longinus followed his eyes and realized what he meant.

He elbowed the soldier next to the cross. "Get his mother." He pointed to where she was.

The soldier ran down the hill. He approached the women, who cowered back at his presence. John tensed, worried they might be coming for him.

"Which one of you is his mother?" he asked.

"I am," Mary said.

"He wants you," the soldier said. "Come with me."

At the words, *he wants you*, John saw Mary start to collapse. He held her steady. She looked up at him with teary eyes. "Will you help me up the hill?"

John took in a deep breath. He was terrified to be that close to Jesus, not only because of the soldiers but also because *he ran away*. How could he explain himself? What would Jesus say to him?

His heart beat furiously. No, there was no way he was going up that hill.

"Yes, I will go," he replied, shocked at the words that came out of his mouth. *What was I thinking?*

Every step was an agony. The small hill of Gologtha felt harder to climb than Mount Hermon. He held on to Mary tightly— *am I helping her or is she helping me?* Together, they came to the foot of the cross.

John didn't want to stare, but couldn't help it. He saw the large spike that they drove into his ankles, the lines of blood that ran down his legs, the ribbons of flesh that hung from his back, the skin that draped off his chest like a tattered sail, the twitching arms pinned helplessly against the wood, the cracked lips, the swollen eye, the crown of thorns.

Mary saw only her son.

Jesus pulled up and drew another breath. "Woman," he said to his mother, "behold your son." Another painful breath. He looked at John and said, "Behold your mother."

John put his arm around Mary and nodded. Tears flowed from Mary's eyes as she whispered, "Your will be done."

Jesus' vision blurred, and he realized that he was crying, too. But it was done. Now, on top of all he had lost, he was also an orphan.

He leaned his head back and looked up into the gray swirling clouds above his head. He felt the despair, the loss, the agony of having *everything* he loved in this life being taken away from him. His head fell down and he looked at Mary, the woman whose obedience to God brought him into the world. And he remembered the psalm she sang when last he saw her.

With shallow breaths, Jesus softly sang in Hebrew, "*My God, my God, why have you forsaken me...*" But he could sing no more.

Is it time?

Yes, came the response, *it is time.*

His eyes moved from Mary and John to Longinus, who was clearly moved by what he witnessed. With a raspy, quiet voice, Jesus said, "I thirst."

Longinus grabbed a spear from a soldier, put a sponge on it and dipped it in a jug of wine the soldiers brought for themselves. He lifted it to Jesus' cracked lips, and he sucked from it. The alcohol stung his lips and much of it spilled down his beard, but he had enough for a taste. He closed his eyes and prayed for strength.

When he opened his eyes, he saw mostly blackness. His body longed to fall into the sleep of death. *But not yet.* He had to let them know. He had one more thing to say, and he wanted them all to hear.

He pushed up with shaking legs. "It..."

A sharp pain from his right leg carried through his body and he collapsed. The weight of his fall pushed the air out of his lungs. He prayed again for strength as he began to rise again, lifting himself up on his right arm.

"...is..."

The arm gave out and he swung limply against the wood. His body slammed against the cross and it shook like a tree tossed in a violent wind. Mary took a step toward him and reached out, but there was nothing she could do.

His breath was almost gone. His vision almost black. The pain in his body was starting to tingle away into numbness.

Not yet, he prayed. *Not yet!*

He turned his face to his left arm and willed it to move. For the first time in hours, it responded. Jesus looked up into the sky and lifted himself forward, almost standing on the nails that they had driven into his feet. His legs awoke with searing pain. He pushed forward, arms fully extended behind him. His face was tense and his body shook, but he was able to open his mouth and sharply inhale in a breath that filled his entire lungs and he cried,

"FINISHED!"

And breathing his last, Jesus surrendered his spirit.

In the distance, Simon could see Jesus' body lurch forward. He could even hear the sound of his voice, though he couldn't hear what was said. Then the body slumped on the cross and Simon knew Jesus was dead.

He began to violently beat his chest, not caring about the pain. "What have I done?" he cried. "What have I done?"

Suddenly, the ground beneath him shook and he fell to his knees. Pieces of the wall behind him fell to the ground. Before he understood what was happening, another tremor threw him face first into the rocky soil.

Everything went black. He felt the wind and rain beat against him more violently than any storm at sea.

He wondered if he had been struck blind until he saw the flash of lightning and heard the thunder roar. It was as if everything in creation cried out in horror at what had just been done. Simon covered his head with his arms and expected to die.

And then... silence.

All he could hear was his beating heart.

Simon looked up and the world was gray. The sun was hidden behind heavy clouds and it looked more like early evening than mid-afternoon. The cold wind still blew but the rain was gone.

The people on the hill slowly stood and turned toward each other. The women seemed all right.

Of course they are all right, he said to himself. Jesus loved them.

He loved me, too, Simon thought. *And I betrayed him.*

He knelt, and stared at the distant body of Jesus.

"Forgive me," he whispered, lip trembling with sorrow.

A part of Simon wondered if maybe Jesus was still clinging to life. Maybe he could still run to him and tell him how sorry he was. He didn't care if the soldiers arrested him, or even if Jesus was angry with what he did. Even a word of condemnation would be welcome in his ear. Simon just needed to hear Jesus' voice one more time.

But as he stared at the unmoving silhouette on the cross, Simon knew he would never hear that beautiful voice again.

His tears stopped. His sorrow and fear was replaced with... nothing.

He felt *nothing.*

And that was the worse feeling of all.

"TAKE HIM"

Matthew 27:57-60

The soldiers were eager to leave. They could see a faint circle of sun beneath the clouds, and realized to their dismay it was only mid-afternoon. They didn't bother to push the women away, though John could tell by their looks that the wailing got on their nerves.

But he didn't care about the soldiers. John was numb with shock and stunned with the responsibility that Jesus had given him. As the women wept and comforted each other, his mother Salome hugged him and cried in his arms.

"I heard what he said to you," she said, cupping his face in her hands. "He made the best choice. Of all of my children, you are the most sensitive, most caring." She looked at the corpse of Jesus and then back at her son. "You are the most like *him*."

His chest heaved with tears at the compliment. Was there anything kinder she could have said? "I love you, mother."

A Pharisee appeared, but at first John didn't recognize him because he wore no turban and his face was swollen with tears. "Rabbi Nicodemus!" John said.

The old Rabbi knelt before the mother. "I am so sorry," he said. "I am so sorry," and he burst into tears.

The tears eventually ceased but the sadness remained. A well-dressed Jewish man came through the gate and headed up the hill, followed by two servants. John thought he remembered seeing him in Simon the leper's courtyard, but couldn't remember his name.

The man called for the centurion and spoke to him in an official manner. As he came to speak to the women, he stared at the body on the cross before him and was overcome with emotion. It took him some time to compose himself. His servants wept as well.

"Where is the mother?" he asked.

Mary nodded, and he went before her on one knee. "My heart goes out to you… words cannot express…" and his tears flowed again. She put a gentle hand on his shoulder. He looked up into her eyes.

"I have only followed your son for a few weeks. But I have learned more these past few weeks than I have in my entire lifetime. His words… they changed me. I'm not sure if I can explain."

"You don't need to try," Mary said.

"My family has a tomb, not far from this hill. I can't imagine you taking him all the way back to Nazareth. I have some prominence in Jerusalem and have already gotten permission from Pilate. Will you let him be buried in my place?"

She smiled. "I will, and thank you." She reached down and hugged him. The women were overjoyed. John said a prayer of thanksgiving to God for his providence. This was the first good thing that happened today.

Mary spoke again. "Sir, I don't even know your name."

The man was startled, embarrassed that he hadn't introduced himself. "Joseph," he replied, "from Arimathaea."

"Joseph," she repeated, and then smiled with teary eyes. "That is a good name."

Longinus couldn't see the faces clearly, but he could hear the emotion in their voices. A part of him was deeply moved—another part of him was angry that he was.

Quintus walked over to him. "What's that about?"

"The governor gave him permission to bury Jesus in his tomb."

"That will upset the high priest."

"Probably why he did it."

Quintus rubbed his arms to shake off the cold. "Let's get this over with, then. I'm thinking we deserve some of the better wine tonight, don't you?"

Longinus didn't respond with his usual enthusiasm. Everything had been turned upside down on him today. He stared at the body of Jesus.

"Longinus?"

Hearing his name again released him from his trance. "Yeah, let's do it."

Quintus handed Longinus a huge mallet. The tall man on the cross began to scream and curse as he saw him approach.

"Last words, thief and murderer?" Longinus asked.

The man howled with obscenities, curses, and rage. Longinus closed his eyes to listen. Normally, this was a great moment for him, to listen to the wails of a prisoner before taking his life. But there was no rush of power, no excitement. It felt like nothing.

Without any emotion, Longinus opened his eyes and swung the hammer, landing it hard against the man's thigh.

CRACK!

The women gasped and covered their eyes. The leg broke and the man stopped swearing. His body dropped unnaturally down and bounced a bit as his torso no longer had legs to hold it up. As he gasped his final breath, his face froze with a look of shock and pain.

The soldiers cheered at his skill of doing it with one blow. Longinus ignored them and walked past Jesus to the other man.

He had intended to do this one quickly—he hated it when they whimpered. But when Longinus stood before him there were no tears, no pleas of mercy. His poor eyesight prevented him from seeing him clearly, but there was something all together calm about him.

"It's all right," said the man on the cross. "I'm going to see my God."

This statement enraged Longinus. "I don't need your permission!" He swung the hammer so violently against the thief's legs that they almost snapped through the skin and off the cross.

The man collapsed against the wood and fell with his face toward Jesus. Longinus stared at him, then looked down at his shaking hands. Quintus came close to whisper to him. "Are you all right?"

The centurion couldn't answer. This was not how it was supposed to happen. *Even on the cross, the Jew has more power over life than I do.*

Longinus threw the hammer to the ground. "Let's get out of here," he grumbled. The sooner he was off this cursed hill the better.

"But what about him?" Quintus said, pointing to Jesus.

"He's dead already."

"Yeah, but…"

"Want proof?" he said. Longinus grabbed a spear from one of the soldiers and he thrust it into Jesus' heart.

A torrent of blood and water gushed forth and he jumped back in surprise. After bleeding so much all day, how could there be anything left? The blood and water covered Longinus's face, and he dropped the spear in shock.

It was in his hair. It was in his *mouth*. He spat and wiped his face. Blood dripped off his hands. He wiped them with the tunic beneath his armor, but wouldn't seem to get clean. There was even blood in the crevices of his knuckles.

My knuckles?

Longinus stared at his hands as if he had never seen them before. He was unaccustomed to seeing that kind of detail, and he shook his head to see if he wasn't imagining it.

He looked up from his hand to the cross and could see the rough way in which the wood was cut. He noticed the rusty orange flecks on the nail that pierced Jesus' ankles. Longinus moved his eyes up Jesus' body and noticed every wound and every detail. Then he came to Jesus face.

"Centurion?" Quintus asked.

When Longinus turned to him, Quintus's face went white with fear. Longinus didn't need to ask why. He could see out of both eyes now, and better than he ever had before.

The women gasped and the soldiers drew near, hardly able to believe what they saw.

Longinus looked around, amazed at his new sight. He saw wrinkles on tunics, tears in eyes, stubble on faces, and could even see the Temple in the distance.

He looked up again Jesus. *What have I done to you?* he thought.

Then he looked down at his hands, stained with Jesus' blood. *What have you done for me?*

"Truly, this man was the son of God," Longinus said. He bowed low and saluted him.

He saw Quintus and the others step back from him in fear. "Take him down from the cross," Longinus said, "but do it *carefully*. You break one of his bones, I'll break one of yours."

The soldiers immediately obeyed.

Mary pondered it all in her heart. *Even in death he still changes lives.*

As the soldiers took off the crown of thorns and carefully removed his body from the cross, Mary looked kindly at Joseph of Arimathaea. He not only shared the name of her late husband, but he looked a little like him, too. Even among the horror of the moment, thinking of Joseph made her lips curl into a slight smile. *It is God's providence he was not alive to see this,* she thought. *He would have fought to the death to prevent it from happening.*

She could still remember the look on his face when she told him that an angel of God appeared to her and she was pregnant. He didn't believe at first—who could blame him? But he also didn't believe she was unfaithful, either. Both ideas were beyond his comprehension. Then an angel appeared to him and he fully embraced his mission.

Those early years were tough, but Joseph was tougher. Oh, how long was that ride from Bethlehem to Egypt! He had to work hard at his trade to make money in a foreign land. Thankfully, he was a master when it came to wood. He built a cradle for his young son. It had twelve slats on it—the name of each tribe of Israel was beautifully carved into each one. And just when things started to work well in Egypt, they came back and moved to Nazareth.

It was hard for him. He could have been a master craftsman in any major city. But his main concern was to protect his wife and child, and the best way to do that was by staying as far away from King Herod's reach as possible. *Such an amazing man,* she thought. *I wish he was still here.*

They had lifted the corpse off the cross and lowered it to the ground. The women gathered around Mary as she stood and walked toward her son. She trembled with each step.

Then one of the soldiers, who held the body by the arm, lost his grip and the body spun and fell.

Mary's fear and trepidation immediately left and she jumped forward to catch her child. Longinus swore at the soldier, and the man repeatedly apologized under his insulting barrage. The gasps of horror and outrage turned quickly to silence as they all stared at the mother holding her dead son.

His head was in her lap, and she cradled it like she would a newborn baby. In her mind, she was no longer on the hill of Golgotha but the manger in Bethlehem.

"Joseph, isn't he beautiful?" she asked.

Joseph wiped the sweat from his brow, amazed at what he had just seen. "Beautiful," he said, but was unable to say another word. It had been such a long journey to Bethlehem, and it was so difficult to find a place to stay. He feared she would have to give birth in an open field.

But the manger provided some shelter, and the animals didn't seem to mind. He stepped near her to take another look. The baby gnawed at Mary's breast, knowing there was food but not sure how to get it. Mary winced as he bit down hard, but then relaxed her face as he began to feed. Joseph carefully ran a finger across the child's wet, matted hair as he nursed.

"Jesus," he said. "Your name is Jesus, little one."

Mary smiled and looked up with love to her husband. She took his hand and touched her face with it. "Are you all right?" he asked her.

She smiled and nodded. "I love you, Joseph," she said and she began to cry with joy. Then she looked down at the baby who happily nursed at her breast. She caressed his small head with her hands. "And I love you too, little Jesus."

"Little Jesus," she said as she ran her hands through his blood soaked hair. She rocked him back and forth, and softly sung the psalm that Jesus didn't have the strength to finish.

"He has not despised the poverty of the poor,
Has not turned away his face,
But has listened to his cry for help..."

Her face was wet with tears and her voice was thick with emotion. Jesus lay motionless in her lap, like a baby sound asleep.

"Do you want to hold him?" she asked. Joseph's eyes grew wide and he took a step back.

"Well... Uh, I'm not sure..."

She smiled, and held the baby toward him. "Take him. You're his father."

He shook his head. "Mary, you know I'm not really his—"

"Take him," she gently said again. "You are his father."
Joseph nodded and she carefully placed the baby in his arms. Looking at the face of Jesus, he lost all fear and smiled.

She would never forget the joy on his face.

"Take him," she said to Joseph.

The man from Arimathaea bowed and motioned to his servants, who laid a linen cloth on the ground, picked up the body of Jesus and put him on it, then covered his nakedness by wrapping the cloth around him. Joseph and his servants led them to the tomb. John was on her right, Rabbi Nicodemus was on her left. The women lined up behind her in their solemn procession.

Rachael was at the end of the line. She had never seen anything so horrible or... beautiful? That couldn't be the word for it. But she was moved in a way she never felt before.

Something inside told her to look around. She raised her head and did so. There was nothing new to see. The crosses were empty now. The soldiers worked their way toward the gate. Everyone else had left... except for one man who sat (or did he kneel?) in the distance by the edge of the city wall.

She took no further notice of him and continued on. Then she looked at him again. He was nothing more than a shape to her at this distance. But she was more confident that he was kneeling, not sitting.

The wind picked up. It beat against her ear with a strange sound, as if it tried to say something.

Go to him.

She stopped moving and the procession continued, too consumed with grief to notice her. She took a few steps toward the man, and then stopped.

Simon!

She began to run. She wanted to scream his name but her throat felt too thick to say a word. Simon was kneeling, staring at the ground. He didn't see her running toward him.

"Simon!" she finally squeaked when she was closer.

Simon looked up with a blank expression. Then he stood and stepped back, waving his hands in front of him as if he didn't want her there.

Rachael didn't care. She plunged into his arms and held him tightly. "Simon, I have been so worried about you! Oh, Simon... how could this happen!"

Simon did not return the embrace. "It's my fault."

She raised her head and looked at him. "Don't... don't say that."

"I denied him," he said. He was cold and distant.

Rachael was stunned to see her husband like this. "No," she said, "you didn't. You couldn't' have. I'm sure–"

"I DENIED HIM!" he shouted, and birds that had perched on the wall took flight at the noise. He began to fall and Rachael helped him to his knees.

Simon's eyes stared at the distant cross. He breathed a heavy sigh. "Did he say anything?"

Rachael nodded, and told him how he had given his mother to John's care. Simon nodded as she spoke. "John was faithful. He'll be in charge of the apostles now."

"But he's just a boy—"

"And I'm hardly a man!" he said, and the rebuke caused her to jump back in fear. Rachael couldn't take any more. She had just lost Jesus, must she lose her husband, too? She bowed low to the ground and sobbed, covering her face with her hands.

Simon stared at her. He knew what she needed. She needed her husband to hold her, to tell her everything would be all right. But things weren't all right and they would never be. The Master was gone.

If he is no longer here, then who am I?

Jesus had given everything to him, and now everything was lost. Simon stared at the cross. He looked down at his wife, sobbing uncontrollably on the rocky Jerusalem ground. He touched her, but she seemed not to notice. The sky grew darker.

"We should go," he said. She nodded and controlled her tears. She rose by herself and Simon stood with her. They were next to each other, but Simon felt a great distance—similar to the way he felt before Jesus entered into their lives.

If he is no longer here, then who are we?

They walked back to Bethany together, neither of them saying a word.

SABBATH

Matthew arrived in the upper room with his brother James. John, James, and Andrew greeted them somberly. But Peter didn't move. He sat in the windowsill, staring out toward the city.

One by one, the others gathered. By noon they were all assembled but Judas. Even as the others arrived, Peter didn't say a word.

Matthew couldn't bear the silence. "How did they find him?"

"It was Judas," John said. "He led them to the garden where the Master was praying."

Matthew shook his head. "No, we were sleeping and he was the one who warned us that the guards were coming!"

"He was the one who led them there," James said. "I saw it."

"But why would he do such a thing?" his brother James said. "Why would anyone?"

The Zealot's face grew red with anger. "What does it matter? He betrayed us all." Then he stood and headed toward the stairs.

"Where are you going?" Matthew asked.

"To kill him," the Zealot said. He said it with such force that no one doubted his words.

"I'll come with you," Jude said.

Finally, Peter spoke. "He's dead."

They turned and looked at him.

"What?" Philip asked.

Peter turned from his view of the city to the ten apostles. For the first time that day, Matthew saw his face. He almost didn't recognize him. Gone was the joy from his eyes, the determination in his voice. He looked twenty years older.

"He's dead," Peter said again.

"How?" John asked.

Peter shrugged. "Does it matter?" Then he resumed his view of the city.

They stood in silence for a moment.

Bartholomew slumped down onto cushions on the floor. "It's over then," he said.

"It's over," Thomas said, "for all of us."

"What do you mean?" Andrew asked.

He waved his hands around the room. "This," he said. And then he pointed his finger at everyone and finally pointed to himself. "Us." The others stirred uncomfortably. "Did anyone here truly believe that he was the Messiah?"

Matthew could see John get red in the face, and other apostles tenses as well. He looked to Peter to do something, but he sat on the windowsill like a statue.

"That's enough of that talk, Thomas," James said.

"Why, because you don't want to hear the truth?"

Matthew tried to calm things down. "I don't think this is the right time—"

"No, you're right! I should have said this long ago. I should have said this in Caesarea Philippi, where the *rock* over here made his brilliant declaration."

Andrew opened his mouth to protest, but Thomas cut him off. "Why are we so surprised? How else could it have ended? The man was mad."

John would hear no more of this. "He spoke the truth!"

"And now he's dead."

"But... he told us it would happen! The fact that it did only means that–"

"Don't you dare say that *Jesus is always right*!" Thomas said. "He *made* it happen. He turned tables over in the Temple and angered the religious leaders so they would have him killed. And he chose a bunch of cowards like us to follow him because he knew we would run away."

James shook with anger, but kept his voice calm. "Say one more word…"

Intimidated by James's size, Thomas grew silent.

But John couldn't let it go. "He also said in three days he would rise again."

"How is he supposed to raise *himself* from the dead?" Thomas said. "Are you mad? It can't be done."

John would not back down. "But Jesus is *always*—"

WACK!

Thomas struck John in the face, and his head was turned by the blow. Matthew couldn't believe it. It looked like Thomas was surprised, too. He opened his mouth to say something, but John quickly thrust his fist into Thomas's face and he fell backward, with John on top of him. The others dove forward in a pile to try to separate the two.

Only Matthew and Peter were not involved. Matthew stood on the outside of the pile, Peter sat motionless on the ledge.

"Please do something," Matthew said to Peter.

Peter said nothing.

"Peter, do something!"

Peter muttered an inaudible response.

"Peter!" Matthew said.

"I... AM... NOT... PETER!" he roared. "NEVER CALL ME THAT NAME AGAIN!"

The apostles froze, all eyes upon him. There was madness in his eyes and he breathed heavily, much like the demoniac they encountered in the Gerasenes. But after a few seconds, the fierceness faded and he returned to a shell of his former self. He sat back on the windowsill and looked out again, but his body still trembled.

Thomas used the distraction to break free of the pile and wipe the blood off his nose. "Cursed be the day I met any of you," he said. He went down the stairs and they heard the door slam.

There was no sound except for Peter's heavy breathing, which eventually quieted itself.

The apostles tried to begin some conversation with each other, but the words felt awkward and forced. None of them wanted to stay, but where else was there to go? The fear of being captured still lingered in their hearts. And all of them could not help but ask themselves that one, horrifying, gut-wrenching question:

What if Thomas was right?

After a time they left as they came, with no plans to see each other again. As Matthew and his brother closed the door behind them, Matthew broke down in tears.

"It's over... it's truly over."

His brother said nothing and held him tightly.

RESURRECTION

John 20:1-18, Luke 24:13-43

"They've taken him!"

Simon sat up, groggy and disoriented, feeling Rachael shake him awake. He didn't know what she was talking about and he didn't care.

"Quiet," he muttered.

"Jesus is gone! They've taken him!" she said through tears.

At the name of Jesus, Simon became alert. "What happened?"

"We took some spices to the tomb, and when we got there the stone was rolled away and it was empty. Empty! Was it not enough that they killed him? Must they defile his body as well?" She began to sob.

Simon was on his feet and out of the room. John and James were up as well and just heard the news from their mother, Salome. The three of them threw on their outer tunics, jumped over sleeping bodies in Simon the leper's courtyard, and were quickly out into the street.

They ran toward the tomb as fast as their legs could carry them. John was fast, and quickly outpaced the other two. James couldn't keep up and had to stop, but waved for Simon to go on before limping back to the house. Simon ran as fast as he could.

The rising sun was behind him and he noticed color for the first time in days. The grey shadows that hung over Jerusalem since Friday were gone, and the sun emerged radiant in color—more radiant than Simon had ever remembered seeing. The cold was gone as well. It was a beautiful spring morning and the birds sang a glorious song of praise to welcome it.

This joyful expression of creation was contrary to Simon's mood and the fear that ravaged his heart. He could not imagine what kind of desecration the Roman soldiers, or maybe even the Temple priests, would do to Jesus' body. His legs burned and begged him to stop, but he willed them forward.

He turned the corner of one of Jerusalem's walls and looked around to see where the tomb might be.

"Over here!" John cried, waiving his arms.

Simon waved back and quickened his pace to reach him. He came upon the tomb. The large stone had been rolled to the side and lay flat on the ground next to it.

"Did you go in?"

John shook his head. "I thought you should see it first."

Simon cautiously put his head inside and inhaled a quick breath with his nostrils. The air was stale, but not the expected smell of decomposed flesh. He bent down into the entrance. He hadn't thought to bring a lantern, so it took him a moment for his eyes to adjust to the darkness.

He was in a small antechamber that led to the room where the body would be held. The room was circular and had empty niches to put favored items of those deceased. He walked a few steps and entered into a rough hewn room with a large, flat slab of rock on the right hand side. A folded pile of blood-stained linen was on the edge of it, but no body.

Why would they have removed the linen? he wondered. It would have been easier, and less messy, to keep him wrapped in the shroud. He looked down to see if there were marks on the ground where someone might have dragged his corpse.

John came in and gasped. While Simon's attention was focused on the ground, John pointed at the slab. "Simon! Look!"

Simon did but wasn't sure what he was supposed to see. "What?"

John pointed at the linen. "*Look!*"

The linen shroud was folded into a tight square—the same way that Jesus folded his tunic when they travelled.

Simon shook his head. *It can't be.*

He looked around for any evidence that the tomb had been broken into or the body was forcibly moved. There wasn't any. But any other reason was inconceivable to Simon. They stood for a few more moments and then left. The two of them put their hands in front of their eyes as they walked into the sunlight, blinded by the beautiful day.

"What do you think happened?" John asked.

He knew what John was thinking, but couldn't bring himself to believe it. "He must have been taken," Simon said. "Whether by the Pharisees, the Temple guards, or the Romans... I don't know."

"But what about the sheet?"

Simon didn't care how the linens were folded. Someone had Jesus' body and was planning to do terrible things to it. "We should get the other apostles together and talk about this."

"I doubt Thomas would come," John said.

"Not after that beating you gave him."

"He deserved it," came the mumbled response.

Simon sighed. "All right, everybody *but* Thomas. He made his position clear. Can you get the word around?"

John nodded.

"Good. Tell them to meet in the upper room tonight." John ran into the city to spread the message.

As he slowly walked back to Bethany, he passed Mary of Magdala. She was clearly distressed.

"Do you know where he is?" she asked.

Simon shook his head. She bowed her head and continued to walk toward the tomb. Simon thought about stopping her, but left her alone with her sorrow.

Mary reached the tomb and began to sob heavily again. She was the only one of the women who hadn't gone into the tomb when they first arrived in the morning.

She was afraid of the tomb's darkness.

Darkness had filled most of her life. She had some memories of happiness in her childhood, but that was before her parents passed away. Mary was put into the care of her father's brother—but he was nothing like her father. Unspeakable things were done to her, and that is when she began to let the darkness in.

She thought the darkness gave her power, so she yearned for more of it. By the time she was a young woman and ready for marriage, she was possessed by not just one, but *seven* demons. Who would marry such a woman? No one. The man to whom she was betrothed broke off the engagement, angering her "father" to no end. She became an outcast to her family and to her community.

During those many years, Mary felt like a prisoner in her own body. The demons were in control. She wanted to scream but nothing came out of her mouth. She wanted to stop but her body continued to go. She felt helpless and alone, cut off from the world.

Until meeting Jesus, she had been entombed within herself. And the thought of walking into the tomb scared her to death.

What if the stone rolled behind her? What if she was sealed in and left to die? What if the darkness of death overtook her again?

The man who saved her from that darkness was gone. But even after she saw his dead body carried into the tomb, she found it hard to believe. How could a man so touched by God have been killed?

The sun was higher now, and the tomb did not seem so dark. She told herself that the stone wasn't going to close behind her. More importantly, she had to see for herself. That's what brought her back. She had to see.

She stepped into the tomb. Being a smaller woman, she didn't need to duck. She froze in the antechamber and breathed in the stale air for courage to go further. As she stepped into the place where he had been laid, she saw two men sitting there, one at each end of the slab.

Mary gasped. The men were dressed in white and had an unnatural glow about them. She was afraid, and yet these men seemed to radiate peace. It was like she walked into a dream.

One of them spoke to her. "Woman, why are you weeping?"

She wiped the tears from her eyes before she spoke. "They have taken my Lord away, and I don't know where they have put him. Do you know where he is?"

He pointed toward the entrance. Mary turned and saw the figure of a man in the doorway. *It must be the gardener,* she thought.

The man in the doorway asked a similar question as the two men dressed in white. "Woman, why are you weeping? Who are you looking for?"

Mary looked back toward the two men, but they were gone. Her heart jumped. Were they angels? And why did they point to this man? Maybe he knows where the body is...

...or maybe he's the one who moved it.

She stared back at the man and fell to her knees. She could only see his silhouette with the rising sun shining through the entrance of the tomb. "Sir, if you have taken him away, tell me where you have put him, and I will remove him."

The man didn't immediately answer, and fear came into her heart. *If this man stole the body, what is to stop him from killing me and leaving me here?*

Then the man spoke,

"Mary."

And she knew the voice.

"I am *not* lying."

"Nobody said that you were."

"Then you think I'm crazy."

Simon shifted his weight awkwardly and looked for one of the other nine apostles to help him. It was evening and they were back in the upper room, trying to decide what to do next.

Mary of Magdala folded her arms and tried to contain her rage. "Either I'm lying or I'm crazy. Which is it?"

"It's been a long few days," Andrew said. "Are you sure you didn't dream it?"

She stomped her foot on the ground. "I *saw* him! I *touched* him! Why won't any of you believe me? John, you believe me, don't you?"

John looked down and avoided eye contact.

"Tell us again what he looked like," Matthew asked.

"He looked like him! Except not like him. I didn't recognize him at first, I thought it was someone else. But then I was sure."

Her answer was hardly convincing. "And he still had his wounds?" the Zealot asked.

"No… and yes. Some of them, but not all of them."

Simon was convinced that she had lost her mind. It must have been clear on his face because Mary screamed at him, "I saw him! I'm telling you I saw him!"

Andrew walked over and put a hand on her shoulder. "Calm down, Mary—"

She backed away from his touch as if his hand was a hot branding iron. "You stubborn, stubborn men! After all you have seen, and you still don't believe!"

Simon couldn't take much more of this. He had listened to her talk all day and had enough. "Thank you, Mary. We need to talk alone."

"But I *saw* him," she said.

Simon nodded. "I know."

She looked around at their faces and grew cold. Without another word, she turned and left. Andrew locked the door of the upper room behind her and came back up the stairs.

"Simon, what did you see?" Jude asked.

"An empty tomb. Nothing more."

"So what happened to the body?"

Simon struggled for words to say. "I don't know."

The Zealot pounded his fist on the table. "It was the Romans. It *had* to be the Romans. They had a guard posted at the tomb, you know. And they are starting to say that *we* were the ones who did it."

This caused a great deal of anxiety among the apostles, especially Andrew. "If the Romans are coming for us, we should stop meeting together—"

They were startled by a loud pounding at the door. "Is there another way to leave?" Jude asked.

"We can get out the window and run across the rooftops," Philip suggested.

A muffled voice called out for them. "Is that father?" Matthew asked. He walked down the stairs to see who it was.

"Don't!" Andrew cried. But Matthew unlocked the door and Cleopas and son Joses came in, shouting like mad men.

"He is alive! He is alive!" Cleopas said.

Simon's heart filled with anger. This was a cruel lie.

"What?" Matthew said.

"Jesus is alive!" Joses said, face beaming with joy.

"What do you mean by this?" Simon demanded.

Cleopas walked forward to address the apostles. "We saw him, Joses and I. We were heading to see my father in Emmaus when a man came up to us on the road, surprisingly ignorant of anything that happened. We told him about Jesus, about how he was killed, and how one of the women had said she saw him alive. Then he explained the Scriptures to us, how all of this was *supposed* to happen!" He could hardly contain his excitement.

"And when we got to the house, he broke bread at the table and we realized it was *him*! He is alive!" Joses exclaimed.

Matthew clutched his hand on his chest. "Joses... you believe?"

"Of course I believe!" Joses said. "Don't you?"

Simon was in shock. The others were as well.

"But you didn't know it was him until he broke the bread?" Bartholomew asked.

Cleopas scratched his white beard. "Well... yes. I mean, looking back I guess we always knew it was him."

"Who did you think it was, before you realized it was him?"

"We didn't ask."

"Let me understand," Bartholomew said. "You walked with a man almost an entire day and never asked his name?"

Joses got defensive. "What does that matter? Jesus is alive! Doesn't anyone believe us?"

Cleopas looked at his two sons. "Matthew? James?"

Matthew and his brother were silent.

"Hypocrites!" Joses said.

"That's enough," Cleopas said. "I wouldn't have believed until I saw it myself, and neither would have you. Let's go. They have much to discuss."

They walked away, but before they reached the stairs Cleopas turned back and said, "Jesus *is* alive." Then they left. Matthew made sure the door was locked and returned to the others.

Simon had no idea what to say. Could they be right? *Impossible.* For a moment, no one said a word.

"Are we going to talk about this?" Matthew asked. "I didn't believe Mary, but it's hard to argue against my father and brother."

"Why?" the Zealot asked. "Because they're your family?"

"Because there were *two* of them," he replied. "If Mary had a vision, that would be understandable. But they both experienced it. Could they have had the same dream?"

"Did they say he ate the bread after he broke it?" Bartholomew asked.

Matthew scratched his beard in the same way his father did. "No, I think he disappeared right after he broke that. They said nothing about eating a meal."

Bartholomew nodded as if that was meaningful information.

"What does that have to do with anything?" Jude asked.

"They might have seen a ghost."

"A ghost?" Andrew said.

Bartholomew nodded matter-of-factly. He picked up a grape off the tray of food that the owner of the house had provided for them.

"See this?" he asked, then put the grape into his mouth and chewed. "Ghosts can't do that. They don't have a body to eat food with."

"But Mary said he *touched* him," John said.

"I still think Mary had a vision," Bartholomew said. "But the others saw a ghost."

The apostles began to argue over his theory. Simon could feel Andrew and Matthew look at him, hoping he might lead. But he would not. *Let Bartholomew take charge*, he thought. *He is much smarter than I.*

Questions without answers were thrown across the room. Was Jesus speaking to them from the grave? Was it a trick of the devil? And what of the Romans saying that *they* had stolen the body?

The argument grew in intensity as they came to different opinions on what it all meant and what they should do about it. Then the blaming began.

"Why did you have us meet together? We might all be captured by the Romans!" Jude said to Simon.

"If I had known Judas was the traitor, I would have killed him on the spot. How could you have stood by while they took him?" the Zealot said to James and John.

"We knew what was going to happen. Why did we let him come to Jerusalem?" Philip said.

Fists were slammed against the table and they shouted at each other. Though many of the comments were directed toward Simon and his failed leadership, he said nothing.

Simon blamed himself for not realizing Judas's betrayal. He knew he was supposed to protect Jesus, but didn't. And the others didn't even know about his denials. As the Zealot and Jude grabbed their tunics to leave, Simon was sure he would never see them again.

So this is how it ends, he thought.

And then he saw Jesus.

Simon jumped up in terror and tried to speak, but no words came to his mouth. The apostles were too busy arguing to notice Jesus' arrival, but they noticed Simon's sudden movement and the pale look on his face.

Jesus stepped from the shadows and moved toward them. They all stared, jaws hanging limply from their mouths. It didn't look like him, and yet it did. He was… beautiful. Simon realized that he looked like what he saw when he looked into his eyes, yet now he looked that way from every direction.

Jesus raised his hands and he saw the holes in his wrists. They gasped.

"Peace be with you," he said.

They gripped each other's arms, but couldn't tear their eyes from what they saw. Simon wasn't sure to laugh or to cry.

Jesus smiled. "Peace be with you," he said again. Tears ran down the apostles' faces. Some fell on their knees. Simon couldn't move. Jesus came closer.

"I knew it," John whispered.

"I can't believe it," Bartholomew said.

Matthew and Little James collapsed in each other's arms. The Zealot was on his knees with arms open wide. Andrew clung to his brother's arm so tightly that Simon's arm became numb. But no one dared to touch Jesus.

He was at the edge of the table they sat around, the same table where they celebrated the last supper. He looked at Bartholomew. "Do you have something to eat?"

Dumbfounded, Bartholomew lifted up the bowl of grapes. Jesus took hold of the bowl and popped a grape into his mouth. His teeth broke through the outer skin and it's juice spilled a little down into his beard.

The apostles watched in amazement. "Why has doubt disturbed your hearts?" Jesus asked. "See by my hands and feet that it is me. A ghost has no flesh and bones as I do. Touch me and see for yourself."

Jesus looked at Simon, as did the other apostles. Simon knew why. *This is the kind of thing "Peter" would do,* he thought. *But I am not Peter.* Simon looked away.

After a moment, John stood. He came close and reached out his hand to touch. John looked to Jesus for permission, and Jesus nodded.

John's finger touched Jesus' hand. He looked at the wound in his wrist. John took a step closer to examine it, and slipped his finger inside. Then he jumped back with an excited scream and buried himself in the Master's arms, sobbing with joy.

They all moved closer now, grabbing him by the arm, touching him on the back, putting their hands on his shoulders. They surrounded him and hugged him until they formed one large pile that shook with the force of their tears.

Simon moved closer, placed his hand on his brother's back, but couldn't bear to touch the Master. Like the others, his face was wet with tears. But theirs seemed to be tears of joy, while his were mixed with sorrow and guilt. Jesus looked him in the eye and almost said something... but didn't.

The others began to marvel at his wounds. Jesus raised his hands and prayed over them. Then, as suddenly as he appeared, he was gone.

They sat in stunned silence and checked with each other to see if they hadn't lost their minds, if they weren't sleeping and in some wonderful dream.

Then Philip began to laugh hysterically. It was contagious, and soon they were bent over, holding their sides, and crying with joy. All of their pain, all their fear, all their frustration was released in that laughter. They felt like children again, and the world was new.

Simon laughed with them, though his heart was still torn. To see Jesus alive again was something beyond his wildest dreams. The joy of the resurrection softened the shame of his failure, but it didn't remove it completely. If anything, it added a new question: *If Jesus can raise himself from the dead, what could he possibly need me for?*

Andrew put his arms around his brother's shoulders. "He is alive!" he said to him. "He is ALIVE!"

Simon looked around at the apostles. They were different men. Joy and peace radiated from their faces, and the truth began to sink in. This was no dream. Jesus had risen from the dead. The Messiah had come back to life!

"Hallelujah!" Simon said, and they echoed back the song.

The apostles left together, unafraid of being recognized. They stumbled through the city streets like drunkards, arm in arm and laughing loudly.

They made their way to the house of Simon the leper. It was late, and most of Bethany was asleep.

Simon was the first to enter. Mary of Magdala was pacing back and forth in the courtyard and headed straight toward him with a fury when he entered. But she froze when she saw the look of joy on his face.

"He's alive," he said with tears in his eyes. "We have seen him. And HE IS ALIVE!"

The house erupted with such a joyful shout that it awakened all of Bethany.

Neighbors ran into the house. Those who were sleeping came out of their rooms to hear the good news. There was crying and hugging and laughter.

People rushed Simon to get an explanation, but he didn't care to talk. "Andrew will tell you," he said. He pushed through the gathering crowd to get to his wife. She was so overcome with emotion that she curled up into a ball in the corner and wept.

Simon bent down and reached his big arms around her. Both cried heavily. "Everything is going to be all right," he said.

She looked up and smiled, her face swollen with tears. "I believe," she said. "I believe."

He began to say, "I'm sorry..." but she shook her head and put her finger to his lips.

"I love you," was her reply, cupping his large face in her hands.

Simon smiled. *This is why I love her.*

They kissed, and that night of their marriage was even more joyful than their first.

RECONCILIATION

John 20:24-21:9

Eight days later, the apostles gathered again in the upper room. Simon did a quick head count. There were eight there—Simon the Zealot and James hadn't yet arrived.

"What did he say?" Matthew asked.

"He was still pretty hostile," Bartholomew said. "I told him what we saw, and he looked at me as if I had gone mad."

"I would have felt the same," Simon said, "if I hadn't seen it myself."

Bartholomew nodded. "I told him how John put his finger right in the holes of his hands. Thomas told me that 'Unless I can put my hand in his side, I refuse to believe.' He was pretty obstinate about it."

"So he's not coming?" Matthew asked.

Bartholomew looked at Simon, who tried his best to repress a smile.

"Well, I wouldn't say *that*, exactly."

Matthew was about to ask what he meant when there was a commotion by the door at the bottom of the stairs. Simon the Zealot came up the stairs backwards, holding Thomas's legs. James had him by the chest. The unusual sight caused many of them to break out in laughter, which only angered Thomas more.

He cursed and swore. As they got to the top of the stairs, he demanded to be put down. They gently put him to his feet and his face was red with anger.

"How dare you!" he yelled. "Who do you think you are? You are all insane! Insane! How do you justify bringing me here against my will!"

But the apostles didn't return the hostility. They all had smiles on their faces.

This reaction stunned Thomas, and he looked wildly about them.

"Why do you look at me like that? You truly have lost your minds. I am leaving, and you will not stop me!" He spun and slammed into one of them, almost knocking him over. "Get out of my way!" he said, and grabbed the apostle's tunic to push him aside. But the tunic came open, revealing a bare chest.

And on that chest was a wound.

And in that wound was a beating heart.

Thomas looked up into the face of Jesus.

"Peace be with you," Jesus said. Thomas and the others fell to their knees.

Jesus pulled his tunic out wider to give full view of the wound. "Give me your hand," he said.

Simon watched as Thomas lifted his trembling hand, and put it in the hand of Jesus. "Put it into my side," and he guided Thomas' hand to his chest.

As it got nearer to the wound, the trembling ceased. His curiosity overcame the fear.

Simon leaned forward to see. The Roman spear had made a large gash in his side. They could see the two pieces of rib on the edge of the wound, and Thomas ran his finger across the bone. Simon wasn't sure, but he thought he could see light emanate from the wound. Thomas moved forward and peered inside. His hand still on the wound, he lifted his eyes to Jesus, who looked at him lovingly.

"Do not be unbelieving anymore, Thomas," he said gently to him. "Believe."

Thomas removed his hand from Jesus' side and looked at him in awe. "My Lord, and my God!" he exclaimed. And then he laid face down on the ground before him.

The others looked at each other in shock. *Did Thomas just say that Jesus was God?* To be a Son of God was one thing, but to be God himself… it was the highest form of blasphemy.

Jesus did not correct him. And in the presence of his beating heart, they all bowed their heads and fell to their knees.

"You believe because you have seen," Jesus said. "Blessed are those who have not seen, and yet believe."

Then there was silence. Simon was the first to raise his head and look around.

"He's gone," he said. And the others lowly raised their heads and whispered in amazement.

But not Thomas. He was still on the ground, sobbing. The others surrounded him and put their hands on him. Their show of support only made him cry harder, if that were possible. Eventually, he sat up and looked at them with tears still streaming down his face.

"Forgive me, brothers," he said. "Forgive my disbelief." He looked at John. "John, I'm so sorry—"

John jumped forward and embraced him. "It's all right, Thomas," he said. "All is forgiven."

Then Thomas looked at Simon and bowed his head toward him. "Peter, I'm sorry I failed to be a disciple."

Simon recoiled at the statement, and all eyes were upon him now. "Me? Why apologize to me?"

Thomas looked bewildered, as if it was obvious. "You are the head of us, and I failed in my commitment."

Simon waved his hands and shook his head. "No, I'm not the head anymore. That was before—"

Andrew spoke up. "But *you are Peter.*"

"Not anymore."

"Come on, Simon," James said. "We all ran away."

"Mine was worse," he said. There was no reason to hide it any longer. *They should know the kind of man I am.*

Simon confessed to them what happened that night. He told them how he cursed and swore that he didn't know Jesus, only a stone's throw away from where he was being beaten.

They listened without interrupting him, and when he was done he found he was crying. He breathed in a heavy sigh. "So I must ask forgiveness of you, my brothers."

They put their hands on his shoulders and nodded.

"You are forgiven," the Zealot said, and they all echoed the same.

"But you are still Peter," Jude said. Other heads nodded.

Simon was stunned at their response. "Did you not hear what I just said?"

"I am not discouraged by it," Little James said.

"Nor am I," Bartholomew said.

"Stop," Simon said. "I am at peace with this decision. When I first followed Jesus, I did not know who I was. When I was named… that name… I began to think of myself as better than you. But I have seen who I truly am now, and I have come to accept it. You should, too."

Matthew folded his arms. "You've made your choice, have you?"

Simon nodded. "I have."

"Then I will accept your decision. I will even go back to calling you Simon, as you wish. But I want you to think about one thing."

"What is that?"

"What makes you think it is your choice to make?"

Simon was floored by the thought. "What?"

"None us asked to be apostles. We were *chosen*. And looking around this room, myself included, we could all argue that our Master could have chosen better. But he didn't. Not only that, but he chose *you* to lead us. And as our young friend is fond of saying… *Jesus is always right.*"

Simon was struck dumb, and had no response.

A week later, Simon was back on the sea.

This is where you belong, it said to him.

Was it? Maybe he should go back to this life now that Jesus had risen from the dead. What could a poor fisherman have to offer someone like him?

Simon stretched, and the early morning sun felt good on his bare chest. It was a hot day, and his tunic was tied around his waist. He looked at his friends who came fishing with him. His brother, Andrew. James and John. Bartholomew and Philip. And most surprising of all… Thomas.

"How you holding up?" Philip asked.

Thomas looked uncertain. "It's not so bad," he said. "But the boat is smaller than the ones we've used before."

"So is our net," James said. "This is more for fun."

"There won't be any storms, right? You promised no storms."

The others laughed. James waved his huge arms toward the clear sky. "No storms, Thomas. I'm proud of you for joining us." He looked down at the empty net that floated limply next to the boat. "Sorry we haven't seen much action today."

The conversation continued and Simon looked back at the water. The boat shifted a bit as Andrew came over to where Simon was sitting. They nodded to each other and looked out at the scenery.

"Is it me, or does everything look different?" he asked.

Simon knew what he meant. "It does," he replied. "But I can't tell you what's changed. It's the same water we've fished on since we were kids."

"Then I guess *we've* changed."

They sat in silence for a moment, as the sea gently rocked them back and forth.

"Are you... all right?" his brother asked.

Simon sighed. "I don't know what to do. I can't express the joy I feel knowing that Jesus is alive, but I also feel a sense of loss. Things will never be the same."

Andrew nodded. He looked at the other end of the boat and saw John trying to teach Thomas how to pull in the net. "What do you think about what Thomas said?" he whispered. "About Jesus being God?"

Simon's eyes fell on Thomas and then came back to his brother. "I don't know," he said.

"But you knew that Jesus was the Messiah."

Simon wasn't sure if that was a question or a statement. He remembered the voice that whispered *Messiah* to him, but no such voice spoke to him now. "I don't know," he said again.

The sea rocked them gently back and forth. Simon was overcome with sadness.

"Simon?" his brother asked. Simon turned away.

Andrew touched him on the shoulder. "Please, I'm your brother. You can talk to me."

He couldn't look Andrew in the eye, so Simon stared at his reflection in the water. "He hasn't talked to me, you know."

"You mean Jesus?"

Simon nodded.

"He's talked to all of us."

Simon shook his head. "But not to *me*. I know it sounds selfish and it's stupid to say. But he always used to talk to *me*. He was my friend and I betrayed him. And now..." Simon took a heavy breath. "Now he doesn't need friends. He doesn't need anything. And he certainly doesn't need me."

They sat in silence for a few moments and Andrew scratched the hair on his face. "You were closer to Jesus than any of us," Andrew said. "I know I was jealous of that, but I was also… proud."

"Proud?"

He nodded. "Proud that I was an apostle. Proud that you were so close to him." Andrew paused. "Proud that you are my brother, no matter what happens."

Simon looked into his brother's eyes and smiled. "Thank you, brother." He leaned over to embrace Andrew, and the boat shifted under his weight.

"Careful!" Thomas yelled from the other end of the boat, causing the rest of them to laugh.

"All right, all right," Simon said as he sat back down in his original position. "It's not like were in very deep water. What, don't you know how to swim?"

"It's just that I'd rather not," Thomas said.

"Any fish?" Andrew asked.

James held up the empty net. "Bread and fruit tonight, boys."

"Have you caught anything, friends?" came a voice. They looked to their left, and saw a man on the beach sitting by a fire.

"No!" James called in response.

"Try throwing the net on the right side! You'll find something there!"

The fishermen looked at each other with a confused expression. *How would he know?* But James shrugged and threw out the net.

He didn't have a tight grip on it and it immediately pulled from his fingers. Andrew reached out and grabbed the net and James regained his hold. They pulled, but the net pulled back. Simon jumped up to help. The ropes of the net strained as though it might break. With a heave, they lifted the net over the side of the boat and fish spilled everywhere.

John gasped. He looked at the figure on the shore and pointed. "It is the Lord!"

At that moment, Simon's heart leapt. He threw his outer garment on and dove into the lake.

The sea rumbled in his ears as he went underwater. It was dark—darker than it should have been at that time of day. Simon flailed his arms forward but felt like he didn't move. The sea not only pushed him back, but tried to pull him *down*.

He thought of when he almost died in the storm. He thought of almost drowning after walking on the water.

But then he thought of Jesus.

I will not give up.

Simon kicked his legs and stabbed his hands against the current. And suddenly he found himself crawling on the shore. He looked back at the boat and saw them rowing in his direction. Then he looked at Jesus.

Jesus sat by a charcoal fire. Simon walked out of the water and his wet tunic clung awkwardly to his body. He sat down on the other side of the fire from Jesus.

"Shalom, Master," he said, still catching his breath.

"Shalom, Simon."

Simon's heart beat wildly. He stared at Jesus, who looked so different from the man he had first met. His eyes couldn't help but stare at the wounds on his hand.

Jesus saw this and raised his hands toward Simon Peter, inviting him to come closer. But Simon shook his head and looked down. "I don't need to touch them, Master. I believe."

"Do you?"

Simon nodded.

"What do you believe, Simon?"

Does he want me to say that I believe he's God, like Thomas did? "I believe… that you know everything," he replied.

"I do," Jesus said.

Those words brought Simon to the brink of tears. He wanted to say how sorry he was. He wanted to admit how he felt, but soon the boat would be on the shore. This was their first moment alone together, and who knew if there would be another? *It's now or never,* he thought. He took in a deep breath and opened his mouth.

But before the words could come out, Philip yelled, "Master!"

And the moment was gone.

The others pulled the boat on the shore, and they ran to embrace Jesus. James and John dragged the boat of fish by the fire.

"Let's eat," Jesus said. He broke bread with them, and they shared the fish with each other.

Simon sat silently and ate, chastising himself for not saying anything when he had the chance. Jesus stood up as if he was going to leave.

"Are you leaving, Master?" John asked.

Jesus nodded.

"When will we see you again?" Thomas asked.

"Soon," Jesus said. "Stay close in prayer with each other. I still have more to teach you."

Simon looked down at the rocky sand and moved his finger around in it. He expected to look up and find Jesus gone, as he had before. He looked up. Jesus was not only still there, but he stared right at him.

"Walk with me, Simon," he said.

Simon and Andrew exchanged glances, and then Simon stood and followed Jesus as they walked away from the others.

This was his chance. Tears rolled down Simon's face. "I'm sorry, Master," he said. "I'm sorry I denied you." His nose ran and his throat was dry. He had to use his tunic to wipe off his face.

"I forgive you," Jesus said.

Simon shook his head. "You shouldn't—"

"But I do."

"I'm no better than Judas."

Jesus was silent for a moment. "You are no better than anyone," he said. "But you are different."

Simon could barely hear him through his sobs. "I wasn't there for you when you needed me."

"Needed you?" Jesus asked in surprise. "Simon, I *never* needed you."

Simon looked up in horror. *Did he really just say that?* All of his worst fears were confirmed. He wasn't better, he wasn't needed. Then what was his purpose?

"I never needed you," Jesus said again. "I *wanted* you."

The tears stopped. Simon stared at him with no response.

"Simon, son of Jonah, do you love me more than those others do?" he asked, pointing to the apostles gathered around the fire in the distance.

He looked at his friends. Simon felt ashamed when he remembered how he said that *he* would be faithful even if *they* were not. He admired James's strength, Thomas's honesty... and could anyone love Jesus more than John?

Love. Simon realized that Jesus used the same Greek word for love that he did when they celebrated Passover: *agape.* Ultimate, sacrificial love. It was how Simon wanted to feel toward Jesus, but knew he failed at it.

"Lord, you know that I... love you," he responded. Simon also used a Greek word of love, but a lesser one: *phileo.* The love shown between brothers.

If Jesus noticed the difference he made no mention of it. "Feed my lambs," he said.

While Simon wondered what that meant, Jesus asked him another question. "Simon, son of Jonah, do you love me?"

There was that word again. *Agape.*

Simon couldn't look him in the eye. "Lord, you know that I love you," he said. *Phileo.*

Jesus nodded. "Look after my sheep," he said. Jesus stopped walking and Simon felt his gaze upon him. But he couldn't look up from the ground. Simon stared at his feet and remembered when Jesus washed them.

Then Jesus asked, "Simon, son of Jonah, do you *love* me?"

This question struck Simon right through the heart, for this time Jesus used the same word that Simon had: *phileo.*

Tears began to flow again. "Lord, you know everything," he said. "I'm not the man I thought I was. I thought I was better than everyone else. I thought I would die for you. I didn't. I do love you. I wish I loved you more..."

He fell on his knees and could not control his sobs.

"Lord, you know everything," he said through his tears. "You know that I love you."

Simon buried his head in his hands and half expected Jesus to disappear and leave him like that. But he felt a hand on his shoulder and looked and saw Jesus was kneeling next to him.

Simon looked into Jesus' face. There were tears in his eyes. And then Jesus said something he was not expecting:

"Feed my sheep."

Simon was stunned. "But, didn't you hear—"

"In truth I tell you," Jesus said, "when you were young you went where you wanted to. But when you grow old, you will stretch out your hands and someone will bind them, and take you to a place where you would rather not be."

It took him a moment, but Simon realized that Jesus just told him how he was going to die. He would die… for *him*.

Sacrificial love.

Agape.

His heart beat wildly with excitement. Jesus smiled. There was no fear, no shame when he looked into the face of his Master. There was only joy.

Simon looked around and noticed the beauty of creation. The sun was up, and the clear sky radiated a bright blue. The green hills that surrounded that sea were filled with wild flowers of every color.

The sea gently rolled against the beach, and he heard its sound. It spoke to him, but for the first time he heard its true voice, not the distorted reflection of himself that he was used to talking to.

Shhh… it said as the waves crested upon the shore.

Be still and know that he is God.

Simon was still before Jesus.

And he knew.

Jesus extended his nail-pierced hand.

"Follow me," Jesus said.

Simon reached out to him, and his fingers touched the wound.

"I believe," Peter said.

And the sea never called to him again.

AFTERWORD

My intention with this book was not to make profound theological statements or share some kind of "private revelation". I wanted to write a novel about the Gospels, focusing on the relationship between Jesus and Peter, that was faithful to Scripture and historically plausible.

Why Peter? Msgr. Eugene Kevane wrote a book called "Creed and Catechesis" where he causally mentioned that though the Gospel's primary intention is to let the reader know about the life of Christ, its secondary intention is that the reader would get to know Peter. This simple statement floored me. I had been reading the gospels almost every day since I gave my life to Jesus at a Young Life camp back in high school and I never noticed that before.

I immediately started flipping through the Gospels and found it to be true. The focus is on Jesus, but the "co-star" is Peter. Nobody else comes close. Even the other apostles pale in comparison. Sure, James and John are often with him but they rarely, if ever, say anything. Many of the other apostles are completely silent throughout the Gospels.

The Holy Spirit wants to make Peter known to us through the Gospels. In asking people what they think about Peter, I've commonly come across three images. The first is the "St. Peter in heaven" line of jokes, portraying him hanging out by the pearly gates, making the choice to let people in or not. Hardly a serious picture.

The other is Peter as the bumbling fool, always putting his foot in his mouth. True, he did often speak before he thought, but what he said was often inspired: "You are the Christ," "Lord, to whom can we go?" "Lord, you know I love you."

The third image, the most common, is Peter as an *everyman*. He is us. Some assume that the Gospel writers put him in there so we can have someone to relate to. This, I think, is closer to the truth. Of everyone in Scripture, Peter gives us the most vivid portrayal of conversion and the ups and downs of following Christ. Surely we can draw our own comparisons!

But thinking of him *only* as "us" robs him of his unique identity. And he boldly did many things I don't think "we" would do. Were I in his shoes, I'm not sure I would walk out on the water or fight soldiers in the garden. Nor has Jesus asked me to be the rock on which the Church is built.

Speaking of the *rock*, I overheard the leader of a tour group read the Matthew eighteen, "You are Peter," verse when I visited Caesarea Philippi. Happy to hear someone speak English, I stopped to listen. He said that most people think that "Peter" means "rock", but really, it meant "pebble". He concluded that Peter wasn't that big of a deal, and he was just a little part of the beginning of the Church.

It's poor scholarship. Yes, the Greek for "rock" is "petra", and "petros" can mean pebble. But Jesus couldn't call Simon "Petra", because he would have called him a girl's name. "Petros" is the masculine for "rock". The real question is how was his name translated into other languages. Both John and Paul call him "Kephas" which is Aramaic for *rock*, not *pebble*! So tell all your friends—Peter is the rock. And if they argue, throw a pebble at them.

While writing this book, I didn't want to get too deep in theology or speculation, I just wanted to stick to the Gospels and elaborate on them using things that were historically plausible. I spent a lot of time on research and even took a personal trip to the Holy Land to check out archeological sites and museums to get it as right as I could.

But there's an awful lot of fiction in there. I imagine someone could take the same Gospel stories and write very different characters with them. People get touchy when you fictionalize things about Jesus, and understandably so. What can be more personal than our personal Savior?

Whether or not you think these depictions of Jesus and the apostles are accurate, I hope you will see them as faithful. It was a tremendous blessing to write this book, research it, visit the Holy Land, pray over the Gospels, and imagine what it might have been like to be there. I didn't try to get too fancy with things. After all, this is the Greatest Story Ever Told. My constant prayer is that I wouldn't mess it up.

Here are some questions that people have asked after reading this book.

Did *that* happen *then*?

Chronology, the backbone of modern storytelling, meant little to the Gospel writers. It was not uncommon for them to tell stories out of order from each other. For them, *when* it happened wasn't as important as *that* it happened. Matthew seemed to compile the stories and teachings of Jesus by themes—John focused on His trips to Jerusalem. The fact that the order of the miracles and teachings occasionally contradict each other in the Gospels doesn't mean the Gospels aren't true, it just wasn't the author's intent to give us a detailed chronology of what happened. They seemed to take the attitude: *Here are a bunch of stories about Jesus that are generally in the right order.*

What wasn't a big deal for the Gospel writers was a big challenge for me. I needed to decide which came first and what followed if I was going to develop the characters and build on the inherent tension of the Gospel story. As a default, I chose the Gospel of Mark. At first glance, it's an ironic choice because Mark has the least about Peter than the other Gospels! But it's often been suggested that Mark was a disciple of Peter, and narrates the gospel based on what he heard from the fisherman's lips. That was good enough for me.

The most egregious chronological error I committed was putting the story of the woman caught in adultery during Holy Week. The Gospel of John (the only gospel where the story is told) makes it clear that it was during the feast of Tabernacles, several months before. But the truth is I really *like* that story, and embraced the attitude of the Gospel writers: *when* it happened isn't as important as *that* it happened.

Did Jesus meet Simon before the miraculous catch of fish?

Bargil Pixner, in his book, *With Jesus Through Galilee According to the Fifth Gospel* gives a fascinating time line for the public ministry of Jesus. Pixner lives on the sea of Galilee, and he uses the way the storms were described, the scant descriptions of weather, and the Gospel events to piece together what might have happened in what month. In his timeline, Jesus was baptized by John in January, comes back and calls the disciples in March, then passes through Cana and spends some time in Capernaum until the Passover in April. Then things quiet down and the fishermen go home. But when the Baptist gets arrested in the late fall, Jesus comes back to Capernaum to start his own ministry in November.

I thought there was a lot of great insight to this timeline, and it beautifully reconciled the Gospel of John (who mentions that Jesus first met the fishermen when they were disciples of the Baptist) with the other Gospels (which start with the miraculous catch of fish, though none of them claim it to be the first time they met). So I made that the background that preceded the calling of Simon on his boat.

To be honest, though, I tried to leave it vague. I didn't want to begin the book with details or timelines the reader may or may not agree with, and then be turned off from the rest of the novel. I just wanted the reader to get a sense of what the Gospels tell us: the fishermen had spent some time helping John the Baptist and had some familiarity with Jesus before their more formal calling by the sea of Galilee.

Why did you make Jesus ugly?

That question was from my wife, and I *didn't*. I just made Him "not stunningly handsome", unlike some of the blond hair, blue eyed, flowing hair-with-highlights pictures that we have here in America (and in my house). There are no Gospel descriptions of what Jesus looked like, though Isaiah prophesied that the Messiah would have *"no charm to attract us, no beauty to win our hearts."* So I went with that.

Was Peter's wife's name Rachael?

Made that one up. It was a popular Jewish name at the time for a woman. There is some tradition that her name was Perpetua and traveled with Peter on his later ministry, but Perpetua is clearly a Roman name, and it's safe to assume she originally had a Jewish one (like Simon did).

Were Peter, Andrew, James, and John the "four men" who lowered the paralytic through the roof?

There is strong evidence to support it. I was on a retreat when a priest mentioned that the Gospel of Mark doesn't mention "four men" but simply, "the four". Simon Peter's home has traditionally been the place where the miracle occurred. So I think it makes perfect sense that "the four" would have been them.

Besides, how rude would it be to trash a stranger's roof? I don't care if you are really itching to heal a paralytic or not. It's not like he's going anywhere.

Were Matthew and Little James really brothers?

Maybe. C. Bernard Ruffin in his book, *The Twelve: the Lives of the Apostles after Calvary* suggests that they were brothers and that Cleopas and Mary were their parents. I loved the idea of a family following Jesus together, and having James the Lesser as Matthew's brother (who also worked with him) gave me an identity for James the Lesser that I enjoyed writing about. It's plausible, but not certain.

Ruffin also makes the connection between the families of Matthew and James the Lesser with James and John, and all of them with Jesus. Since family was such an essential part of Jewish life, it seemed to fit that Jesus would have family members as his closest companions.

Did Jesus have brothers?

The Gospels talk about the "brothers" of Jesus, but there isn't a word for "cousins" in Hebrew. So cousins and second cousins were referred to as brothers and sisters. This is why the characters in the novel say John the Baptist is Jesus' brother, not cousin—I was trying to be true to the feel of the original language. So Scripture is ambiguous about Jesus' family, but Tradition is not. The early Church believed that Jesus was the only son of Mary, so that's how I wrote it.

Wasn't the transfiguration on Mount Tabor, not Mount Hermon?

Honestly, I have no idea. People seem to draw blood when they fight over it. Scripture doesn't mention the specific location. The traditional site is Mt. Tabor and they have a beautiful church on top of it that you should visit if you're in the area. But one problem is that archeologists discovered a Hasmonean fortress on its summit, suggesting it was fairly populated at the time and maybe not the best place for the Transfiguration to have occurred. Mt. Hermon is closer to Caesarea Philippi, but is a pretty big mountain, and at that time of year might have been snowy. Some people think it was neither of the two, and they go on to name places that I've never heard of.

I went with Mount Hermon because Mount Hermon was prettier to write about than Mount Tabor. Color me shallow. And if you ever do a pilgrimage to the Holy Land, say a prayer for my soul at the Basilica of the Transfiguration on Mount Tabor.

When was the Last Supper celebrated?

On my first trip to Jerusalem over ten years ago, one of the guides mentioned that it might have been actually been on Tuesday. I've since read other authors I respect that say the same. The Essenes had a different calendar than the other Jews, and it's conceivable that Jesus celebrated the Passover on Tuesday instead of Thursday when everybody else did. When you consider all that Jesus went through after the Last Supper (trial by Annas, trial by Sanhedrin, going to Pilate, going to Herod, going back to Pilate) it makes a more realistic timeline. (There are other reasons, too. For more, read Pope Benedict XVI's wonderful book, *Jesus of Nazareth*.)

I'm inclined to agree with this, though I confess to not be enough of a scholar to make a stand. But in the end, my decision to write the Last Supper on Thursday was more liturgical than theological. Thursday is the day when we as Christians celebrate the Last Supper of Christ. Friday is the day we remember his suffering. My hope is that, by writing the events in the context of those days, that it would be more meaningful for the reader, especially for someone using the book as a meditation toward Easter.

Did Judas receive the Eucharist at the Last Supper?

It was interesting to read people's opinions on this. Pre-twentieth century writers seemed unanimous that Judas *had* to leave before receiving the Body and Blood of Jesus. How could a traitor be a part of such a sacred moment? But more modern theologians disagree, citing the mercy of God for even the worst sinner.

Not coincidentally, modern writers have tended toward a more sympathetic view of Judas, suggesting he was trying to do the right thing but it got out of control. The only motivation Scripture gives us was that he was a thief and he betrayed Jesus for money. I tried to make Judas human in the book, but I didn't want to veer from that central motive.

Matthew, Mark, and Luke make no mention of Judas leaving the Passover feast. But John, whose account of the Last Supper is longer than the other three Gospels combined, says he left right before the breaking of the bread. I don't think that the other Gospels were trying to suggest Judas was present at that moment, it was just a detail they didn't care to include. So I went with John's more detailed account.

I thought "It is finished" is just one word in Greek, but you make a big deal about him saying each word.

Yeah, you got me.

Was the *agape/phileo* thing at the end accurate?

Yes, though I didn't use the proper tense in the Greek. I wanted to keep it simple.

Why didn't you include the story of _____?

You might think that a three hundred page book should easily cover the Gospels (which are surprisingly brief,) but my first draft was over four hundred pages and I still hadn't covered it all. So I took a machete to it and eliminated anything that didn't directly have to do with Jesus and Peter. There were many casualties. One night, I was visited in my dreams by the woman at the well and King Herod, asking why they were good enough for the Holy Spirit but not good enough for me. I tried to explain that the Holy Spirit didn't have to work with page counts. The woman at the well understood. Herod was kind of a jerk about it.

I'm offended because of _____.

I'm sorry. I truly am. I approached this story with reverence and prayer, but I know that once you put words into Jesus' mouth (or mind) that aren't in the gospel, you are bound to offend someone. I hope this work inspires more than it offends.

Which of the book is fiction and which is the Gospel?

Ah, the best question of all. Many chapters have Scripture references at the beginning; that's a good place to start. But just because I used a story from Mark doesn't mean I didn't borrow from Matthew, Luke, or John's account as well.

I'm afraid you'll just have to read the Gospels yourself to find out. You can do it—they are a lot shorter than the book you just read! And if reading *this* book gets you to read THE book, then my years of working on this novel will not have been wasted.

May all of us, caught in the fisherman's net, learn to *agape* each other as He did for us, and *agape* Him above all.

ACKNOWLEDGEMENTS

My wife is amazing. She encouraged me to do all sorts of crazy things to get this book written, even though it seemed clear we might never recoup the money we put into it. She let me go to the Holy Land for a week, by myself, to do research. I attended writing conferences, paid people for edits on the book, and spent countless hours writing while she kept the kids busy. It's an understatement to say that I couldn't have written the book without her. It's more accurate to say that I can't do *anything* without her.

My mom and dad are the most supportive parents a person could hope for. They were a constant source of support and gave great advice. My dad turned out to be a pretty good proof reader, too.

Were it not for Bert Ghezzi, this book wouldn't have been written. He cornered me at a conference and accused me of wasting a gift that God had given me, all because I had a bad experience with my first published book. He was right. I'm grateful for his challenge and his constant encouragement and advice throughout the process.

Dr. David Craig, who teaches creative writing at Franciscan University, read every draft I gave him, and always pointed out what was wonderful and what wasn't. His wife, Linda, also read it to help with my many grammar mistakes. Special thanks to my Uncle Tom Tisa who helped find typos, syntax errors, and even did some historical fact checking.

Dr. John Bergsma is a colleague of mine at Franciscan, an absolutely brilliant Biblical scholar. I went to him to make sure I didn't write anything heretical. He not only gave me great theological advice, but advice on the story as well! He went above and beyond what I asked him to do and the book is much better for it.

I sent various drafts of this novel to friends along the way, many of whom replied with helpful feedback. I'm especially grateful to "*The Wrinklings,*" (especially Mike Fitzgerald, Andy Bonjour, Richard Smith, and Marcus Grodi,) Mike Carotta, Richard

Bullwinkle, Mike Patin, Gene Monterastelli, Steve Angrisano, and Kristin Witte.

Jeff Gerke did a fiction edit of the manuscript, and that's when this novel went from being a veiled catechesis into a legitimate story. He wrote a great book called, "The Art and Craft of Writing Christian Fiction," which you should get if you want to know how to write great Christian fiction.

But it's said that the best edit you can do is to read the book out loud. That's what I got to do with Dan Bozek, who produced the audiobook version of this novel. We had a lot of fun doing it and he did an excellent job.

I read a number of books to better understand what the world was like in time of Christ. The ones that I'm most grateful for are Bargil Pixner's *With Jesus Through Galilee According to the Fifth Gospel,* C. Bernard Ruffin's *The Twelve: the Lives of the Apostles after Calvary,* Miriam Vamosh's *Daily Life at the Time of Jesus, Daily Life in Palestine at the Time of Christ* by Henri Daniel-Rops, and *The Temple* and *Sketches of Jewish Social Life* by Alfred Edersheim. Benedict XVI's *Jesus of Nazareth* and *The Apostles* gave great insight as well.

The beautiful cover of this book is by Rembrandt. If you take a closer look at the painting, you'll notice there are fourteen people in the boat. Rembrandt wanted to put *us* in the boat with Jesus, and that was something I hoped this book would do, too.

Then there's you. Yes, *you.* Thanks for reading this book, and I'd like to thank you in advance for telling a few friends about it. As a self-published author, this book will only survive by word of mouth. So if you liked it, tell your friends and post a good review at Amazon.com. And thank you for supporting my ministry and my family.

Finally, I'd like acknowledge the obvious: All praise and all thanksgiving be to Jesus Christ, the Word who became flesh and dwelt among us, with grateful affection to those Apostles He called who were so faithful to him, especially St. Peter.

ABOUT THE AUTHOR

 **Bob Rice** has a passion to share the love of God. An internationally sought after speaker, Bob has published numerous articles on youth ministry, is an accomplished musician and songwriter, and a popular blogger. He teaches about Scripture, evangelization and youth ministry at Franciscan University of Steubenville, Ohio, where he lives with his beautiful wife Jennifer and his seven adorable children. You can find out more about him at bob-rice.com.